It's possible to hide much of who we really are.
But the things which seem to fascinate us
can be very revealing...

Darrol and Magnus stopped as a demolition ball, small but potent, swung forward—elegantly, almost formally—and savaged another portion of wood, plaster and cement. As it swung back on its chain, the ball danced a lively jig of celebration.

"Impermanence," Magnus said. "We think we build for forever, but then..."

Seemingly on its own, another section of wall tumbled, a glacier calving. Dust billowed toward the street.

Darrol smiled enthusiastically. "Ever read that story by Graham Greene? About the kids destroying a house? Called *The Destructors.*"

"I wouldn't have taken you for a literary man, Mr. Yount." Magnus' smile held no warmth.

Darrol blinked, persisted. "Have you read it?"

"I'm afraid not." Magnus wiped a small chip of wood from his face. "I must get back."

He brushed past the foreman and strode into the temporary pedestrian lane. Darrol jogged after him, caught up as they regained the sidewalk.

"It's a great story," Darrol said. "These boys take over a man's house while he's gone for the weekend. They demolish it completely in the inside. From the outside it still looks OK. When the guy comes back, the whole place totally collapses in one huge, wonderful smasharoo. Pretty much right before his eyes."

"Why would they do that?" Magnus seemed more curious than shocked.

"Because they could."

They turned onto Chestnut. A sharp-edged breeze rollicked down the hill.

Magnus tugged at his collar. "All that creativity going into pure destruction. Does that appeal to you, Mr. Yount?"

Darrol's shivered. "Oh, yes," he said, grinning. "I think destruction can be a very creative act."

EMPEROR'S REACH

A Novel of San Francisco

Eric E. Wallace

2018
Rabbit Creek Creative
Anchorage, Alaska – Eagle, Idaho

Published by BookLocker.com, Inc.,
St. Petersburg, Florida,
USA

Printed on acid free paper.

With the exception of Emperor Norton, the characters and events in this book are fictitious. Any similarity to other real persons, living or dead, is coincidental and not intended by the author.

First Edition

Cover design: Todd Engel, www.toddengel-engelcreative.com
Cover photography: Golden Gate Bridge © Rene Türk_123rf.com

Rabbit Creek Creative
2018

For Kathy

In loving memory of
**Linda Sutherland
Ian Wallace**

also by Eric E. Wallace

UNDERTOW
HOAR FROST
STONERISE

EMPEROR'S REACH

Chapter 1
Mischief is the Name

Early on a fine summer morning, every dog on San Francisco's Russian Hill shut up at the same startling instant, yielding an exquisite moment of total canine silence.

Then: a low, cringing whine. Barking, howling, baying, keening. Utter cacophony.

Far to the north, a playful epicenter sent out a rippling tectonic wave. As the shock hit the Bay Area, one tendril gave Russian Hill its own seismic goose.

High rises jitterbugged, new cracks capered in the streets. Twitching wires flung up irate crows. Pigeons and parrots collided, squawking. Car alarms shrilled and shrieked. Panicked tourists staggered sideways. Trashcans tumbled, clattered. Empty bottles and rotten oranges rolled downhill in a conga line.

The air sang of irritated skunk. Asphalt. Loam. Wet mulch.

The quake careened into the neighborhood grocery, Emperor Norton Provisions.

The resident spider, high in a corner behind the checkout counters, felt her web do the lindy. She started forward, found there was no prey and backed into her sticky white tunnel.

The shaking ended.

A last red gumball in the candy machine rolled forward, clicked down over its cowering peers and landed against the closed slot with a quiet *plop*.

"Wow! See what I caused?" A half-second before the tremor hit, Darrol Yount had flicked his long red licorice whip at nothing in particular, at life in general.

"Somehow I cued it just with this?" Feigning grave respect, Darrol considered the licorice carefully.

"Such power you have, Mr. Yount." Magnus Quist picked up the posterboard figure of the Emperor Norton and returned it to its place near the entrance.

1

Once more the life-sized Emperor, in his ostrich-plumed beaver hat and his bold-epauletted Union officer's jacket, stared out intently, unfazed by the unsettled nature of his city.

"At first glance, nothing too bad." Alma Quist came from the main aisle. "Perhaps a few broken bottles." She looked behind Magnus. "But I see the sword has slipped again."

On the back wall, a leather-sheathed cavalry sword dangled precariously from one end of its faded gold sash.

"Another nail needed, I think," Magnus said, his blue eyes enlarged by thick glasses. He rummaged in a drawer. "I believe Christ got three nails, so the Emperor's sabre is allowed at least two."

"There's no logic to that, Mr. Quist," Alma said mildly.

"Precisely my point." Magnus waved a hammer at his wife before driving a nail into the wall with one firm blow.

Darrol bit into the licorice with his perfect teeth. "Is that sword the real thing?"

Magnus rebalanced the sword between the nails. "A real sabre, yes. And very sharp too. But did it belong to Emperor Norton? Hah! May I please to sell you the Golden Gate Bridge?"

Alma straightened a candy display. "What Magnus means is, when he bought the sword, they claimed it belonged to the Emperor, but..."

"...but we've since seen a dozen more of the damn things." Magnus flicked lint from the gilt sash. "As we said in Sweden, 'Låt köparen akta! Buyer beware'."

"Which also means," Alma added, "not everyone's as smart as an antiques dealer. Not even a Swede."

Her husband scowled. He was starting to mutter something when a stocky man bustled in from the street.

Magnus slid his glare into a semblance of a smile. "Good morning, Colonel Jesperson."

Jesperson nodded. His angry eyes and leathery jaw gave him the face of a pit bull. "What a humper-bumper, eh? Reminds me of being under fire. The whole damn delta quaking. VC Mortars. Most of 'em were nasty little Chinese-made bastards."

He turned to Alma. "Pardon my language, Mrs. Quist. Old habits. Have those sardines come in yet?"

Alma smiled. "I think so, but let's go see." As they left her raised voice trailed after them. "I hear worse language daily, Jump, some of it in Swedish."

Magnus adjusted his apron du jour, a deep blue. Like every apron he wore, it seemed too short for his tall, thin frame. He peered at Darrol, who was still standing near the counter.

"Something else, Mr. Yount?"

"Whyn't you call me Darrol?"

"Very well. I shall try." Magnus nodded at two more customers entering the shop.

Darrol presented a dazzling smile. "So, guess what?"

"I am not much for guessing."

"Big party at the restaurant last night. Filthy rich characters. Tips like you wouldn't believe. So this month I'm delivering the rent smack on time." Darrol shoved a rumpled brown envelope toward the older man.

Magnus held up a hand. "Please. I'd appreciate if you'd deal with my wife, *ja?* She handles all the apartment things."

He picked up his fly swatter, swung quickly at the glass counter top. A loud smack. "Ach! *Jäkla fluga!*"

He shook his head, his thin silvery hair catching the light. "And you..." He turned and looked up at the spider. "You are not doing your job, *spindel.*"

"How's my dear ancestor? Did he survive the quake?" Accompanied by a swirl of lavender, a tiny, elderly woman emerged from the coffee bar. She removed lipstick-stained cake crumbs from her powdered cheeks, licked them from her fingers.

"The Emperor is well, Mrs. Durr," Magnus told her. "He had a small spill. That is all. He takes his bruises with good spirits. If only I were cardboard, then perhaps I could say the same."

Mrs. Durr looked puzzled. "Is Magnus making a joke, Darrol? I'm getting so old..."

Darrol glanced at Quist. "I didn't get the joke, either, and I'm only 31. And I still have all my marbles."

3

Mrs. Durr tittered. "Are you suggesting I don't have all mine?"

Darrol had the grace to blush. "Oh..."

"Really," she went on, her tone teasing. "I may be ancient, but unlike my great-great grandfather"—she patted Emperor Norton's shoulder, causing the figure to quiver—"I have marbles enough to spare."

Quist steadied the Emperor. "Do you have the correct number of 'greats' there, Josephine?"

"I'm no mathematician, but that hardly matters, Magnus. Blood is thicker than math, you know. Or marbles."

"Please, madam." Magnus gestured to a small Asian woman holding a shopping basket. "Let me help you. These people are just clogging up the store."

"I do not clog," said Mrs. Durr, affecting annoyance. "Though that reminds me about my kitchen sink. It's getting hinky again."

Magnus rang up the woman's purchases with the deftness of a croupier. "Please to take sink problems up with Alma. Apartment matters go to her."

Mrs. Durr sighed.

Darrol wiped his mouth. "Are you really Emperor Norton's great-great whatever it is?"

"Oh my, yes. No one else believes it, but the lineage is very clear to me."

Quist, who was starting his bagging, didn't look up. "A fine trick, as Norton died unmarried and childless."

Mrs. Durr leaned toward Darrol. "Magnus never allows for the bastard. No one does. Norton's son was illegitimate, you see. Kept a secret. But I'm sure the line still flows right down to me."

Darrol smiled. "Well, I'll call you Empress."

That earned him a giggle wrapped in another puff of lavender.

"I don't know much about...your ancestor," Darrol said, "except that he was crazy and had the whole town giving him freebies."

Mrs. Durr nodded. "He was rich, but he lost everything. He also lost, as you'd say, all his marbles." Another small giggle. "He declared himself Emperor and became the city's favorite eccentric." She smiled. "More than 10,000 people attended his funeral."

"That's quite something."

She went on enthusiastically. "As an Imperial Majesty, he issued his own currency. He collected 'rent' from 'his citizens'. He enjoyed free food and lodging and loads of attention for about twenty years."

"So, crazy but smart." Darrol bit at his licorice and studied the posterboard figure with renewed interest.

Quist gave the Asian woman her credit card. "If you'd like a cup of coffee, please help yourself in The Nook over there. The coffee is free."

The woman smiled and moved toward the small side room.

Darrol tossed a stage whisper after her. "Yeah, but they charge you for the pastries."

Magnus snapped the fly swatter at the air. Mrs. Durr flinched. Darrol frowned. Magnus flashed a tiny smile.

Colonel Jesperson clattered five cans of sardines onto the counter.

"Look at my catch! *Banh mi* for dinner tonight! Swallowed my first sardines in the Mekong River, raw too. Forget what the little buggers were called over there, but..."

He saw he didn't have an attentive audience. Magnus, quickly done with bagging, was reloading the register paper. Darrol and Mrs. Durr were examining a display of photos of the Emperor.

Jesperson squared his shoulders. "Put 'em on my account, would you, Quist?" He took his bag and strode out.

"Good timing." Alma had come back up front. She turned to Mrs. Durr and Darrol. "I can give you two an early alert. Mr. Quist and I are thinking about having a dinner party for our tenants sometime this month."

"Lovely," said Mrs. Durr.

Darrol cleared his throat. He glanced at his watch.

"Nothing fancy," Alma went on, "but we thought the little band of us who live here ought to get to know each other better."

"She thought," corrected Magnus, moving the cardboard Emperor closer to the window. "Alma is our thinker and planner. I merely dust the shelves."

"Be that as it may," Alma said, "we'll send real invitations when everything's figured out. And Darrol, don't worry. We'll fit it around your work schedule."

"I wasn't worried." Darrol saw Alma's small frown and quickly added. "But thank you." He took a longer look at his watch. "Time for my walk." He opened the door.

"And I have to go meet my lover," said Mrs. Durr. She swept out, leaving the other three agape.

"All right then," Darrol said after a moment.

He went outside, took a couple of steps up Chestnut, stopped, looked back at the store window. He moved closer and stared in at Emperor Norton.

The black eyes seemed fixed on nothing and on everything, a wild, knowing darkness.

Darrol saw his own reflection on the glass. He moved to superimpose his face onto Norton's. He tilted his head slightly, and his reflection neatly fit over the Emperor's image.

Alma watched him from inside. Shaking her head, she turned to Magnus. "I'm not sure if I like that young man."

Magnus climbed onto a stepstool. "He's a bit stuck on himself, I think. He wanted to take credit for this morning's earthquake."

"Yes, that would be Darrol. But there's something else..."

"Something?"

"It's just that...Well, *vem vet?*"

"Who knows, indeed." Quist dusted an upper shelf. He sneezed.

Alma, going closer to the window, watched Darrol swagger away into the morning sunshine.

"A fault line," she said after a moment. "I think perhaps he has a fault line running right through him."

The building which housed Emperor Norton Provisions was just over a hundred years old. Constructed only a few years after the Great San Francisco Earthquake, it was close to achieving the status of venerable. At least that's a term Alma Quist liked to use: *venerable*. More than once she'd tried to have the building listed on the San Francisco Heritage Register, but so far, in a city of many splendid old edifices, it had been deemed 'not unique enough'. Alma was determined to nominate it again.

The building had seen life as a boarding house, as a private dwelling, then as a duality—apartments above, a series of businesses below: a dry goods emporium, a hardware store, a bicycle shop—almost self-defeating in this extra-hilly part of a hilly town—a health food store, a yoga studio, a laundry and a neighborhood grocery.

Alma sometimes thought she could detect a strange, musty mélange of the odors all those enterprises must have produced—everything from rubber to sweat to soap bubbles— still lingering above the earthy smells of fresh vegetables and the waxy pong from uncountable layers of floor polish.

Long ago, before the lower floor held any businesses, the entire building had acquired the name Mischief House. Alma diligently searched historic records to try to learn the name's origin. Eventually she found a small article in a vintage Russian Hill news sheet, which said the cramped, dead end alleyway behind the building had for a time been called Mischief Lane.

This sobriquet was likely awarded, the article posited, because of the repeated warnings to their ten children by the building's owners, a Mr. and Mrs. E. Latham. "Don't get into mischief," they said.

One child, the unfortunate Tad, didn't heed his parents, sneaked into the nameless alley at dusk, and was severely beaten, by 'a bully or bullies unknown', apparently wielding, the writer marveled, a 'horseshoe of prodigious size'. Tad's prognosis was not revealed, nor why the name Horseshoe Alley or Tad's Folly hadn't attached.

But henceforth the blind alley became informally known as Mischief Lane, and some later owner affixed a small brass plaque near the doorway to the apartments proclaiming the building to be Mischief House. The plaque was barely noticeable.

Far more prominent was the sign further along the wall for Emperor Norton Provisions, nicely done with a hint of 1800s lettering. When Magnus and Alma Quist bought Mischief House, lock, stock and store, they renamed the grocery (then known as Discount Dan's Market) after one of Alma's favorite historical figures, the deranged but beloved businessman who'd declared himself to be Emperor of the United States.

The Quists added some Norton-themed elements: the life-size standing figure, a dozen photographs of the Emperor, a genuine piece of Norton's imperial currency and, eventually, a replica of Norton's sabre.

Later, Alma came up with the idea of 'Norton Notes' promotions—issuing scrip which gave customers small savings in exchange for a degree of loyalty in their shopping.

It was never easy going for the 'Norton, as the regulars called the store. It struggled in the presence of a mini-mart a few blocks down the hill, two supermarkets within easy driving distance, and, arguably their most-troublesome competitor, a Trader Joe's not far across Columbus Avenue.

But this was a walking neighborhood, filled with many people who'd lived on Russian Hill for years, and as long as the 'Norton kept prices reasonable and the staff engaged and friendly, the customers kept coming.

The Quists also had the advantage of owning the entire building, and their apartments, despite the city's rent controls, provided additional income.

Mischief House had five apartments. The Quists lived on the second floor in a large unit directly above the grocery, and 'old Mrs. Durr', as everyone called her, rented a smaller place across the hall.

There were three apartments on the top floor. The smallest was rented by Brick Zimmer, a commercial airline pilot who appeared to bring home a different young woman every week—if not every day—and, perhaps not surprisingly, didn't seem to mind that all his windows looked over the mildly-infamous back alley.

A middle-aged couple, the Collins, rented the next unit. They were very low-key, virtually invisible, and no one else in the building knew their first names except for Alma Quist, who processed their rent checks, and Darrol Yount, who made it his business to find out such things.

He learned that the Collins' names were Tom, which made Darrol snicker—was the guy a cocktail?—and Phoebe, which made him shake his head at the quaintness. He wished her name had been Rum just to complete the set of drinks. The one time the couple came into the restaurant where Darrol worked, he comped them with a Tom Collins and a Rum Collins, but they didn't get the joke.

Darrol shared number five, the biggest third-floor apartment, with his girlfriend, Maria Grimaldi, who paid more than a fair portion of the rent, and with their roommate-of-necessity, Duff Lee, a young Chinese man who worked as a cable car gripman.

Long ago, Darrol should have worn out his line "Get a grip, Duff," but Duff continued to wince when he heard it, so Darrol continued to say it.

The final tenant of Mischief House was the Quist's cat—or more correctly Alma's cat—a big tortoiseshell-with-orange-splotches female named Lyckatill, who had the run of the building. Technically, Lyckatill was not supposed to go into the grocery store, but if Magnus was out, the cat knew to slink in when Alma used the internal door from the apartment vestibule on the main floor.

The cat also had the habit of apartment-hopping. She appeared in Darrol's apartment so often that Darrol, not a fan of cats in general, got very angry.

Assured by a sobbing Maria and an abashed Duff that they weren't letting Lyckatill in on the sly, he went hunting for a secret passage, going through every room and checking every wall, window, vent and baseboard. Not even a mouse hole.

He did learn that Duff hid a large box of pornographic magazines under a gym bag in a closet. Deep on the top shelf of the closet, Darrol also found a box of newspaper clippings about something headlined 'The Golden Dragon Massacre'. Nodding quietly, Darrol vowed to read through the stuff when he had the chance. In the meantime, he mentally tucked his discoveries away for possible future use.

Once, reminded by the KitKat bar he was buying, Darrol had complained about the cat to Magnus. "I don't want that little beast in my apartment," he grumped. He tore at the wrapper with his teeth. "How does she even get in?"

"Think of her as the Cheshire Cat," said Magnus, who liked Lewis Carroll and also liked seeing Darrol irritated. "She smiles, she vanishes. Invisible, she goes anywhere. We could all profit from such a talent, *ja*?"

He smiled broadly as if about to vanish himself. "However, the main thing is, that Mrs. Quist..."

"I know, I know," Darrol said offhandedly, "Mrs. Quist takes care of apartment matters." He'd lost interest, his mind drawn to the idea of invisibility. He separated the chocolate wafers and snapped part of one into his mouth.

"Indeed she does," Magnus said, restacking the round iron weights beside his old-fashioned scale. Click. Clack. "And the animal is also her cat, so..." Clack. Click.

It was clear to Darrol that the cat ruled the roost—or whatever the feline equivalent might be.

Alma had special feelings for Lyckatill, feelings of which Magnus was only partially aware and certainly never acknowledged. Alma, as some sort of compensatory action, had brought the cat home from a shelter soon after their daughter Thea suddenly moved out.

They'd adopted Thea when she was seven months old. Her childhood was uneasy, her early teens tempestuous. At 17, following a long series of escalating arguments about boys, drugs, curfews and whatever annoyance of the moment Thea could find, she sought peace, and maybe salvation, not only in leaving but, after several painful and confusing phone conversations with Alma, in complete estrangement from her parents.

The Quists thought Thea might be over in Berkeley—they examined and reexamined a careless remark by one of their daughter's acquaintance for further clues—but they weren't sure. T.K., as the staff had called Thea when she helped in the store, was obdurately silent. Not even an email from her.

One afternoon Magnus had taken his little-used silver Volvo out of the garage he rented, driven across the Bay Bridge and had repeatedly gone along Telegraph, down Bancroft and back and forth on Shattuck, thinking he'd somehow spy his daughter, and that he could persuade her to come home, all forgiven.

Who needed that forgiveness most, he wasn't quite sure.

Alma taught herself to use social media, but found Thea was no longer active with her old accounts. Their daughter didn't wish to be found.

Alma's dammed-up maternal affections soon spilled out. The new cat was the immediate and obvious beneficiary. At first Alma wanted to name her Thea or T.K., but even before Magnus had boiled very far into apoplexy, Alma thought better. She suggested combining the Swedish words for 'good luck' and calling the cat Lyckatill. Magnus stopped fomenting and agreed.

Good luck was something they both knew they needed in more than a few aspects of their lives.

"But I will not rub that cat like a rabbit foot, *gumman*," Magnus said. Alma gave him the little laugh he expected, but she wasn't sure if he was calling her an old woman to be affectionate or if he was belittling her. As she sometimes did, she gave him the benefit of the doubt.

Later on the morning of the earthquake, Darrol returned from his walk, hopped up the small stoop, entered the street door to the apartments. The vestibule was empty.

He moved to the internal door to the 'Norton. Only Quist and his wife used that door, and it was always locked.

Darrol looked closely at the keypad. He'd picked up most of the code from twice engaging a careless Alma in trivial chat, but he hadn't caught the last two digits. It didn't really matter. Eventually he'd find out, and he'd file away the information for some possible use. Information gave you a better offense, sometimes even a better defense.

Giggling. Clumping. Baritone chuckles. High soprano laughs. Darrol quickly backed away from the keypad and crossed to the mailboxes.

Down the stairs thumped Brick Zimmer and his latest, a blonde, mid 20's. Zimmer had a fondness for blondes. This one was very pretty. Darrol, always quick in his observations, also saw she was slightly cross-eyed. He noticed a brown mole lurking at her jaw. Those little defects made her even more attractive.

Darrol believed an oddity or a blemish could up the ante. His Maria, for instance, occasionally mangled the language, and that pleased him. He was particularly drawn to women with limps, tics, hints of childhood scoliosis. It usually worked in the other direction too. Most women seemed to think Darrol's broken nose enhanced rather than diminished his good looks.

Zimmer flipped a small wave toward Darrol with his free hand, abundant red hairs smirking from above his knuckles. The pilot's other hand was occupied somewhere to the rear of Miss Cross-eyed.

Darrol, shuffling junk mail, gave them a broad wink, which drew a little scowl from Zimmer and an alert, amused look from his date. As the couple bustled outside in a wash of gin and expensive cologne, Darrol felt a tiny jab of envy. The blonde's brief look suggested smart, and smarter women were often out of Darrol's reach.

He went upstairs, precisely watching where he stepped. On the first flight he used the right edge on tread three and stepped lightly on the left of tread seven; on the next flight he stuck to the left side on treads one, four and five. No creaks. Always useful to know where the quiet places are. Knowledge is not just power. It saves your ass if you're trying to sneak up or down and one set of your not-so-beloved foster parents are light sleepers but heavy on leather belts with brass buckles.

Reaching the third floor, he stopped to look at the tracks on the hallway carpet. Last evening Maria must have trailed in flour from *La Dolce Via*. He thought it odd, as the bakery was some distance away, but maybe Maria had shaken out her pockets on approach or was already unwrapping the pastries she stole for him.

The ghostly tracks led in the direction of his apartment. Idly, he wondered if Maria would nab him a couple of Napoleons again soon. He liked Napoleons.

He moved toward his door and stopped again. The carpet was marred by a few dark greasy spots, undoubtedly courtesy of Duff and his cable cars. Grit and grease seemed to follow Duff. Clang, clang, clang goes the oily trolley. Alma would have a fit when she saw those spots.

Darrol himself left few tracks, the barest impression on the carpet. He liked to think of himself as gliding, dancing above it all, a useful subset of stealth.

As he reached the apartment, he noticed tiny flecks of kitty litter not quite managing to hide on the faded floral pattern. His temperature shot up. Lyckatill had been on the prowl. What's more, those insolent cat tracks led directly to the threshold.

Darrol unlocked the door with the stealth of an experienced cat burglar, which in a sense he thought he was, as he was debating finding the damn cat, stealing it and taking it far away, details to be worked out.

He sometimes wondered why Lyckatill annoyed him. He knew it had partly to do with the cat's sublime independence, which Darrol envied, with its disinterested attitude toward him, which he resented, and with the struggle between an atavistic boyhood pull urging him to wield power where he could and the natural caution not to get in bad with his landlords. Old Lady Quist in particular seemed to think that Lyckatill was God.

If Alma Quist was right, God was aloof, meowed at the night sky and didn't know how to clean the kitty litter off his paws. Well, maybe her paws.

Lyckatill, true to her name, was lucky. When Darrol whispered the door open, he first looked to the right. From the left, Lyckatill, in silent mode, burst toward him. She shot between Darrol's legs and bounded unscathed into the hallway. Dislike the animal though he might, Darrol gave it credit for having topnotch instincts. The finer your instincts, the better off you are. One of his mantras.

As Lyckatill fled, Darrol's own peculiar set of instincts kicked in. A minute noise, an out-of-place smell, a fluke of light, pure ESP—something put him on the alert.

He forgot about the cat, quietly closed the door and, light on his feet, levitated towards the bedroom he shared with Maria.

The bedroom door was ajar. A silken sliver of sound. A mixed iota of sweat, fear, oil and unwashed roommate. Darrol eased forward.

"Well. Well. Well." Long ago, Darrol had perfected the art of the drawl. "Look who the cat let in."

Duff Lee straightened, turned and froze. A drawer leaned open, accused him. Duff blinked.

Darrol thought he could see a blush spreading even under that rough-sand skin. "A little panty exploration? Who'da guessed? I thought you were more for..."

"My gloves. Lost a pair." Duff held up his hands, trying for proof. "Need my gloves."

"Well, they sure ain't in that drawer." A snicker. "Not in Maria's drawers they're not."

"I will look somewhere else."

"I guess you should. Jeez, get a grip, Duff."

Duff shoved the drawer shut. He looked down and mumbled something in Chinese. It had the vague sense of an apology.

Darrol nodded. "Aren't you working?"

"Late shift this week." His head still lowered, Duff shuffled out past Darrol, crossed the hall to his own room, closed the door.

Smiling, Darrol moved further into the bedroom. Surprising someone can be so...satisfying.

He watched sunlight sliding delicate tree shadows over the bedroom wall.

Satisfying.

Chapter 2
Street Talk

Russian Hill extracts a fee from walkers. It takes its recompense in aches and stress and cramps and bent-over gasping for breath. Your ankles, shins, calves, knees and lungs all pay.

The pavements are unyielding, the grades ungenerous. Stairs, where you can find them, are ready to test foot flexion, lung power, balance and overall stamina. Walk any distance on the Hill and you'll rediscover your sweat glands, even in winter.

But in exchange for all that you pay to walk on the Hill, you are given great views, many of them exquisite surprises between tall buildings. You are given shade trees, birdsong, a fine panoply of scents. You are given parks—some quite sudden—many quite small, but no less inviting. You are given the crisp California air, somehow more vibrant up here. In some areas you're given the cheery clang of the cable cars and the slow steady song of the underground cable.

Darrol Yount loved to walk on Russian Hill. He knew every road and alley, every odd little half-street, every cul-de-sac, every steep staircase, every viewpoint, every park, every bench. He knew where he'd step on concrete, asphalt, cobblestones, brick, grass. He even knew where he might have to step to avoid the daily dollops of owner-ignored dog droppings.

The Hill was his to command. Since his work at Lanterman's usually started in the late afternoon, he had almost all the time he needed to roam.

Today, Darrol was packing. In his pockets, addition to his small sketchpad, he'd carefully placed two bags containing a few of Maria's latest stolen pastries.

He remembered how, as a boy, he'd very rarely had a chance to stuff his pockets with bits of bread and go feed the ducks. Those few times—fun, brightness in his dark world— would have been with Him #2.

That foster guy didn't seem a bad sort until he wanted to play the tickling game too much. At first it seemed all right. But soon...

Even Darrol's dumb kid-self thought something felt wrong, was wrong, but Him #2 assured Darrol it was just fine. *Tickle, tickle.*

More than once Darrol's adult mind had grabbed Him #2, chucked him into the slimy pond and held him down, sodden white chunks of bread bobbing among the thrashing black water, ducks noisily flapping their wings and quacking in approval.

Today, it wouldn't be ducks he would choose to feed. It would be his favorite street people. As he went on his long walks around Russian Hill and Nob Hill and down into North Beach and sometimes in big loops close to City Center, he'd often encounter one or more of his favorite crazies.

Some of them—social services and the cops willing—inhabited the same small squares of sidewalk day in, day out. Others walked the same little routes over and over, more dependable than the damn city buses.

A few simply popped up here and there, you never knew where. Billy Pickleface was like that, a gypsy jack-in-the-box, his smallpox-scarred features at first slightly-menacing but immediately almost sad or even oddly saintly in their vacuity.

Maria asked Darrol if he had a favorite among his 'unfortunates'—she much preferred that to using his word 'crazies'—but he couldn't pick one. Most of the time, he liked them all. He often stopped to hold what passed for conversations with them, and now and then he brought them Maria's pilfered treats. He wasn't ashamed to say that some of the best goodies went to Jeepers Peepers' flatulent Chihuahua, Perro Caliente.

It was a pleasant, fog-free morning, and Darrol extended his walk down Larkin. Ahead of him, sure enough, Psychedelic Sally was pirouetting beside her pet fire hydrant. As usual, her extreme gestures, her wild flounce of colorful clothes and her maelstrom of straw-brown hair were turning drivers' heads. She was not as distracting as the nude woman

16

who'd once caused a string of accidents over on California Street, but she was distracting enough.

Supposedly Psycho Sally had been a professional dancer before something went wrong. Darrol wondered if there were such a thing as dancer's CTE: leap, slip, tumble, smack your head on the heartless floor. Regardless, bonkers. Nowadays Sally twirled on the streets, performing incredible fragments of self-choreography. She was still lithe enough to manage fantastic leaps and dramatic bends. Her beloved, incredibly-soiled Giants cap often fell by her feet, and it was hard not to drop in a coin.

This morning, Darrol's offering for her was a three-spice cannoli. Sally wide-eyed the pastry, did a bourrée toward him and neatly nabbed it from his hand without squirting any cream. Rancid body odor collided with a whiff of nutmeg. Sally twirled back, stuffing her mouth with cannoli and long strands of hair.

"Let me know if you like the anise," Darrol said. But Sally, not four feet from him, was miles and miles away.

A few blocks over, spotlighted by sun shards reflecting from a glass building, Ain't Marley was broadcasting ska from his big duct-taped boom box and panhandling for batteries.

Ain't Marley was a startling double for the long-gone reggae musician. To those bold enough or foolish enough to mention that to him, he replied with only two words, thus his name.

The guy obsessed on batteries, but he never turned down one of Darrol's treats. Today, he kept nodding in time with the beat, reached for the pistachio biscotti, nodded again, his dreadlocks dancing. He disappeared into the music, muttering "Ain't Marley," which Darrol this time took to mean some form of thank-you.

Darrol turned towards Nob Hill, thinking he'd go back home via Grace Cathedral. The pulsing reggae quickly faded, smothered by traffic rumbles.

He wondered again how Emperor Norton would have fit among today's street people. Crazy or not, the Emperor seemed to have had a real con going, apparently charming merchants, restauranteurs and hoteliers alike, not to mention ordinary residents, the newspapers and even politicians.

Not one of today's crowd—Psychedelic Sally and all the rest—could pull off swiping a banana from a street vendor much less enchanting a whole city. Hell, any of the parrots up on the Hill had more cunning. Darrol liked the crazies he met on his walks, even if they were essentially clueless, but he admired Emperor Norton a whole lot more.

As it often did, the cathedral pulled him up the hill. He felt drawn to go there on his longer walks. Darrol thought it was the huge, beautiful building itself beckoning, not a rascally deity, certainly not any vestigial sense of religious duty. He'd long ago rebelled from that.

When he was a boy trapped in the system, there had been too much religious claptrap crammed into him—at times he felt force-fed—too many layers of dogma slapped onto him— even literally: one sanctimonious prick had backhanded him with a bible—too much Gospel rubbed into his pores, gallons of unctuous oil. He felt sure all these people must belong to the same cult, a First Church of the Truly Grim Foster Parents or a Holy Covenant of the Pious Hypocrites.

Today, breathing lightly after a steady walk, he stood at a favorite spot near one edge of Huntington Park and looked across the street to Grace Cathedral.

Once more he admired the architecture, what he took to be a blend of modern and ancient styles. He liked the twin sturdy bell towers and the slender spire puncturing the sky. In a city of steeples—all saying, Darrol supposed, "Hey, God. Look at us! Reach down your finger and give us a favoring tickle, would you? Oh yes, a tickle. But, p.s. we've got lightning rods installed just so you don't get any cute ideas"— this spire seemed the most...succinct.

Succinct. That was a word Darrol liked, finding it useful, like other nifty words he purposefully acquired. You could get ahead in this world not just by what you said, but by the vocabulary you used.

He particularly liked the way the cathedral claimed dominance up here. It owned the spot. Not the remaining old mansions, not the newer buildings, no matter how grand, not the tallest trees, could make that claim. But it wasn't a bold statement of dominance. It was power asserted quietly. Darrol liked that.

An annoying gaggle of Chinese tourists crossed in front of him, chattering, waving their expensive cameras in all directions. Darrol didn't like tourists in general—although he prided himself on always giving them excellent service in Lanterman's, another self-imposed test of his will power—but it was the Chinese tourists who most irritated him. They clustered too much, rolling about like a big single, jabbering organism, crowded everyone else out. And they wore those silly surgical masks. Did they think San Francisco was full of germs?

Darrol had decided he wasn't prejudiced—after all, didn't he have a Chinese roommate? Didn't he go often to Chinatown with Maria to eat *dim sum*? Didn't he hang out on Grant Avenue each Chinese New Year watching the colorful dragons dancing? No, it was just the way their damn tourists conducted themselves in his town.

As he stared sneeringly at the babbling throng, Darrol noticed a familiar figure beyond them. Lo and behold and verily, verily—he could always remember an assortment of ministerial phrases—there was Gerta Twoshoes on the plaza, sloshing about in one of the low, flower-shaped fountains. He skirted the Chinese and crossed to her.

Gerta was one of Darrol's street favorites. Age about fifty, going on a hundred. Stringy yellow hair like a clump of Emilio's discarded pasta. Face like a twice-crumpled grocery bag. She was wearing her usual green sack dress, the torn bottom edge trailing just above the water. Her trademark mismatched shoes—today a pair of Crocs, one blue, one black—were neatly aligned on the plaza. In a rare moment of coherence, Gerta had claimed she wore odd pairs of shoes for good luck, that budget had nothing to do with it.

"Getting baptized, Gerta?" Darrol asked. She turned, stared at him quizzically, gave him a little wink. He rummaged in a pocket, found a semblance of a ladyfinger, offered it to her. "Well then, here's a communion wafer."

"Ah, Mr. Darcy," she said, her voice surprisingly sonorous. She stepped from the fountain and reached for the ladyfinger. "I accept your Twinkie."

She took the treat, shoved one end in her mouth and ate it with sleight-of-hand speed.

As Gerta wiped her lips with a sleeve, the remainder of the ladyfinger dropped to the ground. "Fiddlediddle!" she said. One of Gerta's oddities was the infrequence of rough swear words. Though she lived in a blue-streak environment, the Emily Post in her misfiring brain almost always kept some civility in her speech.

Gerta frowned. "Well, pooh-hoo!" She bent, considered the shattered confection, carefully picked up the largest piece, regarded it, ate it. She squashed the smaller bits with her bare foot, stepped back into the fountain edge and figure-eighted the water.

Nob Hill was not prime territory for homeless people. They preferred the flatlands around the Civic Plaza or hanging about in the Tenderloin, near the shelter which some called the 'residue mission'.

"Why are you 'way up here, Gerta?" Darrol asked, genuinely curious.

Her head took over making the figure eights. Her hair rolled around, dirty noodles tumbling. He thought she wouldn't answer, but suddenly she did.

"Nearer to Goliath."

He was startled. "Who's Goliath?"

Gerta stood still. "The big one." She licked her lips and stared skywards.

"You mean God?"

"That's the cheese." She resumed swirling.

"Hm. I hope he takes care of you."

She looked down at the water.

"Bye, Gerta." When she didn't respond, Darrol moved away. He was almost to the street when she called after him, more coherent than usual.

"Bless you, Mr. Darcy."

He gave her a big wave over his head and kept walking.

His street people always kept him a little off balance. One moment totally unfocussed or completely irrational, one moment lucid. Their conversation—if that's what you could call it—might range from bizarre to profound, from supplicating to sly. Darrol found it entertaining. Unsettling but entertaining.

He remembered talking to Jeepers Peepers a few months back. JP was perched on a broken shipping crate, staring vacantly at the world. The famous Thinker statue, San Francisco style.

As usual, Perro Caliente was sitting bug-eyed at JP's feet. This dog was the least-hyper Chihuahua Darrol had ever seen, practically comatose. PC's tongue hung out like a beggar's tin cup. Darrol wanted to drop a dime onto it just to see what would happen. Something, no doubt, in canine slow motion.

But he had nothing for the dog that day, coin or otherwise. Instead he offered JP a treat wrapped in tinfoil. The man's big eyes flared even wider behind his cracked spectacles. He grabbed at the offering, dropped the foil onto the sidewalk and regarded the slice of currant bar like a museum specimen.

"Pride," Peepers said. "First thing to go. Out here. And then..."

He took a speculative bite, savored the taste. "Raisins? Cockroaches? No matter." He chewed slowly. He tilted his head looked at Darrol. "What was...?"

"You were talking about pride, pride going," Darrol said, not really expecting JP to pick up the thread. But the guy did.

"Yeah. I had thoughts." JP chewed. "This cockroach is fine. What? Oh, pride. You see, it comes back, Jack." He stared at Darrol. The Chihuahua was gawping up also, waiting for the first crumb to fall.

"You lose it, but then a different brand comes along. Street pride. I got pride, street pride. Don't you forget it." JP's tone stopped just short of hostile.

"No," Darrol said. I'm with you, JP. We've all got our brands of pride."

A loud squawking slashed through Darrol's thoughts. The goddam parrots again. Darrol was in the transition zone between Nob Hill and Russian Hill. Let the realtors battle which block was really which and skyrocket the prices accordingly. You step across just one slab of sidewalk, across just one crack really, and property values shift gears bigtime.

But the damn parrots didn't care which hill they were on. They were busy infesting.

Supposedly years back the birds started out near Telegraph Hill. Some idiot let his pet escape. At first only an innocent screech or two in the neighborhood, jungle lovebirds screwing happily in good old San Francisco. Then more and more—oh how cute!—but now there are flocks, and they have the run of the place. People even put out food for the things.

Darrol fed his street people. But he'd never feed these birds. He'd like to wring every feathery little neck. When he'd moved to the Hill and first noticed them, he admired the bright cherry heads and the lime-colored bodies, thought their swooping antics were fun. But soon he found that they annoyed him. They were a total blight. They fluttered and screamed, filled the eucalyptus trees with bickering, destroyed the calm of his walks.

But it wasn't just that. He envied their freedom, their insouciance—another word he loved, although he regretted that it applied to the parrots—and they mocked him. This was his territory, and he hated intruders beyond his control. He cheered on any hawk or cat who got one of the bastards.

As he quickly moved to the next block, the parrots behind him screamed goodbye. He resisted screaming back.

In front of him, a parade of ants was crossing the sidewalk. He watched for a moment, then crushed the line with his feet. A few survivors scurried in circles.

Darrol was still fulminating when he passed the top of the Vallejo steps. He decided to stop in the small hillside park. It was a clear day, and he expected the views to be grand and satisfying. This might be an opportunity to do some sketches. His smartass art teacher always wanted students to bring drawings to class. Mostly to make fun of them. *Sardonic.* That was the word for the bastard. But Darrol would show him.

He hadn't expected to run into someone he knew. But there on a bench, her face to the sun, was Alma Quist.

Darrol was debating whether to quietly step the other way, when Alma opened her eyes. She turned toward him as though she'd sensed his presence.

"Darrol?" she said. She gave him a small, polite smile. At least she didn't have her husband's cold habit of saying 'Mr. Yount.'

"'morning, Mrs. Quist." Darrol said. "Store closed? Burned down?"

She took a moment before she laughed. "Hardly. No, Georgia and Hilda are working this morning, and I thought I'd get some fresh air. Playing hooky, and you caught me."

"I've been slaughtering parrots," he said, not sure why he might want to provoke her.

Alma was alarmed. "Slaughtering...?"

"In my head. I don't like the way they're taking over the Hill."

"You're not a bird lover?"

"Those parrots aren't birds, Mrs. Quist. They're invaders. I hate the noise."

"Well, I've been listening to chickadees, sparrows and such. Really sweet, really nice." She hesitated, thought, patted the bench. "Want to sit? And please call me Alma."

He sat beside her and looked down across the sunlit slopes, through the trees and over the whitened city to the bay. It all seemed so still. But when he paid attention, he could hear the constant hum rising, the busyness.

The bench slats were cold. He shifted. Something rough tugged at the back of his trouser legs.

Alma was watching him. "Quite a lot to look at, don't you think?"

"Yep."

She stared out again. "When I find myself thinking about my place in the world—up here, for a moment, I can feel almost like I'm the queen of it all, everything else is so small."

Darrol nodded. His kind of sentiment.

"But paradoxically..." Alma tucked back a wisp of hair. "Looking at this expanse, and knowing how much diverse life is scurrying about down there, then it also makes me feel like I'm only a tiny, tiny part. Queen no more!"

"Speaking of royalty—do you suppose Emperor Norton ever came up here?" Darrol asked.

"Oh, I'd think so," Alma said. "Probably not for panhandling. But maybe surveying his domain. Are you interested in the Emperor?" She seemed surprised.

Darrol flicked a eucalyptus leaf from his sleeve. "He's caught my attention. Quite a character."

"Talk to old Mrs. Durr. She's the expert. Claims she's related to him, which is extremely doubtful. But she's up on his history."

Darrol nodded. He watched a distant airplane moving silently above the bay. The breeze dropped, and the air immediately felt much warmer. The scent of pine drifted lazily around him.

He glanced at Alma. She had closed her eyes again and tilted her head to the sky. Her face seemed tired but kind.

He thought about Her #4, a dumpling like Alma, maybe even smaller. But Her #4 was anything but kind. She was able to rapidly summon the gods of wrath, inflating her angry body like a puff adder. He remembered the hot, lumpy oatmeal raining down on him after he'd said he wanted none, the oily retch of soapsuds after she punished him for a supposed lie. Did he lie back then? Maybe so. He wasn't sure. Sometimes a lie was the only defense.

"Easy to get lost in your thoughts up here, isn't it?" Alma was watching him again.

"I guess. I was back in my childhood."

"Happy times?"

"Anything but."

Alma waited, but Darrol added nothing more.

"I'm sorry," she finally said.

Shrugging, he mustered up a little politeness. "And you? Grow up in Sweden like your husband?"

"No, I was born here. Right in San Francisco in fact. But both my parents were Swedish immigrants. They clung pretty heavily to the old traditions." She laughed. "That's probably why I have a small purple birthmark in the shape of Sweden on my derriere. Willed on me by my mother."

Darrol gave her a small grin. "If that's how it works, my mother—whoever she was—must have willed my birthmark too."

"Oh?"

"Yeah. I got something looks like one of those inkblot tests on my thigh. I reckon she wanted me to spend my life guessing what it meant." He snorted. "Or maybe who I am."

"You sound like you're a little down on yourself."

"Down on...? I don't think so."

"You got anybody cheering you on? Your girlfriend maybe? She seems like a nice person."

"I don't need cheering on."

Darrol stood, stretched, and moved back onto the path. A chastising squirrel scrambled to avoid him.

"Everybody needs at least one cheerleader," Alma said quietly.

"Naw. You do it for yourself. That's the best way. Maybe the only way." Darrol began jumping up and down. "See? I go rah! Rah! Rah!" He flailed his arms. "Gimme a D, gimme an A!"

He stopped and moved hair away from his forehead.

Alma chuckled. "OK, OK. I'm convinced. If you ever want to be a cheerleader for the 'Norton, let us know. I bet we could use you."

"I'll remember."

Darrol said goodbye and returned to the street. The odors of hot tar and juniper welcomed him.

Above him, a hawk was circling. He stared up at it.

Hope you got your sights on something good. Maybe on a goddam parrot.

Chapter 3
Fine Dining, With Footnotes

Scorned women notwithstanding, hell hath no fury like a noisy restaurant kitchen during the dinner hour. Especially when a chef, already overdue for one of his bi-weekly tirades, had set the lamb chops on fire.

Flames burst heavenward like an angry NASA rocket scorching up from the launch pad.

"Pecore in cielo!" Joe Rosa, wearing an enormous, bobbing *toque blanche* almost as huge as his ego, cursed in two languages, grabbed a fire extinguisher and whooshed the grill with a white storm of chemicals du jour.

"Charge 'em extra," Joe snarled when the lamb chops re-emerged through the miasma. *"Doppia merda!* See if they don't taste better this way!"

He left the smoldering meat for an assistant to repair and whirled toward the béarnaise. *"Roba calda di mio agnello, si?* Oh, close your mouth, Chips."

Chips Blaine, the sous chef, thoughtfully sampled the sauce.

Darrol grinned. He liked watching the nightly dramas in the kitchen. Fastening his apron, he turned back to the assignment board.

He was about to start his shift as a waiter—there were no 'servers' at Lanterman's. "If you want a 'server' go watch tennis," the restaurant's founder had quipped. By his still-standing edict, the wait staff were always called 'waiters', were always male, were always dressed in traditional black and white.

For San Francisco diners, Lanterman's of North Beach was the perfect combination of well-established and contemporary. It had a solid menu balancing long-running favorites with plenty of surprises, a cuisine which was current but never too-edgy.

Lanterman's was quiet, ideal for romance, intrigue or closing a deal. No garish neon signs or giant letters announced the place: a simple brass plate by the elegant handcrafted mahogany door bore the restaurant's name.

The staff was sincere but not snooty, a class act. Darrol liked to think he had something to do with that. He was a charmer to both women and men. He'd mastered the art of being obsequious without groveling, of being attentive without hovering. He remembered the names, the tastes, the quirks of the regulars. He impressed newcomers and made them feel genuinely welcome. He was gracious with the uncertain, courteous to the boorish, sympathetically-firm with the tipsy. He memorized complicated orders, easily dealt with changing minds. He knew when to smile politely, when to raise an eyebrow, when to nod just so.

Darrol was professionalism itself, wrapped in good looks and quiet good humor, Cary Grant reincarnated. He knew it. And he especially loved it that no one—not customers, staff or management—knew his disdainful heart.

No way was this his stopping point.

He stepped from the kitchen and surveyed the dining room. At this early hour, there were only a few customers. Spike Duggan was tending to all of them, floating about with his smooth, almost-standoffish proficiency, his head held high like a danseur posturing.

One of the elderly regulars, Oscar Labellarte, sat at table three, engrossed in a novel and in his first cocktail, undoubtedly a Rob Roy. Oscar's twin puffs of wild white hair looked like big earmuffs trying to escape his gnarly skull.

At table five, a well-dressed young couple held hands and shared meaningful glances, likely awaiting those devil-seared lamb chops. Honeymooners, Darrol thought. Hungry for meat, hungry for each other. Juices all around. When the big juicy bill arrived, it might even be a turn-on.

A rumpled business type sat at table four juggling a spreadsheet and a martini. Two olives lay forlornly to one side, creating a small stain on the white linen tablecloth. Darrol frowned inwardly. Customers also needed to adhere to rules of propriety. The open spreadsheet was already pushing it, but dropping olives on the cloth was pure bad manners.

Darrol suppressed a sigh and turned to the front of the restaurant.

The manager, Radisson Vero, was at the hostess station, talking quietly to Tekla Hart as she checked the reservation rundown. Vero was far too slick for Darrol's taste—and Darrol didn't like that the man's black hair literally was slick with brilliantine—but there were two or three things to envy.

Vero's tuxedo was top-quality, the daily yellow rose in its lapel always mysteriously fresh. The roses were real enough— Darrol had checked, surprised by a sensual tingle as he ran his fingers twice across the soft, lightly-scented petals on Vero's jacket as it hung on the office door. Yes, real roses.

Darrol wasn't so sure about the genuineness of the hint of European accent—country not known or ever mentioned—or about the origin of the small scar on Vero's cheekbone—more than once it had been tossed off as a 'dueling matter'—but Darrol had to allow that the man had style.

And Radisson Vero seemed to hold Tekla Hart in thrall. Whether that came from being boss and employee or something more, Darrol had yet to learn. Vero was married— and his wispy, high-voiced wife had a habit of dropping in to Lanterman's ad hoc—but Tekla was single.

Darrol found the tall hostess beguiling—that was the exact word he wanted, *beguiling*. He'd looked it up, hoping to enchant her with it—but although she was always very polite to him, even cautiously friendly, Tekla kept her distance. Darrol decided she was shy, or knew he was living with Maria, or was a lesbian, or she had a secret. Or a secret lover. Maybe all of the above: thus, just as he thought, *beguiling*.

This evening, Vero had provisionally assigned Darrol tables two, eight, twelve and thirteen.

Table thirteen, a corner five-top, was the subject of much discussion and not a little superstition. When Vero graciously allowed them the privilege, some waiters traded it. Carey Modoc in particular didn't want to serve at thirteen. If Vero was in a snit, he took pleasure in assigning Carey the table, no trades allowed, and making Carey suffer.

Darrol was amazed at the number of people on the staff who had no desire to serve at thirteen.

"Judas Priest, you're a superstitious bunch," he'd say. The religious ones weren't sure if they could laugh at such little jokes. But it wasn't just the old hoohah about the number. Even Darrol had to agree that the table seemed jinxed.

At thirteen, there were more drinks spilled. More orders screwed up. More customers who were rude and irritating. More lousy tippers. Over the years, it was said, the table had landed two heart attacks, one stroke and three Heimlichs. Strange shroud of Turin markings appeared on thirteen's tablecloths, candles set fire to seasonal decorations, a bee stung a busboy when the kid adjusted the fresh flowers.

Darrol felt that the table had real character and gravitas (another word he had looked up; a good vocabulary was a very useful thing). *Gravitas.*

It would have been easy to renumber, to call the table anything but thirteen. However, whenever that idea arose, Vero nixed it. On orders from higher up, he always said. Some thought he meant God, but most realized he was talking about the son.

Supposedly the restaurant's founder, the great and mighty August Lanterman himself, had eaten at table thirteen the night he died. Possibly just hours before his unusual death. Some wondered if that was the jinx at work again. But August's son, Vinnie, still a majority owner though rarely in evidence these days, continued to insist the number be kept, for reasons only a psychiatrist might divine.

Good old thirteen was often assigned to Darrol. He was not unreasonably superstitious, though he'd had his share of spilling water and wine at the table. He simply took care of things by being even more careful and meticulous than usual.

Recently, he'd doubled his guard after almost dumping pumpkin soup on a suddenly-moving child. Only Darrol's amazingly-discreet pivot had saved the day. Later he was sorry the accident had been averted. The kid was really obnoxious and doubtless would have benefitted from a sticky dousing with hot, rusty cream. Maybe from a few home-made croutons chucked on for good measure.

"Hi, Darrol." Xavier Shea, the principal busboy, scurried by, neatly balancing a tray of clean glasses.

Darrol followed Xavier to the serving banquette. "Hey, listen, X. If Miss Hugo comes in tonight, keep an extra eye on her water, will you? Last week she got really snotty when we were two seconds behind on a refill."

Xavier nodded. "Gotcha. I appreciate the alert."

Darrol grunted. "She's probably flushing her system. Colonics. Hydroponics. Tectonics. Something."

"Ebonics?" Xavier flashed a big smile. "But what's a black dude to know anyhow?" Even though he was at the bottom of the pecking order at Lanterman's, Xavier sometimes risked showing a sense of humor.

Darrol nodded. "In any case, I guess she's one rich bitch and not to be tangled with."

"Aw, man, Darrol, you got her twisted round your little finger."

"Think so?" Darrol made a production of checking his fingers and nails. Clean and absent any evidence of Miss Hugo or her furs.

"You gentlemen plan on working tonight?" Radisson Vero had glided over with his trademark stealth.

"Just a small coaching session, Mr. Vero," Darrol said mildly. He squelched the impulse to twirl Vero's annoying little moustache. Or to push one end up into that unlikely scar.

The manager seemed mollified. "Well, good, then." He made a minute adjustment to a table cloth.

"Before more guests arrive," he said to Xavier, "get on your knees, pull out the stupid matchbooks and kindly stick a real shim under that damn leg on 22. Wobbling again."

"Yessir."

Vero slid away towards the kitchen.

"Where you gonna stick that shim, X?" Darrol said, studying the nearest chandelier.

Darrol, like the best of waiters, was a dancer, a diplomat, a clairvoyant, anticipating without being the least pushy. He could be ever-present, yet virtually-unnoticed. He understood when to speak or simply to nod; when to laugh, when to smile or merely to politely acknowledge. He knew every menu item.

He sampled all specials, told of each like a master storyteller. There were times—often—when, as he described the food, he could hear his customers' salivary glands rejoicing, their gastric juices jumping in anticipation. He took great pride in all of this. And he expected a fair measure of reciprocity.

Give Darrol a receptive diner—a polite, attentive, interested, taste-attuned, appreciative, gracious, respectful diner—and he was perfection.

Give him a nosher, a food-shoveller, a boor, a clown or an arrogant prick who looked down on him, and Darrol could be like the Titanic's favorite iceberg: smooth, easy innocence above, fulminating, dangerous and malicious beneath.

Unfortunately, most of his reprisals couldn't be recognized by the diners—Darrol couldn't foul his own nest with traceable acts like confusing orders or shortchanging—so mostly he had to settle for little covert bites of revenge, inner chuckles.

He might substitute regular coffee for decaf, full-calorie drinks for diet sodas. Spitting in the food was juvenile, he knew, but sometimes he did it anyway, and when he could, he'd watch a complicit fork or spoon deliver his finest hawkings to an offender's unaware mouth. *Life's small pleasures.*

Dishwater was a dandy additive for certain spicier dishes. In his locker he kept a small, opaque vial of urine, ideal for sprinkling into Chips' sauces or Emilio's soups—adding a *soupçon*—another word he loved, and so apt, he thought—of acid retribution.

Diner be good or diner beware. That was the unseen motto of many a restaurant.

Occasionally fate gave Darrol a hand in small paybacks. Whenever a jerk left his cell phone behind, as often happened, Darrol was solicitously concerned—"Sorry, sir, we didn't find anything"—or if some bastard had left his car keys, Darrol would hunt like a gillie—"No, regrettably not under the table either, sir. Shall we call a taxi for you?"

Car keys Darrol gleefully tossed in the dumpster. But his little collection of misplaced phones was growing. You never knew when you might need to make an anonymous call.

Often very satisfying, those little paybacks.

Tonight went quickly and smoothly. Decent tips. Amiable diners if a few sloppy ones. No drunks. Even Mr. Labellarte ate quietly, exited quietly. The irascible Miss Hugo didn't show. No accidents at table thirteen. Radisson Vero left early.

Closing time arrived. Darrol was almost disappointed.

"How's this for a laugh?" Carey Modoc said as they were helping Xavier with the remaining bussing. "The other night at that fancy Italian place on Clement, a whole table of shmucks were hassling the server—sorry, dear, dead Mr. Lanterman, I mean the waiter—and they were rowdy, rude, pushy. Giving him trouble from the get-go. It was Greg Purchase, you know, the kid who blushes so easily."

"Yeah, I know Greg," Spike Duggan threw in. "Worked with him once. He ain't got a chance in hell of making it."

Darrol frowned. "Let Carey tell the story, would you?"

Carey was blushing himself, but he went on. "Anyway, poor Greg, who was having a bad night to begin with, serves the main courses. He's offering the parmesan when the chief schmuck hits the rudeness button.

"'Don't bother me, just put it on everything, dammit,' the schmuck says.

"Greg sprinkles some parmesan on the pasta, thinks about it, then he dumps parmesan over the guy's head and shoulders. In his lap too. They're all sitting there with their mouths open.

"Our Greg starts to leave, but then, still not saying anything, he comes back and scatters the rest of the cheese on the other idiots for good measure before making himself scarce."

"That's really great!" Darrol said. "Primo come-uppance! I'd loved to have seen that."

"See, I told ya," Spike growled. "Greg dug himself a big hole in the ground. Word spreads fast. Who'd hire him now?"

Xavier was laughing. "What a way to go."

"I'd hire him!" Carey said.

Spike stared. "Yeah, well, when you're in a position to hire anyone, Fairy, we'll see."

Darrol stiffened. "His name's Carey."

"Whatever." Spike tugged at his apron and strode away, whistling.

Xavier and Carey turned to collect more glassware. Darrol, grabbing tablecloths, went toward the hosting station, where Tekla was putting on her jacket. She waved off Darrol's attempt to help.

"What was so funny?" she asked.

"A waiter at Ciao lost his cool. Very satisfying. Long story. How 'bout we go for a drink and I tell you about it?"

"Can't. Sorry." She zipped up. "And don't you have a girlfriend, Darrol?"

"Sure, but we have an understanding."

She picked up her purse. "Is that understanding a two-way thing or a one-way thing?"

"Hey...it's just a drink."

"Anyway—believe it or not—I have to go walk my mother's dog." Tekla looked at her watch. "And I have twenty-two minutes to get over there before disaster. G'night, Darrol." She swept off.

Darrol smiled. He liked a challenge.

Maria was waiting for him just inside the hall of their apartment. Maria was always waiting for him, living for the crumbs of his affection.

Tonight she seemed especially glad to see him, giving him a huge hug, squeezing him in small flurries of cinnamon and vanilla. Long ago Darrol had told Maria not to shower right after work as he liked to come home to the bakery smells hovering around her.

The smells gave him pleasure in their own right, but eventually he realized there was also a connection to one of the rare happy times in his childhood.

Her #5, Mrs. Santa Claus herself, fat and jolly, baked almost daily, and her scrawny little foster kid was allowed to revel in smells, tastes and textures, the flour sometimes turning his eyebrows white. Naturally, the State, instinctively sadistic, decided that Darrol needn't remain in that home very long. He still missed the sugared raisins.

"Guess what, Darrol?" Maria looked like she'd scored a winning lottery ticket.

"Why don't you just get to it, Mimi?"

He watched the familiar little pout appear. "But OK," he said. "I'll play your game. Tips were good. I'm feeling generous."

He led her into the small living room. They sat together on the lumpy sofa.

"Ah, lemme think," Darrol said. "Someone finally got up the nerve and smacked Lenz on the kisser with a big cream pie?"

Maria giggled. "Mr. Lenz doesn't deserve that!"

"All bosses deserve that. But let's see." Darrol pretended to think hard. "I know! Your mother has decided she likes me."

"Oh, I wish, I wish. But no, it's not that either." She tugged at a strand of her hair. Motes of flour danced into the air.

Darrol's spidered his fingers up her leg, inside her skirt. "Ah, you tease," he said. "I know. You're not wearing any underwear. Is that it? Let's find out."

Maria's hand halted his, though without much conviction. "Darrol, you're not being serious."

He pushed his hand further up her thigh. "Oh, but I am."

She wriggled free. "Well, I'll tell you, silly. I got a raise today! A good one!"

"What'd you have to do? Help Willy Lenz get his own raise and sit on it?"

Maria's face fell. "Darrol, that's not very nice. I thought you'd be happy. It's more than two dollars an hour extra. The Merry Widows said profits are good, and we're all sharing the benefit."

Darrol got up and walked toward the window. "I don't get those two old ladies. Husbands kick off, bakery gold mine falls into their hands. They can have their cakes and eat them too. So why share?"

"Some people are nice, Darrol."

He stood at the window and stared out. Fog lazed down under the streetlights. The distant, deep moan of a Golden Gate foghorn slid across his thoughts. Grumbling in harmony was the faint hum-rattle of the cable car chain turning under Mason. Darrol refocused on his dim reflection on the dark pane, saw Maria move toward him. She put her arms around his waist.

"Another little surprise," she said. "I didn't have to sneak any goodies out for you tonight. The merry widows said everyone could take a treat. *Au gratin.* I brought you a chocolate cream cake. Pretty good, huh? I put coconut and chopped nuts on it, just for you."

"I think you mean *gratis.* I wouldn't want cheese on my cream cake."

Maria laughed. "Gratis, grass, gratin. Easy to mix up!"

Darrol turned to face her. "You're OK, Mimi." He gave her a kiss. She snuggled into his chest. "But I'm wondering..." he said.

"Mm. Wondering?"

"If it tastes as good when it's given us for free. It won't have the flavor of excitement like it does when you've swiped it...."

"...with my sticky fingers?"

"That's an old joke, Mimi. But yeah."

The foghorn lamented again. Maria shivered. They walked toward the kitchen.

"So what about this?" Darrol said. "Someday I want you to steal the whole damn bakery and bring it to me. Will you do that for me?"

"You know I will."

Chapter 4
Magnus Dei

This afternoon, the 'Norton was jumping. Alma Quist said it seemed like a medieval village during a raucous harvest festival. Or the inside of a wildly-populated Brueghel painting.

Many of the regulars had chosen this hour to come in and were combining shopping with chatting noisily as though they'd not seen each other in ages.

Newcomers hunted for items, none afraid to interrupt the staff or the regulars to ask what was where.

Tourists gawked at the poster-board Emperor and tried to encourage Alma to take the sword off the wall. She declined, but always with a smile. "Too valuable an antique that. Emperor Norton's very own sabre," she'd say, not the least concerned about the lie, her false pride of ownership bolstered by each viewer's envy.

It was almost staff changeover time, and Georgia Vining and Jazz Turner had arrived early to do their own shopping before beginning their shifts.

Magnus Quist, in a new green apron, astonished customers at the main register with his dexterity in using the antique scales and weights. At the smaller checkout counter, Hilda Brown was busy with a steady line of shoppers.

In the Nook, Jump Jesperson and Lukas Knudsen guzzled the free coffee, trying to top each other with war stories and to hold the attention of an elderly Russian-American couple, Ilia and Olga Grekhov.

"So tell me what was so bad about Viet Nam, a war 'way over there," said Lukas. "My grandparents had goose-stepping Nazis living right in their village, taking over. Nazis, good God, up close and personal, ready to line people along the wall and shoot them. Brutal."

Jump waved that off. "You want brutal, try the stinking jungle. Booby traps ready to impale your face or rip you right in the nuts, pardon my French, Mrs. Grekhov." His voice was grating.

Olga raised her teacup but said nothing.

Jump leaned close to Lukas. "You try parachuting into that kinda godawful mess or onto ground so infested with tunnels you'd think brigades of gophers had gone mad. That's war, sir. Highly up close and personal."

Lukas raised an eyebrow. "Parachuting into Viet Nam? You really do that, Colonel?"

"Special ops, special missions." Jump folded his arms and sat back in his chair, his eyes intense and challenging.

On Aisle 10, Mrs. Durr was bending the ear of Ramu Grendhal and Della Rossiter as they shelved specialty pastas.

"I traced my line right back to one Benjamin Kearny, you know," Mrs. Durr said. "Born, oh, about 1856. Someday I'll prove Benjamin's father was Emperor Norton." She popped a peppermint into her mouth.

"I don't even know who my grandfather was," Ramu said, clicking the old labeling machine into submission. "I only know that he dumped my pregnant grandmother on a ship, pointed to America and said *alavida, qismat* or maybe just *cheerio* and disappeared with his mistress into Bombay."

"Oh dear." Mrs. Durr shook her head. "What about you, Della?"

"My living relatives give me enough trouble," Della told her, "so I don't pay any attention to the dead ones."

Mrs. Durr laughed. "Well, ancestry matters," she said. "At least to me. Besides, who wouldn't want to be related to such an interesting man as the Emperor?"

At the register, Magnus was explaining Norton Notes to a slim, wind-burned woman who was holding an orange cycling helmet and a white netted bag. She looked ready to play some sort of hybrid basketball.

"Norton Notes are like coupons, *ja*?" Magnus told her. "Use them for a little bit of savings, you know. My wife's idea. It's tied into our namesake, the Emperor. He issued his own currency. One bill of which, you can see here, so."

He pointed to the wall near the sword. A dark wooden frame held a piece of yellowed scrip. Magnus quoted from memory. "'Issued by The Imperial Government of Norton I.' That bill's the real thing, worth exactly—well, worth nothing in exchange value—but, I suppose, worth quite a lot as a collectible." His glasses gleamed.

"History adds value," said Alma, leading a customer to the second register. "At least for some of us. Here, Hilda will help you with this."

The bell above the door jingled brightly—Alma had insisted on installing this old-fashioned signal—and the Green girls dashed in amidst a burst of sunlight. Paige, 11, and Patricia, 9—better known as Pig and Pug—often showed up after school, sent almost daily on shopping errands by their stay-at-home-with-a-bottle mom.

The girls seemed to enjoy their visits. Magnus kept the big gumball machine well-stocked and was known to slip them quarters.

Pug also liked hearing Magnus recite passages from Lewis Carroll, though lately her older sister seemed less enthused about that. If Magnus began to expound, Pig tended to examine the Norton figure or to peer into the glass case at the display of 19th century toys Magnus kept near the front.

"Excuse me, Mrs. Quist," Pig said. "Where are the sponges?"

"Not yellow," Pug announced loudly. "Mom don't like yellow."

"Doesn't," Pig told her. Pug shrugged.

Alma smiled. "We have pink. That'd be nice. They're in the little hardware section in the back."

"Back?" Magnus leaned over the counter toward the girls. "It's no use going back to yesterday, because I was a different person then," he said.

"That's silly," said Pug.

"That's Alice," Magnus told her. "But never take Alice at face value, käraste." He pronounced the endearment with a slight hiss. "Lots of ambiguity there. Do you know that word, Paige? Ambiguity?"

He swept up his swatter and demolished a too-slow fly atop the gumball machine. The girls flinched.

"We need to get our sponges," Pig said, dragging her sister away from the counter.

"Let me show you where," Alma said.

"What's a human sponge?" Pig asked. "Mom says we have some of those in our family."

"You'll have to ask your mother," Alma said. "But I think those come in all colors too."

Laughing, she led them up an aisle.

"You really do need a better quality *kapusta*." Olga Grekhov plunked a fat red cabbage on the counter in front of Magnus. "Ilia's borscht requires only the finest."

"We do our best," Magnus hefted the vegetable. "This one certainly would work just so in *kokt rödkål,* a pickled cabbage delight from Sweden. It goes nicely with pork or—"

"—yes, all well and good, but we're Russian," Olga said.

"The only genuine Russians on Russian Hill, it appears," Ilia added, "or there would be more demand for better cabbages. Mind you, your beets aren't bad." His gaunt face wore a permanent stamp of weariness.

Magnus weighed the cabbage on his old manual balance scale, accurately countering it with the correct two iron weights, and only needing to add a tiny third weight to achieve equilibrium.

"I'm forever amazed how you do that," Ilia said.

"Life is all about balance, don't you think?" Magnus weighed the beets. "Did you notice we have fresh dill?"

Moments later, Darrol Yount breezed in. He noticed Hilda. "*Wooden tag,* Mrs. Braun," he said, clicking his heels.

Hilda, flustered as always by any attention, gave him a shy little half-smile and fumbled with the box of crackers she was pricing. Darrol stepped to the candy display, found a licorice whip, tried to snap it in the air.

"I'm disappointed. No quake this time." He waved it again as he approached the counter. "Wouldn't want to lose my touch."

"You like whips, Mr. Yount?" Magnus asked, his voice soft and ambiguous. He sounded like Laurence Olivier in *Marathon Man.*

"Whips, yes," Darrol said affably. "And chains and...studded leather. Of course. Just like everyone. Does the 'Norton carry any of that kinda stuff?"

Magnus took Darrol's bill and made change. His voice dropped even lower. "I believe there's an excellent little shop over on Polk near Pine, if you're serious, Mr. Yount."

"Serious? That's my little secret. And call me Darrol. Meantime, this whip I eat." He tugged a bite free, turned, and almost collided with a pretty young woman leaving Hilda's register. They made polite excuses.

Darrol held the door open. "Would I've seen you down at the Art Institute?" he asked.

"Possibly," she said. "I fool around with ceramics."

They went out into the street. The motionless air was warm, smelling of star jasmine.

The woman inhaled, smiled, looked at Darrol. "You taking classes too?"

"Yeah. When I can fit one in," Darrol said. "Right now I'm in basic drawing." He stuck out his hand. "I'm Darrol Yount, aka Michelangelo."

She laughed. "Karin Holt, aka myself."

She juggled her shopping bag and they managed a brief handshake. "Nice to meet you. Sorry, but I gotta dash." She turned up the street, chasing the clang of a cable car.

Darrol watched her for a moment. He smiled, bit hard at the licorice whip.

Magnus was sipping aquavit, sitting upright at the *Svea Rike* board, his head held high. Alma, drinking tea while awaiting Magnus' next move, studied her husband. His more distant ancestors supposedly were of the Swedish nobility. All Magnus lacked was a crown, nicely bejeweled. Or perhaps a gold scepter.

Sweden Rules always brought out his imperious side, even when they were playing with other couples from the Swedish Society. But during those games Alma could enjoy the changed dynamics.

She and Anja Olson, for instance, ignoring the intense intricacies of the game, always gossiped for pleasure and, Alma long ago realized, to aggravate the men. The women's chatter and lack of focus could lead their husbands to errors or to quiet, polite forms of enraged confusion or, on a good evening, to both.

Tonight it was just the Quists, Alma playing as the Sturr Family and Magnus as the noble Grips. Magnus was accumulating a fine balance of money, land, fiefs and cultural achievements and was on his way to winning the most status points.

Three convoluted centuries of Swedish history lay before them on the complicated, colorful board and in the gorgeous cards and tiles. Alma often said that the visual treat alone was enough for her, but she never let Magnus run away with the game.

At the moment they were at war with Poland, and Magnus was amassing troops. Alma, however, paid less attention to the war than to her longer strategy, building up points in culture and science. And to distracting her opponent.

"So, a good day today?" She reached over to stroke Lyckatill, kibitzing from a third chair. The car purred like a fine old Saab. Alma missed those cars, though, in an ironic moment of fate, it had been a Saab which hit her father. He'd been born in Trollhättan, very near the factory where they once made those automobiles.

Magnus pursed his lips. "Not a bad day. But the month has been weak, yes?" He peered at the board. "Do we wish to ally our forces here?"

"Not if the Grips are going to stab the Sturrs in the back again."

"That's ancient history," Magnus said, chuckling softly at his oft-repeated joke. "OK, then, as Exchequer, I need to roll for Poland's first attack."

They ran a military sequence and Sweden won. Magnus grunted and sat back.

"Sell," he said. "It would be a good time."

Alma studied the board. "Sell what? Palaces? Troops? Those queens? Aren't your holdings pretty diverse?"

"I mean the store, the apartments. The whole thing."

"Magnus, enough. Can't we just enjoy the game?"

"Ah, the game." He took off his glasses, squinting as he polished them with a brown chamois he'd pulled from a pocket. "Always fun, always challenging. But where are we in the bigger game, *käraste?* Over 25 years now and we never get ahead."

"What does that mean, 'get ahead'?"

"That's one thing I admire about you, Alma, your intentional obtuseness. The first King Gustav had that trait, I believe, and often confounded his courtiers with it." Magnus put his glasses back on.

Alma smiled benignly. "I'm neither king nor queen, Mr. Quist. I'm just dull little me."

"Never dull, Alma. Never would I have married dull. But tell me, aren't we slowly draining your inheritance rather than building on it?"

"Ups and downs. I wouldn't say draining." Alma drank her tea. It was cold and a little bitter. "My turn, I think." Her hand vacillated between the piles of undrawn cards.

Magnus finished his aquavit. "Very well, another time. But eventually we must stop to reassess our lives. That's something I expect many fail to do before one day they wake up and discover they're dead."

Alma laughed. "Now who's being Gustavian? He loved his little paradoxes."

She reached for an Event card. "But yes, we will talk." She flipped the card. "Oh, look! *Fantastiskt!* I must have the magic touch!"

Magnus leaned in, saw the Peace card, nodded.

"Ah. Then let it be so, Alma," he pronounced. "For this round." He pushed back from the table. "I'll go down and help lock up, ja?"

"Ja, *sötnöt.*"

As he stood, Magnus bumped into Lyckatill's chair. The cat mewled, thumped to the floor and fled toward the kitchen.

"*Han är så ledsen, katt!*" Alma called after it. "Around King Clumsy you need all nine lives."

"Perhaps ten lives, *katt,*" Magnus murmured, opening the door, "perhaps ten."

Chapter 5
Sweetness and Light Overtures

*L*a *Dolce Via* was an enviable place to work. The popular Marina District bakery was convenient to bus lines, provided employee bicycle racks—one of them a striking piece of Victorian curlicue iron rescued from the old Sutro Baths—and even offered three off-street employee parking places, assignments democratically-rotated every month among those few who drove to work.

The pay was reasonable, the benefits generous and the work hours flexible provided you asked for time off or a schedule change a little in advance.

It hadn't always been this way. The bakery opened in 1969 as *Pane di Vita*, founded by two close friends and business partners, Emilio Lombardi and Anthony Russo. They were a tough pair, tight with money, ruthless with vendors, demanding of their employees, less-than-imaginative about the possibilities of the business.

During the first decades, the place saw plenty of turmoil, mostly of the aggrieved staff variety. But the bakery was in a fine location. It put out decent breads and acceptable cakes and pastries, and it survived.

Emilio died in late 1999, smiling in the arms of his mistress. Anthony died only a few months later, grimacing in the arms of his bookie.

During services for Anthony at St. Dominic's, along came the kind of miracle most Catholics can only dream of.

The two widows—*Le Due Vedove*—Rosa Lombardi and Sophia Russo, put their black-veiled heads close together in the front pew. They were thought to be in deep, shared grief, but by the miracle—the arrival of exhilarating freedom—they were reaching a quick understanding and experiencing uncommon joy, considering the occasion and the doleful oratory of the priest.

When they burst into giggles, everyone thought they were weeping, and loud sobbing flooded the church.

Soon after the husbands were tucked safely away, *Pane di Vita* was reborn as *La Dolce Via.*

Rosa and Sophia leased part of the adjoining building and enlarged the premises. They brightened the space with windows, more light and cheerful colors. They brought in new display cases, new equipment, new tables and counters, and they made the work areas more comfortable for employees.

Insurance money works wonders.

In the most important change, the widows created a whole new approach to the merchandise. They kept an Italian emphasis but added international goodies, encouraged improvisation and rewarded culinary innovation. And they hired a new manager, whose main brief was to make sure all the employees were content.

"I want everyone to taste happiness in our products," said Rosa.

This time, the employees remained. 'Turnover' was no longer a personnel problem but a wildly successful treat available in apple, peach, cherry and—a big hit—mandarin almond.

The bakery always smelled wonderful, filled with an engaging waft of spices, butters, creams, herbs, sweets and fruit. It all triggered so much saliva that, in a less health-conscious era, brass spittoons would have been in evidence along every wall.

The staff, much like well-chosen ingredients in a good *pannacotta con frutti di bosco,* blended nicely, even though each had a very distinct personality.

The chief baker, Tito Fiorenze, a small, energetic man of about 60, knew he was good, in fact very good, but took on no airs. The others adored him, although they cringed when he smiled, as his teeth looked like the ruins of the Colosseum in Rome.

"Overindulgence has its price," Tito once said cheerfully, catching Maria staring.

Gracie Ocean, the chief pastry chef, was a middle-aged woman as sweet as the confections she created. Her laminated pastries, each layer light as fairy wings, were the envy of San Francisco. It was Gracie who was most likely to notice Maria's daily pilferings, and Maria was pretty sure that Gracie was simply ignoring them. Sweet, indeed.

Joyce Bacigalupi, the senior pie baker, told off-color stories, somehow never repeating a one, and was always cheerful despite an apparently-boring but long-lasting marriage to 'Pin-Prick'.

"Never marry for love," Joyce told Maria more than once. "Make sure he's good in bed, then study the Karma Sutro."

"The Karma what?"

"That Indian sex book. Everything you need to know. Put it to good use, stay ahead of your guy, and your relationship will be perfect as apple pie." She began dimpling a crust. "Or at least your sex life will."

Maria blushed. She frequently blushed around Joyce.

The only person remaining from the old days was Maureen 'Red' McIlhenny, once a counter worker and now an assistant pastry chef. She was not red of hair—it was enhanced brown—but she was frequently red of face and cheek. On days when there were tight deadlines or big special orders, Maureen was known to known to nip a little Irish whiskey, preferably Bushmill's, and not that covertly, but it never adversely affected her work. In fact it seemed to give her new energy. Tito once offered Maureen a little *grappa*, but that made her sick, so Irish whiskey it was.

Back in 2000, when Maureen heard who her new bosses were, she snorted. "Ah why call them 'The Two Widows'? Let's call 'em 'The Merry Widows'. You can bet they're merry now that their cigar-smoking, philandering, dickhead husbands are gone."

Maureen, Maria learned, had thrown out her own brand of undesirable husband when she turned 50 and since then had lived with a succession of younger men.

"There's always a supply of testosteronics who appreciate experience," Maureen said. "If that Darrol guy of yours gives you trouble..." She shoved a thumb toward the door. Maria blinked, but she still filed away the thought.

Luc Thanh Giang, *La Dolce Via*'s ageless general factotum and main delivery driver, rarely said much, but when he spoke he might offer small fragments of wisdom or advice. At those times, his otherwise expressionless face creased into a thousand simultaneous smiles.

"Did you really go to Berkeley?" Maria asked Giang one morning. "I heard you studied philanthropy."

He laughed. "You mean philosophy?"

"Oh, dear. Maybe I do."

"Regardless, close but no cigarette." Giang tilted his head—Maria thought he looked like an attentive terrier—and smiled at her. "Everything you hear is not gold," he said. "Worth remembering."

He slid two bread racks into a gleaming stainless steel cart. "But I went to Berkeley High for a year. So, part truth." He nodded. "I read some Confucius, Luong Kim Dinh and, most important, Peanuts. So, another truth."

Maria's slight favorite among her co-workers, just because the woman was so inadvertently entertaining, was the principal counter clerk, Nia 'Cookie' Kronos, a meek, worried-faced Greek woman in her mid-40's.

Try as hard as she might, Cookie could not pronounce many of the Italian pastries and treats. Virtually every time she uttered the words, her mind reared, if not in terror, at least in confusion.

Terms like *cannoli, bruttiboni, panforte*, and *zuppa Inglese* tended to come out as *canniggly, beauty-bony, panfruity*, and *zipper glacee*.

Even simple confections like biscotti and tiramisu could get Cookie flustered. And she was always totally floored by the bakery's gorgeous, shell-shaped filled pastries, *sfogliatelle*, though, as a true San Franciscan, she usually got the 'fog' part correct amid her tangled mispronunciations.

Regular customers loved hearing Cookie mangle the words. Some mischievous types purposely asked for the most complicated items.

After a really serious round of garbling several goodies, at the end of which a flustered Cookie couldn't even properly get out *filone*, The Merry Widows were reported to have consoled her. They said that her unusual pronunciations clearly stimulated sales; customers asked for more than they came in for so they could hear her speak. In any case, Cookie's embarrassment was always followed with good-natured laughter. Including her own.

Overseeing everything was *La Dolce Via's* affable manager, Willy Lenz, who also pitched in wherever needed, often singing opera with a sensuous voice which might have led to a musical career had not his range fallen into what Willy ruefully described as mezzo-tenor.

His voice could only drop to bargain basement baritone—oh, he had pleaded with God, oh for half an octave deeper!—and in the upper direction he could only reach the bottom edges of the required stratosphere for true tenors—oh, for seven or eight higher notes and the extra lung power to support them!

But God granted nothing. Undaunted, Willy, forever a mezzo-tenor, modulated expertly and was extremely listenable, regardless of the language in which he sang. He modified arias from the baritone, bass and even soprano repertoires, so he always had lots to perform.

Some days the bakery staff got to listen to all of the major arias from a complete opera. Willy might sing Figaro in the pastry room, Cherubino around the ovens and Count Almaviva at the assembly stations or the pie tables.

For good measure—and Willy was astute at keeping tempos—he might throw in a little conducting, although more than once he forgot that he was wielding tasting spoons or forks or spatulas, and he was known for flinging butter icing or cookie dough or warm crusts of *pane rustica* into the air.

One spectacular afternoon he was out in the shop, humming *La donna è mobile* and using a long tube of bakery sprinkles as his baton. The cap of the tube flew off, and the customers standing near the counter were showered with colored bits of sugar.

"Fireworks!" Willy declared happily, not missing a beat. "And a free marzipan fruit for each of you, my friends! Cookie, please give one to each of them."

Cookie, who had ducked her head into a display case, quickly came out, embarrassed, but ready to dispense the treats. What's more, 'marzipan' was one word which for some reason never troubled her.

Maria liked everyone at the bakery. And she loved it that the one ingredient in almost everything they did was laughter.

This Wednesday, *La Dolce Via* was just into its semi-annual Viennese Week. Tito had wanted a focus on tortes, and the staff had outdone themselves with Sacher-tortes, Esterhazys, Dobos and Malakovs, along with Tito's own invention, a five-layer cake masterfully intertwining Austrian marzipan, hazelnuts and coconut.

They worked a day ahead on most things, but yesterday, almost everything had sold, so today it was double production. They'd survived a few slideovers, a number of collapsed centers, one tray of cakes upset on the way to the whipping cream station, not to mention a sudden moment of cream-slinging between Red, Gracie and Joyce, their giggling wide-eyedly interrupted by The Merry Widows who arrived unannounced.

Maria, who was at an adjoining table whisking batter, silenced her mixing machine. One of Willy's arias rose up from the next room, softly counterpointed by a tiny burst of Gracie's chronic flatulence.

Rosa Lombardi sampled the whipping cream, looked thoughtful, appeared to offer a ladleful to Sophia Russo and instead dabbed a blob of cream on Sophia's nose.

"It suits you," Rosa said. "*Molto bello!*"

Sophia wiped at the cream. "*Molto divertente! Basta guardare fuori quando ho le mie mani sulla marmellata di fragole!*"

She smiled at Maria. "I told her to watch out next time we're anywhere near a pot of strawberry jam."

"Carry on, ladies," Rosa said. "Which is to say, back to work, perhaps? But have fun!"

The widows walked towards the front of the bakery and the others resumed their tasks. Red McIlhenny took a not-so-discreet sip from a small silver flask.

Maria, stirring and tasting, again fell to puzzling how to fill another of Darrol's special requests. Often he simply accepted whatever treats she was able to sneak out. But occasionally he placed an order—emphasis on the word *order*, she thought—and last night, knowing this was Viennese Week, Darrol had asked for an entire cake.

"I'll have to buy it," Maria had said. "There's no way I can just cart one off."

"What, tight inventory control?" Darrol had a tiny hint of a sneer under his neutral tone. He was as good at vocal layering as Gracie was at laminating pastry.

"No," Maria said. "It's not that. They never really count things. It's only that the torte...it's too big. How do I carry it out without being seen?"

"You'll figure something," said Darrol. He fondled her long black hair. "I told you the bakery stuff always tastes so much better if it's not legal. Don't you go buying it, now, Mimi."

"I won't." She looked at him. "Darrol, for all the sweets you eat, you're pretty buff."

"My busy brain burns calories like a jet burns fuel."

"Huh." She yawned and rose from the couch. "I need to go to bed. Gotta be in even earlier tomorrow."

Darrol pulled her back down. "Here's an idea. It's brilliant! We make like you're pregnant, fit you out with a false tummy. You can hide all sorts of things in there. Fool 'em for several months, right?"

Her smile was brief. She twisted sideways. "Would you like a baby, Darrol? I mean, for real?"

He sat up straight. "God. I dunno. Maybe. Someday, maybe. Got a lot to do first."

She studied him. "You love me, Darrol?"

"'course I do, Mimi." He slapped his thighs. "Hey, let's go to bed. I got art class tomorrow and you've got...a busy day of smuggling."

Carefully watching the big mixer making lazy loops in her batter, Maria was almost hypnotized.

"How do I tote the torte?" she kept asking herself, using one of Darrol's self-described clever lines. As a first step, she'd already managed to carefully place a Sacher-torte in her locker, the cake inside one of the unmarked boxes the bakery kept for some bulk deliveries.

The phrased nagged at her. "How do I tote the torte?"

Tote? She had an idea.

When her break came up, she told Gracie she was going to run over to Mother Earth on the next block to get some things.

"Darrol wants odd fruits and veggies for an art project," Maria said. "And the 'Norton doesn't have quite the right things."

How easy it was to lie sometimes. She wondered if she was learning that from Darrol. She suspected he lied now and then, and he was really good at it. She was never positive.

Fifteen minutes later, she had a nifty Mother Earth tote bag—ironically it had cost her almost as much as buying a torte—and she put the cakebox on the bottom of the bag, hiding it under a small assortment of cumquats, ugli fruit and kohlrabi. She doubted these exotics would have any use for Darrol's drawings, although he told her he wanted to experiment, but she could try making some new kinds of salads or something. Maria had long taken pleasure in being inventive in her cooking.

As she placed the bag in her locker, Willy Lenz came into the staff room, preceded by snatches of what sounded like Italian. Maria managed to push at her locker door casually enough, but she was breathing heavily.

Lenz saw her and stopped mid-aria. "Poor Mimi," he sighed.

Maria was taken aback. "You mean me, Mr. Lenz?"

"No. I mean Puccini's doomed heroine. *La Boheme.*" He laughed. "No, I didn't mean you, Maria."

"My boyfriend sometimes calls me Mimi."

"Dear, oh dear. Are you consumptive?"

She was puzzled for a moment before she thought she understood.

"You mean do I do the shopping? Yes, mostly I do."

Lenz laughed again. "Maria, you're a delight. No, 'consumptive' means having tuberculosis."

"Oh..."

"Poor Mimi is dying of TB." Lenz leaned toward her. His white linen suit gleamed under the lights. "You're not...are you? Dying of consumption?"

"Gosh, I don't think so." She tried to be funny. "But maybe I'll die from inhaling too much sugar."

He laughed lightly. He glanced around the empty staff room. "You're sweet all by yourself, Maria." He tapped his forehead with a palm. "God, too corny? But you're very sweet nevertheless."

She blushed. "Em, thank you. I'd better get back to..."

Lenz held up a hand. He smelled liked he'd been rolling in cinnamon.

"Perhaps a drink after work some day?" His voice was friendly, pleasantly musical. No sound of leering, no come-on.

Maria knew leering, she knew come-ons. Whenever any of the men at the Culinary Academy had spoken to her, they'd had only one thing on their menus and their voices always betrayed them.

"That'd be very nice, Mr. Lenz, but my boyfriend..."

"...he wouldn't approve? Not even for a simple drink?"

"He really wouldn't."

Lenz sighed again. "Jealousy is the stuff of operas, you know. Pity it has to show up in real life."

"Aren't you married, Mr. Lenz?"

"Willy, please." He looked at his well-manicured nails, frowned, brushed flecks of flour from the back of his hand. "Mine is a 'yes-but' marriage."

"A yes-but marriage?"

"As in 'Yes, I'm married, but...'" He stepped back. "Well, maybe I'll tell you about it someday."

"Maybe. Thank you."

Lenz surprised her with a short bow, smiled, walked into the hall. His singing resumed.

Maria, about to leave, noticed her locker door wasn't completely closed. She gave it a guilty little push.

It had been more trouble than usual, but Darrol would have his special treat.

Darrol always got what he wanted.

Chapter 6
Deconstructing

The last of the early fog had ghosted away. Impatient sunlight rushed down the hillside and began to paint the buildings with morning radiance.

Darrol, digging in his jacket for a mint, ambled around the corner onto Jones. He saw Magnus Quist walking just ahead, holding his silly little blue satchel by his side. It flopped against Magnus' leg, limp, impotent. Deposit safely made, presumably.

Idiot. Nine out of ten could guess you carry cash in that thing. Darrol found the lozenge and slid it into his mouth. He sucked coolness across the mint. The tingle was very pleasant.

Magnus, moving slowly, raised his head. He seemed to be sniffing.

Darrol was amused. *What are you, a dog?* But he followed Magnus' example and sampled the morning air with a big sniff. Nothing unusual. A hint of the ocean, a whiff of burnt coffee.

He caught up to the other man in a few vigorous strides. "Been to the bank, Magnus?"

Without slowing, Magnus glanced sideways. "Ah, Mr. Yount. So observant." The sarcasm was light. "But yes."

"Not afraid of robbery?"

Magnus turned his head again. His thick glasses became almost opaque. "I don't think so."

Darrol laughed. "No, I suppose not. You have quite a reputation."

"Reputation?" Magnus continued walking.

Now Darrol felt like the dog, trotting alongside. "Well, in the 'Norton. I've heard stories. About you fending off the bad guys."

"I have my ways." Magnus pronounced it *vays*.

"Is it true you used that sword once, the Emperor's?"

"Not as efficient as my revolver." Magnus allowed a small smile. "But perhaps sending a sharper message, yes?"

"They say you cut the guy's ear off?"

Magnus shrugged. "One's legends are best made by others, *ja?*"

Just ahead, a thump, a low rumble and a crash. The sidewalk was blocked by construction sawhorses and by a short, frowning foreman whose battered orange hardhat kept sliding toward his nose. Watched by a small retinue of gawkers, his crew was demolishing an apartment wall, a deft bit of surgery in between two other grim-faced buildings.

Darrol and Magnus stopped as a demolition ball, small but potent, swung forward—elegantly, almost formally—and savaged another portion of wood, plaster and cement. As it swung back on its chain, the ball danced a lively jig of celebration.

"Impermanence," Magnus said. "We think we build for forever, but then..."

Seemingly on its own, another section of wall tumbled, a glacier calving. Dust billowed toward the street.

Darrol smiled enthusiastically. "Ever read that story by Graham Greene? About the kids destroying a house? Called *The Destructors.*"

Magnus' smile held no warmth. "I wouldn't have taken you for a literary man, Mr. Yount."

Darrol blinked, persisted. "Have you read it?"

"I'm afraid not." Magnus wiped a small chip of wood from his face. "I must get back."

He brushed past the foreman and strode into the temporary pedestrian lane. Darrol jogged after him, caught up as they regained the sidewalk.

"It's a great story," Darrol said. "These boys take over a man's house while he's gone for the weekend. They demolish it completely in the inside. From the outside it still looks OK. When the guy comes back, the whole place totally collapses in one huge, wonderful smasharoo. Pretty much right before his eyes."

"Why would they do that?" Magnus seemed more curious than shocked.

"Because they could."

They turned onto Chestnut. A sharp-edged breeze rollicked down the hill.

Magnus tugged at his collar. "All that creativity going into pure destruction. Does that appeal to you, Mr. Yount?"

Darrol shivered. "Oh, yes," he said, grinning. "I think destruction can be a very creative act."

"A man who likes paradox, I see." Magnus' eyes were mocking.

"Don't know about that," Darrol said. "But what I love is all the power those kids have."

Magnus glanced at him but said nothing.

They puffed up the hill towards Mischief House. Darrol was replaying some of Magnus' remarks. He wasn't sure he liked the man's tone. Treat a guy as an equal and what do you get?

With a brief nod, Darrol turned at the door to the apartments. Magnus grunted and continued toward the 'Norton.

D arrol had grown to like the San Francisco Art Institute. It was convenient, just a short walk down Chestnut from Mischief House. That allowed him to squeeze in classes on work days without wasting his valuable time getting there.

But far more than convenience was the look and feel of the place: he liked the Spanish colonial architecture, the arches, the skylights, the tiled courtyards, the central fountain, the rooftop sun terrace, the overall sense of Mediterranean warmth.

The Institute was big and rambling, filled with activities which seemed to Darrol to make much more sense than in the everyday world. *Meaning.* The place was filled with meaning and purpose.

You created. You controlled. You put your mark on things. You could express just who you were.

He liked the smells. Near the entrance were hints of lavender, cypress and rosemary. Inside were oils, turpentine, paints, and sawdust overlain with odors of coffee, savories and pastries from the Institute's café.

He liked the sounds: the drilling, chiseling, sawing, hammering. He often felt he could hear the syncopated swish of brushes on canvas, the eager scratching of pencils on paper, the rush of fire in the kilns.

He liked that there were women everywhere, attractive students and handsome faculty. Not to mention the models. Bodies chosen for regarding thoughtfully, inspecting artistically. The looking-at-lustfully aspect you kept to yourself.

When Darrol first came here to find out about the Institute's public classes, he charmed the assistant registrar, a middle-aged woman with a sad face, and she gave him permission to explore a little on his own.

"Don't get me into trouble," she said, blushing doubly when he blew her a kiss.

But Darrol himself could blush at the result of his first foray. He'd wandered into one of the biggest classrooms and found himself in a busy sculpture class. More than a dozen students were working at individual stations set in a circle around the room. Darrol moved from station to station, looking intently at each emerging piece.

The students were shaping modeling clay into what appeared to be variations on a nude female figure. A few of the emerging sculptures seemed realistic, but many ventured into abstraction. The contours and protrusions were puzzling.

Having almost completely strolled around the room, Darrol came to a bearded young guy who was using a stylus to detail full female breasts rising from a Dali-esque roulette wheel, warped and surreal.

Darrol couldn't help asking "Where do you get your inspiration for this?"

The sculptor gave him an incredulous glance and said "Hey, man, from the fucking model, where else?"

Darrol looked up. To his lifelong chagrin, he realized that on a dais-raised stool in the exact center of the room, sitting boredly—but still provocatively—there was a beautiful young brunette. Totally nude. She was slowly revolving the stool to give all the student artists equal opportunity.

He quickly tried to cover his stupidity, "Well, yes, I meant your casino element, your roulette thing. But I get it. We all gamble on women, right?" His little chuckle earned only a blank look from the student.

Darrol cleared his throat. Holding his head high in what he thought was an instructor-like manner, he checked out the remaining sculptures. Trying to remain detached, he also managed repeated glances at the gentle, inviting swell of the model's ass.

When he could fit them around his work schedule, he began taking drawing and painting classes. Though he disliked the looming presence of the instructors and hated their condescending remarks, he loved the power the implements gave him.

He wanted immediate freedom with his pens, pencils and brushes, but his teachers told him repeatedly that technique and certain premises came first.

"You're not a baby bird, Mr. Yount," said the ageless Ms. McKeown, a regretful virgin if ever he saw one. "You can't just leap off the tallest tree and expect to fly. First some rules of aerodynamics are required."

Flapping her own paint-spattered wings, she moved to the next student. She left behind the odor of stale cigarettes and an indelible impression of dirty nails chewed to the quick.

Although Darrol was taking only the occasional public education class, he managed to latch onto a regular student ID card, carried it dangling on a lanyard. He was never challenged by the security staff or the teachers when he wandered about. The Art Institute became another of his domains.

He kept his initial embarrassing failure of observation to himself, not even telling Maria about his visit to the sculpture class. But he was a quick learner: he never again failed to look at the center of any classroom to see if a Venus might be rising there. And he chatted up his fair share of models.

"We're not really supposed to, you know, hang out with the students." Sheryl Duncan was gripping her dressing gown as though a freak wind might rip it away.

They were standing in an alcove outside the drawing classroom. As usual, the Art Institute was busy, but Darrol's instincts had led him to this little backwater corner with its incomprehensible clump of twisted bronze perched on a small display stand. The sculpture looked vaguely like a tribute to someone's intestines. The stink of recently-applied industrial floor polish savaged Darrol with memories of grim school authorities. His nose rebelled.

"So..." Sheryl shifted her weight, and the gleaming floorboards creaked. "It's a rule. Models can't go out with the students."

Darrol flung his knockout smile at her, thinking about what he knew was underneath the white robe. As in nothing. Everything. *White for innocence, that's a laugh.*

"Well, I'm not a fulltime student," he said. "I'm a service professional. So actually..."

Sheryl was very pretty but she wasn't terribly quick. Darrol watched her mind processing his irrelevant technicality. "Oh, then, I guess..."

"Besides," he cut in smoothly, "you look like a rule-breaker, Sheryl. Us rule-breakers should stick together, right?" He could tell he had her. Or did he?

A sudden sly look appeared on her face.

"Here's the deal, then," she said. "You've been staring at me jaybird naked for the last hour. Show me you drew something good and that you ain't just a perv with a pencil, and maybe I'll go out with you."

Perv with a pencil? I got a pencil, all right. "My sketches are pretty rough. I'm new to this class, but OK." Darrol opened his portfolio and pulled out three sheets.

Sheryl took them and shuffled between the drawings. She shrugged again. "Hey, maybe you got talent. What do I know? These seem OK."

Darrol looked over her shoulder at the drawings. He decided his work really wasn't bad at all. He'd taken an art appreciation class in community college, and he recognized these were a bit like the quick and casual style of Picasso— fluid, loose lines mostly emphasizing generalities but hitting all the high points. Like Sheryl's perfect breasts.

Two drink dates and one week later, that perfection was close at hand. In his hands. In his bedroom. He loved it that Maria's work schedule and his own were so conveniently divergent.

Sheryl propped herself up on one arm and peered at him. "You gotta be the best-looking guy I ever... Why aren'tcha in the movies?"

"'Best looking where? Best on Russian Hill? Best in San Francisco? Anywhere?" Darrol really wanted to know.

"Tom Cruise got nothing on you. I seen him in person once, so I know first-hand."

"You went to bed with Tom Cruise?"

Sheryl squealed and poked Darrol in the ribs. "No, stupid! I seen him outside a movie house. And you're taller, not a little squirt like him."

"But I'm the best-looking, huh?"

"Better 'n best."

"Mm."

Darrol gazed at the silver cross dangling between her breasts. It was pointing directly at her genitals. He lazily mulled this over. Was God wanting her to be sexual? Was the cross an atonement? A protection? What?

He reached out and touched the chain. "Why'dya wear this thing?"

"I dunno. Had it for years. Raised Catholic."

"You believe in God?"

"Sure. Doesn't everybody?"

"I doubt it. But you—do you really think about it, God, heaven, all that stuff? You work it all out for yourself or just take what they taught you?"

Sheryl frowned. "What's wrong with what I was taught? You a religious weirdo or something?"

Darrol laughed. "Not on your life. I'm just trying to understand. Am I the boss, or is someone up there"—he pointed at the ceiling—"running the show? And I don't mean my landlord." A downward gesture. "He lives down below."

"I never heard the Devil called the 'landlord'."

Darrol hooted. "Sheryl, you're a kick." He flicked her cross. It swung back and forth.

He put his arms behind his head and leaned back. "So, what's it like having men ogling your tits and your pussy while you just sit there?"

Sheryl steadied the cross and sat up straighter. "Geez, Darrol. It's not about tits. I provide texture and shape. Form, you know. The human form."

"You sound like a textbook. Or like that paintslapper Cortez."

"Who?"

"My teacher. The Mexican. Something about him rubs me the wrong way."

"You mean Miguel? He's cute."

"You screw him too?"

"No way. Faculty's off limits."

"Just like us students?"

"Don't make me regret breaking the rules, Darrol." Sheryl's tone turned petulant. "But what I said is true. I'm a model. Not a piece of ass."

Darrol grinned. "Can't you be both?"

For a moment she was blank-faced. She smiled. "I guess." The smile broadened. "And I can rub you the right way, can't I?" She began to show him again what she meant.

Darrol came out of a dream, sweating. He'd been in Lanterman's, gleefully pouring warm lemon custard over a blonde movie star. Then over himself. He turned to the clock and muttered low syllables. He needed to get ready for work.

"Who's Mimi?" Sheryl was propped on one elbow, her big breasts dangling close to his face, not as alluring as they seemed an hour ago.

Darrol groaned. He needed to kick her out. Needed a shower. "What?"

"You was dozing, kind of cute little baby like," Sheryl grinned. "And you said something to a 'Mimi'. Or maybe it was 'Jimmy'. Coupla times. Who's that?"

"Dunno."

"Oh, come on, Darrol. Is it a gal or a guy?" She winked. "I wouldn't care if it was a guy, you know."

He sat up sharply. "Then watch out for HIV. I'll give you AIDS."

She didn't rise to the bait. "I tried women a coupla times. Not as good as the main event, but pretty fine. Sorta like playing with yourself, only you get to reach lots further."

"Jimmy's my roommate." Darrol swung off the bed. "Sheryl, we got to get the hell going. We sure as fuck don't want Jimmy coming in and finding you here. Be worse than the HIV I just gave you. He's a mean dude."

She rummaged for her clothes. "That's what I like about you, Big D. You're funny."

As soon as Sheryl left, Darrol showered and dressed for work. He took his time in front of the bedroom mirror, leaning in to admire his thick black hair, his depthless brown eyes, his classically-handsome face made more interesting by the broken nose.

"Imperfection makes perfection," he often told himself. Many of the women he met thought so. One said he was a reincarnation of the young Marlon Brando. He didn't bother even pretending to disagree.

Before he closed his white tux shirt and fastened in the black studs—all part of Lanterman's stringent dress code—he examined his profuse chest hairs. Why did women seem to be drawn to them? It mostly didn't work the other way. There was Maria going to electrolysis each month—in secret, she believed, but he knew about it, just didn't let on—because she thought she'd otherwise turn into a cavewoman.

He fired a burst of Aramis towards his chest, fastened the shirt, and finished dressing.

Slipping his lifts into his shoes, he thought again about the Hollywood types who wore lifts all the time. Politicians too, that was a given. Darrol was far from short, but he liked the extra two inches of stance the lifts gave him when he stood before his customers or at the kitchen service counters, begging for favors from the chefs. And he liked being eye to eye with Radisson Vero. Stance was power.

Emperor Norton popped into his thoughts. There was a guy who wasn't that tall, at least not if you went by the dumb cutout in the store. But the Emperor fooled you with that high plumed hat, distracted you with the froufrou uniform, intimidated you with his cavalry sword, and transfixed you with those black, manic eyes. Regardless of Norton's height, there was power, and then some. Of course it was all an act, all walking on water. But the crazy guy really believed he was the big shot, and it worked. No one called him on it, no one yelled about the Emperor's new clothes. He was the man. King of the hill, king of the city.

Looking in the mirror again, Darrol fastened his tie. He patted down an errant strand of hair. Smiled. Winked.

He thought about Sheryl. Pretty. Good body. OK in the sack. Amusing in an offbeat sort of way. A fair enough listener. Maybe not really a stepping stone, but good to have around for a while.

He went to the bed, checked for hairs, earrings, any other telltale signs. Not that Maria would really notice, but it always paid to be careful.

He patted the pillows, shook out the top sheet and coverlet, sniffed. He thought he detected a trace of Sheryl's patchouli stuff. He fetched his cologne, spritzed a tiny shot towards the bed, tidied up. *Next!*

He laughed at himself. *What am I, a fucking barber?*

The following week, Darrol, chewing the last of his afternoon licorice, arrived at the Art Institute early. He was eager to get to his drawing class and show some cityscapes he'd done up on the Institute's rooftop patio.

He knew that Sheryl was at her regular job, hostessing on Pier 39, and he was a bit surprised at how her not being around seemed freeing.

An earlier class was still at it in the drawing classroom, so he went back out to the main courtyard. A slash of sunlight arrowing along on the red tiles drew his attention to the hall to his right, the Diego Rivera Gallery. He'd been in there several times. He liked the hall's skylights, the high, open-trussed ceiling, and especially the huge Rivera mural which took up almost one whole wall. He went into the gallery to study it again.

The mural was a multi-paneled optical illusion, a fresco within a fresco. Diego Rivera himself and several of his assistants were portrayed working from *trompe l'oeil* scaffolding on panels dominated by a huge figure of a workman. The man's giant hands were controlling some sort of machinery. Below and to the side were other large panels filled with busy planners, architects, riveters, mechanics and laborers, all busily engaged in aspects of building a modern city.

"Creativity caught in the act, yes?"

Darrol turned. The attractive woman he'd met in the 'Norton was beside him, gazing up at the mural.

"Pretty daring," she said, "mostly just showing us their backs." She looked at Darrol. "David, right?"

"Darrol."

"Oh, yes, sorry. Darrol. I'm Karin."

"I remember." He said it too quickly. It sounded a bit snide. He added a big smile. "You like this mural?"

She nodded. "Very much. I love the earth tones, just gorgeous. And I admire the way he mixes different kinds of reality. I'm tempted to try that in my ceramics."

"Ah." Darrol was rarely tongue-tied. This wasn't only his unfamiliarity with the art. It was the woman. Even in her grubby, clay-stained gray smock, she was stunning. He loved the way one of her eyes had the tiniest droop. He managed a half-stammer. "Your ceramics, yes..."

"My work's usually pretty delicate," Karin said. "And since everything about this mural is the opposite of delicate, maybe that's why it intrigues me. It forces me to wonder how I could render mass and solid shapes in my own style."

Darrol could only nod.

Karin became more animated. "Don't you think we far too often look for inspiration in things we're comfortable with? That greater ideas might come from exploring things that are unfamiliar, far from our usual?"

"You mean...familiarity breeds dullness?" He didn't know where that had come from, but he blathered on. "I guess there's lots to be seen in another person's mirror?"

Karin beamed. "Yes, that's part of it. Exactly."

His successful shot in the dark emboldened him.

"I was thinking...that this might even apply to my drawing studies."

"It would," she said, helping him out. She pointed at the mural. "See where he's intentionally left outlines of his underdrawings exposed? Something to think about. You work in charcoal?"

"Um, yes, some. And pencils. I'm pretty new to it."

She looked at the little watch she wore on a gold chain. "Darn it. I got a piece cooking in the kiln." She lowered the watch and smiled a goodbye.

"Would you like have a drink with me?" Darrol hated blurting—it so often came from a position of weakness—but he didn't want her to get away.

Karin paused and considered him. He noticed her eyes were lilac. It was the left one which had the slight droop. A lovely touch of asymmetry.

"How about maybe coffee instead?" she said. "But not right now. Track me down in the ceramics studio in the next couple of weeks, OK?"

She smiled again and strode off, chased by tiny plaster sunbeams.

His class did not go well. Miguel Cortez, oh so hip in his designer jeans and leather-fringed shirt, seemed to pick on Darrol, trashed his latest set of drawings.

"C'mon, Mr. Yount, you should be far past finger painting. This looks like you've been jacking off with a piece of charcoal."

Darrol cringed, though Cortez' students heard this kind of language all the time. Someone sitting off to the side had the gall to snicker.

"All of you, pay attention." Cortez ripped a used sheet away from his big easel pad. The exposed white page flared angrily. Darrol pursed his lips.

"OK," Cortez said. "Engage the right side of your brain, really see your subject, sight like I've told you."

Cortez looked for no more than a moment at the bonsai and the jade dragon on the display stand. He swept his arm quickly across the virgin paper, stepped closer and, without a pause, began moving his hand gracefully and fluidly, a symphony conductor leading an allegretto.

"Let the essence flow right into your drawing implements. *Through* them!"

In seconds there was a remarkable semblance, not just of the bonsai tree and the dragon, but a lithe, mysterious abstraction hinting of something much more.

Darrol stared in annoying envy. The prick had talent.

"Don't outthink it, don't try to control it." Cortez said, stepping back. "Just *be* it."

Be it? Darrol slumped. *Shit, what does that mean?*

"You mean like in really good sex?" someone finally dared to ask. Everyone laughed. Even Darrol.

Cortez allowed himself a smile. "Not that far off." He flicked something from his perfectly-groomed mustache. "Losing yourself is part of it, *amiga*."

Darrol got home sooner than he expected. On this rare day off from Lanterman's, he had a date with Maria, but she wasn't due for another hour.

He chucked his drawings onto the kitchen counter, reconsidered, picked one up and looked at it. The little dragon he'd sketched seemed real enough. Darrol thought he'd even captured some of that demonic face. At least a hint. Isn't that what Cortez wanted?

The dragon reminded Darrol of something. Dropping the drawing, he chewed slowly on a fingernail. He stared at the kitchen clock, a black cat with a swinging tail. One of Maria's kitschy decorations. Plenty of time. Duff would be at work too until seven.

Darrol went down the hall to Duff's room, opened the door and went in. He was attacked by an unpleasant odor. He made a face. He guessed incense and engine oil. Not his cup of smells.

He opened the closet, reached high, felt on the top shelf, found the box, levered it down. He checked that it still contained the newspaper clippings and letters. It did. He carried it to his own bedroom, closed the door, sat down to read. *Yes, a dragon. The Golden Dragon.*

The fall of 1977, San Francisco. Two Chinese gangs. A longtime feud. Retaliation for an earlier murder. A really screwed-up assassination attempt in a Chinatown restaurant. Five dead, eleven injured.

In twenty minutes, Darrol not only knew a lot about the restaurant shootout, but he realized that someone in Duff's family—Duff's grandfather, as best Darrol could determine—likely had been involved in what the press eagerly called *The Golden Dragon Massacre.*

Darrol understood a little about the idea of saving face. If Duff was much invested in his Chinese side—and Darrol thought the guy was—this could be heavy stuff. The little mental file on his roommate was building nicely.

Maria rattled open the door right on schedule. She was smiling broadly as she came into the kitchen. She clattered her keys onto the counter. "Are we really going on a date, Darrol?"

Darrol closed his journal, secured the band, and stood up for her kiss. "Yep. Burgers and a movie. Can't beat that, can we?"

He reached for Maria's big brown bag. "Something interesting for me today?"

She pushed his hand aside. "Oh, it's buried. I'll get it."

She rummaged, pulled out a napkin-wrapped object, put it on the counter beside Darrol's drawings. She opened it slowly, attempting a fumbling moment of suspense. "Ta da!"

Darrel peered down. A substantial rectangle of firm dark chocolate topped several sturdy layers.

"Baking cow patties now, are you?" he drawled, testing the unyielding chocolate with a finger.

Maria chose to laugh. "It's chocolate week," she said. "Tito wanted us to make this Canadian stuff. Pretty good. Sold a ton. Custard, coconut, lots of things you like, D."

"Canadian, huh? So it's a hockey puck?" He thumped his fingers on the chocolate.

This time a little scowl escaped. "You know, I don't have to bring you things."

"Yes you do." He pulled her close and ran his hands over her bottom. "You have no choice. You've also gotta laugh at my jokes, Mimi."

"Oh." She moved in and nuzzled his neck. She sighed. "I like these evenings when you don't have to work, Darrol."

He gave her a brief squeeze, released her. He picked up his journal. "Yeah, well, some are gonna be taken up with more art classes." He gestured at the drawings. "Apparently I need them."

Maria bent over to look at his work. She oohed and aahed appropriately. He glanced over her shoulder. Yeah, the drawings weren't bad.

But he was thinking of Sheryl. Thinking even more about Karin. *Lilac eyes.*

Difficult as his classes were, art still had its rewards.

Chapter 7
The Night Fantastic

D ancing, ever dancing.

In 1986, Alma Falk, 23, and Magnus Quist, 27, met for the first time on the dance floor at the Swedish Society's Freya Ballroom on Market Street.

They sized each other up. He was quite tall and she decidedly was not. Her expensive high heels made little difference. But the *dansband* was playing enthusiastically and the prismatic ball was casting bright, hypnotic jewels about, so they took a trial turn—Alma remembered that the dance was a foxtrot; Magnus always said it was a waltz—and they discovered their height disparity was of no consequence.

They finished that dance, then another, then danced the rest of the evening to the exclusion of anyone else.

That night several people came up to them, lavish with compliments, some in English, some in Swedish, asking how long they'd been dancing together.

Less than an hour? Couldn't be! You met when? *Omöjlig!* Impossible!

Alma had been dragged to the dance, almost literally, by her mother Sigrid, who wanted her daughter to *gifta sig med en fin Svensk pojke,* i.e. 'marry a nice Swedish boy.' That Alma had been born in San Francisco and had only been to Sweden once—although her parents had infused her with the language and customs of their homeland—didn't deter Sigrid, who even then was dealing with the cancer which took her life the following year. She desperately wished to see Alma in a happy marriage and producing grandchildren. Ideally Swedish blood from both sides would be in their veins.

Magnus had the right blood. He'd been born in Stockholm to a professional couple, Bengt and Helwig Quist, who were quite surprised at—and unprepared for—the pregnancy.

Hoping to bring their son good luck, they named him after an ancient Swedish king who'd been clever at acquiring land from other countries. They paid no attention to the rumors that Good King Magnus, ominously nicknamed 'the Caresser', was also very much into hanky and panky.

When Magnus was fourteen, the Quists emigrated to Chicago. Helwig, a CPA, did well for several years, but ran into trouble with the IRS and retired early, grateful at avoiding Joliet. Bengt became a successful architect and eventually an even more successful alcoholic. However, he was not successful at skirting trouble while chasing teenaged girls. Several lawsuits depleted the family resources.

Magnus graduated with a business degree from Northwestern, but he had neither a decent role model nor a clear direction for his life. He wandered out to San Francisco, where Swedish friends helped him find an administrative position with a supermarket chain.

Like his royal namesake, Magnus had the urge to extend his holdings. He was at the dance as part of his campaign to find a partner. A well-off partner. Better still, a rich one.

Alma Falk fit the bill. Not only did she come from a well-to-do family—and she was also an only child, so helpful when wills are to be probated—but she was extremely pretty. She had a soft, sweet voice. And she had lovely, slender ankles and tiny, well-formed feet, which Magnus had watched earlier from across the dance floor with considerable pleasure and a hint of arousal.

Once in Magnus' arms, Alma was light and nimble at following his every command, even anticipating perfectly when he improvised, which he often did.

Magnus, not completely mercenary, was delighted that love of a sort came with the bargain. Her Swedish heritage was a minor bonus; he could make jokes in Swedish and be understood.

What Alma gained was equally clear: a tall, nice-looking Swedish man with impeccable manners, well-educated, with a fine style on the dance floor, including knowing how to do the lively Swedish *bugg*, something her father Christian had taught her when she was a teenager. She was fascinated by Magnus' eyes, bluer than the Scandinavian glaciers she'd seen in her mother's books. Icier too, at times perhaps, but that only added a touch of mystery.

Between dances, when they talked, sipping cherry punch laced with aquavit, Alma began to think of Magnus not as Quist but as Quest, as a young man questing for something, and she found that appealing.

Magnus, afraid to let her slip away, babbled on. That she actually listened to him made her additionally charming. That he wanted to keep talking to her intrigued her. Together, they realized, there might be possibilities...

Within a few decades, Alma, speaking both from wistfulness and wisdom, said that young love and young folly are but sides of the same coin.

Over thirty years after their first dance in that stately Swedish hall on Market Street, Magnus and Alma still went dancing almost every week, a bond with their past, a connection, she thought, to lost innocence.

The old Freya Ballroom long since had given way to a noisy nightclub, so the Quists found their dances elsewhere, generally in more sterile environments. But any dancer knows that if the lights are down low enough and romantic music is playing, some sort of magic can still seep up from forlorn, undusted corners.

Two nights before they hosted the Mischief House dinner, Magnus and Alma were at Filbert Hall, 'The Nuthouse' as Magnus often called it. The dances there drew eccentric or slightly-demented seniors, some totally focused on regaining youth on the dance floor, often to the exhaustion of their partners, others furtively scanning the wallflower section for the person of their dreams, the one who not only could dance sublimely, but could transform the future, what was left of it. Some, of course, just craved a few bittersweet hours of human touch.

"So," said Magnus, expertly guiding Alma in a moderate two-step, "it really will happen? All those people will troop into our home just for your *köttbullar?*"

"Not just the meatballs. For nettle soup too," she murmured into his chest.

"I speak as figuratively, Alma," he said. "It means I will have to be nice, *ja?*"

She leaned out a little and glanced up at him. "Is that so hard for you, *sötnos*?"

He pulled her back in. "I don't mind Jo Durr and her delusions about the Emperor. Or—what's the girl's name?—Maria. She seems sweet enough. But that smart-aleck Yount, and the sour-faced Chinaman and the Collins couple, they're not my cups of tea."

"Then drink something stronger."

"*Tres* witty, Mrs. Quist." He executed a quick turn. "As to the *fördömd* Collins, have you noticed those two rarely shop with us? I think they go to that Joe the Trader place. I've seen their shopping bags."

"They're only our tenants, Magnus. We can't control where they buy their groceries."

He spun her out rapidly. Alma's odd piled up-hair—Magnus often thought it looked like a dollop of merengue—remained firm atop her head. In past years, her hair would have come loose, swirled sensuously down to her shoulders. Tonight, it played stubborn and stayed put.

He twirled her back in, no longer his child bride. These days Alma was plump as a *Julegrot* pudding, but still remarkably light on her feet.

"Ah, yes, control," Magnus said. "*Fördömd* rent control. The Collins are among those getting off for cheap. And who loses out? We do."

Alma said nothing. This conversation could only tumble downhill and crash into the walls of an argument. She focused instead on the treacly clarinet riff. When Alma and Magnus danced, especially the slower numbers, Alma liked to disappear inside a romanticized past, not only her own, but into pasts she'd read about. She hadn't been a history major for nothing.

Recently, she'd been thinking of herself as Napoléon's first wife Joséphine. That didn't really put tall Magnus in the role of squatty Napoléon, although Magnus shared traits with Napoléon, imperiousness being one. Tonight she'd been trying to cast Magnus in the role of one of Napoléon's advisors, maybe Marshal Ney, or perhaps to assign Magnus the part of the gallant Swedish ambassador to France. That had cachet.

"What do you think?" Magnus yanked her back to the present.

"In this instance, Sweden should give way to France," she said, startling herself as much as Magnus. Too much *Svea Rike*. Too many private thoughts.

"Time traveling again, *ja*?" He voice seemed surprisingly affectionate. "I understand that's a skill of imaginative people." He smiled down at her. "And of the addled elderly."

That sort of remark called for a duel at dawn behind the statue of King Gustavus.

Alma deftly followed his sudden series of side steps. "Ask again," she said calmly. "What I'm supposed to have an opinion on."

"Have you thought more about selling everything?" He took them into a sort of grapevine. She shadowed him step for step. Other couples gave way.

"Magnus, I've thought about no such thing. In fact, I'd like to talk about some upgrades to the shop."

He stopped mid-beat. "Upgrades?"

Another couple had to brake and make an abrupt move around them. He guided Alma forward again. "That takes money."

"And we have it. Besides, it's not just the 'Norton to consider. It's all of Mischief House. I think there's a neighborhood tradition to consider, to support, to invest in. Think about that, Magnus—tradition."

"Alma, you should have been a preacher," he said sourly, giving her a final expert twirl.

The music ended to a dribble of applause.

The night was still young, but their frequent topic, unresolved, was not. They both knew it was getting very old indeed.

The evening before the dinner party, Alma was again dancing. This time in her kitchen. And without Magnus. She'd invited Maria to come down after work to learn about making a certain Swedish dessert.

To Maria it all seemed to be as much about footwork as about ingredients. She watched as Alma danced from cupboard to cupboard, to the counter, to the island, to the refrigerator, sometimes with a bag in hand, sometimes a spoon.

The dessert's name alone had intrigued Maria. "Vacuum cleaner rolls?" she asked.

"They're marzipan and chocolate outside," Alma said. "Inside, they get filled with all the leftover crumbs you can find. Like a vacuum cleaner sucks up bits of stuff."

"Ick." Maria made a face. "There's lint in there? Dust balls?"

Alma needed a second to realize that Maria was kidding. They laughed together.

"In Sweden, they're known as punsch-rolls or *dammsugare*," Alma said. "My mother, bless her soul, taught me how to make them, along with everything else Swedish she could think of. Figured that would help me catch a Swede even here in America."

"And it did, didn't it?"

"Yes." Alma carefully place a large blue bowl on the center island. "It helped me reel Magnus in like a long lake trout. I had all the hooks: my cooking, my dancing and my family money."

Maria couldn't hide her double take.

Alma smiled. "Too candid for you? Sorry, we make no secret of who holds the purse strings. That's my role. Magnus, as you may have noticed, literally wears the apron strings. That's his role."

She shook the ingredients of two plastic bags into the bowl. "This is the filling. Lots of cake crumbs...and these are cookie crumbs, bits of biscotti. Magnus does have a sweet tooth."

"Boy, Darrol does too."

"That's good. Make your men salivate any way you can, my dear. I guess with you working in a bakery, you can keep Darrol in good supply, yes?"

Maria's blush was extensive.

Alma didn't appear to notice. "All right," she said, working as she talked. "Now we're mixing in the butter, our cocoa, a little powdered sugar and the all-important liqueur. Have you ever had punsch?"

"No, I don't think so."

"It's made from arrack, brandy and sugar." Alma found the bottle and a glass on the counter behind her, poured a tiny amount. "Here, try a little."

Maria sipped. "It's really sweet!"

Alma, nodding, stirred. "Where'd you learn to bake?"

"Oh, I went to the California Culinary Academy. Could you use a mixer for that?"

"Yes. But I prefer what my mother called *vinklad fett*, elbow grease."

"That's what my boss says he prefers, but most of the time we need the big Avantco and Hobart mixers."

"Well, anyway," Alma went on, "machine or hand, you keep mixing, sampling." She scooped up some dough and tasted it. A satisfied smile. "Getting there. It's got to be nice and firm."

She stirred some more. "You went to CCA, huh? Your mother must be proud. Pretty good credentials."

"I guess. So, do you and Mr. Quist have children?"

"Unfortunately, I couldn't conceive." Alma set out a tray and began rolling the dough into small logs. "But we adopted a lovely little baby girl. We called her Thea Kachina." A wistful smile. "Thea Kachina Quist."

"Nice name, quite lovely."

"I think so. Thea translates as 'God's present' and Kachina means 'dancing spirit'. We tried to be good parents, and at first Thea was a fairly good child, but in her teens, she started drifting away from us."

"Oh dear."

Alma rolled the last log. "At the moment, for reasons I don't understand, we're estranged. Thea's choice."

Maria touched Alma's arm. "I'm so sorry."

Alma put a crumb-dusted hand on Maria's wrist. "Thank you. We're surviving." She picked up the tray of logs. "Well, let's not keep the pastries waiting." She placed the tray in the freezer.

"We'll firm our little logs up some more before we wrap them with this." Alma pulled another bowl from the refrigerator and put it on the island. "Voila!"

Maria peered into the bowl. It was filled with a thick, dark lemon-lime dough.

"The all-essential marzipan," said Alma. "I've always believed the green in this variety stands for the envy of those who don't get to taste it. I made it yesterday. I much prefer my own to store-bought."

She pulled a saucepan from a cupboard and placed it on the stove. "You ever think how all this is just like trying to put together a good relationship?"

Maria was puzzled. "No, I hadn't..."

Alma produced out a plate of dark chocolate squares. She dropped the chocolate, block by block, into the saucepan.

"For a good relationship," she said, "you need to have the right ingredients, the right amount and balance. You need to mix them together properly. Need to apply a little muscle, a little tenderness, a little heat or passion"—Alma turned on a burner—"and overall, to be creative, be very attentive and, of course, love what you're trying to do."

Maria nodded. "I like that." She moved around to look into the saucepan. "If only it worked."

"Sometimes it does." Alma pushed a wooden spoon at the chocolate and began to stir slowly, thoughtfully.

"And soon, perhaps after a cup of tea," she said, "we'll assemble our masterpieces. Whatever else works or doesn't work in our relationships, we can still enchant our men with sugar."

Chapter 8
We Gather Together

Dinner for seven at seven p.m. The date also happened to be the seventh. Alma, bustling about, tallied that up and declared the auspices to be excellent.

Magnus checked his shadowy reflection in the microwave door. "When did you become superstitious?" He practiced his smile.

"I'm not. But you know how I notice details." She carefully placed a stack of glass dessert plates on the island.

"Ah, but..." He reached toward her. "May I point out one detail you missed?"

He plucked a large tuft of orange and white hair from her shoulder. He held it up in front of her face. "*Din katt.*"

He tried to flick the hair into the trashcan but had to shake twice before it fell.

"I suppose," she said placidly, "you'd be happy if I put roast cat on the menu."

"I salivate at the thought." He poured aquavit into a small crystal goblet. "But I'll settle for your delicious *köttbullar.*" He drank, gasped in satisfaction. "Fire in the hold, as they say."

Alma sorted through a box of dessert napkins. "Are you going to be nice to our guests, *sötnos?*"

"I am forever nice, Alma."

"At least you won't have to deal with the Collins. Not able to come."

"Very likely down at Joe the Trader's spending what could have been our money."

"You're funny even when you're sadistic, Magnus." She fanned out dark floral napkins.

Magnus held up his goblet and examined the clear liquid. "And this will fortify me, *ja?*" He downed the remainder. "Ahh! So I will play the gracious host."

"I hope so."

The warm apartment was filled with savory odors.

The first to arrive was Mrs. Durr, beaming, holding a pot of pansies cradled in purple foil, then Duff Lee, bearing only a tight little smile. Close behind him came Brick Zimmer, looking incomplete, Alma thought, without a woman on his arm.

A few minutes later Darrol and Maria came in, Darrol a study in black, Maria completely in white.

Alma was amused *My goodness, chess pawns. On opposing sides.*

As Magnus closed the door, Maria smiled at him. "It was kind of you to fit this into Darrol's night off."

"It worked well for most. Even Mr. Zimmer over there has not to fly tonight." Magnus pronounced it *Tssimmer.*

The pilot was sitting in an overstuffed easy chair, slowly bouncing one leg on the other. His black utility boots were highly-polished.

"Just needs a joystick and he'll take off," Darrol said. "Or maybe all of us will." Zimmer sent them a grin and a small wave.

"Welcome, everyone." Alma came into the living room, wiping her hands on her blue half-apron. "Welcome to the first ever Mischief House dinner."

She took Magnus' arm. "I know you all pay rent, as Mr. Quist might point out, but we think of you as family. We should have done this years ago."

"Totally Mrs. Quist's idea," Magnus said. He seemed very tall. The coved ceilings in the apartment were much lower than those in the store.

"Well, regardless, thank you both." Mrs. Durr said, leaning forward. Behind her, a white tatted antimacassar slowly slid askew. "As Emperor Norton said, 'Better late than never.'"

"Norton said that?" Darrol couldn't hide his incredulity. "Surely..."

Mrs. Durr fluttered her small hands at him. "Oh yes, I believe so. A very smart man for all his craziness."

Magnus smiled. "Ah! Smart and crazy: a formula for success." His thick glasses gleamed. "Take note, Mr. Yount."

Darrol dredged up his best professional smile.

Alma clapped her hands. "Well," she said, "find a seat you two, and I'll get the appetizers. Magnus, will you help?"

Maria sat on a dark green loveseat. She gave a tiny squeal as the cushions enveloped her in unexpected softness. Darrol sank down beside her. He rubbed the velvety material. It gave a resilient purr. He leaned forward and rapped his knuckles on the teak coffee table. Solid as Scandinavia.

They looked around. Every space seemed used. Oriental rugs on the deep-pile carpet. Small tables, two short bookcases, some of the titles not in English. Many surfaces had succumbed to invasions of old-world knickknacks.

The interior walls were a deep red-earth color. They were decorated with romanticized landscapes, a few gilt-framed architectural drawings and one large, modern oil portrait of a teenaged girl.

This painting was an odd combination of realism and abstraction. The girl was curled on a spacious mauve satin cushion. Behind her was a blurry suggestion of cityscape, hinting that perhaps she was on a wide window seat.

Her age was ambiguous—somewhere, perhaps, between fourteen and eighteen. Her over-large eyes, wide-open, looked directly at the viewer. Her expression seemed pleading, yet almost seductive. Her blond hair, long and lustrous, cascaded down one shoulder. She was dressed provocatively in a blue-green, filmy tunic which revealed a little too much leg and a little too much shoulder.

"Tinker Bell grown up?" Darrol sniggered.

"But there aren't any wings," Maria said, taking him seriously.

Brick Zimmer had the sharpest eyesight. "You notice she seems to have bitten some of her fingernails?" he said, "But not all."

Mrs. Durr who was closest, peered at the hands. "Yes, and the other nails are bordello red." She tittered. "At least that's what I'd call it."

Duff merely stared.

Their hosts returned, and the art critiques quickly faded away.

Magnus distributed small plates and napkins. Alma brought out a silver tray laden with pieces of caraway cheese topped with pickled beets.

Darrol, reaching for a napkin, looked up at Magnus. "Strange to see you without an apron."

"Am I such a creature of habit, Mr. Yount?"

"Aren't we all?" Alma said brightly, shouldering Magnus aside. "Creatures of habit? And some of those habits not so good."

She held the tray in front of Darrol and Maria. "Try these. A Swedish favorite."

"That's what Mrs. Quist used to call me," Magnus said. "Her Swedish favorite. But alas... Time fidgets, as I've heard it said."

He cleared his throat. "Now, who'd like a beer? Or maybe aquavit? Home-made schnapps?" He took their orders.

"Something smells wonderful," Maria said.

"Oh, butter, garlic, onions, the usual," Alma said airily. "But thank you."

"And nettles," said Magnus, calling from the kitchen. "Don't forget the nettles."

That made even the taciturn Duff sit up. "Nettles? In the food?"

"Oh, wait and see," Alma said, offering a second round of appetizers. "You'll be surprised."

As Magnus served the drinks, Maria asked about the artwork.

"Well," said Alma, "the old paintings are from my side of the family. Mostly half-decent reproductions, I think, but that larger farmhouse scene is an original John Bauer. Late 19th, early 20th century. Besides his landscapes, he painted, of all things, a lot of trolls. In the original use of that word."

She laughed. "For all I know, there may be trolls hidden in that image..."

"...much as there are trolls hidden in real life," Magnus added. He poured himself more aquavit.

Alma ignored him. "Anyway, apparently that painting's much like the farm my father grew up on. That's why he bought it."

"Speaking of fathers," Magnus said gesturing with his goblet, "these architectural pieces over here were done by my own esteemed father. Pride of Chicago. Once."

"This big picture of the young girl," Zimmer said, "I think we're all curious about it."

"A little odd, isn't it?" said Alma. "A bit mysterious. Magnus found it on one of his treasure hunts. Around the time Thea left, wasn't it, *gubben*?"

"Perhaps. Yes, about then," Magnus said. "But before anyone asks, I just liked it. I can't explain. There's an old Swedish saying, '*Om ditt sinne spelar tricks, den har en anledning.*'" Essentially that means, 'trust your mind; it knows what it's doing.'"

Alma couldn't resist. "Of course, another old saying is *Lätt fånget, lätt förgånget.*"

Magnus scowled. "Mrs. Quist is saying 'Easy come, easy go.' Yes, it was an expensive piece, but I was drawn to it. I still am."

Mrs. Durr nodded. "Does it remind you of your daughter? I think it's about how I remember her."

Magnus flinched. "*Himlar, nej!* She's...it's nothing like Thea."

"No, not really" Alma added. "But Mr. Quist said he fancied it, so I let him hang it there in exchange for putting up a few more of my dreary old landscapes." She laughed. "Such are the tradeoffs of a happy marriage, yes?"

They squeezed into the small dining room, which was separated from the kitchen by a pony wall. Alma brought in an elegant white porcelain tureen, decorated with small blue flowers.

"All right, you doubters," she said, raising the lid. She flourished it amidst ascending steam. "Our first course. Those nettles! And the most delicious soup you'll ever taste."

"My parents called it *naässelsoppa*," said Magnus, as he passed a plate of black bread to Mrs. Durr. "Decorated with hard boiled eggs and crème fraiche, *ja?* And enjoyed with *svartbröd.*"

Alma ladled out the soup. "I found the nettles at the farmer's market by the Ferry Building." She began passing the bowls.

There were murmurs suggesting apprehension. "Do they sting?" Duff asked, staring suspiciously at the dark green surface.

Alma laughed. "No, not at all. The stinging tendency is boiled out early in the cooking. But if you think about it, there's a lesson here..."

"...Mrs. Quist loves her little lessons," Magnus said through a mouthful of bread.

"I do indeed," Alma said. "When I'm allowed to offer them. So, nettles. Consider the nettles of the field. Even they can be tamed, and they are good for us. Thus: how you approach something makes all the difference."

Magnus nodded. "She boiled me to remove my sting."

His wife pointed the ladle at him, catching a drip with a napkin. "In his case, it didn't quite work. So beware."

The others laughed but said nothing. Everyone tried the soup. Even genteel Mrs. Durr couldn't avoid a bit of slurping. Duff Lee's expression moved from suspicion to surprise to what might have passed for pleasure.

The main course was meatballs and potatoes, accompanied by lingonberry jam.

"My mother's influence, naturally," Alma said. "I cook to honor her and our heritage. And to keep Mr. Quist here in line."

Magnus rubbed his hands together. *"Köttbullar och potatis och lingonsylt."*

"Mind you, Magnus suggested we serve a different dish." Alma passed heaping platefuls in from the kitchen. "A food our cousins in Iceland eat. It's a splendid delicacy called *hakari.*"

"Essentially," Magnus said, "it's fermented shark. Really wonderful. You bury a dead shark in the earth for several weeks, dig it up, hang it out to dry, serve it cubed."

"A nice healthy dose of ammonia, I'm told," said Alma. "A bit overwhelming."

"A bit?" Maria asked.

"Shark, huh?" Darrol glanced at Magnus, then looked back at his plate. "I've known a few sharks."

"And I've known plenty of meatballs," Brick threw in, earning laughter from everyone.

"Our parents," said Mrs. Durr, stirring lingonberry jam over the potatoes in joyful swirls of red. "We've mentioned parents a time or two tonight. I'm curious to hear more." A sly twinkle. "I always have an interest in ancestors, you know."

Alma looked at Maria. "What about your parents, dear?"

Maria was caught off guard. "Oh. Em. Not much to say. I was six when my father disappeared into a heavy fog and never came back. My mother, when she's not shacked up— sorry, I mean living with someone—scrapes out a sort of a life in Daly City. I'm ashamed to say I don't see her very much."

"Common enough problem," Alma sighed. "Now me, I had good luck in parents, until my twenties, when my mother died of cancer, and not that long afterwards my father walked in front of a cable car he'd just stepped off and met an idiot speeding up California Street."

She paused for the murmured commiserations. "Of course, Pappa would have been pleased that at least it was a classic old Saab 96." She paused for the laughter. "And that the driver was a Unitarian, not a Lutheran." Smiling, Alma ate more of her dinner.

Darrol's voice rode over the chuckles. "All of my parents were religious. All eight or twelve of them." That brought silence.

"Foster homes," he explained. "I don't rightly know who Foster was, but he must have had an in with God considering the self-righteous way all those people behaved."

This time the laughter was merely polite.

"So you're not related to the famous George Yount of Yountville?" Alma asked.

"Never heard of him."

"Yount was a California pioneer, among the first white settlers in the Napa Valley. I think he founded an early winery. Yountville is named after him."

"Thus..." Magnus waved his knife. "...thus endeth Alma's latest history lesson." The others laughed.

"Maybe I'll adopt him," Darrol grinned. "You said George Yount? I'd love the connection. And the inheritance, if it's a big one." More laughter. "But I believe my names were picked out at random by some dumb social worker. Couldn't even spell Darrol properly." He drank more of his beer.

"And you, Mr. Zimmer?" Mrs. Durr asked.

Zimmer had a mouthful of meatballs. He nodded his head, swallowed. "Army brat," he said at last. "Dad was a lifer, Mom a school teacher. We moved and moved again. Unsettling, I guess literally, but they always tried to make it easy for me and my sisters."

Magnus looked at him. "That's why you keep at it as a pilot, *ja?* Travel, travel."

Zimmer wiped his mouth. "Could be. Never looked at it that way."

"Is your name really Brick?" Maria asked.

"Actually it is. Well, sort of. It's Bricknall. Old family name."

Alma smiled. "So you're not like the long-suffering Brick in *Cat on a Hot Tin Roof?*"

"Hardly," Zimmer said. "Life is good. As are your meatballs. Any seconds?"

Lyckatill chose that moment to leap onto the pony wall.

"*Gå, fan katt!* Magnus hissed, throwing his napkin. The cat jumped back down.

"You must forgive Lyckatill," Alma said, spooning out more food. "She's the true ruler of this house."

"Which puts me to be very low on the pecking order," Magnus groused.

"What's the name mean—Lyckatill?" Zimmer asked.

"It's Swedish for 'good luck.'" Alma said.

Maria started laughing. "When Darrol first heard that word, he thought it meant that the cat licks the cash register. Get it—lick-a-till?"

"Yeah, we get it." Darrol said quickly. He wasn't able to head off the laughter. "That's several debits," he muttered to Maria.

Maria sat back and slowly wiped jam from her lips.

Mrs. Durr turned to Duff. "You're awfully quiet, Mr. Lee," she said. "Tell us a little about your family. How about your name for starters? Duff, is it?"

"Scottish mother, Chinese-American father. They met in Singapore."

Mrs. Durr clapped her hands. "How exotic! Were you born over there?"

"No, right here in the City. Children's Hospital. Nothing exotic."

"Now wait a minute, said Darrol innocently, "The Golden Dragon. Wasn't that a little exotic, Duff?"

"What's the Golden Dragon?" Maria asked.

Duff shook his head and studied his food.

Darrol made an apologetic face. "Mm, somehow I thought Duff's family was connected to a little Chinatown adventure. My mistake. Who knows what strange *drawers* our minds keep these things in, eh, Duff?"

Duff managed a small blank smile. He looked at his watch. "You know," he said, "I forgot an appointment. My martial arts trainer. I must go."

He stood. "So sorry." He reached across the table and shook Magnus' hand. "Thank you, Mr. Quist."

Alma saw Duff to the door. He gave her a small awkward bow.

"I'll save some dessert for you," she said. "I'll send it up with Darrol and Maria, but they have to promise not to eat it."

She closed the door behind Duff and returned to the table.

Mrs. Durr was puzzled. "Did we say something to offend him? I certainly hope not."

"Good old Duff keeps very odd hours," Darrol said. "Between his work and the gym, he's always going somewhere." He speared another meatball.

"OK, Jo." Alma put down her fork and looked at Mrs. Duff. "You've been the interlocutor far too long. Now it's your turn to reveal all."

"Oh, my dear, I've not revealed all in years." Mrs. Durr gave them her patented giggle. "Too many wrinkles showing."

She turned to Brick Zimmer. "I always recommend turning out the lights after you're 50." Zimmer laughed.

"But briefly to other matters," Mrs. Durr went on. "I was born right down there on Bay Street." She leaned towards Zimmer. "Never you mind when, dear, unless you're going to turn out the lights *and* wear a blindfold."

After this bit of laugher subsided, she went on. "Daughter of Theodore Starr Kearny and Evangeline Zelda Cross. Married to Samuel Burton Durr for far too long, but he's dead. My only sibling, Norah, died quite young. And, alas, my only child, Esmy, also died too early. Both were childless. So here I am, the sole set of chromosomes on the end of the long genetic trail which goes right back to...you know who."

She turned toward Zimmer and mock-whispered. "Allowing for a bit of bastardy along the way."

She rummaged in her pearl reticule. "Very few believe me—oh, don't pretend any of you do—even though I can produce as supporting evidence..." She held up something small. "This button, right from Norton's very jacket!"

They handed the button around. It was wooden, small, and soiled almost black from too much handling.

"This is about as authentic as the Emperor's sabre downstairs," Magnus said, handing the button to Maria. "I hope, Josephine, you didn't buy it from the crook who sold me that sword."

"Oh, I didn't buy it at all. It has passed down through the generations. From great, great whatever to me."

"Do you really want to be related to a crazy man?" Darrol asked.

"Crazy, maybe," she said, "but famous, and wildly popular in his day." She dropped the button into her bag. "One could do worse for an ancestor."

Alma pushed back her chair and stood up. "All right! The meatballs have vanished! So please let us clear up a bit and we'll have coffee and a dessert with a most unusual name." She put out a hand. "Darrol, no, please sit down. Thanks, but you don't need to help. It's your night off."

She led Magnus into the kitchen, looked over the pony wall at Darrol. "But maybe you'll tell us what it's like working in a restaurant."

Maria jumped in. "He looks so handsome in his uniform. He..."

Waving Maria off, Darrol thought a moment. "It's a complete universe, lots going on. Tragedies and triumphs. Petty politics. Major dramas and, well, plenty of funny stuff."

Maria was enthused. "Tell them about the purse snatcher. I love that story."

"I can decide for..." He gave her a sharp look. "But OK. Well, last Mother's Day, we were doing our annual brunch. Full table service but also a buffet and omelet line.

"A very snooty woman is up by Emilio, one of our chefs, and he's putting on a show, creating her the omelet of a lifetime.

"Somehow this creep comes in, grabs the woman's purse and races out. Screams, confusion, all that. Emilio drops his omelet fixings, I mean for real, literally—like pans and eggshells and cheeses and artichokes flying everywhere, and he takes off after the guy.

"In a few minutes, Emilio comes back with the lady's purse. Turns out he tackled the creep a block away. The guy punched Emilio and ran, but Emilio saved the purse.

"The whole restaurant bursts into cheers and everybody, I mean everybody, lines up wanting omelets and to shake Emilio's hand."

"Great story," said Alma, setting out elegant cups and saucers.

"Yeah, only one catch," Darrol mused. "Cost me in tips— all my table customers jumped ship and became buffet junkies. Emilio was the star, the hero."

"Left you in the cold, *ja*?" Magnus voice came from the back of the kitchen.

Darrol stared over the pony wall. Magnus was absorbed with a coffee pot.

"Well," said Mrs. Durr, "when Samuel and I went to Peru, the restaurants in Lima chained our bags and purses to the table legs."

"Chains? Maybe I'll suggest that at Lanterman's." Darrol's tone was not sweet.

"All right! Here they are!" Alma placed two plates of the pastries on the table. "Vacuum cleaner rolls!"

Maria clapped her hands. "These are what I helped with, Darrol! Dark chocolate and green marzipan—Alma made that herself—and inside, cookie and cake crumbs, biscotti pieces and liqueur. I forget the name."

"It's called punsch," Alma said. ""Coffee coming soon! Right Mr. Quist?"

"*Ja, ja!" Hälla din hästar!*"

Alma passed a plate. "Maria was a big help. I didn't know she was a Culinary Academy grad."

"Technically," said Darrol, reaching for a pastry, "she's not. Can you imagine our little Maria broke the rules? Had to turn in her spatula early."

"Oh, I'm sorry," Alma said. She gave Darrol a frown.

Maria was blushing. "It's nothing. Worked out for the best. I got hired at *La Dolce Via* anyway, and I'm very happy there."

"Did you call these 'vacuum cleaner rolls'?" Zimmer asked. "They're really great!"

Mrs. Durr reached for another. "I second the motion!"

"Mimi," Darrol had the tiniest bit of contrition in his voice. "maybe you could show the bakery how to make them? Might mean big brownie points for you."

Zimmer laughed. Magnus poured coffee.

Maria looked at Alma. "If Alma would give me the recipe..."

"Or course, dear. It's a good idea. Nothing better than buttering up your boss." Alma said. "My goodness, we're all full of bakery jokes, aren't we?"

Magnus refilled his aquavit. "So, Mr. Zimmer. Do you ever fly to Sweden?"

"Occasionally to Stockholm. Nice place."

"Mostly I remember it," said Magnus. "as a cold and dark town. Cold and dark schools. Cold and dark parents."

"That part I wouldn't know about." Zimmer sipped his coffee.

"Come now, Mr. Quist," Alma said, with a toothy smile, "your childhood is one thing. Stockholm today is quite another. You should rise again like the *Vasa*!"

"What's that?" Maria asked.

"Quite amazing." Alma looked around the table. "The *Vasa* was a Swedish warship which sank in the Stockholm harbor in the 1620's. It was to be the pride of the Swedish Navy and of King Gustavus. But only minutes into its maiden voyage, the ship tipped over and sank."

"My goodness!" Mrs. Durr's eyes were wide.

Alma went on. "Somehow it was forgotten until the 1960's, when archeologists brought it up and built a museum around it. Right near downtown Stockholm. It looks much as it did almost 400 years ago. Stunning to see."

"So ultimately Alma's saying I'm really 400 years old," Magnus grumped. "But behold! I've risen again!" He raised his arms triumphantly. "And stunning to see."

"And more power to you, Magnus," Alma said. "So lighten up."

"Why'd the thing sink?" Darrol asked, biting into a marzipan roll.

"Bad design. Top heavy. Overloaded with cannons and dignitaries. You name it. But I think hubris, greed, even stupidity were all part of it." Alma grimaced. "A metaphor for today, yes?'

Darrol nodded. "Stupidity, it's all around." He sounded angry.

"Alma, how do you know all these things?" Maria asked.

Magnus flashed a benign smile. "Perhaps she identifies with sinking ships?"

Alma aimed a finger gun at him. "I love history," she said. She pulled the trigger.

"Was Gustavus another crazy king?" Mrs. Durr asked. "The world is full of them. Crazy kings and crazy presidents. Really bad eggs, not nice like my crazy ancestor."

"Gustav probably wasn't any crazier than any other king or politician," Alma said. "Greedy for power, perhaps, but aren't they all? It's a disease."

"And no cure," Mrs. Durr chuckled.

Alma nodded. "Now, Gustav's daughter, Queen Kristina, on the other hand, may actually have been crazy. For sure she was wildly-eccentric. She gave up the throne, traveled all over, trying to find something, find meaning, something."

"I don't find much meaning in my travels," Zimmer said. "But I do get a paycheck. Such as it is." There was generous laughter, except from Magnus.

"Travel a lot," Magnus said, "or stay in one place—like our spider downstairs—it can be hard to find true meaning. Alma has a cousin, for example..."

Alma nodded. "Oh yes, my cousin Thetis. She's the personal assistant to a minor but self-important VP at Bank of America. Been with him for over a quarter of a century."

Magnus went on. "Thetis is—what's the word?—*slaviskt,* slavishly, yes, loyally devoted, to the man. She is completely focused on the tiny *detaljer av* his work. But I am willing to say not one bit of what he does—or what she does—is important in the bigger scheme-of-things. Not one bit."

"Probably she has a very full life outside of the bank," Maria said.

Magnus looked at her. "Away from the bank? Not so. What is there for Thetis? Very little."

"Flowerboxes," Alma said musingly, "canasta, keeping records for the Swedish Society, and a small, not-very-bright dog. Of course, we ask her here for dinner. She rarely accepts."

"So," Magnus continued, "a life built on flowerboxes, *ja?* No! Her life is all about serving her boss. What meaning does that have? What meaning, truly, is there for either of them? Slaves to commerce, to higher-ups, to anonymous stockholders." He stared at his drink. "Or slaves to a grocery store, *ja?*"

Alma touched Magnus' hand. "*Gubben,* what's the Swedish word for 'morose'?"

A puzzled look. "*Dyster* or perhaps *vresig.*" Now a rueful look. "Ah, is that what I am being?" He turned to the others. "*Förlåt mig!* Apologies. Next time, I think a little less aquavit?"

"Heady stuff!" Mrs. Durr laughed. "Both the aquavit and the conversation." She creaked to her feet. "Well, before we all try to find meaning in our lives—if not the meaning of life—I for one must call it a night."

"And I have a date," Zimmer said, getting up.

Maria looked up at him. "So late?"

"Her flight came in only an hour ago." He winked at her. "But never let your love life be at the mercy of dispatchers or air traffic controllers."

"A redhead?" Darrol's smile included a touch of envy.

Zimmer winked again. "That's for me to know, isn't it?"

Pushing back from the table. A round of thanks. Handshakes. Trooping out, with Darrol and Maria the last to go.

Maria and Alma hugged as Darrol strolled off toward the stairs.

Alma closed the door for the final time. She went to the dining table and began gathering the remaining plates and saucers. Lyckatill appeared from nowhere and rubbed against her legs.

Magnus was already in the kitchen, filling the sink. "So..." he said, "...a success?"

Soap bubbles rose toward the counter. The room was becoming lemony.

"A good first," Alma mused. "Though I was sorry Duff seemed in a hurry to leave."

"It's clear Darrol Yount has Duff's number." Magnus put on a red apron. "What was that dragon business?"

"Not sure." She brought him the dishes. "And you? Did you survive our little gathering?"

He shrugged. "Your *köttbullar* were deliciously top-heavy. Like the *Vasa*." He lowered the saucers into the suds. "As to our guests—tomorrow they will again be customers and tenants. The clock strikes midnight and the carriage is once more a rutabaga."

"Do you like them? Our tenants?"

"In varied degrees." Steam fogged his glasses. He removed them and wiped them with a dish towel, his large eyes momentarily vacant.

Alma transferred the remaining pastries from the tray to a plate and put plastic wrap around them. "All that stuff about Thetis. I've not known you to quite be so philosophical or metaphysical. Are you hunting for meaning in your life, *sötnos*?"

Magnus blew a soap bubble toward her. "Aren't *you* my meaning, *käraste*?"

The tiny iridescent world floated downward, bloomed, burst.

Chapter 9
Shell Game

Darrol dreamt that he was driving a cable car down a very steep hill. There were no passengers, no brakeman. Alcatraz beckoned from far out in the bay. Suddenly the car rode free of the tracks, sped down the hill, glided through a park, flew into the water. And floated. Ahead now was the Golden Gate Bridge, and beyond that was the open Pacific, glistening.

Careening toward Darrol, levitating over the waves, was a huge wooden warship, with tall masts, large flapping sails, big cannons poking from the portholes. At the bow was Emperor Norton, in full Union regalia, his sword pointing forward. He turned his head toward Darrol. The eyes were dark and flecked with madness.

The cable car vanished. Darrol instantly was aboard the warship, his bare feet skidding on raw planking. Everything tilted, and the gray waters of the bay rushed over the decks toward him. A seagull kept screeching.

Maria's alarm.

In his frayed blue sweats, cupping a mug of Peet's, Darrol sat at the kitchen counter and tried to describe the dream to Maria. She was rushing to make her lunch.

"I can't remember the name of that Swedish ship," he mused, watching her rear as she bent to find something in a lower drawer. He liked how Maria looked in her bakery whites.

A muffled "What?" Maria popped up holding a rumpled paper bag. She pushed the drawer shut with her foot.

"The ship they told us about last night. The Swedish one that sank. I've forgotten the name."

"The *Vasa*." She stuffed things into the bag.

"How the hell you remember that?"

"It's not hard. Sometimes I think I've got sort of a pornographic memory."

"What a great thing to have!" He slurped his coffee. "But I think you mean *photographic* memory."

Maria sniffed. "I thought that's what I said. But no matter. I got an OK memory. But names are easier to remember than where I put my sunglasses." Searching, she shuffled papers about on the counter. "You think I'll need sunglasses today? It's supposed to be cloudy."

"Am I the weather man?" He caught her little frown. "Hey, I'm kidding. You're looking good this morning. Rain or shine, you always look good. C'mere."

Maria smiled. She came around the counter. Darrol, remaining on the stool, pulled her close. She smelled of jasmine. He liked her perfume. And he liked that it was inexpensive when she expected him to buy her some.

"I gotta go," Maria said. "But we could have a little fun tonight when you get back from work." She wiggled in his arms. Her version of provocative.

"It's a date," Darrol said to her breasts. He looked up. "Or you could just cut work and we'll have fun right now." His hand ran across her rear.

"Tonight, silly!" She kissed him quickly and moved away. "Ciao."

That word always seemed stupid coming from her, but so far Darrol had held his tongue about it. Pick your battles.

"Hey!" He stood up." Don't forget to tell them about those vacuum cleaner rolls."

"If I can." She was at the door.

"And bring me something extra sweet, would you?"

"You want me, rolled in sugar?"

"That'll do it! That and a cannoli or two."

Maria laughed and went out.

Alma was descending the apartment stairs when Darrol bounded down from above. He slowed and joined her. They had just stepped into the vestibule when there was a hurried clumping behind them. Brick Zimmer and a pretty blond woman rushed from the stairwell. They were both in uniform, both carrying flight bags, both laughing.

"Good morning! Goodbye!" called Brick, opening the street door. "Thanks for dinner!"

The two bustled out. The heavy door clicked shut behind them.

"I wish I had his...stamina," Darrol said, shaking his head.

Alma smiled. "No ill effects of last night's Swedish onslaught?" she said.

"Only in some strange, pretty active dreams. They're mostly fading."

"A lot like life itself, dreams?" Alma mused. "All glorious action and promises then so quickly receding."

"You sound a little bleak."

She shook her head. "No, I'm not really bleak, but last night's conversations got me thinking about my parents. Both of them died far too young."

"I'm sorry. And Mr. Quist's parents—I assume they're gone too?"

She nodded.

"He seems a little angry about them."

A tinier nod. "He is that."

"One of his blind spots, huh?"

"Oh, I don't think Magnus has any blind spots."

"Mr. Perfection?"

"Hardly. Mr. Inscrutable." Laughing, she walked to the private door to the 'Norton. "Don't tell him I said that!"

Darrol followed her. "Well, he—"

"Look, I've got to go in, Darrol." She reached for the keypad, turned again. "Are you headed for the store right now?"

"Yes."

"Then come on through with me. It's against the rules—Magnus' rules—so we'll keep it a secret, yes?"

"I like secrets." He tried not to be obvious about leaning forward.

Alma made no effort to block where her fingers went. As she keyed in the code, Darrol, nonchalantly vigilant, saw every number.

Ah! He tried to breathe normally. *9-1-7-4-6.*

Alma opened the door and gestured to Darrol to go first. They entered. She quietly closed the door.

The interior hallway was narrow and dimly lit. There was a muted, complex odor. Darrol sniffed. Must and vegetables. And something else.

"Smells of history, doesn't it?" Alma said in a soft voice.

Darrol nodded. "I like it. I don't know why."

"I swear I sometimes detect the layers," Alma said. "New bicycle tires and barrels of minty candy and dry cleaning fluids."

Darrol muffled a sneeze.

"And of course dust," Alma whispered. "Historic dust." She took his arm. "OK, let me give you a tiny tour, then you need to get out into the store before Magnus wanders this way."

Opposite where they stood was heavy steel door. It was brownish-black except for a pair of thin, blood-red lines inset a few inches from the perimeter. A circular mechanism—two large connected steel rings—dominated the door's center.

"In some past life this was a vault," Alma said. "Magnus uses it as an office or den or heaven knows what. No one else gets in there. Not even me. I guess every man needs a private space, yes?"

"We sure do." He stared at the vault. "We sure do."

Alma had moved on. She pointed at a door with an inset rippled glass window.

"This is Della Rossiter's office. Bookkeeping, inventory, payroll, you name it. Our little secret—the 'Norton couldn't run without Della."

Darrol knew Della. Fifty going on forever. Oversexed and obvious. She put the overt in overture. But she was as harmless as one of his street people. He always let her down easy with a joke.

"And here we are!" Alma was still whispering.

The last space, door-less, belonged to a small break room. "My desk," Alma pointed. "I get to share it with ham sandwiches and small talk. But that's fun. I like our staff. And mostly I'm out in the store."

She went to end of the hallway and peeked through a square window in the metal door. "OK, coast's clear." She opened the door. "Don't let on you've been here or I'll be smacked with a flyswatter. Or worse."

"I won't."

She let Darrol into the store, and closed the door behind him.

9-1-7-4-6.

"I didn't see you come in, Mr. Yount." Magnus was filling the gumball machine.

"I flew in on my very own cable car," Darrol said, reaching for a stick of licorice. "You ever have flying dreams, Magnus?"

"I keep my dreams private." Magnus snapped the dispenser lid shut, put the gumball box under the counter. A feather duster stuck up from one back pocket, a fly swatter from the other. Today's apron was green. Stitched across the chest in big gold letters were the words *Jag vet.*

Hilda Brown was at her register, a middle-aged Heidi with flaxen braids. Darrol gave her a raised hand salute and clicked his heels. She managed to look both embarrassed and pleased.

"That part of history is best forgotten." Lukas Knudsen held his basket like a fullback protecting a football.

"Eva here doesn't mind," Darrol paid Hilda for the licorice. "Do you, Mrs. Braun?"

"Her name is Hilda," Magnus said softly, adjusting the figure of Emperor Norton. "And it's Brown, not Braun."

"I don't mind, Mr. Quist," Hilda said, unloading Knudsen's basket. "Darrol makes me laugh."

"See?" Darrol waved his licorice airily.

Knudsen looked at him. "As a lawyer, I'd say you're within your rights. As a person whose Danish grandparents suffered under the Nazis, I'd say differently."

"Swedes and Danes," Magnus said, dusting the hanging sword, "hardly see eye to eye on anything, do they Mr. Knudsen? But in this case..."

"OK, OK. Point taken." Darrol said, "And I'm not making a joke about your sword." He nibbled on the licorice. "So, do you ever take that thing out of its sheath, condom, whatever it's called?"

"I very rarely do. It is sharp. Like your wit, Mr. Yount."

"Call me Darrol, for Pete's sake. Haven't I seen people taking pictures of themselves with the good old Emperor here? Taking selfies with his sword too?"

The bell over the door jingled as Jump Jesperson entered.

"Yes, good for business," Magnus was saying." Sometimes I may take it off the wall for them. But not out of the sheath. Too dangerous."

"Did I hear dangerous?" Jesperson took a gunslinger pose. "I'm your man! But I'm mostly here to spend some Norton Dollars." He waved a fistful of the discount coupons.

Magnus wiggled his duster. "Good morning, Colonel. We discuss the danger of the Emperor's sabre."

Jesperson nodded. "That thing's probably as nasty as a punji stick."

"A what?" Darrol asked.

"Viet Nam. Punji sticks were vicious little stakes that got you unawares. Poisoned tips. Punctured your legs, your face, your guts." He grimaced. "One time I remember chuting in, just missed landing in a pit of the bastards."

"Wow!" Darrol looked impressed. "A war hero right here in the 'Norton?"

"No, not really," Jesperson smiled, "just a guy doing his duty." He stood up straighter.

"Well, this sword is safe in comparison," Magnus said. "But it stays in the sheath for any who take self-photos."

Jesperson was staring at Magnus' apron "Are you a veteran, Quist?"

"What?" Magnus glanced down. "Oh, the words? *Jag vet* simply means 'I know...'"

Magnus saw Darrol's questioning look. "You like ambiguity, Mr. Yount. You figure it out."

Columbus Avenue was clogged with tourists, and their big busses seemed to have taken over every curb near the three-street intersection of Columbus, Chestnut and Taylor. As Darrol walked along his chosen loop, clusters of chattering Chinese people were pouring onto the sidewalks. He dodged around two noisy groups and cut over to Lombard.

He cursed under his breath. Many of the tourists were already heading up the few blocks toward the so-called 'Crookedest Street in the World', a very steep section of Lombard in which virtual switchbacks zigzagged between low landscaping. Even this early in the day, cars were making their slow, silly turns down the road. Tourists, waving cameras and selfie sticks, stood at the bottom of the slope.

This was not Russian Hill as Darrol would have it. Not his Russian Hill.

He returned to Taylor and walked south, trying to focus on his art assignment, due next week, but interrupting himself by thinking about Magnus Quist.

The man was beginning to irritate him—just a little, but the signs were there—and Darrol wasn't quite sure why. Not knowing why doubled the effect. He didn't like people getting under his skin, especially if he couldn't immediately do something about it.

Take Anne of Green Goobers, for instance. Darrol saw Anne on the sidewalk just ahead. Her gray skirts billowing, she was bending to pet something—a stray cat or a big rat or a really small midget.

Or maybe a dead art teacher. His mind played with the possibilities.

Anne, or Annie as most knew her, was one of the few street people Darrol didn't much like. He thought it had partly to do with the green and yellow snot which often hung from her nostrils like exotic plants dangling from cliffside caves.

Most of his street people had grooming issues. Most of them reeked, although often with faded, individual pongs which after a time became not-unpleasant personal identifiers. Darrol suspected he could walk up to any of them blindfolded and know who he was meeting.

But Annie, who'd earned her sobriquet soon after Darrol realized her nasal horrors were chronic—and who'd done heaven-knew-what with the packet of old handkerchiefs he'd brought her—really rankled with her disgusting appearance.

On top of that, Anne of Green Goobers, much more than any other street person Darrol knew, expected things from him. She was the one who always thrust out her hand like a greedy child ready for a treat. Not just ready. Not just hoping. Demanding. He didn't like it. Not one bit.

As he approached, Annie was still bent over, focused on petting the Gollum, the groveling pygmy, whatever it was. She was going to look down there forever. Maybe she'd already died in that bending position. One could hope.

Darrol, not wanting another big detour, decided to plunge on. He quietly stepped into the gutter, crossed his fingers and got ready to pass by.

"Prince Charming," Annie wheezed, bobbing up like a toy drinking duck. Her dirty hand was already out. Today's snot was minimal, but the neon green was effectively sickening.

"Prince Charming," she said again, pronouncing it like the brand of toilet paper, "whatcha bring yer old Cuddly?" She smiled, remembered her manners, and wiped away the green crust with the back of her sleeve. The hand thrust out again.

"Oh, Annie," Darrol said, "I didn't know I'd see you. I don't have anything." Not quite true, as there were sugared cruller pieces in two of his pockets.

A sly look emerged on her face. More greenish awfulness peeked out at the day. "Ah, April foolsy. Trick or treaty? You want me to sing?"

He'd heard her screeches before. In comparison, the parrots on Green Street were a chorus of angels. "No, no, Annie," he said quickly. "I just remembered I have something."

He fumbled in his right pocket. "Yes, here." He dropped half a cruller into her palm. Her fist closed faster than a Venus flytrap.

"More?" It was not really a question. The other hand was out.

"Sorry. Gotta go." Darrol stepped around her. The creature begging at her feet flapped its wings at him.

A trash bag, its ends waving in the wind.

He heard Annie call out. He didn't look back. No, it wasn't the goobers at all. What annoyed him was the lack of respect, the absence of deference.

Unbidden, Emperor Norton came to his mind again. What a juggling act the guy managed! Face it, Darrol thought, Norton was a crazy street person, no better than Annie or Jeepers Peepers or the rest. But he was also the illusory boss of the city. He claimed deference, respect, even submission, and he got it. A distinct case of mind over matter. Or lack-of-mind over matter.

As Darrol turned west again and continued winding his way up Russian Hill, he was back on the subject of Magnus Quist.

The Swede was generally polite enough, but there was an edge of something there too. Superiority? Scorn, even? At times it almost felt like malice, although that feeling probably came, Darrol decided, from the effect of Quist's creepy eyes lurking behind those thick glasses.

Magnus Quist was smart, not without humor, and he seemed to have interesting things to say. Darrol liked smart people. When they treated him as an equal. Minimum. But Quist...

The morning was still cool and surprisingly humid, but Darrol was sweating. He stopped for a moment. Cigarette smoke made his nose twitch. Somebody sneaking one behind the high redwood fence. Something strong and pungent. A Turkish terrorist hiding through there? More likely some rich kid avoiding his parents.

Darrol couldn't stand smoking. He'd tried it in high school when the other boys thought it was cool to flaunt the rules. He quickly decided the real act of rebellion was to break from that crowd, stand on his own. Then he read more about smoking and said screw it, who needs cancer, and that did it. But he had to admit the smell weaving toward him up here in the cool, pine-tinged air was just slightly seductive.

He could hear a few birds singing, the taller trees rustling in the slight breeze. He looked up. The sky, bleached of all but the most stubborn blue, was mostly clear, except for a few high clouds. A white contrail smoked across, dissipating leisurely. Odd thing, Darrol thought, to reach the age of 31 and never have flown. Blame his absentee parents. Blame the Fosters, the creeps in the institutes. Blame the system. Never to have flown. Well, except in dreams.

He took his bearings, yawned, decided to climb another few blocks.

The snail was in Darrol's way. Taking advantage of the cool morning, it was sliming across the sidewalk, completely exposed to accidental death from an overpriced Nike or some kid's grungy skateboard wheels.

Or from Darrol's purposeful tread.

Darrol could imagine the satisfying snapping and thin crackling, feel the slurpy squish, the futile life nicely oozing away underfoot. He stopped right beside it. The thing was either courageous or stupid or just totally out of it. Like so many people.

Most people, though, didn't leave a trail of slime behind them. Or did they?

Darrol liked to ponder such questions. Yes, he thought, maybe there was a certain sliminess in the wake of a few of his regulars at the restaurant. Unctuous people who looked down on him, if they even really noticed him in the first place.

Darrol, standing still, watched the snail. In the last two seconds, in human terms, the creature had made little progress. Darrol laughed. In snail terms, maybe the thing had just a set a world speed record, but who was to know? Slow contracting waves gradually were arcing its rubbery body and its tiny mobile home towards the edge of a sickly bit of grass, someone's poor attempt at a lawn.

He wrinkled his nose. Waffles, maybe, or pancakes. The nauseating smell of maple syrup took him back to an Oakland foster home and the cloying, smothering woman who burned everything she could get her pans on and then required Darrol to gag down every mouthful. She was putrifyingly-sweet with an aggravatingly-false smile and, he was sure, a deadly heart. How can a kid hate pancakes? How can a kid hate a sweet old foster mother?

He looked again at the snail, remembering the hundreds, thousands, of bugs he'd squashed in his boyhood. And the two bees he'd stuck in a bottle to fight it out. Back then, the only real power he had was over insects, small animals and the occasional kid dumb enough to wander down an alley alone.

Nowadays...well, his power had increased, was increasing ever more. He grinned.

So, *sayonara*, snail. He raised his foot.

And stopped.

He stooped low and looked closely at the snail. He could almost admire the construction. The cinnamon shell with its perfect dark chocolate whorls. The yellow-brown body, scrotal and elastic. The twin main tentacles tipped with tiny eyeballs or sensors or whatever they were.

Shit, was it looking back at him? What did it see? Some giant alien or the best-looking guy on the Hill—hell, in the City? He gave it a wink just in case it really was aware.

Darrol nodded and stood up. What the hell, run your mucous-y trail smack into that guy's feeble rhodies. Chomp away. Have brunch on me. Go to sleep. I don't care. I'm choosing to give you a pass, snail.

He almost staggered backwards. Not from the slope but from the force of an epiphany. In that moment he realized that what he had was even more significant than having power over other things, power over other people.

He could *choose* whether or not to wield that power.

He realized that rather than acting instinctively, he could operate on a higher level and make a choice. Ending a snail's life, for instance. He could choose to squash it or choose not to squash it. Choose to be civil to Annie and the rest or to show them his back. Choose to wield knowledge he held over others, or to choose to be beneficent.

The true power lay in that willful act of choosing. *His* willful act. Thumbs up, thumbs down: he could make such truly powerful choices. He saw this as a subtle distinction which elevated him into the ranks of CEOs, kings, emperors, gods.

Hell, maybe he had the power of the big God himself. He took a huge breath and savored the revelation.

The sun fought with a cloud. The sun triumphed.

Grinning, filled with power, Darrol looked at the snail one final time and turned back down the hill.

Chapter 10
Seeing Nothing, Seeing Everything

That afternoon, on the way to Lanterman's, Darrol reflected on the grand order of things at work. He called up some of the religious stuff crammed into him at that smug place in Hayward, Holy Crap School. The whole pecking order pretty much fit:

There was the Father, i.e. the restaurant's founder, the still-revered August Lanterman, long dead—but wasn't God supposed to be dead anyway?

Next came the son, Vinnie Lanterman, co-owner and semi-silent partner, but continuing to be around and ornery, worshiped by some and feared by most.

The Holy Ghost pretty much had to be co-owner and manager, Radisson Vero, whose presence was felt even those rare times he wasn't in the restaurant.

The head chefs were the angels and devils. The sommelier and bartenders would be minor deities or maybe the saints— they certain thought they were.

The waiters and other staff were the hungry multitude or maybe the Israelites hunting for a permanent home.

At the bottom of the chain were the busboys and the dishwashers, the rabble waiting for grace and enlightenment.

Which left only the beautiful Tekla Hart, the hostess. *Shit!* Darrol slammed a fist into a palm. *That's it!* Tekla was Mary Magdalene.

He was so bemused and amused he stepped from a curb on Grant into busy traffic. An enraged horn returned him to the present, and he jumped back.

He was happy to note the vehicle which might have hit him was a dark green Jaguar XKE. If you're gonna get creamed, he thought, at least do it in style.

Darrol arrived at work early. He was the first server to come in. This was a non-lunch day, so everything would start up for dinner. The kitchen was slowly bubbling back to life. Darrol could hear Joe Rosa and Chips Blaine going at it with the kind of friendly aggression they'd likely been part of for years. *They might as well be married.*

The dining rooms were empty, but Jarrett Soucie, one of the bartenders, was at the main bar taking inventory. He nodded as Darrol passed but said nothing. Soucie, tall, gaunt and ageless, was a strange one. Darrol suspected he had a habit which went beyond alcohol. But the guy mixed superb cocktails and was fast about it, a jackrabbit among the bottles.

The windowless staff room was dark. The place always smelled of the previous night's cooking and not in a pleasant way. At best, the air was sullen. So much for high-tech kitchen fans.

Darrol flipped on the lights, hung his coat in a locker, admired himself in the full-length mirror. The modified tuxes, designed by Vinnie Lanterman and inspected nightly by Radisson Vero, really looked quite classy. Slim lapels, quality-cut, one-button Regent jackets cleverly-tailored for easy arm movements; broad satin accent stripes on the pants. Lanterman's had to have the best-dressed wait staff in the city, and Darrol knew he was the best of that best.

He gave his hair a final check, turned off the lights and wandered out to his primary service podium. There were no arm napkins, and he decided to stock up. Normally it was X's job, but the kid wasn't here yet and Darrol didn't mind helping him out. He went back down the hall towards the linen storage room.

As he neared the door he heard a soft swishing and panting. The swishing could have been tablecloths being folded, but the panting—and now a low grunting—well, Darrol was pretty sure he knew what was going on in there.

The only question was who.

Propriety was not an issue, nor respecting privacy, nor avoiding anyone's embarrassment. The issue was gathering information. Darrol opened the door and took a step inside.

Exhilarating, if a tiny bit envy-producing.

Radisson Vero and Tekla Hart were going at it, she face down on the linen-folding table, he doing the dancing goat behind her.

104

Darrol took it all in, swiftly snapped mental photos. As Vero half-turned, Darrol faked a mumbled apology, backed out and closed the door.

Well, well, well, he thought. *Snails, both of them.*

There was that power of choice again. One word to Vero's wife or to Vinnie Lanterman and...two shells crushed, mangled. Or keep mum and who knows what the two of them would owe him.

He retreated quietly down the corridor, thinking they could hear his inward laughter. If they assumed he was laughing at what he'd seen, they'd be wrong. He was laughing about the restaurant's religious hierarchy he'd mapped out. Here was Mary Magdalen doing her thing, but not as the mistress of Jesus. She was making it with the Holy Ghost himself.

Darrol entered the kitchen, chatted with the chefs, memorized the specials. He earned a rare smile of approval from Emilio when he asked confirmation on pronouncing *Strangozzi al Tartufo Nero*, which he got right on the first try, and *Tonnareli alle uevo di riccio*, right on the second try.

"You really put urchin eggs in that stuff?" Darrol asked.

"I dive for the urchins myself off Point Reyes, what you think?" Emilio said. He tossed a round of soft cheese to Joe Rossi. Joe caught it with the cool flair of a veteran Giants' first baseman.

Darrol went to the wine cellar to look for the sommelier. Hank Barrett was a gray-faced, funereal man who only came alive when describing wines to the customers. Hank was from Bayonne, New Jersey, but when a diner pressed his buttons, he became charmingly cosmopolitan and uncorked a believable trace of a French accent.

Hank's nametag, insisted on by Vinnie Lanterman, read *Henri.* "A fair degree of snobbery is tolerated, even expected," August Lanterman reportedly said the day he first opened the place.

Explaining the featured wines to Darrol, Hank reverted to his glum demeanor and his New Jersey accent. Darrol dutifully memorized two French wines and two from a high-end Sonoma vineyard.

Darrol always liked to have a little extra knowledge in his back pocket. But with a sharp-eyed, critical manager hovering, he was careful how and when he used it. He remembered one of Radisson Vero's little lectures to the staff.

"A great waiter backs up his sommelier," Vero pontificated, "but he doesn't try to replace him or try to know more than he does. So don't show off. Don't put on airs. Offer the wines if necessary, pour as required, then step back into invisibility."

Darrol laughed, guessing that at this moment Vero must be wishing he himself had been invisible in the linen room. *God, the guy wears garters. Shoulda known.*

As the rest of the staff arrived, it was easy for Darrol to stay busy and to stay out of Vero's way. Make the bastard squirm in anticipation of their eventual encounter.

The kitchen released hints of butter and garlic and spices. Darrol salivated. He drank some water and made the round of his assigned tables to look at the initial place settings. Shortly afterwards, Xavier would do the same checking. And then, redundant as ever, Mr. Black Garters would glide among the tables, perfecting.

It was hard for Darrol to keep a straight face thinking about Vero shifting a teaspoon one millimeter to the right, rotating a wine glass a precise five degrees to the left or tweaking the corners of a tablecloth oh so carefully—all sans his pants.

It was equally hard to keep a straight face as Vero, waving a small clipboard, gathered the front staff for his nightly coaching session. Vero held his head held. He avoided looking at Darrol.

Tekla remained at the hostess station. Normally she joined the group and exchanged a little friendly banter. Tonight, head down, she seemed to have found an unusual amount of paperwork with which to occupy herself. Darrol, in a generous mood, didn't really fault her anything. Other than for her lousy taste in men.

"All right, people." Vero trundled out his best managerial voice and a touch of a Slavic accent. His cheekbone scar was glowing. Anger? Embarrassment? Who knew? Darrol guessed Vero was wishing to be anywhere but here right now. Probably wished he were in the 49ers' locker room, issuing a genius game plan to the hungry offense. But here he was, stuck in a dining room repeating himself to a bored wait staff and to at least one guy who knew too much already.

Vero checked his clipboard. "Important guests for tonight. Mr. Lanterman may be dropping in. Keep sharp. Commissioner Dunstin and the Assistant Mayor at seven. Miss Hugo has a reservation at eight. Jon Gulliver will be here at 8:30, party of two. Apparently he's just published another book. Mr. Modoc, I think he's your table."

Carey nodded.

Spike folded his arms. "I wish you'd assign him to me, Mr. Vero. I read all his "Abandonment" novels. Really racy."

"I wouldn't know about 'racy', Mr. Duggan," Vero said. "I only know those books are doing very well. And I don't care what you read. In any case, Gulliver is Modoc's tonight. But Carey, don't swish around him."

"I don't swish," Carey said quietly.

"That's right." Vero adjusted his lapel rose. "We're all genderless professionals."

Darrol stared. *You hypocrite.*

It was easy to tune out as his boss rattled off the usual list of do's and don'ts, the slick black hair catching the light.

Vero often reminded Darrol unpleasantly of Him #4, who slathered himself with brilliantine. One day, the Foster had caught young Darrol investigating a tube of brilliantine borrowed from the medicine cabinet. Even though Darrol protested he was only fascinated by the fun brand name, *Bumble and bumble*, the jerk had whaled the living hairdo out of him. That guy was a bummer all right, may he rot in hell.

As usual Vero wrapped up by saying he wanted the busboys to be 'lightning fast and totally invisible'. He gave Xavier a condescending grin.

"X marks the spot, right?" he announced. No one was ever sure what that was supposed to mean, but the few sycophants in the room always chuckled. Xavier and Tommy Scott, the other busboy on duty, looked at each other and drifted away.

Vero clapped his hands. Coaching session over.

The slight echo of his dismissal had barely ended when one of San Francisco's patented tremors rattled dishes, tumbled glasses, jingled chandeliers and managed to tilt two paintings, including the restaurant's prized Diebenkorn cityscape, purportedly bartered by the artist himself in exchange for meals.

No one was particularly startled. There was the familiar frozen moment, a still frame, as everyone waited for a possible second shock.

None came. Vero clicked his fingers, pointed, and sent Tommy and Xavier to check for displaced table settings. The manager, pulling his cuffs, went over and personally straightened the art.

"Good thing I wasn't serving bouillabaisse," Spike Duggan said. He didn't get any laughs.

Darrol was thinking about licorice whips and hand claps and coincidental earthquakes. How wonderful it would be to be able to summon up a quake whenever you wanted one. He watched Vero fine-tuning the Diebenkorn, and he mentally pointed at the man's back, mentally clicked his fingers.

No dice. One could only dream. But then again, Darrol thought, the things he knew about people could start mighty fine tremors indeed.

A food fight. Another of Darrol's frequent fantasies. More than once he'd envisioned the restaurant breaking out into one marvelous gastronomical battle zone, crepes and pasta and lobster zinging about, the satisfying plop of an slippery oyster or tri-berry panna cotta catching someone—say Radisson Vero—right on the kisser.

But tonight he had little time for such fantasies. Lanterman's was busier than ever.

Darrol worked his tables with exemplary skill, even eliciting praise from the dread Miss Estelle Hugo when—speaking of coincidence, he thought—he happened to be in just the right place to catch her skittering dinner roll before it hit the carpet, swivel, wield his silver tongs and serve Miss Hugo a fresh roll.

"Your instincts, young man, are positively Faustian," the lady said, her evil little diamond earrings bobbing in agreement.

Darrol wasn't quite sure what she meant, unless had something to do with dealing with the devil, but he hope it might translate into a really generous tip.

When Miss Hugo was pleased, she was extremely generous. When the lady was pissed, watch out. Beyond her stiletto tongue lay the power of numbers. Her 90 pounds—part of that full furs and heavy jewelry—was nothing. But her 90 gadzillion dollars packed incredible heft.

On his best evenings, Darrol believed he must be in what he knew jocks called 'the zone'. His focus and poise and speed were incredible. He showed diners complete mastery of the menu. For every dish, even Joe Rosa's complicated one-time specials, he could recite ingredients, spiciness, possible allergens, ease on the palate and suitability with various wines. He served with grace, good humor and a perfect balance of deference and charisma.

As engrossed as he was, Darrol didn't quite eliminate observing the world around him. Tonight his antenna were up over the way Spike Duggan was bouncing about in a flurry of attentiveness and overt attempts at extra flair.

Spike had never been Darrol's favorite. From the beginning, there was something about the guy that Darrol didn't like. What exactly it was, he wasn't sure, but the dislike was palpable.

His antipathy was reciprocated. Spike, a career waiter, was full of thinly-masked disdain for Darrol, easy to think of as an upstart, a mere dabbler, a non-professional who happened to have some skill.

Usually Darrol could ignore Duggan. But tonight it finally hit Darrol what bothered him most about the other man: Spike was really, really good at his job. He was competition.

That hadn't mattered much before, but now it was rumored that doddery old Claude Gallatoire, who'd been working at Lanterman's for half a century, if not forever, was at last thinking of retirement or dropping dead, whichever came first. That meant a senior waiter position would come open. More money. More perks. A gold nametag. The two most-likely leading candidates for Claude's job: Spike Duggan and Darrol Yount.

And over there was ancient Claude himself, breaking every house rule, leaning back momentarily against the wall before tottering between tables six and ten while the hungry young knights craving his crown jousted in the lists. Darrol was amused at Claude and annoyed at Spike.

But he forced himself to rise above those feelings so he could deal with the familiar couple at table thirteen. *God, the Shrinks.* For the second time this month he was stuck with them.

Dr. and Dr. Holmes, Ian and Janis, in their late sixties, semi-retired psychiatrists, dined at Lanterman's with some frequency. Darrol suspected neither of them could cook. He thought of them as Dr. Prim and Dr. Proper or Dr. Grim and Dr. Reaper.

Usually they wore closely-matching sage tweed suits, the guy often with an ecru shirt and dark green bow tie, his wife with a white blouse topped with a burgundy cameo. They had long, thin, newspaper faces imprinted with columns of worldly care, drained of humor. Nasal, monotonous voices, both, check. A way of staring right through you, both, check.

It didn't help that Darrol had a low opinion of the couch profession, as he called it, since his boyhood encounters with psychologists and psychiatrists and other voodoologists had ranged from very uncomfortable to torturous. He didn't like people trying to pry into his mind. Or the invariable stuck-up manner.

When he'd mentioned the Doctors Holmes to Maria, scoffing at their bleak demeanors, she asked if they might have endured tragedy, the loss of a child for instance, or if one of them was perhaps dealing with some dreadful illness. Maybe, she speculated, maybe their entire families disappeared in the Holocaust. Darrol sniffed, said he thought Maria was showing more imagination than she usually did.

"Oh, I'm not artistic like you, Darrol" Maria said, pouring coffee, "but I think a lot about people, about their lives. At work we talk all the time, you know. There isn't a person in the bakery who's not had to deal with real troubles, bad ones."

"You cry into the jelly donuts? Sob over the bombolonas?"

"Don't make fun. And we don't have jelly—"

"—whimper over the whiffleschnaffen?"

Maria stared. She started giggling. "Whiffle...what's that?"

"You got me, but I think I'd like some. Yum."

Darrol stopped smiling. "OK, so Doctor Holmes and Doctor Holmes: here's what I think. They're really a twisted brother and sister masquerading as a married couple, but not quite pulling it off. Incest is best, you know the rest."

Maria put down her coffee. "Darrol! That's not nice."

He pointed his mug at her. "In any case, they rub me the wrong way, those two."

"You say that about everyone you don't understand."

"Do I?" he said, suddenly thoughtful. "Maybe you're right. I thought I understood you, Mimi, right down to your bellybutton. Now I learn you have an imagination. Worse, I find out you're a psychoanalyst."

"Does that mean I rub you the wrong way too?"

"Mm, not usually. Sometimes you surprise me though." He jabbed her in the ribs. "God, more than ever I need some whiffleschnaffen."

Darrol thought about that conversation tonight as he served table thirteen. Rub him the wrong way indeed. Tonight, the Drs. Holmes were downright irritating. They ignored him when he first arrived, made him wait. *OK, I get it, I'm a waiter.* They frowned more than usual. Asked him to clarify multiple dishes. Made him repeat each special. *Aren't you listening?* Listlessly challenged his pronunciation of *orecchiette*. Remained glum-faced when he tried to play with it. Wanted more lemon. Extra butter. Pointed out water spots on a spoon, good God.

He heard Maria's voice: *think tragedy, tragedy.*

In his mind he asked them "Your house burn down? Lose your life savings? Discovered your Viagra's run out?"

Darrol was balancing dealing with three other tables—each of those a triumph, he thought—but every time he returned to table thirteen, his normal perfect rhythms were just slightly off.

And, judging by the way they picked at their food, neither Dr. Holmes seemed to like much of anything. It was hardly Darrol's fault, but he felt responsible.

"Everything all right here?" Radisson Vero had skulked over.

"Fine, just fine." Ian Holmes barely looked up. Janis studied her plate.

Vero paused, waited for more, got nothing, nodded. As he glided away, he managed to give Darrol a stony sideways look without actually making eye contact. Clearly he blamed Darrol for whatever was troubling his customers. In Vero's mind 'fine, just fine' would represent an oblique complaint. Lost points for Darrol.

This required payback for the doctors. Darrol was always on the ready for payback.

He found a moment when his tables were taken care of and no orders were pending. He told Xavier he was taking a quick restroom break. But instead of going to the employee bathroom he went to his locker, found what he needed, returned, and started working at the coffee service area. The evening's brew smelled great.

Doctored, he thought. *Nice word.* Maria's diuretics always came in handy.

"Didn't order coffee," Dr. Janis muttered as Darrol brought them an elegant silver tray laden with a carafe, cups, a cream and sugar salver and a silver dish holding two dark chocolates.

"Compliments of the house," Darrol said, full of charm. "For our special guests."

He poised the carafe over a cup and opened the lid slightly, sending seductive hints of superior French roast curling toward the doctors.

Dr. Ian murmured to Dr. Janis. "Might help us focus." He gave Darrol a half nod. Darrol promptly poured and served. He was rewarded by the other half of the nod, no verbal thank you.

Resuming the rest of his work, Darrol was rejuvenated, back in the zone, again in the groove.

He happily thought of Dr. Holmes and Dr. Holmes up peeing all night, maybe with few other little side effects, a palpitation or two. You could always hope.

It was rarely possible to witness the results of his paybacks, but Darrol loved how his imagination always went to town. He smiled at Spike Duggan across a table. Spike couldn't keep the hint of puzzlement from his face.

When the Holmes left, Darrol checked their credit card slip, expecting a lousy tip. He was surprised. The amount was right at 20%. Maybe they really liked the coffee, enhanced and all.

With considerable commotion, the writer Jon Gulliver had meandered in, arriving at table twelve after much handshaking. His bestselling status apparently allowed him to break Lanterman's unexpressed dress code. Gulliver looked neo-bohemian in his thick blue fisherman's sweater with a vintage paisley scarf fluffing out from the neckline.

His companion, a young, fair-haired woman, at least was wearing a decent-enough dark wool business suit. As Gulliver talked, she scribbled in a small notebook. *Not a date*, Darrol thought. He noticed that Gulliver was covertly eying Carey. *No, not a date.*

There was a bigger commotion, at least among the staff, as Vinnie Lanterman oozed into the room, his corpulence only partly-masked by his custom silk Versace dinner jacket. Vinnie walked chest first, his short legs waddling to catch up. Radisson Vero rushed in to help seat Vinnie at a back corner table which conveniently allowed a view of much of the main dining room.

The Son was on his holy throne.

This was a rare appearance. Vinnie was saggingly old, increasingly grouchy and likely going senile, but he was unwilling to relinquish his majority ownership to Vero and their silent partner.

Tonight, Allan Schultz drew the short straw and was tapped as Vinnie's waiter. Darrol would have liked the assignment for the possible extra kudos, but he knew it was a very dangerous one. He knew that, even with top-notch work, it was far too easy to screw up in Vinnie's eyes. So let Allan rise or sink. Either way, Allan was no threat to Darrol's position.

At closing, Vinnie was still there, drinking his second or third bottle of wine. When he finished guzzling, he surprised everyone—and made many nervous—by wandering about as the staff finished up.

Darrol turned from helping Xavier clear a banquette and found himself face to face with the old guy. More accurately, Vinnie's face came up to Darrol's top stud. Both were shiny.

"So, remind me...Darrol," Vinnie said, reading the name tag. "Remind me of your last name." His low, rough-weave voice was only partially-softened by the wine.

"Yount, sir. Darrol Yount."

"Right. I been watching you. You've got a way about you. Got some pretty smooth moves there."

"Thank you, sir." Darrol hoped that Vero, hovering nearby, was taking notes.

"Yount, was it?" Vinny scratched what was left of his pewter hair. "I'm quite a history buff, you know. Yount. You any relation to that old pioneer up in the wine country?" Vinny hiccupped.

Why not? "Ah, yessir," Darrol smiled, "George C. Yount was my great-great grand uncle. I'm proud to carry on his name."

He hoped Vinnie was in no shape to know what Yount's middle initial really was. Darrol needn't have worried.

"Related, huh?" The hiccup became a little belch as Vinnie laughed in anticipation of his own joke. "Well, then, why ain'tcha rich?" His hot breath carried a respectable local zinfandel towards Darrol. "Just kiddin', fella. Keep up the good work."

He aimed his chest toward the kitchen and trotted after it. "OK, gotta go hug those guys in the stupid hats."

"Hey," Carey said, stepping beside Darrol. "You're batting a thousand tonight, Darrol. That little bigshot loves you, and Jon Gulliver wants you to join him for drinks at Random Schotts."

"Me?"

"Well, you and me, maybe coupla others."

"I'm to be a chaperone?"

"Very funny," Carey said with no rancor. He and Darrol understood each other.

Darrol tossed his serving towel to Xavier. "OK, but why me? I don't read the guy's books. And I'm not gay."

"Pity," Carey said, clearly meaning it. "I think Jon likes to surround himself with good-looking men, whatever their inclinations. He's celebrating the new book and wants you there."

"Why not?" Darrol said. His presumed triumph over the psychiatrists notwithstanding, he needed a drink. "Meetcha over there in a bit."

Carey went to help Tommy gather the table vases. Darrol felt another presence materialize at his elbow. *Here I am, the Emperor himself holding court.*

"Yount," said Vero. He cleared his throat. "About, em, about what you saw earlier..." His scar flared.

"I saw nothing, Mr. Vero." *Like hell I saw nothing.*

Vero blinked sweat from his eyes. His trademark rose had wilted. "Nothing? Nothing at all? The linen..."

"No, sir. Nothing." *Except she has a fantastic ass. Wears black panties. Well, around her ankles.*

Darrol slowly shook his head, avoiding the temptation to wink. "Don't remember seeing anything. Sir." *And you, of course, in those snappy black garters.*

Vero let out a breath. "Ah, well. Good man, Yount. Keep it up!"

"Thank you, sir." *You keep it up, Radish—if you still can.*

Later, as Darrol was buttoning his coat in the locker room, he heard Tekla talking in the back hallway.

"My roommate told me," Tekla said. "I guess her father's an EMT working Pacific Heights."

"*Doppio?* Double suicide?" Emilio Fiore's voice was soft and kind compared with his sustained barking in the kitchen.

"Jeez. Both were their patients?" That was the Radish. No accent.

"At least one was. Her patient, I think," Tekla said. "Isn't that bad enough?"

"No wonder they were so...I guess withdrawn." Even the Radish sounded subdued.

"Why would they even come out dinner?" Fiore asked. "*Buon dio!*"

"What else you are going to do?" Tekla sounded like she was about to cry. "Look, I should go."

"We'll walk you out," said Vero.

Darrol heard the trio moving away. He almost wanted to feel something for the Holmes. Couldn't. But he did feel his calves hurting. He bent, removed his shoe lifts. He tucked them away and finished buttoning his coat.

Moments later, as he walked over to *Random Schotts*, he remembered he was supposed to meet Maria at home for some after-work fun.

He stopped, thought. Resumed walking. Cut across Washington Square Park toward the bar, enjoying the welcome softness underfoot and anticipating a free drink or two.

Contrition was not on his menu tonight.

Chapter 11
Jumping to Conclusions

When Darrol walked into Random Schotts, his ears cringed at the racket. Had they been off-leash, they would have howled and fled.

However, for those who preferred quiet, there was one remarkable plus at this popular bar. The owner, Herbie Schotts, in a moment of brilliance enhanced by his finest brandy, had designed something special.

The Cortex, as Herbie called it, was a separate, soundproofed back room suitable for quiet drinking and serious conversations. Entry for the right patrons and for the unobtrusive servers was through a small hallway functioning as a sound lock. Drunkards, louts and bellowers in general need not apply.

Herbie Schott's roots went back to the days of San Francisco's Barbary Coast, when noise was king, rules were jokes and bribes and graft trumped codes and enforcement. Herbie's ancestors ran brothels, saloons and gambling holes, done in only by the tumultuous 1906 earthquake and fire and the unfortunate shift after those calamities to a semblance of law and order in the city.

The walls of the current bar, built on the site of one of those saloons, held neatly-framed photos from the lawless good old days. Herbie put the images up less to intrigue guests than to remind himself that respectability could be both an atonement and a profit center.

Jon Gulliver, as an emerging star of quick-read titillation, had no difficulty in reserving The Cortex, a fine place for him to hold court.

It was Herbie himself who walked Darrol to the back room to join Gulliver's party. Herbie was a wispy little man of about 70, his surprisingly-big head adorned by a billowing toupee. He also wore too-obvious dentures and large, retro hearing aids.

After he took Darrol into the antechamber, Herbie looked up and grinned. Darrol saw a well-dressed monkey with large, perfect teeth.

"So," Herbie asked, "you a writer also?" He didn't wait for an answer. "Even at my age, Gulliver's books turn me on. That guy knows how to stroke you with just a handful of words. And who'da thought ketchup and lace could be such aphrodisiacs?"

Cackling, he opened the door to the inner sanctum and sent Darrol in alone.

Darrol was enthralled. Deep armchairs, long red velvet drapes, bookshelves crammed with big, leather-bound volumes. Heavy tables of dark wood inset with green marble. A gas fire was murmuring welcome heat across the expensive red wool carpeting.

The room smelled of cognac and luxury. This was the kind of gentleman's club Darrol knew was his due.

"Come in, come in! You're the last to arrive." Jon Gulliver waved. "Darrol, right?"

Gulliver sat next to the fire. His female companion from Lanterman's sat on his right, the notebook still in her hands. Carey Modoc, his face glowing, sat to Gulliver's left. The other two were Allan Schultz and, Darrol was surprised to see, Xavier Shea. X was comfortably sprawled in his chair like he was lord of the manor. Darrol sat beside him.

"Couldn't ask the whole staff," Gulliver said. "Just my favorites." He smiled. "I sure wasn't going to invite that career waiter of yours, the one with the chipped granite face. I don't like him, starting with his name. Spike? You gotta be kidding. So forget him. I mighta asked the other career waiter, the old guy, Claude, but it's 'way past his bedtime. Gonna put Claude in my next book though, the way he holds up the walls. I might make him a geriatric Samson with the fate of the whorehouse literally resting on his shoulders."

He turned to the woman. "Don't write that down, I'm only musing. Besides, someone might steal the idea. Oh, gentlemen, this is Brittny—with no 'a'—intern from *The Chronicle*. Follows me around hoping to get insights. Or to get into my pants. Oh, don't blush, Brittny."

He sipped his wine. "These days everyone wants in my pants." An afterthought. "That one you can write down, kid."

A Houdini waiter appeared. Darrol ordered the most expensive Scotch he could think of. Let Mr. Success pay. Too bad smoking was outlawed or he'd have asked for a fat cigar.

"I'm celebrating," Gulliver said. "And I thought, why celebrate with the same old crowd of sycophants? So you're my groupies for the night." He laughed. "That's just a joke. I really admire all of you, working your asses off, and in style. I figured I'd get you out of the salt mines for once. You don't drink where you work, right? Like being your own lawyer or something. Don't write that down, Brittny. Have another drink and just listen."

"So here's what I've learned so far." Gulliver looked at the group. He raised his glass to Allan.

"Allan there is an actor—every other waiter is an actor, yes?—waiting, no pun intended, for his big stage break. More power to you, Al."

Gulliver patted Carey on the knee. "My boy Carey here doesn't know what he wants—or who he is, really—but he's got pro-clivities for certain ac-tivities dealing with fest-ivities. Sorry. I was gonna be a poet until I discovered it didn't pay. But I'm guessing Carey's thinking hotel management."

He cocked his head toward the reporter. "We learned," he said, "that Brittny—with no 'a'—wants to be the next Lois Lane before newspapers go completely belly up. Better make that fast, Brit."

Gulliver turned the other way. "And as for Xavier, our token...busboy. What do you want?"

Xavier gave a slow, exaggerated shrug. "A new president." They all laughed. "Yeah, besides that, I'm trying to be the first in my family to finish college." He studied his drink. "Then I'll run for president myself." More laughs.

"Which brings us to you." Gulliver peered over his spectacles at Darrol. "I've watched you. You're good at what you do. Damn good. Darrol the Magnificent. But Lanterman's ain't the end of the line, for you, no sir. I can tell. You're not headed in old Claude's direction, a big white napkin on your arm the rest of your life. You got plans, don't you, Darrol? So spill the beans."

Darrol looked past Gulliver towards the fire. The orange flames bowed to him. He tasted the buttery, reassuring scotch. Inhaled the warm leather of the books. Finger-traced the cool, strong, eternal edge of tabletop marble.

The others waited. Darrol was the man of the moment.

"Power," he said. *Christ. How'd that slip out?*

"By that I mean..." He sought inspiration and delay in another sip of his drink. "By that I mean...being in a position where I can do some real good."

"You wanta be president too? President of Twitter?" Gulliver led the laughter at his own wit.

"Sure," Darrol gave a wide-eyed, comic nod, relieved that he was off the hook.

Gulliver gestured to the hovering waiter to refresh the drinks. "And finally as to me, yours truly. My new book's gonna be the biggest hit yet. Readers are like sheep. One idiot critic leads the way, bleating, and now they're all chewing on my novels like the best pasture grass anywhere."

"What I can't figure," said Brittny, "since I don't see how it relates to your books, is why you go to Lanterman's so often." Her voice was startling, low as the Fort Point foghorn. "No offence to the rest of you, but it's not exactly a hotspot."

"Kinda stuffy? Uptight?" Gulliver asked. "Too much money swirling around in the vichyssoise? That what you mean?"

Brittny nodded. Gulliver put a hand on her leg. *Mr. Touchy-Feely.*

"Truth to tell," Gulliver said, "the food's great. Ancient as the joint is, they don't think *nouvelle cuisine* is a dirty word. But here's the main thing: Lanterman's is awash in stories. Granted, it's not for most writers. Ferlinghetti said it was too fucking formal. Rexroth and Brautigan turned up their noses.

"One time Thom Gunn and two of his pals waltzed in wearing motorcycle pants and chaps, and that threw Vinnie Lanterman in a doozy of tizzie, not only about their outfits, but because they were, you know..."

Gulliver smiled at Carey. "That's exactly when Vinnie put in his fussy dress code, though he couldn't do much about the other."

"But," he said. "To the matter of stories. Going to Lanterman's is like being bi—it means the best of both worlds. There are plenty of places in town to find edgy stuff, but Lanterman's, in its own stodgy way, gets my imagination stoked up. It makes me ask: What's under the surface? Who here has secrets? Does Vinnie like little boys? Is he tied into the mob? Is that snooty chef stealing sides of beef? Why do I sense sparks flying between certain waiters?" He winked at Darrol. "Is the manager with the dumb moustache and the fake dueling scar banging the hostess?"

Darrol flinched. This clown with his big ego was treading dangerously close to Darrol's stash of invaluable knowledge.

"But, you know," Gulliver was saying, "one of the things which most intrigues me is the death of your revered founder. Supposedly he fell from the Golden Gate Bridge. An accident. But everyone wonders about suicide. I've been playing with his death in my head. Maybe someday I'll put it into a novel." He flourished his wine glass. "Are you curious how I imagine it? If you let me try to improvise it for you, you won't need to buy the book."

"You want to tell us a story?" Brittny asked. "Now?"

"Yeah, sure." Gulliver grinned. "Why not?" He patted his knees. "Any of you kids care to sit on my lap?"

When no one moved, he pretended to pout.

That's why we're here, Darrol thought. *His captive audience.*

"Well, OK then. I'll tell it anyway." Gulliver gulped more wine, put down the glass. He clasped his hands, folded his arms across his chest, closed his eyes, began to create his tale.

San Francisco, 1957, early on the evening of Saturday, August 31st. Still brightly sunny, but unseasonably cool. You can't help shivering. The masts in the yacht club harbor are rocking and rolling to a music of clinks, clanks and clunks. Along the Marina walk, busy with arm-in-arm couples, the sneaky breeze lifts young ladies' dresses with salacious abandon. Their dates would get hardons except that their cold pricks are like popsicles. But I digress.

August Vincent Lanterman, businessman and restauranteur, who yesterday marked his 55th birthday, drives past the Marina and heads out toward the Golden Gate Bridge. He stops near Vista Point. He parks his big cream Buick on the Presidio side and gets out, shaking his head when the expensive engine pings.

He stands for a moment to follow the sad, fierce notes of a bugle coming from the base. The sound rises majestically like an eagle seeking the clouds. The soldier is only improvising jazz chromatics, but August thinks of Taps. That thought makes him grin in a grim sort of way.

He sniffs the air. The blend of sweet eucalyptus and sap-heavy evergreens reminds him of his pampered boyhood in the sunny Oakland hills. Today, August's mind has been returning a lot to his boyhood.

He crosses over the roadway and ventures out on the eastern promenade leading to the bridge. He watches a few sailboats braving the bay before nightfall arrives to chase them away.

The fidgeting sails remind August of the sheaves and sheaves of business papers he tore apart that afternoon in his office, of their white tatters floating in the dust-mote light.

He walks out above old Fort Point. There's a snarling noise overhead. August stops, looks up and sees a red biplane dragonflying toward Alcatraz Island.

Watching the old aircraft sets him to imagining his father Peter buzzing over World War I France, skilled but scared shitless, and also terrified he might shoot down a Lantermann from the German side of the family. Or be shot down by a Kraut cousin, unfair and ironic.

August nods his head grimly again. As it happened, both sides survived and prospered dramatically until that black October Tuesday when Oberleutnant Hans Lantermann climbed the tallest building on the Kurfürstendamm in Berlin and took his last flight, wingless, strutless, hopeless.

Thinking of that leap, August shivers. Or maybe it's the wind.

On this side of the ocean, August's father, Peter Lanterman, whose luck held, clambered high on the misfortunes of others, not only surviving but prospering even more until his heart attack in 1945 in a classy bordello while he was celebrating V-J day. Even then, Peter probably died happy and on top of things. He set a high bar for his son.

August starts moving again. He is like any other Saturday stroller heading out to walk on the bridge, if wealthier-looking than some. His tassled shoes are a shiny brown full-grain leather. He's dandied by a tawny vicuna topcoat. As a nod to the common people, a blue and gold California Golden Bears scarf sprouts from the neckline, one end tossed jauntily over a shoulder, devil-may-care. August's milk-chocolaty hat is an imported Italian fedora, jammed down a bit on his head so the crosswinds won't peel it away.

He takes a substantial breath, smells ocean tang, oily exhaust, an odd burst of roses and lawn cuttings. He steps onto the bridge itself. Immediately, he thinks he can feel it swaying in counterpoint to his heartbeat.

The flow of cars is uneven. They seem to come past in little convoys, protecting each other in this brave passage over the void. Tires clatter across the expansion joints in a syncopation at times merry, at times reminiscent of short bursts of gunfire.

Dangling from a strap on his left shoulder is one of his birthday presents, a gift from his young son Vincent. It's a new Brownie Hawkeye camera with an attached flash, already armed with a fat bulb, a cyclops eye in the middle of the reflector. Bobbing as August moves, the shiny flash parabola snares the sun and throws tiny shards of light onto the sidewalk.

Why August Lanterman is walking out on the bridge this Saturday evening is not something even August can say. He believes he's going to take pictures of his beloved city, he's going to contemplate his life, he's going to figure out how to start anew, he's going to have a mystical experience, he's going to think about ending it all. He's not really sure.

Murmuring lovers come toward him and pass him, wrapped in each other, wrapped in illusion. He's too preoccupied to be very envious.

Wind-whipped gulls screech overhead, the traffic rumbles its low borborygmus, a tanker horn blares a moody departure, the breezes sing thinly in the soaring cables. August's hard soles rap the pavement, the cadence still steady. Coins jingle in his pockets.

Slowly, the sun is being lured toward Asia, but it's reluctant to leave, and the light glows, gently pouring in soft, gold streams across the radiant orange bridge, spilling slowly into the bay and over the hills, caressing the city with diffused lusciousness.

Seeing this panorama, August begins to weep. Or perhaps a roguish breeze summons his tears. He stops, blinks. He steps near the railing, raises the Brownie and aims it at San Francisco. He presses the shutter.

The flash goes off with a quick puffsnort and silvers a cable. It startles August. He grunts a laugh, removes the dead, charred bulb too soon and singes his fingers. He tosses the hot little globe over the railing. A gust from below holds it, even raises it. It's a plump cherub hovering. August wonders if he too would simply take to the air, float, glide, find a shortcut to heaven. Abruptly the bulb drops from view.

Gloaming approaches, and the city shimmers. Lights firefly here, there, everywhere. The first faint upwash of spotlights climbs Coit Tower. A red cherry watches from the top. Reaching out from Alcatraz, searchlight beams sweep, flare, vanish. Sweep, flare, vanish. Perpetual motion.

All is suddenly alpenglow. August winds the film forward and takes a second photo. There's a muted click, no flash. He winds the film again, inserts another flashbulb, not really sure why.

Sweep, flare, vanish.

August will never know it, but over there in the city, Alfred Hitchcock is lining up his rooftop shots for the movie *Vertigo*. Jimmy Stewart and a cop will chase a bad guy from roof to roof at sunset, one soon to plunge to his death. Acrophobia will play a big part in that movie.

Out here on the Golden Gate Bridge, August, looking down, not acrophobic, still has a lurch in his stomach, bile in his throat, but he keeps peering. The waters of the bay are losing their luminescence. They appear colder and colder. He trembles. He doesn't like cold.

Is that an irony, he half-wonders, beginning to walk further out, the pathway continuing to rise. How high above the bay is he now? A hundred feet, one-fifty, two hundred, more?

Sweep, flare, vanish.

He stops again and defies the breeze by spreading a broad lapel of his topcoat as he lights one of his expensive Cuban cigars. Rich, earthy smoke, momentarily satisfying, coils around him, flings itself away. Cigars mean confidence, surety, a sense of all's right with the world. But August can't help also thinking of the last smoke of the condemned man. Tonight his mind is jumping—and right now what word is more ironic, more appropriate?

He walks and he smokes and he shivers, and the first orange tower looms above him and he thinks of his cheating wife, his in-his-image son, his financial misdeeds, his overextended businesses.

He thinks of his vanity restaurant, huge steaks flown in from Argentina and rare French wines. Not for the customers. For him. Even now he salivates. And he smokes his cigar and he shivers in pride, in doubt, in fear. The desire to live and the craving for peace swirl around each other as the wind blows smoke back into his eyes.

He thinks of the extravagant insurance policy. The incontestability-clause is the silver bullet, or is it the silver lining? No matter, Vinnie's pockets would be lined with silver. If.

The amber roadway lights flicker and turn on. Amber for ambiguity, for half-go, half-stop. Isn't that what most of life is built upon, ambiguity? Everything about death is ambiguous too, August thinks, no matter how mighty the oratory, how assured the faithful. And he has never been faithful—not to a creed, not to his family, not to anything.

Now August is in the middle of the bridge, standing halfway between the counties of San Francisco and Marin. No man's land, he thinks, how appropriate. He looks to the west and sees a greeting card sunset setting fire to the infinite Pacific, but after two long breaths, he turns to face east, where the light is more tranquil, more circumscribed, more fashioned by men such as he could have been.

He walks to the railing and touches the cold upper edge with his free hand. The rail is solid, unyielding, uncaring, but he clasps it more firmly to withstand the malevolent push of the wind from behind. He thinks how, for this moment, the cold, obdurate metal band ties him deep into the earth on both sides of the Golden Gate, the bridge anchored far down in ancient rock. That connectedness strangely pleases him but soon frightens him as he imagines the crushing pressure, the numbing silence, the deadening, unbreathable blackness below.

He recoils from the rail to stand mid-sidewalk, panting, looking unseeingly at the darkening city. Still gripped by one tense hand, the cigar feeds on restless air and glows.

The bridge sways more than ever. August feels his heart trying to steady its own uneven rhythms. A cruel tension strains in his chest. His breathing lumbers. The hairs on his arms rise, spears thrust up in defense against an enemy approaching from the horizon. He struggles to control his bladder. His legs are leaden, reluctant to move.

But move he does. He deadweight-walks to the railing, leans over, looks down. The distance to the gray water seems incredible, each foot a yard, each yard a mile. Sickening. He can barely make out swells, waves, the seductive curl of the tide. Or a trick of the light. Again he shivers.

The crosswinds are, indeed, cross. August's brown fedora is wrenched up and out. It spins away, away, falling, falling, almost carefree, almost flying, until, upside down, it drops into the water, far off, its white lining puffed out like sails. August watches it ride a swift current toward Alcatraz, ready to rescue the prisoners. August no longer wants to be a prisoner of indecision. But he's held by confusion.

Sweep, flare, vanish.

He doesn't know why, but he suddenly wants a dusky image of the city. He looks up, raises his camera. The cigar tumbles from his hand, hits the rail, cartwheels and falls, a leafy meteorite showering tiny orange sparks all the way to the water.

August's mind is sparking also. It's telling him 'now I know, now I know. They won't think ill of me. I won't jump, I won't jump, but if I fall, fall in the name of art, fall with pride, they won't think ill of me. And if I don't fall, it's a sign, a sign.'

He reaches for a cable strut, ignores the sharp, palm-slicing pain its sprouting wires inflict, pulls himself up on the railing. Holding the strut with his right hand and the camera with his left, he leans out and swivels toward the cityscape to take the shot that no one else would dare to try. He is weeping again, crying at the beauty he wants to hold in his mind forever.

Gulls scream, yelling voices rise over the wind, footsteps clatter. August pays no attention. The wind tugs his Cal scarf free and whirls it away, go Bears. He fumbles to slide a frigid finger toward the shutter release without dropping the camera. He winces, tries his thumb. Succeeds. With a snarky *pffft!* the flash goes off.

It illuminates nothing, yet it illuminates everything. Something in August's soul awakens to full, blinding awareness.

Life is all there is.

However, that taut cable strut bears not only his blood but heavy grease. As August tries to lean back, his hand slides, slips free. He falls, flailing out and down.

His coat whips and balloons. It does not provide a parachute. His sudden regrets and hopes don't keep him aloft.

He plummets. Two hundred and thirty-seven feet measure the remainder of his life. Two point nine seconds are his eternity.

The dark, impatient, insatiable waters wait below.

Sweep. Flare. Vanish.

Gulliver opened his eyes. "And that's how I imagine it, the death of August Lanterman."

He leaned back, crossing his arms behind his head, affecting modesty.

The applause was prolonged, but the sound was quickly absorbed by the thick drapes.

"Geez," Allan muttered, "my heart did a few summersaults there."

"Mine too," said Carey, "It makes me shudder."

Gulliver leaned forward again, reached for his glass, drank some wine. "I've a few postscripts," he said.

"Yes," Brittny said, "did they call it suicide or not? There must have been an inquest."

"There was. Accidental death. Gave him the benefit of the doubt. They decided he was trying to be Ansel Adams and slipped. Helped the whopping insurance claim go right through, with our boy Vinnie as the sole beneficiary."

Darrol had been sitting hunched, intent. He had no sympathy for August, but the thought of drowning in freezing hell and darkness made him cringe. "Nobody stopped him, out there on the bridge?" he asked.

"Nope. Those were far different times. Today on the bridge you got cops, Homeland Security, suicide patrols, curfews. Now they're busy installing a suicide barrier net thing down below. They've made it harder."

Gulliver winked at Darrol. "But you wanna do it, you can figure it out."

Darrol's smile was fleeting. He did not wink back. Jon Gulliver was a smug son of a bitch.

"In the meantime," Gulliver was saying, "Young Vinnie was an aggressive little bastard, and he eagerly took over the restaurant. Newspaper headlines blared things like *Noted Restaurant Owner Plunges from Golden Gate Bridge*, and there was a ghoulish increase in business.

"Vinnie got a copy of a big-headlined article, put it in a fancy frame and hung it prominently in the lobby.

"Supposedly it stayed there for ages until a competitor put out fake slogans like *Take the plunge & try Lanterman's*, and *Death is always on our menu* and—my favorite—*At Lanterman's, we dive for our own oysters*. In any case, one of Vinnie's partners—or a rare attack of good taste—eventually made him take it down."

"Sounds like it all means another novel for you, Jon," Carey said, pouring more wine.

"I'd buy it," X said, waving a cheese stick. "Hell, I'd buy two."

"So, then lemme try something out on you," Gulliver said. "That last flash of August's camera interests me, and I've asked myself who might see it go off." He leaned forward.

"What I came up with is a convict in his cell out on Alcatraz. Exactly when August climbs on the rail, the convict is half-straddling the cell wall, the toes of one foot jammed in a crumbling concrete niche, and he's straining to look partway out a small slit to the outer world. All it allows him to see is wedge of the center of the Golden Gate Bridge, but he'll take it.

"At that very moment, August presses the shutter release. The staring convict sees a microscopic blip of white light, a starpoint 'way out there. Whether it's a camera flashing, sunlight ricocheting from a car window or the quick gleam of a turning bird's wings, that minute glint signifies freedom to the con. He's blasted with intense pain and longing, almost literally knocked off his perch.

"Skinning his knee on the cell wall, he tumbles to his cot and huddles there, resenting the world and hating everything about his life. He has no way of knowing the flash he saw was the precursor to someone's death. And thus, you'd say, showing him a very different sort of freedom."

Carey was nodding with enthusiasm.

"Wow," Allan said. "Put that in too."

Brittny was all grins. "I love thinking about synchronicity," she announced.

Gulliver smiled. "Yeah, well, good. And you might be interested to know that from the bridge to Alcatraz is about a 3-mile shot. I measured it on a street map using the most advanced technology that a whiskey glass and a blunt pencil could supply."

He got the laugh he wanted. He looked up. "Hey, gotta go, Darrol, my man?"

Darrol was putting on his coat. "Yeah," he said. "My girlfriend's expecting me at home." *About two hours ago.* "Thanks for inviting me." *Enough of this lovefest.*

He flicked his hand, the best goodbye gesture he could muster and left The Cortex. As he passed through the main area of Random Schotts, a cannonade of noise assaulted him, an ocean of hops welled over him.

Out on the street, it was cooler, quieter, and decidedly less alcohol-infused. The nascent fog bore the smell of bay brine and oranges and damp pavement and the sweetstale exhalations of hundred-year old buildings.

Walking home, Darrol tried to figure out why he was feeling both uneasy and annoyed.

The annoyance was the simpler of those to gnaw on. He quickly sensed he was annoyed that he let himself be envious of Gulliver. Envy? In the long term, there was no reason for envy. Sooner or later things would be reversed.

But it was more. Jon Gulliver, talented or not, was patronizing and condescending. No amount of charm could trump an engorged ego.

And it was worrying the way the writer had pulled stuff from the air, so similar to hidden truths Darrol had labored to find and to hoard. Granted, Gulliver was creating fiction, but his inventions ran too close to the secrets which gave Darrol power.

Darrol's thoughts brought up payback. Could he, dare he initiate something bigger and better than little nasties at the restaurant? Of course he could. That prospect, even if his ideas were unformed, gave him momentary cheer.

But the other: the uneasiness. Darrol thought it had to be that story itself, the rich jerk wandering the bridge, lost in confusion and cigar smoke, thinking about giving it all up instead of twisting the world his way. And then, shit, if you really must do it, Augie, what's this bit about taking a camera along and trying to make people believe it was an accident? *You in control or not, man?*

Up the street a cable car clanged. Sounds of the past.

Darrol thought of Emperor Norton. There was a man who lost it all, even lost his mind, then still came out on top, if in a different way. That's how to do it. And, compared to most of us, Darrol thought, Norton is remembered. A sort of immortality.

Darrol jaywalked across Columbus and drew the wrath of a car horn. But he kept walking, and the humpbacked black Lexus slowed. As he passed in front of it, Darrol gave it a leisurely royal wave. The fog felt damp on his hand.

His shiver dislodged another insight. The suicide story bugged him, he thought, not just about the loss of control but about death itself. Especially that kind of death, the long, breathless fall, the awful, splattering collision, the voracious, swallowing sea. He could almost taste the angry saltwater.

But what he was puzzling over was that a voice deep inside told him that, of all people, he had the right to be in charge of his life. And his death. Suicide was not cowardice. It was another form of power.

He let himself into the dimly-lit Mischief House vestibule. He paused, remembering that he now had the code to the inner door to the 'Norton. It was after midnight, a perfect time to do a little exploring.

As he moved to the door, it swung open. His heart exploded. He staggered back and fought to evince calmness.

Someone came out, his back turned as he closed the door. He sensed Darrol, whirled. It was Magnus Quist.

"*Min Gud, man!*" Quist said, his face whiter than usual. *Vad*...what are you doing here, Mr. Yount?"

"I live here, remember?" Darrol's breathing was returning to normal.

Quist gargled a small laugh. "Ah, *ja!* Forgive me, you startled me. My mind was on...on so many loose endings, ends." He tried to smile. "No rest for the wicked, *ja?*"

"I guess not." Darrol's return smile was a spotlight. "But how would I know?"

Quist tested the door lock. "You young people keep such late hours. Life is a party, yes?" He went toward the stairs.

"Not tonight. Suicide watch." *Ambiguity at its best.*

Quist froze. His forehead furrowed. "I see," he finally managed. "Well, good night then." He started up. He rounded the turn.

Darrol strained but couldn't hear him. Quist was moving amazingly quietly, a phantom ascending. *Does he avoid treads also?*

What had sly old Magnus been up to? Who does the books at midnight? What's in that vault? By the time Darrol had reached the third floor, he'd tucked the incident into one of his favorite files, *gotcha-but-needs-further-study.*

Still smiling, he walked along his hallway.

Maria, her fingernails nicely chewed, would be waiting, a treat ready in the grease-stained bag she undoubtedly was holding.

Suddenly, Darrol was hungry.

Chapter 12
The Happiness of Pursuit

On warm days when she had enough time, Maria carried her sack lunch outdoors and strolled the few blocks over to the rec center park.

She liked to wander about, sandwich in hand, looking at the plants, puzzling over the modern sculptures, watching the kids in the playground and dreaming of life to come. Kids, yes. With Darrol, she hoped. Soon.

Today, she'd settled under a tree, her back supported by a stout sycamore. Or was it a gingko? She was never too sure about her trees. But the firm, rippled trunk held her reassuringly. It seemed to massage her spine. She could chew her mustardy egg salad sandwiches in comfort and with a reasonable measure of crumb control. She protected her bakery whites from grass stains with a small waterproof cloth she always carried in her pack.

Birds sang in what sounded like contentment, a small military band—Maria thought they looked like young Navy guys—played familiar tunes, and the children squealed and jabbered in more languages than Maria could count.

She had turned to watch a skinny little black boy in wild tropical colors do comical handstands when a shadow moved over her. She looked up.

It was Willy Lenz. Coincidence? Or had her boss chased her down?

"Miss Grimaldi. Maria. Mimi." Lenz sang the last name, improvising notes, extending the word for several long measures, unembarrassed to be singing in public. Or to be in competition with a Navy band.

Maria's mouth opened. Bread crumbs escaped and rappelled down her chest. She flicked them away.

"Mr. Lenz," she said.

"It's Willy. Always Willy. Always will be." A tenor's warm laugh. "May I join you?"

He didn't wait for her hesitant yes but turned and plunked onto the grass. Maria worried about his white linen suit. How would he get the stains out?

"So," Lenz said. "I've been wanting to talk to you, Maria."

All she could manage was a lame "Oh?" She was glad he hadn't suddenly burst into her namesake song from *West Side Story.*

"First off," Lenz said, "we wanted to thank you for the vacuum cleaner rolls idea. Tito and Gracie are going to make some next month."

"That's wonderful," Maria said. "But I'm sorry you had to chase me out here just to tell me that."

Lenz turned and watched a thin squirrel run past. "Actually, there's something else..." His voice trailed off.

For the first time since Maria had known him, Lenz looked a little uncomfortable.

"The thing is," he said, "the thing is. Well..." He picked up a small twig and toyed with it.

A piccolo shrilled above the other instruments. Maria, breathing hard, said nothing.

Lenz dropped the twig and turned to her. "Well, I'll come right out with it. I know you've been stealing from us. And likely doing it for a long time." He exhaled noisily. "There, that's said."

Maria's eyes teared. The piccolo trilled, hit a bad note, broke off.

Lenz took Maria's hand. It still held most of a sandwich. Egg salad burped onto the edge of his jacket. Maria stared at the mess, aghast.

Lenz laughed. "Don't worry about it—the stain I mean. I've worked at the bakery a long time. I've learned how to take care of worse."

"Mr. Lenz, Willy, I don't know what to... I can't... I..." She bit her lip.

The band stopped playing.

"I don't mean to upset you," Lenz said, still holding her hand. Pickle fragments dripped through his fingers and fell to the grass. "We can protect your job."

Maria pulled her hand away. The sandwich plopped into her lap. "I only take little stuff, just little treats for Darrol, that's all."

"He's not the issue. And, unfortunately, your 'little stuff' adds up." Lenz pulled out a handkerchief and wiped his hand. "My main concern is what the Merry Widows would say. They're really lovely ladies, generous and fair. But I know they draw the line hard about certain things. Theft is one of them."

"Oh, God. Is it really theft? Did you tell them? Are you going to?"

'No, of course not."

She flipped at the half-eaten sandwich. It slid from her lap onto the grass. "I can pay it back."

Lenz drew a breath. "Probably not. No, I don't think so."

Maria slumped. A scruffy black and white terrier darted from nowhere, looked determinedly up at them. They offered no resistance. The dog grabbed the sandwich and scrambled away.

"But," said Lenz, cautiously brightening, "it doesn't have to end up with the soprano dying in the garret."

"I don't know what you..."

"Like Mimi, I mean." His enthusiasm built. "Or like poor Gilda dying in the bag....or Tosca falling from the battlements."

"Willy, I don't understand. I really don't."

A snare drum rolled and the band attacked *Anchors Aweigh* at a ferocious tempo.

"What I'm saying is..." He let the rest rush out. "We can come to an understanding, you and me—you and I—and really you wouldn't have to stop taking things either."

"Understanding?"

Lenz took her hand again. 'You know I've always liked you, Maria."

He didn't need to say anything else. Everything clicked. Maria paled.

"Oh, God. Are you...? Are you offering me some sort of trade?"

"Well, I wouldn't go so far--"

Maria's voice was strangely calm. "Aren't you married? I know you're married. You said so, the 'yes-but' thing..."

"My marriage was deader than Aida years ago." He grinned. "The icing's long off the cake."

Maria removed his hand and got to her feet. Lenz struggled to join her.

She looked intently at him. "Are you blackmailing me?" There was no anger. It was curiosity. "Or what's that other word? 'Exporting'?"

Lenz laughed. "Maria, how funny you are! I believe you mean 'extorting'. No, I don't think I'm doing that. I just think we can reach an accommodation. It could be very nice for both of us."

Maria bent and picked up her ground cloth and backpack. She sighed. "I don't know if I should kick you in the shins or feel flattered or what."

"'Or what' sounds good to me."

"You do make me laugh, Mr. Lenz, I'll say that."

"Willy."

She surprised herself by what she said next. "Can I think about it, Willy?"

He beamed. "Indeed." He slipped back into operatic mode. "Yes, indeed," he sang. "Take your time." His vocal flourishes drowned out the Navy band.

"Caruso," he told Maria, "a favorite of mine. Did you know he was visiting here in San Francisco during the great earthquake? Scared out of his wits?"

"Like I am," she said quietly. "But I promise to think about it."

They decided they should return to *La Dolce Via* separately. Lenz kissed her hand and moved away. The grass stains on his trousers made Maria smile. The lime color, she thought, nicely complemented the mustard she'd smeared on his jacket.

She left a minute or two later, the band music slowly fading behind her. As she passed the far corner of the park, she saw a slender, silver-haired woman dancing barefoot on the lawn. Wearing a long, brilliantly-white gown and a rippling headdress of white bird feathers, the dancer was arching and gesturing in sinuous slow motion.

Maria peered down at her own industrial-white uniform, sandwich-stained and rumpled. She made a wry face.

She looked again at the dancer, envying the pure, fluid grace. But the longer she marveled, the more she realized she understood the dancer's metaphors.

It was all about transformation. Yearning became determination. Hesitation became action. Life could give you—if you reached for them—promise, possibilities, freedom.

For just a moment, Maria's heart danced.

A red-shouldered hawk chased a sparrow—innate, relentless skill pursuing a rush of avian adrenalin—across the bright panorama of city and bay.

Had the sparrow chosen a straight line, it would have become a quick appetizer. But it dropped, fear-driven maneuvering taking it under telephone wires and sideways between two close-standing cypress trees.

The hawk thought better. Aloof, it rose toward the sun, turned toward Golden Gate Park, where easier meals awaited.

Darrol, watching, was conflicted. He'd like to have seen a strike, the perfect talons plucking that little bird right out of the air, holding it trapped in a bloody cage of bone and sinew, carrying it off to oblivion. The way of the world. But part of him was happy the little guy won out. For once.

He was on the uppermost deck of the Art Institute rooftop terrace, dodging, he admitted, Sheryl Duncan. Did that make her the hawk, him the sparrow? A bit of role reversal, he supposed. It wasn't that long ago he'd hunted Sheryl. But Sheryl was old news. He needed to move her aside to make room for the delicious possibility of Karin Holt. Now he was dodging on account of dumping. That seemed to be what happened in situations like this.

Sometimes he yearned for the days before Maria, the days when he could juggle and finagle and enjoy the excitement of keeping three or four women in the dark about each other. Living with Maria meant severely limiting his intrigues.

But the tradeoff mostly seemed to be worth it. In exchange for reining himself in, he received a measure of steadiness, dependability and predictability. There was also, he had to admit, a measure of sweetness, not only sweetness from all the *La Dolce Via* treats but from Maria herself.

Some people might call that love of a sort.

Darrol drank his coffee, still hot. The terrace café seemed to know what they were doing. Or perhaps the baristas were sadistic, hoping to burn people's tongues. He could understand that urge.

As he sipped, he looked up at the pasty, anemic clouds hovering in indecision high above the city. When he was a kid he liked to watch clouds, especially the bigger, complex ones, and try to imagine floating up there, disappearing into the mysterious tumble, going somewhere, wherever clouds went. Anywhere would do.

Daydreaming was a secret and guilty pleasure. And rare. Few of the Fosters let him simply sit and do nothing. If there was a bit of lawn to lie on, his head back on his folded arms, his face to the clouds, it was lawn which had to be cut and edged—now, not later—grass which had to be plucked of dandelions, one by one. Not just grabbed from up top but from down at the roots. Far down. And right away.

You plucked evil out by the roots, Her #3 liked to say. Were dandelions evil? Darrol once asked and received a thunderstorm in return. In the Foster world such questions were defiance of authority, signs of impudence or that wash-your-mouth-with-soap sin: sarcasm. You might be allowed to speak in tongues, but not in metaphor or symbol. And speculation was a sign of disbelief and disrespect.

The skies of his childhood were often denied him. But today, things were different. He could manipulate clouds, speculate how he wished, dream without rebuke or reprimand.

Those merging clumps up there were Karin's breasts, hidden for now under dingy white cotton, but all the more tantalizing. Below them, that other slowly-undulating shape was the curve of her ass. Darrol's breathing quickened.

But Karin was more than sex. She was classy, really classy. And smart. He was moving up. All he needed now was to run into her again, get that first date. He drained his coffee, crushed the cup.

Yes, moving up. He looked for a trash receptacle. Class acts don't litter.

"Did you really cut off his ear, Mr. Quist?" Little Pug Green was back on a familiar, fascinating subject.

"A deft stroke," Magnus said, putting the sword carefully back on the wall. "Or perhaps just a lucky blow. Do you know the word, 'deft'? In Swedish we would say *skicklig* or *flink*."

Pug giggled. "Weird. I don't know those words." She eyed the gumball machine.

Magnus smiled. "'Deft' means 'handy' or 'skillful', something like that."

"OK. Pig, do we have a quarter?"

Her sister ignored her. "So can we pay for these, please?" Pig waved a twenty dollar bill over her items, a magician about to make things disappear.

"Of course," Magnus rang up her purchases. Two cartons of macaroni and cheese. Two cans of chicken soup. Three oranges. A box of Tampax. He looked at Pig. She stared past him.

"You two seem older every time you come in," he said. "Nine-eighty-six, Miss Green."

Pig handed him the twenty.

"Am I old enough to hold the sword myself next time?" Pug asked.

"Perhaps with a little supervision. You know the word 'supervision', Pug?"

"Yes. I'm almost ten, you know."

"Ah! Practically a lady, but the Emperor's sword still needs supervision." Magnus slowly counted the change into Pig's hand. "With two extra quarters for your little cravings."

"Magnus!" Alma was suddenly behind the counter. "Magnus, why did you order that ginger tofu? Hello, girls."

"Hello, Mrs. Quist." A polite duet.

"Blame Joe the Trader," Magnus said. "They carry such things. We must compete, *ja?"* He watched the girls claim their gumballs. Yellow. Green.

Alma picked up a small nest of plastic shopping baskets. "Compete, maybe. Go overboard, maybe not."

Pig tugged at her sister. The girls turned to leave. Pug gave Magnus a big smile.

"Thank you for showing me that sword!" she said.

Magnus nodded. "Goodbye, *mina kära.* And don't forget what Alice said." He glanced at Alma. "'It would be lovely if something made sense for a change.'"

The overhead bell ushered the girls out. Magnus raised the flyswatter and flicked at a space inches from Alma's unflinching face.

He nodded in satisfaction "Deft, *ja?"*

Alma put down the baskets and glanced at the customers in the nearest aisle. She kept her voice quiet. "Are you trying to provoke me, Mr. Quist?"

"It was only a damned fly. And I got her." He pointed to the floor and started to turn away.

Alma touched his arm. "I don't mean that," she said. "I mean the tofu. Yes, and the Jamaican soda, the rum-pesto crackers. All of it. You know we can't keep going if we're higgledy-piggledy about what we stock."

He put the flyswatter on the counter and wiped his glasses with a corner of his red apron. "Who's Higgledy-piggledy? A fairy tale character, *ja?"*

"Don't be clever. I don't mind our discussions, but I'm not amused when you try to subvert things. When you try to tilt the ledger."

She stepped closer. Her voice softened. "We've kept it going for almost thirty years. Let's keep working together, *gubben."*

He gave her a thin smile. "Alma, you know *min gamla sang.* I'd like to go to places like Jamaica, not just peddle their damned grapefruit juice. And soon."

Alma picked up the flyswatter and regarded it absently. "We have time enough, Magnus. Give us a little time."

"*Knulla allt,* Alma!" "Some days I think you're getting as crazy as him." Magnus aimed his thumb at the Emperor.

The sudden sharp *swoosh* almost took his glasses off.

"Only a fly," Alma said, tapping the swatter in her palm. "Only a fly, *ja?*"

"**Y**ou're lucky to have caught me." Karin's voice was silver, coated with honey. Darrol loved it. "I usually don't take a break, but I needed a piece to cool a bit longer."

They were standing in a wide hallway, students coming and going.

Lucky, maybe, Darrol thought. *But you make your own luck.* Several times this week, he'd stalked the entrance to the 'class members only' ceramics studio. Good thing there was a bench across the way where he could sit, pretending to sketch. Well, not completely pretending. He'd been little surprised at the good things emerging under his pencils.

"Ought to trade phone numbers or something," he said. *Lame.*

Even frowning a little, even dust-streaked, her face was extremely beautiful. "Aren't you jumping the gun a little?"

"I used to do track, you know," he blurted. "One of the few bright spots about high school. I practically never jumped the gun. You develop instincts. Time it perfectly." *God, now I sound like I'm bragging.*

The frown disappeared. The dust remained. "I like offbeat," she said, laughing. "You strike me that way. Well, either offbeat, or small-boy awkward. Are you secretly shy, Darren?"

"Darrol!" It came out as a bark.

Two other students turned. He managed to grin, dropped his voice. "It's Darrol. Darrol Yount."

"I'm sorry, Darrol. Inhaling too much porcelain addles my brain. And I have trouble with names anyway. Away from here, I'm an elementary teacher, and I only keep the kids straight by having them wear nametags for far too many weeks."

"Teacher?"

"Yeah." Karin glanced at her watch. "You know, I can maybe squeeze in enough time for a cup of tea. I was heading up to the quad. Could we go there instead of talking out here?"

"Sure. Great." He kicked himself. Monosyllables seemed to have become his norm. His charm machine had battery failure. As did his sense of time. He realized he had to be at Lanterman's in little more than an hour. *Replace those batteries fast.*

They took the stairs. Darrol let Karin lead so he could enjoy the view of her rear, only partially hidden by her smock. Jeans didn't work for everyone, but they did for her.

At the café they got tea and coffee. Karin was first at the register and paid for both, waving Darrol off.

They sat at an outside table. The late afternoon air was lazily warm. Small birds hopped near, trolling for treats. Smiling, Karin looked at them.

"Earlier," Darrol said, "I saw a hawk chasing a sparrow. I don't know how it did it, but the little thing got away. I was really glad."

Karin tested her tea. "Life's all about pursuit, isn't it?"

Ordinarily Darrol liked the possibilities of that oblique sort of comment. He would have enjoyed responding in kind. But the clock was against him right now. He felt he needed to take charge again quickly. "So, what's the current project? Your ceramics, I mean."

He was rewarded with a gleam in her lilac eyes. "It's my biggie for the term. Going really well. It's an abstract female head, part fantasy, part dreams, part allegory. I'm experimenting with loads of subtle colors and tiny details. If the last firings don't fail me, I might enter it in something. I think I'll call it 'Spring Waiting.'"

"Sounds intriguing. I'd love to see it. Is it an image of you?"

A sparrow of a frown appeared, darted away. "Not really. Just my imagination at work."

She drank some tea. "So, Darrol,"—she enunciated his name carefully—"how's your own art coming? Drawings, was it? Paintings?"

"Bit of both. I think I'm improving, learning. Come quite a ways, actually. Learning to look." He laughed. "I don't think I told you my silly early experience here, did I?"

"I don't think so, no..."

"Well, when it comes to spotting attractive women, I have terrific peripheral vision. But right here at the institute there was one exception."

He enthusiastically told his story about not noticing the nude model in the center of the studio. Karin nodded and even laughed a little, but once or twice his language slipped into coarse.

He missed her first flinch. At last he braked, but not until he'd said, grinning full bore, "Can you imagine, somehow I didn't see that beaver right there in front of me?"

"No, I can't imagine," Karin said, standing. "I'm glad you're alert now. When I don't see things clearly, it's...it's a problem. Well, look, I really have to go." She moved so quickly, he could only half-rise.

"Could we get togeth--" His question-fragment earned only the back of a short, vague wave, and Karin was gone.

He sat down again and stared blankly at where she'd been sitting. He realized he still didn't have a way to contact her.

Darrol picked up his cup. The remaining coffee was lukewarm.

He rushed home, changed, went to work and took out his annoyance, secretly, on the first diner who irritated him. This happened to be the unfortunate Oscar Labellarte, as usual having too many Rob Roys and indulging in more butter-slathered rolls than were good for his desiccating arteries.

It was easy to send the old guy home with lovely butter stains on his pants, a simple trick most waiters learned in Retribution 101. On tottering back from the restroom, Oscar never noticed the pat of butter on the chair slyly awaiting his descending derriere.

As soon as Oscar had paid and left, Darrol called Xavier over, and they inspected the chair. The padded seat bore a really nice greasy insignia. Almost regal. Xavier quickly pulled the chair out of service.

Oscar Labellarte never tipped over the minimum, so Darrol could both tamp his annoyance at Karin and pay back the chronically-stingy diner with a simple pat of fresh MarinGlow Organic.

Most likely Oscar would blame himself for the stain, but if he complained to the restaurant, Xavier or Tommy could take the fall. Isn't that what busboys were for?

Then there was Karin... Darrol, back in the groove, reminded himself he liked a challenge.

Chapter 13
Rising to Occasions

The man had a knife.

Duff Lee and Arty Krebs were rotating good old car Number Ten on the Aquatic Park turntable. The watching throngs were doing the usual oohing and aahing, taking photos and making smartass comments. Duff had heard nothing new since his first day as gripman, but sometimes he awarded the jokesters a dutiful grin. He probably wouldn't have the job without the tourists. Essentially the cable cars ran for them.

The park vibrated. Its trademark contingent of Frisbee-tossers, drifters, lovers, jugglers, tin-cup musicians and Irish coffee addicts fresh from the Buena Vista performed their rituals under perfect pre-twilight skies. A huge slash of solar red lingered high beyond the bay.

All nice and normal, but now at the edge of the turnaround there were noises and movements which seemed out of place. Duff, his arm on a pushbar, glanced up.

A leering guy in grubby jeans and a filthy gray T-shirt was swinging a big knife side to side, the ugly blade parting the sea of tourists, some peeling away, gasping, tripping, others immobilized by that disbelief which locks suddenly-jolted minds.

People later asked: where were the cops? Apparently watching two chicks strip-dancing in the far corner of the park. SFPD disgraced again.

Which left it to the cavalry: one Duff Lee, cable car gripman, and one Arty Krebs, conductor.

Arty didn't realize he should be a hero. He was just as petrified as the skinny kid in the Raiders cap and the woman in the neon jumpsuit. They'd all become solid pieces of public art, neo-realism with running sweat.

Duff tugged at his bulky Muni-brown jacket and stepped away from the cable car.

"Put it down, please. Sir, put down the knife and walk away." Not exactly John Wayne. Duff was five-six and his voice was thin.

The man's face creased with savage delight. "A Chink? Hey, slanteyes! Whadya gonna do? Hit me with them fat ole gloves, fag boy?"

Duff stepped closer. "Sir, please...I don't want to hurt you."

"Shit, bring it on, Eggroll. I need a massage." The man slowly flipped the knife back and forth between hands, not inexpertly. He hadn't simply watched this stuff in the movies.

Duff kept his gaze loose. He took another half-step forward. "I have to tell you I train in martial arts."

This got a snort and a spit. "Who d'ya think you are? Fuckin' Bruce Lee?"

"He was my grandfather, sir."

That comment might have given pause to some, but it aroused this guy.

He charged.

Duff moved, incredibly fluid, eyeblinkingly fast. He coiled slightly. His right leg shot out, hit the guy in the crotch. Stepping forward, Duff linked his arms behind the man's neck, pulled the head down. Duff's upcoming knee exploded into the shocked face. There was an unpleasant crunch. The knife fell. Its owner dropped, blood geysering from his nose, the onlookers learning the meaning of deadweight.

End of episode, except for the two cops, belatedly running over, ready to make the collar.

The applause sent Duff back up into the car. They were off-schedule. He'd have some explaining to do at the car barn. He'd much prefer to fight at the gym, get his whole body glowing.

C*hrist! Is that Duff?* As Darrol walked up Chestnut toward Mischief House, he saw the familiar figure coming the other way. It looked like they would meet exactly at the door. Darrol enjoyed occasional coincidence or maybe *congruency*, a word he'd learned and liked tossing about, but his roommate-of-necessity wasn't supposed to be part of that. Another bummer on a difficult day.

As they neared each other, Darrol first smelled, then visually confirmed that the fucker was smoking a stinkeroo cigar. Duff had his work jacket slung over his shoulder. Not at all typical.

"What gives?" Darrol asked, fanning the smoke aside and pointedly faking a cough.

"Long story." Duff seemed uncharacteristically cheerful. "Maybe you will read about it in the paper?"

He went up the stoop, keyed in the code and opened the door. He strode in, leaving Darrol to catch the door and follow.

Without speaking, they crossed the vestibule and went upstairs, Duff in the lead. Darrol, remembering walking behind Karin, watched his roommate's hips. He'd never before noticed a certain swing, a sway, even a hint of a—*nah, swish? Really?*

He flashed back to the porn mags he'd flipped through in Duff's closet. They weren't all hetero. Down at the bottom were at least a couple that weren't straight at all. Unless you considered a cock with a standup boner to be a straight line, as in the shortest distance between two points. *Hah and hah.* Darrol stifled a guffaw. Is that why the guy went to the gym? *Buff, tough and rough.*

"So you really won't tell me about it?" he said to Duff's back as he reached the upper landing.

Duff paused. "I disarmed a man with a knife, that's all."

"You the big hero, Duff? Mr. Bruce Lee himself?"

Duff looked at him oddly. "Funny you should say that." He seemed about to laugh.

Darrol moved in for the kill. "Or is it Mr. Golden Dragon Lee?"

Duff's usually-impenetrable expression vanished. Wariness and anger fought each other. "I don't know what you think you know. But please..."

His jacket swung forward. He caught it, stood there, expecting more taunts.

"Hey," Darrol said. "I know all about saving face, Duff. Don't worry about it." *Keep the guy off-balance.*

Darrol looked down at the carpet and scowled at the minute trail of kitty litter and sawdust. "God, look. We got more important things. The fucking cat's been up here again."

"Sorry. My turn to vacuum." Duff's humbleness was nauseating. "I will do it now."

"Forget it. I'll make the little hairball lick it up. Let's get inside."

They entered their apartment. Duff walked quickly to his room as Maria came out of the kitchen. Darrol accepted her hug. She seemed extra-clingy and a little shaky, but he jumped to the important question.

"Is that damn cat in here again?"

"Who, Lyckatill?"

"Who else? We got an army of cats here?"

"She's not here, Darrol. I didn't let her in."

He thought a moment, switched gears. "So what's my treat?" He pretended to search her pockets. "I've had a rough day, Mimi. I really need something sweet."

Maria started crying.

Darrol stepped back. "Hey, what is it?"

She shook her head and continued sobbing.

He stared at her. His face darkened. "You're not pregnant are you?"

"No. No, Darrol, I swear." She wiped her nose with the back of her hand. "Not that."

"So what gives?"

"Mr. Lenz talked to me today."

"So...?"

Maria attempted to smile. "They like the vacuum cleaner rolls. Gracie's gonna make some soon."

Darrol took her by her upper arms. "That's really great, Maria. Really super great." The sarcasm flooded in. "They giving you a million bucks? A party at the Hyatt? Must be a fucking big reward for you to be crying so much."

She tried to laugh. "It's not that, Silly..." The tears rushed back. "He's found out."

"Who's found out? Found out what?"

"Willy Lenz knows I've been stealing stuff." She leaned forward for consolation.

Darrol held her off. "What? Are you talking about my treats?"

She nodded slowly.

"That's not stealing," Darrol said, suddenly genial. "Hell, they just throw the stuff away anyway."

"No, they can still sell it." She looked at him entreatingly. "Can we sit down? Please."

"Stealing? Huh! Amazing."

He released her arms and they went into the living room. They sat on the sofa. The smell of fresh coffee drifted up from the 'Norton.

"Lemme get this straight," Darrol said, the geniality gone. "Your pansy singing boss caught you with your hand in the cookie jar?"

"He said he knows I've been stealing things."

"You weren't clever enough or careful enough, huh?"

She muttered into her lap. "And that's not all of it."

"It's not what...?"

"That's not the worst of it."

He glared at her. "What, you're fired? You're going to jail? Christ!"

She spoke quietly. "I think he's offering to forget it if I'll... If I'll...you know."

Darrol sat back. Amazement fought with admiration. "That clever bastard," he finally said. "That's what I'd fucking do. He holds it over you and gets in your pants."

Maria blushed. "He didn't exactly say he wanted me to...sleep with him."

"He didn't?"

"He just sort of hinted. He might mean something else."

Darrol brayed. "What else do you think he means? He wants you to say ten Hail Marys? Shine his shoes? No sir. He wants you to shine something else, like polish his knob."

"You don't need to be crude, Darrol..." Maria sat up straighter. "Mr. Lenz is a gentleman."

"A gentleman?" Another bray. "Gentlemen have knobs like the rest of us, I assure you. They got secrets and lusts and horny dreams. Some of them just hide it better. And that makes them hypocrites, too. Gentlemen, hah!"

For a moment, neither said anything. A dog barked. A cable car clanged.

Maria wiped her eyes. "Maybe he'll forget it," she said.

"Don't count on that. Give a guy an inch he'll take a mile. So what's the deal? One quick roll in the bakery hay and he forgets about the petty pilfers? The petite fours?" He snickered at his pun.

"I don't know, I really don't."

"Unless he's a queen, all that opera stuff you tell me about..."

"He's not gay, Darrol. I really don't think so." She flushed.

"Maybe he wants to watch us going at it, you and me." Darrol put his hand on Maria's knee. "Might be kinda fun. For all of us?"

"Darrol..."

"Or I could get to watch? Or at least get the details." He squeezed her knee. His voice was velvety. "What do you think?"

She bit her nails. "I think it's all pretty awful. I shouldn't have taken anything. I know you like treats, Darrol, but I wish I'd just bought them for you."

"Where's the fun in that?" He suddenly recognized her confusion. "You know, Mimi, maybe you should negotiate with the guy. Offer some small favors if he'll look the other way."

"Look the other way? You want me to keep stealing?"

"Why not? He's trying to blackmail you, right? He ain't perfect either. So you can negotiate. Make it a trade. But keep him hungry."

"Hungry?"

"Allow him a kiss, a touch, a squeeze, the tiniest little something now and then—and you'll have him on a string. And keep taking the pastries. He won't talk. He'll think he's punishing you. He gets his little treats, you get yours. I get mine, sort of. In the meantime, we'll figure out what to do. I'll figure it out."

"I don't know, Darrol." Maria put her hand on his. "I'm your girl. Letting him—well, it doesn't seem right."

Darrol faced her outwards, pulled her close so that her back was against his chest. "I'm your guy too, Mimi. You know it. And we can make this a win-win deal."

He kissed her neck drew back. "You know you can't do any better than me, Mimi." He bent again, lifted her hair and began nuzzling. Gently. Expertly.

"Oh, that feels good."

Darrol breathing was becoming irregular. "You'll tell me about the things you do? With him, I mean."

Maria had closed her eyes. "Would you like that?"

"Win-win," he mumbled, still nuzzling softly.

Chapter 14
Shades of Meaning

The cool morning light, gloriously soft, tiptoed into Darrol's apartment. White gold drifted across the floor. Darrol, yawning, stood near the kitchen counter. He clicked through his high-quality colored pencils. He tried to focus on his drawing assignment.

All he needed, he thought, was a big skylight, a north-facing window, an oil-stained easel and perhaps a beret like the one he'd seen in a photo of Picasso. Then he'd be all set to be an artist with a capital A.

But he still needed one other essential. *A fucking idea.* He scratched his stomach. Sour sleepsweat made his nose wrinkle.

He drank some of the orange juice he'd sneaked out of the 'Norton. He had to admit they had good stuff down there. It might even have been worth paying for if he hadn't had a roomy back pocket and a drowsy Georgia Vining at the register. Easy pickings. These days he rarely stole anything. But he liked to keep up his skills.

The orange juice was pulpy and flavorful. It beat the hell out of the dreck they used to serve in The Place, where he stayed between various Fosters. The older boys contorted their faces, said it came from concentrate thinned with castor oil and urinal scrapings. They made snickery jokes about saltpeter. Back then, Darrol didn't get those jokes. Why would you put salt on your peter? Nowadays he could laugh. So did all the women he told that story to.

He held his juice glass to the light. Could he find that exquisite orange color in a pencil? Create it with his novice blending techniques? The orange juice at The Place had been a coppery pumpkin color. It was urp-provoking then, but today it might make a very effective shade.

But at the moment colors were a secondary issue. What was the subject?

Miguel Cortez had told them this would be both their easiest assignment and their hardest assignment.

"Draw anything," he'd said. "Show me what you got. Some of you will suffer from blank-paper-itis. You'll puke on the paper at the horror of it all. The horror of actually needing an original idea.

"But puke is a start. Blood is a start. Bleed on the paper. Piss on it. I don't care. Call it mixed media. Just dig deep, draw like Michelangelo and show me what you got. Then bring me your masterpiece next week."

In class, Darrol had scoffed, ground his heel on the gauntlet. Who was this sarcastic bastard anyway? But the assignment was due soon, and now Darrol fumed and fretted. He'd been dreaming and thinking too much about other things.

He'd been thinking about Vero and Tekla grappling in the lusty linen room, Karin Holt wiggling her ass but turning up her nose, Maria and Lenz doing the dirty, sugar and flour flying about them like snow, Jon Gulliver throwing August from the bridge, bland-faced Duff performing Jackie Chan heroics, knives flashing, Magnus Quist and his patronizing air, lord of the flyswatter. Darrol had even thought about Emperor Norton, standing to the side in his big plumed cap, above it all, beyond it all.

Darrol tossed a brown pencil, caught it, tossed it again, missed, had to pick it up from the floor.

The Emperor! Could he be the subject of the drawing? The idea faded quickly, like fast-moving clouds pushing the morning sunlight away from the kitchen.

But something else jumped to the fore. A tumult of images assaulted him. Sirens sang from the rocks of his subconscious.

He leaned over the counter, finished taping down the rectangle of illustration board, spread out the cedar pencils, selected a lavender gray and began sketching.

Slowly, faster, faster. Faster.

Patience, lightness of touch and other rules vanished. He raced through his wildly-rough sketch and plunged into drawing. What he wanted was crazily complex, but his mind and his hands seemed willing to cooperate.

Scratching, rubbing, grazing. The steady whispers of pigment conferring with the surface. Tiny papery teeth greedily nibbling morsels of color.

Crimson. Orange. Violet. Tangerine. Prune. Seal brown. Rifle green. Sandstorm.

The hexagonal grips wearied his fingers. He vaulted into his mind. Overdrive met autopilot.

Self-mesmerized, he muttered, hummed, sang, roared. He rattled on to the unseen Emperor about bridges and clouds and swords.

Pencils raced, snapped, broke, collapsed. He sharpened and resharpened impatiently. He threw stubs over his shoulder, dropped them on the linoleum.

He squeezed waxy pigments from the core of the wood. Took no prisoners.

Applying, layering, mixing, blending, blurring. Subtlety shoved aside by rapaciousness. At times it was near frenzy.

He gave up his shower, his licorice, his coffee, his walks, his lunch, his mulling over grievances, his daily planning. He gulped water, rubbed his cheese-grater beard, looked at the work, plunged back in.

His pencils hovered like hummingbirds, darting, darting, darting.

He dove through the textured surface, swam in color, fought to come up for air.

The kitchen smelled of sweat and wax and pencil shavings.

He began toning down the brilliance. Oxford, midnight blue, raw umber, sepia. Dark sienna. Ash gray. Battleship gray. Finally, brooding charcoals and blacks.

And then he burnished, eagerly, with eggplant and white smoke.

He pushed it all the way into the late afternoon, finishing less than an hour before needing to shower, change and rush to work.

He put his initials in white in the lower right corner. Subtle, but there, ready to accept full credit.

And at last he lifted the pencil high in triumph. He was on his way.

"**M**aria, can I see you before you go home?" Willy Lenz sang the words, as usual in fine mezzo-tenor voice. This afternoon he had a sizeable audience, as *La Dolce Via* was crowded with people seeking treats before the bakery closed. The shop smelled of sugary spices, creams, lemons, almonds, warm pastry. It was a smell of contentment and anticipation.

Some of the bakers had been conscripted to help the counter staff deal with the rush. At Lenz' little aria, Joyce Bacigalupi grinned but wisely refrained from her usual profanity. Maureen McIlhenny winked knowingly at Maria and twitched her head slightly at Lenz, who stood behind the workers, awaiting Maria's answer.

"Sure, Mr. Lenz," Maria said over her shoulder. She leaned into the center case, hiding her blushes among the profiteroles and *albicocche*.

She came back up in time to hear Cookie Kronos, boxing generous slices of *salame del re*, refer to the jelly roll as 'deli salami". Cookie's customers, two regulars, chortled in fond delight.

Maria smiled, again thinking what a happy place this was to work. But now, as she served with friendly energy and enthusiasm—she liked pronouncing the Italian, German and Spanish words and talking knowledgeably about the ingredients—her mind kept nibbling on one big slice of worry over what Lenz might want to say. Or what she might say. Or agree to.

After the shop closed and she returned to the back rooms to finish cleaning up, she thought more about the men in her life, past and present. She'd barely known her birth father, Christoph. When Maria was four or five, he'd fallen in love with a ballerina and danced away to New York, not to be heard from again. Christoph's smile, wide as the Golden Gate, was almost all Maria could remember of the man.

After he left, much of her life, she realized, had involved trying to pick her way carefully through minefields laced with prickly male egos and male violence.

She loved Darrol, of that she was pretty sure. He had his faults, probably more than she ever allowed herself to really

156

recognize. But he was a vast improvement on her two previous boyfriends, one of whom who'd been more besotted with marijuana than he was with Maria, and the other of whom seemed to think Maria was his punching bag and his sex toy.

And Darrol, for all his authoritarian ways, was so much better than her stepfather Rico, who, though only a shoe salesman, acted like a Mafia don crossed with Mussolini. Even today, she flinched whenever she remembered Rico's wicked backhand.

So here was Darrol, who'd more or less rescued her after her trouble at the Culinary Academy. He was very handsome. He was a good lover, if not, she sometimes thought, overly imaginative. He was never drunk or stoned and he always came home at night. Sooner or later. He sometimes made her feel really special, never raised a hand to her—although his words could jab and sting—and he seemed constant and committed enough, even if he was a bit evasive about babies, settling down, and the future in general. That Darrol had her stealing for him—no, surely stealing was too strong a word— was only a minor thing. Unless, of course, it cost her this job that she liked so much.

As she rinsed off the last mixing bowl, she thought about Willy Lenz. He'd always been charming, a really good boss, always nice to her. He'd always been the kind of man she'd have liked to have as an uncle or even as a stepfather. But now that she focused more intently, she realized that Willy was not that much older than she was, and, especially after the other day's conversation in the park, he no longer appeared the least bit like an uncle or a parent. It was not illogical that Willy might decide to serenade under her balcony.

Maria sighed. Serenades were for romance, for courting. But Willy wasn't courting. Willy, it seemed likely, was just another lech. And besides, he was a married man. For that matter, she was not available either. Or was she? Darrol hadn't defended her honor as she'd expected. He seemed willing for her to negotiate, to lead Lenz on. All that for pastry, for sugar, for marzipan!

Maria laughed aloud. Gracie Ocean, who was collecting aprons for the laundry, smiled pleasantly at Maria's minor eccentricity. Everyone at *La Dolce Via* knew everyone else was slightly nuts, but in a nice way. Inhaling all those spices did that.

Maria took off her apron, handed it to Gracie and thanked her, went down the hall to Willy Lenz' office. She removed her cap, fluffed her hair, and knocked.

That was Willy's cue for another operatic line, sung at full volume.

"*Fragrant as flowers, she entered and fell into my arms.* Willy's voice was always enchanting, no matter his emergent lechery. "Come in, come in," he called.

Maria opened the door. Lenz was moving two chairs together in front of his desk.

"A little bit from *Tosca*, that," he told her. "Do you know *Tosca*? Unhappy story but great, great music. Here, please sit."

She chose one of the chairs. He closed the door and stood facing her. "Men are such cads, aren't they? In opera anyway."

"In real life too." Maria said, blushing.

"Indeed." Lenz adjusted the other chair and sat beside her. "Well, Tosca took a dagger to one of them. I hope you're not so inclined, Maria. A dagger, I mean."

She'd used her only bit of repartee. "Look, Mr. Lenz, em, Willy. In the park the other day..."

"Ah, the park, yes. I'm sure I confused you. That's what I want to explain. I realized how what I said must have sounded to you."

Maria nodded. She met his eyes. They were a fascinating greenish-brown. She'd not noticed that before. Was that what people called hazel? She exhaled. "I think I know what you were suggesting."

"No offense, but you probably don't. I bet you thought I was Baron Scarpia offering you a very dishonorable trade." He saw her puzzled look. "The Baron tried to extort sex from Tosca."

Another blush.

Lenz reached over and touched her shoulder. Maria stiffened. He quickly removed his hand. "Sorry. But that's not what I meant, bumbler that I am."

She stared at him. A thin strip of early evening sunlight lay across his chest, putting a faint yellow sash on his white jacket. He had dark stubble on his face. There were hints of graying at his temples. Or was that flour? His intriguing eyes seemed to hold less certainty than usual.

He blinked, and his words poured out. "I'm lonely, Maria. My marriage is a mess. I'm pretty sure Jessica has someone else. I need a friend to talk to, intimate conversations, a bit of affection. Oh, I don't mean sex. That's not what I mean. I just mean closeness. A hug. Holding a hand. Quiet talking. You're the gentlest, sweetest person I know, and I'm turning to you. I shouldn't have mixed it up with the, the other question—with the things you take—I should have just asked you." He snorted. "But even us operatic heroes have our failures. We have feet of clay."

"Feet of clay?"

He chuckled. "Meringue then, if you prefer. I'm so stupid at times, I wallow in the stuff. But what I'm trying to ask is if you might be willing to let me talk with you once in a while..."

"Just talk?"

"That's it. Maybe after work now and then. A few moments of...kindness. Could you do that?"

Maria surged into laughter and couldn't control it. He slumped.

Still laughing, she leaned over and grabbed his hands with a ferocity which startled them both.

"I'm sorry, Willy, I'm sorry! It's not what you said. I suddenly couldn't help thinking about you wading about in a tub of meringue."

He sat up and chuckled.

Maria kept going. "And singing at the top of your lungs."

"Perfect!" Willy said. "The clown in *Pagliacci*! All in white! Spraying vanilla and almond with every high note. *Vesti la giubba!* Put on your costume!"

They giggled together for a moment. Maria was the first to calm down.

"Of course I'll be your friend," she said softly.

"What?"

"I said yes." She squeezed his hands, released them and sat back.

Willy gave a great sigh and studied the floor. When he looked up, his eyes were wet.

"Thank you," he said. "Thank you. And please forget about the other. Take what you want, Maria. Just don't let the Merry Widows catch you."

"It's not for me, you know," Maria said. "Taking things. It's for Darrol. He expects me to bring him treats."

"Your boyfriend?"

Maria nodded. "Darrol can be very persuasive."

Willy started to say something, but stopped. He sat back.

"It's funny," Maria said. "I don't have many secrets from him. Not any, really. I told him you'd found out and that it seemed you wanted—well, you know."

"Lord! What did he say? Do I need to hire a bodyguard?"

"It was odd, but I think it turned him on in a way."

Willy laughed. "Well, this will be a big disappointment to him."

Maria thought about that. Her growing smile became mischievous. "Only if I tell him the truth."

The old Volvo was talking quietly in Swedish. Magnus was sure of it. "Hear all the true inflections and cadences?" he said to Alma as they drove east on the Bay Bridge.

"My father used to that call 'misfiring,'" Alma replied, taking a chance on irritating her husband. His Volvo was very dear to him.

But Magnus merely grunted, which some days for him was akin to a sound of pleasure. Tonight he was in a good mood. They were headed to Berkeley and a Swedish Society dinner at Spenger's Fish Grotto, a place which Magnus liked. He said it had to do with a lingering seafood smell which took him back to the docks of Stockholm.

"I thought you didn't like your boyhood," Alma said. "Or Stockholm, for that matter."

"I didn't, mostly. But there are exceptions to everything, *ja?* Always allow for exceptions, Alma. In the summer, Stockholm's waterways had their moments, their attractions for a boy. My great Aunt Greta, who looked a little like her infamous namesake, that Garbo actress, would take me to tea at the Grand Hotel. Then, when she was upstairs tupping some rich industrialist or other, I got to roam the harbor for a few hours."

"A few hours? Her lovers must have been very good."

"Surely it's about quality, not quantity? And I believe there may have been a leisurely bit of drinking time too. But what would a boy know? *Arsel!*"

Magnus honked the horn at a driver cutting in too closely.

They were in the left lane of the old lower deck. The supports and columns flashed by in a hypnotic rhythm, accented by mesmeric bursts of dusty evening sunlight. Alma had to struggle to avoid dozing.

"When I'm on this bridge I often think of the '89 earthquake," she said. "Those poor people trapped in their dangling car. How frightening."

"What frightened me most about that quake," Magnus said, "was how it happened on the very day we closed the deal on the store. Remember? Had we not just signed within the hour? *Ja?* A bad portent, that."

"I hardly think so, Magnus. Pure coincidence." She pulled at her seatbelt and shifted to look at him more directly. The fine old seat leather sighed contentedly. "Besides, we've had a fine run. I'm looking forward to celebrating thirty years of good business, of—"

"—of making ends meet," he said, braking for another pushy driver. *Förbannat!*"

"I was going to say 'of serving our neighborhood.'"

"What does the neighborhood care? All those little lives, day in day out, meat, potatoes, cheap wine, toilet paper, tampons, a slab of bitter chocolate now and then. A procession of births, deaths, garbage trucks and moving vans. The neighborhood is a mindless organism. Seething but mindless. Doesn't think or care one bit."

"My, but 'bitter' is the word tonight. You need your dinner, *gubben.* Maybe plenty of the best aquavit."

"They don't have aquavit at Spenger's." He said that very gently. He'd recognized he was pushing it and was backing off.

Alma accepted that. To a point. "You know," she said, "there's an institution—Spenger's—which has been running a long time. More than eighty years, I think. Isn't that something?"

"It's a lot of oyster shells, I can say that, a lot of fish tails."

Magnus hunched over the wheel, frowning at the glaring eyes of brake lights ahead. "I'm always glad to get onto the open deck."

They came out of the tunnels. Both squinted as they rose into the bright airiness of the newer span. Ahead of them, the East Bay glowed, awash in soft orange.

"Do you think Thea's still over there?" Alma asked. She never knew what reaction she'd get from mentioning their daughter, but tonight the skies seemed filled with longing.

Magnus allowed himself a glance at the distant shoreline. In middle of the pointillist puzzle, he easily found the tall, white university campanile gleaming in the light from the west. "She might be attending, even teaching there now, you think? Graduate assistant or perhaps assistant professor."

"What, at Cal?"

"She has the brains, *ja?* And maybe, with time passed, now the temperament."

Alma smiled. "Professor Quist. I like that. What field would you suppose?"

"Architecture," Magnus' response was quick.

"Why do think that?"

"A guess. I remember when I took her on outings how much the buildings interested her. She had curiosity. She loved going to see those Victorian houses by Alamo Square. She had done serious reading. She knew the styles. She dazzled me with terms like, oh, finial and blind arch and mullion, and she could point those things out. It was almost a passion."

"I wouldn't know a finial from a funnel," Alma said. "Maybe that's because when she and I did things—before boys and such got in the way—Thea always seemed interested in people and what made them tick. I thought that was her passion. We'd walk past some elderly man, for example, and Thea would immediately speculate at length on his life. So: sociology, psychology maybe."

Magnus grunted. "Three degrees then we give her. Professor Quist indeed."

Alma laughed. She stared at the lines of traffic. The bridge slowly slid everyone down toward the darkening shore. "As long as she's happy."

Dinner was convivial. Spenger's private dining rooms were filled with fragments of Swedish, some phrases quite mangled. Laughter rattled about the shiny telescopes and compasses, echoed from the brass ships' clocks. Magnus was gratified to discover the bartender could, indeed, provide some aquavit.

"This is almost like high school prom night," Alma said as they drove the short distance from the restaurant to the Berkeley Marina, where the group had reserved a hotel ballroom for dancing. "Dress up, eat, drink, drive, dance, party the night away."

Magnus tapped his fingers on the wheel as he waited for a red light to change. "After which try to get laid, as I think they called it."

"My, my, Mr. Quist! Such language! Was that your experience? Sex on prom night?"

"Only in my mind, alas. I confess to thinking about it. But what *övererotisk* girl would want a tall, skinny boy with bad eyes and a heavy *Svensk* accent?" He put the car in gear and they moved through the intersection.

"Your traits all appealed to me," Alma said.

"But years later, *ja?* By then I had very nice glasses and cleaned up the accent some."

He glanced sideways. "And you, Alma, on your prom night, did you get laid like a chicken?"

"Odd that you've never asked that before."

"Is it not good to still have things not explored even after our century of marriage?"

"I'll assume you're being affectionately flip. But yes, it's probably good to have things still unsaid, some mysteries, even a few secrets. Probably very good."

"You have secrets from me, Alma?" He turned the Volvo into the hotel parking lot.

"Tit for tat, Magnus."

"I am as open as a book."

It took only a few moments to park, stroll through the lobby, check their coats, stake out a table and move onto the dance floor.

A five-piece combo, Ole and the Oleanders, was thumping out a good beat, and Magnus led Alma in a medium foxtrot.

"Alex Plink," Alma said into Magnus' shoulder.

"What?" Magnus guided them toward the picture windows. Across the dark bay, the lights of San Francisco were dancing to their own rhythms.

"Alex took me to the prom. It was great fun. Afterwards, as I recall, we had a bit of a tussle in the front seat of his car. Remember bench seats? So easy for fumbling about."

"A tussle?"

"Alex's hands wanted to wander. My prim little self was probably very conflicted—I don't remember now—but I fended him off. End of story."

"It makes me a little jealous." He turned her out in a short twirl and pulled her back.

"Magnus, don't be silly. Nothing happened, and anyway it was long before you."

"Still, I might have retrospective jealousy."

"You mean retroactive?"

"Retroactive, radioactive, whatever. Jealousy is very powerful stuff, you know." He led her into a conversation step. But there was no more conversation through the rest of the number.

"So, *sötnos,*" Alma said, as they commenced a very slow waltz. "I can also admit to a little jealousy."

"Can you?"

"Remember that young blonde girl we hired as cashier our first years at the 'Norton? The very young one?"

Magnus guided them around a stalled couple. "Mm, braids, pigtails sometimes? A sturdy bust and a smile to dazzle?"

"That's the one. Anna or Annalise or something."

"And dangerously short skirts? *Nej,* I don't remember her at all." He took Alma into a stately turn.

Alma exaggerated a knee bend. "Very funny, Mr. Quist. Anyway, at times I felt strong pangs of jealously. The way you looked at her. How your hand brushed hers when you were showing her inventories."

He initiated a hesitation step. "Oh, that Annila. I was old enough to be her father, maybe her grandfather."

She glanced up at him. "Some like them young, I think?"

"You were jealous, Alma? Aha! Another tat for tit."

"Yes, I suppose you're right." Alma looked up at him. "And there was Thea."

"Thea?" He lost the beat.

"At times I was jealous of your relationship with her. I felt left out."

Magnus resumed the full waltz step. "There is no equal to father and daughter. There is nothing quite like that, *ja?*"

"No, I suppose not," Alma said. "But I was jealous. The way you sometimes hoarded her."

Magnus frowned. "I wasn't aware I hoarded."

"I'm guessing parents don't always realize these things. Not till years later maybe."

Another series of hesitation steps. "Did we ever fight in front of her?" Magnus asked.

"Not so she'd notice, I don't think."

"I wouldn't like to think we drove her away." He cleared his throat.

"We didn't, Magnus, I'm sure we didn't."

The waltz ended. The Quists wandered to the windows and looked at the mix of ballroom reflections and distant city twinkles. A red beacon blinked from Alcatraz.

"You adopt a child," Alma said, "you try to give her love, you try to give her everything, you expect her to stay. But she changes, she leaves you. And what remains? A vacuum, a black hole."

He looked at their faint reflections in the dark window. "I miss her."

"Me too."

The evening passed quickly. The band played a few traditional pieces, the *hambos*, *buggs* and *snoas*, even one out-of-breath *fjäskern*, which produced two near-collisions and much laughter. Magnus and Alma sat some of those out.

But they danced most of the slower numbers, Alma with her eyes closed and Magnus often focused on somewhere far outside the room. They would have said they danced as always: for memory, for their youth, for nostalgia. They held on to each other, tenderness and tension competing in every push of his hand against her back.

After the hugs, the goodbyes, the promises for the winter event, Alma stood in the hall, waiting for Magnus to return from the restroom. There was an outflow of noise down the hallway. A large, energetic group emerged from another ballroom a few dozen yards away. Alma glanced up with only minor curiosity.

It seemed to be mostly younger people. Some dragged easels and others wrestled with large charts. Many were busy with their phones. There was affection, geniality, laughter.

Alma, with her timeless silk dance dress, lace shawl and pearl-trimmed clutch purse, awash in 1990's perfume, suddenly felt like a little old lady, eons out of touch with the present generation. She smiled, a little ruefully.

My God. Thea.

Wasn't that Thea, tall, frizzy-haired, standing there talking to the young black man in a yellow African robe? At least it appeared to be Thea. Alma's breath caught. She felt her pulse jump.

The man moved off toward the lobby, his robe fluttering, but the Thea person paused, turned and seemed to look right toward Alma. The young woman hesitated, appeared to half-raise her arm, lowered it, hesitated again, took a step in Alma's direction.

At that moment Magnus walked from the restrooms and came over to Alma. She stood motionless, mouth agape. He followed her stare and looked down the hall.

A tall young woman was turning away, striding toward the exit.

"Alma, was that...?" His thick lenses caught the hallway lights.

"Maybe. I think. I'm not sure." Alma's voice was hoarse.

Magnus ran his hand through his hair. He muttered something, moved quickly down the hall. Alma watched him push his way through more groups flowing from the far ballroom. She lost sight of him as he turned toward the lobby.

"Are you all right, Alma?" Adele Ericksson, the Society's president, was by her side. Despite the warm evening—and despite the animal rights activism in Sweden—the woman was in a mink coat.

"Yes, yes. Thank you, Adele. Just waiting for my husband, who's, eh...gone to get something from the car."

"You look at little—"

"—I'm just fine, thanks." Alma dredged up a smile.

Adele touched Alma's arm. "Tired from all that dancing, aren't we? *Kul, ja?* You and Mr. Quist were wonderful. The belles of the ball." She laughed. "Well, you're the belle. I'm not sure what we call a man. Maybe belle ringer?"

Chuckling at her joke, she moved away, giving Magnus a little wave as he passed her. Flushed, breathing heavily, he came up to Alma.

"Disappeared," he said. "I lost her. For a moment, she looked like... I don't know if it was..."

"I'm not sure either. Maybe we've just been talking about her too much?"

He dabbed at his forehead. "But if it was Thea, and she saw us, why wouldn't she...? *Et pussel.*"

As they drove homeward, they were silent for a long time. After they'd passed the toll plaza, and were rising on the bridge, Alma finally spoke.

"Well, I had a good time. Despite. We still dance well together, always have. We blend."

"Blend?" Magnus checked his mirror and changed lanes. "I wish we could blend our ideas more."

"What do you mean?"

"I mean our goals. Where we're going, the future, that sort of thing."

"Oh, Magnus, not tonight."

"Do you have a headache?" He flashed a smile at her, but she was staring straight ahead, emotionless. "Hm. Not ready for my little jokes, I see."

"Jokes, maybe. The old familiar theme, not at the moment. It's been a strange evening. Lovely, but also very disconcerting. I can deal with such emotional extremes, but why throw anything else in right now?"

"Why indeed?" The words came out like a snarl. Magnus clutched the wheel and took a deep breath. "Well then," he said, almost sounding conciliatory, "what to talk about?"

"Mm. How about Lyckatill?"

"Lyck-a-till?" In three fast syllables, conciliatory moved to derisive.

Alma pressed on. "I often wonder if she goes out dancing when we're gone. Or dances around the apartment."

"I hadn't given that that *förbannade katt* the smallest thought."

"She adds joy to my life, Magnus. It's amusing to think of her dancing."

He snorted. "Take your pleasures where you can, yes?"

Alma gazed at the lights of the city. "It's not such a bad philosophy."

Magnus stroked the wheel. ""Then my little joy for this very moment could be that traffic is for once almost reasonable." A sideways glance. "And that we can enjoy it in relative quiet."

He pressed the accelerator. The Volvo, humming louder, eased forward.

Chapter 15
Taking Stock

Inventory days at the 'Norton were always a scramble. Magnus insisted that inventorying usually be integrated with regular shopping hours. Alma, knowing when to pick her battles, didn't choose to argue. Instead, like an inspired field general, she worked out clever ways of deploying their small forces.

This morning had an unexpected interruption. Duff Lee had come in for some minor purchases, and his presence was causing a bit of excitement. This was Duff's first time in the 'Norton since news of his heroism had appeared in the papers—an online front page story in *The Examiner*, a feature piece with a flattering photo in *The Chronicle*—and everyone stopped to talk to him, which made him seem extremely flustered.

Georgia Vining called Duff over to her register. "Golly, Duff," she said. "That was something. Kung Fu, huh? You related to Bruce Lee?"

"Looks a lot like him, doncha think?" This was Georgia's customer, a tall, middle-aged woman with a strongly-bronzed face. A narrow line of auburn moustache accented her huge smile. "Maybe even handsomer."

Georgia nodded in agreement. Duff drew back as if he feared being fondled by these two.

"Ha-ha!" he said, the laugh forced. "You joke. There are many Lees in the Chinese world. The great Bruce Lee was not a relative. However, as it happens, I'm studying martial arts."

"There you go then," said the moustache. She signed for her purchases, grabbed her shopping bags and moved off proudly, her point made to her own satisfaction.

"Duff, would you mind a photo?" Alma waved a small camera. "I could take it by the Emperor."

"All right," Duff said. "Only for you, Mrs. Quist." He walked over and stood awkwardly by the cardboard Emperor.

"We could use these for promotion or something," Alma said. She took several shots of Norton staring distractedly over Duff's shoulder.

Magnus, handing cash to a customer at the second register, shook his head but said nothing.

As she was trying to convince Duff to put a careful arm around the Emperor, Alma was summoned to deal with an inventory scanner issue. She dashed off. Duff looked relieved.

But he had no respite. The Grekhovs immediately cornered him and wanted all the details.

"I've never known a real hero," Ilia said.

Olga poked him. "Yes, but we almost met Vladimir Putin when his KGB unit was raiding the apartment next door. Later we found out who he was."

"Wisely, I think," said Ilia, "we kept our heads in."

"And our heads on," snickered Olga. "Very close to a dangerous sort of hero, that was us."

Darrol came in behind two other shoppers. He headed for the licorice.

"What's the fuss?" he asked.

"Heroism," Magnus said. "Mr. Lee's big moment in the sun." He began restacking the weights for his scale.

"Oh, right. So, come and get me, Duff." Darrol juggled a licorice whip between his hands as though it were a knife. He fumbled it, and he had to lunge to stop it from falling on the floor.

The Grekhovs, laughing, steered Duff toward the Nook.

"You must choose your weapons better, Mr. Yount," Magnus said.

Darrol came to the counter, cutting off a young Korean woman. "All right then. Fly swatters at midnight? Suit you, Magnus?" He put down two quarters.

Magnus gave him a cold smile, scooped up the coins and turned to take the basket from the woman.

Darrol went into the Nook. It smelled of raspberry jam and fresh coffee. He stuck the licorice in a pocket, found the carafe and filled a mug with Colombian.

He leaned against the wall and sipped.

The Nook was crowded. At one table, the Grekhovs and Mrs. Durr were trying to ply an embarrassed Duff with cake and donuts. Jump Jesperson, who had one foot on a chair, was standing close beside them. Any moment his coffee would drip onto Duff.

Darrol smiled. *Waterboarding.*

At the other table, Lukas Knudsen and a pleasant-faced woman were conversing with two elderly men who Darrol didn't recognize.

Two more unfamiliar female customers sat on stools at the small bar nibbling on this morning's freebies, small pieces of raspberry strudel.

Darrol often thought the Quists were giving away the farm. But their foolish generosity seemed to generate business, and he had to assume the 'Norton was running in the black, free coffee and occasional free treats notwithstanding.

He tried to equate this to his giving stuff to his street people, but all they gave him back was occasional amusement, and that was unintentional and entirely dependent on his moods.

"I know what it's like to face down a knife, Duff." Jesperson's annoying voice was raspy. He leaned into the group. "I crawled out of one of those cu chi tunnels near Saigon and there was a little pajama bastard, 'scuse my language, Jo, coming right at me with a big mother of a blade. I got my nickname from jumping outa planes, but I swear I earned that moniker again right there, I jumped so quickly. He hadn't guessed I could move that fast, 'specially after I'd been creeping along on all fours."

"Adrenalin is a wonderful thing," said Olga Grekhov.

"So's a 45!" Jump whooped, firing an imaginary gun. Grinning, he began clipping his fingernails.

Darrol winced. His coffee soured. Two boyhood images rushed up in reflux.

Her #4 was all over little Darrol about cutting his nails in public.

"You don't do that, ever, you got it? It's the devil's bad manners, the devil's horns. I catch you again, I'll cut off your pinkie."

And before that there had been Him #2, clicking and snipping and showering his evil little nail slivers everywhere, one of them hitting young Darrol in the face. Dirt and scum and Darrol's skin were under those fingernails. Darrol had rarely agreed with Her #4, but that time she was right.

"Not in public," Darrol said aloud. No one seemed to hear him. Jesperson clipped away, punctuating one of Mrs. Durr's comments with a sharp little *click*. Duff's rise to hero was irritating enough, but this blowhard with bad manners was just too much.

Darrol put down his coffee. It was time for his walk and big gulps of fresh air. But as he turned to leave, things got more interesting at Jesperson's table.

"Excuse me." One of the older guys from the Knudsen table had stood up and was facing Jesperson. "Ain't you Bobby Jesperson?

Jesperson gave him an icy frown.

The man didn't let up. "Hey, Sarge, dontcha recognize me? Spec 5 Cully Simms, Fort Ord, good old Delta-5-1."

"I'm sorry," Jesperson said stiffly. "I'm afraid..."

"God, I'd know that voice anywhere. Put chills in all of us, not just the trainees, Sarge."

Jesperson shook his head. "Sorry, buddy, but you're completely mistaken." He turned around, sat, said something to Mrs. Durr, laughed.

Simms stood a moment. "Well, I guess you're a fuckin' big dopplewhanger or whatever it's called. My mistake. Let's go, Jerry. I'm losin' my mind."

His companion rose. The two men nodded to Lukas and his lady friend and pushed out of the Nook. Jesperson went back to cutting his nails.

Moments later, when Darrol came outside, the men were still standing on the sidewalk. Simms was staring at the store, muttering. The other guy was trying to fumble a cigarette from a crumpled pack.

"Excuse me," Darrol said. "I couldn't help overhearing. Who did you think that was back there?"

Simms was eager to talk. "I coulda sworn he was my old sarge from Fort Ord. Same platoon and all." He coughed. "'Way before your time, kid, no offense."

"Oh, yeah? Vietnam era?"

"Fuckin' A. We was stuck in that sandblasted post trainin' snotty little California draftees while the real action was over in Nam. Turns out we was lucky, though, wouldn't you say, Jerry?"

His companion blew smoke and nodded. "Jeez yeah, Cully's right, you know. Lucky on account of not getting kilt. Lucky on account of how this damn country turned on us."

Darrol stood with the sun behind his back.

Simms squinted up at him. "What's your angle, chief?"

"I'm just curious. That's Colonel Robert Jesperson in there. At least he says he is. Vietnam hero. Paratroop jumper, tough ground fighter and so on."

"Him? Nah, no way! Bobby Jesperson were no colonel. Non-com, through and through. E-7, busted back to E-6. Served stateside the whole time. Benning, Polk and Ord, if I recall. He saw plenty of Nam all right." A short laugh. "But only in trainin' films and on the news. He was good at scaring the kids, though. That voice and them hard, hard eyes did the trick. Nights he went off-post and drank his way through Monterey. If he jumped anywhere it was off a bar."

"Or onto a whore," Jerry hooted. His hand shook as he drew on his cigarette.

"Yeah, that too. Bobby liked his women. I lost track of him when he went up on a Article 86 or a 112 or something, you know, for being a bad boy. I heard he got off, but then they shipped him to Ft. Lewis or someplace."

"So that's not our man in there?" Darrol said, moving so the sun hit Simms full in the face.

Simms shaded his eyes. "Naw, couldn't be, could it? Not if that old guy was really a colonel. But sure looks and sounds like our Bobby."

"**O**K, I'll be brutal. Brutal appeals to you—right, Mr. Yount?" Miguel Cortez had a very slight Hispanic accent and the off-cadences of someone who'd learned English as a second language.

Cortez had warned them he would do the critiques in front of the entire class. So far, one woman—probably his latest conquest, Darrol thought—was still smirking and doubtless dreaming of gallery showings, but two students had failed to stifle tears and three others were slumping in their seats, licking their psyches.

Now Darrol's work was on the easel. On the spot.

"Here we go," Cortez said. "Let's assess the good points of Mr. Yount's drawing, so provocatively titled, *Untitled.* We're seeing what could be the Golden Gate Bridge, viewed from the middle of the bay. The level of abstraction is pretty high, but he's dropped in some clues—this could be a tower, for instance, and over here a hint of Fort Point. The little, eh, *insinuación* of reality appeals to me."

Cortez moved to the other side of the easel, stepped back, wiggling his laser pointer. "He exploits the space pretty well. There's an air of mystery. Is it day or night? Dunno. That's OK. Is that someone falling from the bridge? Could be. Is that real or metaphor? Again, OK.

"It's interesting that these foreground mists or clouds or squiggles just maybe suggest an anguished face. Intriguingly vague, but it's in danger of falling, pun *todo mío*, into cliché or melodrama. It's all more bleak than redemptive, but I can't begin to guess the dramatic intent.

"The possible suggestion of a sunset makes me literally see 'red', as in Commie, and so I wonder if this is all about Vladimir Putin taking a bath. Ay-ay-ay! There's your title, Mr. Yount. 'Putin Taking a Bath.'"

The class laughed. Darrol grimaced. He smelled turpentine. The odor was aggravatingly strong.

Cortez swigged water from his canteen. He swung the laser back to the drawing. A sniper's dot identifying targets. Darrol braced for more 'but's.

"But lemme talk about technique. Like several of you here, alas, Mr. Yount is another who has far too little patience. You can see countless places he pushes the boundary between drawing and scribbling. The medium requires lots of patience—and sometimes caution—but his work exhibits very little of either. Colored pencils take time, time, time.

"What else? Heavy-handed? Yes, as here and here. Too many haphazard marks? Take your choice. Overdone in place? Yes, as in parts of this alleged sunset. And an unfortunate tendency not to use skillful mixing to create unique colors but to go right to the commercial shortcut, as down here, where the color listed on the pencil probably said 'San Francisco Bay Blue'. Scribble it on and you're done, *si?*"

More laughter. Despite his resolve not to react, Darrol had already joined the ranks of the slumpers. *Bastard.*

"What does he know? Arrogant S.O.B." he said to Maria later that night.

"I had a teacher like that at the Academy," she said, handing Darrol a glass of wine. "Silvie LeBlanc, pastries. Not in your department, so you wouldn't have met her."

Oh, but he had. Darrol remembered the small, firm breasts, the long tassels of incredibly-black pubic hair, the way Silvie screamed in French when he did all the right things. Which was often. Too bad she'd thrown him over for that hairy Greek cutlery salesman. Too bad he'd not been able to properly pay her back. The three revealing photos he'd anonymously mailed to the Greek had probably only excited the guy.

Maria was staring at him.

"Sorry," Darrol said. "I was remembering one of my own asshole instructors at the Academy. You were saying about, em, whatshername."

"Silvie LeBlanc. She never seemed to like anything I did. Oh, maybe some of it was deserved. I guess at first I was a klutz, real clueless, even about the basics. But Silvie could be vicious. Especially in front of the class."

"She probably thought you were too cute, Mimi, too smart. It was jealousy, pure and simple."

"Darrol, you're sweet, but you know that's not true."

He twirled his wine glass and looked at her through it. "Maybe she wasn't getting enough. So she took it out on her students."

Maria laughed. "Why does it always come back to sex? But I saw her once with some dark, muscle-y guy. They looked pretty happy."

"They did, huh?" Darrol gulped some wine. "But you know, I think some teachers and students just don't click. I didn't like Cortez from the beginning, and for some reason he's always looked down his nose at me."

Maria touched his wrist. "So what're you going to do?"

Darrol shrugged. "Maybe sell my drawing to the DeYoung for one hundred K and prove him wrong."

"That's pretty funny, Darrol."

"Or I could get him fired."

"You could do that?"

"I bet I could find a way." Darrol studied his wine. "Or then again I could just do a better drawing, right?"

"That's a nicer idea." She smiled. "You know what I did about Silvie?"

"What?"

"I cried a lot. But then I started paying more attention to what I was doing in class. I even discovered I had a little talent for it after all. Silvie found someone else to pick on."

"OK, I'll learn to cry. Maybe that'll do it."

Maria slid off her stool, went to the refrigerator, returned with a *La Dolce Via* bakery box. "I almost forgot. These should cheer you up."

She opened the lid. Darrol looked down at two fat, sugared creamhorns. He carefully lifted one out.

"See if you like the filling," Maria said. "It's my own experiment. I tried cutting the raspberry with a little orange zest."

"So you're back to taking things?" He regarded the pastry with an almost lascivious eye. "Have you already given Lenz what he wants?"

"No, not at all. We're negotiating. I'm kinda stalling him, and this week he's been busy with the equipment inventory.

We might talk again Friday, but he said to help myself for now."

"Awfully generous of him. Are you telling me he's not been sampling your goodies?" Darrol squeezed her thigh.

"Of course not." Maria put her hand on Darrol's. "And maybe he just wants to talk."

"Talk? Fat chance. Talk dirty, maybe, take it from there."

Darrol's sweet tooth trumped his suspicion. He took a bite.

"Wow!" It came out more like 'Woof!' "Would you lie to me, Mimi?"

"Of course not. I think Mr. Lenz thinks I'll be worth it. If and when." Maria reached over and wiped sugar from Darrol's chin. "Darrol, are you sure about this? I'm your girl, you know."

"I know, I know. But let's see what the deal is. It could be fun for all of us." He attacked the rest of the creamhorn.

Ninety minutes later, with Maria asleep, Darrol slid out of bed. His mind was still far too busy for rest. Too much sugar, he thought. Too many plans pinging around in his head. Like dealing with Cortez: how to make him pay? Like giving Karin Holt another shot. Too many bits of information to process. Like the truth about that lying braggart Jesperson. Someone needed to out the jerk. And what was the deal with Quist? Darrol didn't like the way Magnus seemed to look down on him. That might need attention.

And for the moment, maybe that was how to spend this sleepless time, try to get some goods on the man.

The key code. The way into the 'Norton. This seemed a perfect night to sneak in for a look-see. If he explored now he was unlikely to meet Magnus Quist. The Quists had been at it all day with their inventory nonsense.

Earlier, when Darrol was returning from Lanterman's, he bumped into the Quists in the vestibule of Mischief House. Magnus regarded him blearily and Alma told him they were exhausted and dragging off to bed.

Darrol slowly made his way down the stairs, tread-reading for complete silence. His energy was high, his senses on extra alert.

On the ground floor, he stood for a few moments by the keypad, his heart rate up, almost pleasurably. He tried to slow his breathing. Blood drummed around his ears. There was that nice old tingle of anticipation.

He'd not done much breaking and entering—or as Darrol termed it 'sneaking and entering'—since he was a teen; even then it was not with criminal intent but with the idea of arming himself with knowledge.

You looked through someone else's unguarded private spaces, and you never knew what you'd find. Drugs, sexual sidelines, hints of financial hokey-pokey, intimate diaries, steamy love letters, clues to habits both good and bad. *Hell, you could find a whole massacre at the Golden Dragon.*

He wasn't sure what he could come up with tonight, but he thought at the very least he'd sneak through the store and check out that sword. See if it had the cheap heft of tin, the 'made in China' label.

And maybe, just maybe, he'd learn what Magnus hid in that vault.

His breath caught again. What if they switched the code every week? *God, dead in the water.* But he calmed himself. Why would the Quists bother? There was only one way to find out. He carefully punched in the code. *9-1-7-4-6.*

The lock clicked. He exhaled, opened the door and crept in.

The inner hall was dimly lit, surprisingly cool, silent except for the hum of freezers out in the store. He let his eyes adjust, thinking he could almost hear the old building breathing.

He took in that intriguing smell he liked, the sum of the past, yesteryear's joists, studs and flooring, old wallpaper layers, worn linoleum, overlain with the smells of groceries, fruits and vegetables, cleaning products, sweat and the ghosts of decades.

He turned first to the steel door to the vault. The big lock with its concentric steel circles was impossibly daunting, but when he moved his small flashlight beam about, he saw that there was another keypad on the wall. The original locking system must have been disabled, left there just for show, the door retrofitted for modern convenience.

Would Magnus use the same code on this door? Darrol, hopeful, put in the numbers. *9-1-7-4-6.* Nothing. Seemed likely Quist didn't trust his wife. *Interesting.*

Della Rossiter's office was next. The glass-paneled door was closed, but Darrol tried the handle and the door opened. Letting his flashlight lead him, he went in.

There was a faint odor of stale cigarette smoke imprisoned by sweet air freshener. The store had a no smoking policy, but it was easy to imagine Della sneaking one now and then.

He looked quickly through the desk drawers. Della was compulsively neat. Everything had its place. She liked granola bars—he found a big stash—she was fond of Wrigley's Spearmint—another substantial stash—and she had more antacids piled up than a drugstore. No sex toys. Della gave off such need, he'd expected to find at least a discrete little vibrator.

The personnel files were more interesting and unusually thorough. He held the flashlight between his teeth and rummaged.

He learned that Georgia Vining was only 22. He thought she was black, but she'd checked 'other' for race. Ramu Grendhal was still on a green card. Hilda Brown's real first name was Adelheid. *Adelheid?* And, *looky here!* Jamie Turner had some sort of minor arrest record; it even mentioned 'shoplifting'. Apparently the Quists believed in second chances. Or at least Alma did.

Many of the files had photos attached, as though the 'Norton was so big Della couldn't keep track. Oddly, she kept her own file there. He was startled by her image: the picture must have been taken over fifteen years ago. Once upon a time she'd been gorgeous. *Who'da thought?*

Della liked to keep old files, even for part-time employees. He found one for Thea Quist, middle name Kachina, who'd apparently worked here a few summers ago. A hand-scribbled note said she preferred to be called T.K.

He studied her picture. She was blond, extremely pretty, exuding innocence, looking much younger than her age on the form. *Fucking Lolita.* She looked quite a bit like the strange girl in Magnus' big painting upstairs. *Huh.* She favored neither of the Quists, but then he remembered she was adopted. *Lucky her.*

His mind once more started to dredge up his retinue of foster parents. Not what he wanted. He slammed the file drawer shut.

He cringed. He'd forgotten the need for quiet. He turned off the flashlight and stood in the dark, alert for anyone coming.

After a tense moment, he grinned. There was no one to hear him except for old Emperor Norton out front.

He closed Della's door and moved down the hall and into the store. There was minimal lighting out here too, just a few subdued little safety lights. Ether the Quists were stingy about electricity or they depended on some low-tech alarm system or they thought the people of Russian Hill were trustworthy. *That's a laugh.*

The product aisles were of no interest, and Darrol walked quietly toward the front of the store. Here he had to be slightly-careful in case some late-night passerby happened to look through a window at just the wrong moment. But only slightly careful. Darrol felt lucky, empowered.

For just a moment he stood by Emperor Norton, sorely tempted to do something to the image. Enlarge the already-fat and scruffy moustache and make it really crazy. Draw big glasses round those wild eyes. Add some wiggling snakes to the epaulettes. The prankster from Darrol's childhood had never really gone away. But why reveal his presence in the store for such a cheap reward?

He gave the Emperor a jaunty two-finger salute and moved behind the main checkout counter to the framed Norton currency. It was simply sitting on a small nail. He took it from the wall.

He sank behind the counter and carefully turned on his flashlight.

The yellowed bill under the glass said it had a value of $10. It was 'Issued by the Imperial Government of Norton I' in

March of 1879, and 'Given under the royal hand and seal' with a promise to repay the amount and with interest. On the left was an image of Emperor Norton and on the right what appeared to be the California state seal. No clue as to what, if anything was on the back. The frame was sealed so he couldn't look.

Something nagged at Darrol. He gazed at the bill, puzzling, until that something clicked. This piece of currency wasn't hand-drawn by a lunatic. It was professionally-printed. The nutty old con-man of the streets must have finagled some free printing on top of his free lodging, free meals and his free whatever else. Enviable. The Emperor really must have had the city eating out of his hand. *King of the hill.*

Darrol turned off the flashlight and put the frame back on the wall. Neat.

He moved to the replica of the Emperor's sabre and touched it for the first time, almost delicately, running his fingers from the hand guard down the curving sheath to the gold-tipped end. It all hung by a gold-tasseled braid. Darrol suspected that part was Alma's addition.

Cautiously, he removed the thing from its wall hangers.

He was surprised at the substantial weight, the generous heft. Not what you'd expect from tin or aluminum. The padded sheath seemed to be made of a dusty leather-like material, convincingly old and faded. Not quite soft to the touch, yet still oddly supple. He fondled it again.

It felt like the goatskin canteen he'd pilfered as a kid. It felt like the inner thigh of Mrs. Napier—god, he hadn't thought of her in years—one of his early teachers in the art of lusty sex. Ultimately, a mutual taking-advantage-of.

Slowly, he unsheathed the sabre. It moved out smoothly, a ready cock sliding from its foreskin. Again he was startled. The weapon looked and felt like steel. It had a really nice balance, comforting, emboldening. Darrol risked turning on his light, tried to funnel the beam. He peered closely.

The long edge seemed sharp enough to do substantial damage, and the point ready to begin evisceration. On the lower third of the blade was a thin line of rust. Or was that blood? Darrol shivered. Laughed.

Not a hint anywhere of an incised 'made in China' announcement. This seemed to be an excellent replica. No wonder Magnus had at first thought he was buying the real thing.

Darrol turned off the flashlight, stuck it in a pocket. Slowly, he waved the sabre in the air, dreamed of victories. He sighed, re-sheathed it and put it back on the wall.

It was time to get out of here.

He considered taking a few things. Licorice, for one. Those little Ghirardelli chocolate squares. Maybe razor blades, other odds and ends. No one would ever notice.

But almost immediately he thought better. *I'm not a petty thief. I gather information. I take only when I want to provoke. Or if I want retribution. I'm not a thief.*

"I'll see you, pal," he whispered to the Emperor. He saluted again and returned the way he came in.

Chapter 16
Built for Two

Mrs. Durr didn't quite creak, but she was no longer a two-at-a-time stair climber. Now and then you could hear her puffing as she went up to her apartment. This Saturday morning she let Darrol, who'd come into Mischief House right behind her, carry her shopping bag up the stairs. But she declined his offer of a steadying arm.

"I'd love to be on your arm, Darrol," she said, "but this is one of my daily little exercises. Heaven knows you need exercise at my age." She laughed. "Besides, you're spoken for."

"I suppose."

She glanced at him. "You 'suppose'? Aren't you and Miss Grimaldi practically engaged?"

"No, no, no." Even Darrol thought that sounded very negative. He was quick to amend. "I mean, we've not really discussed that yet." He shifted the bag to his other hand. They turned the corner.

Mrs. Durr winked. "So you just live together, completely in the moment, as they say?"

"I suppose."

"How very 21st Century of you. After my dear Samuel and I met, we courted—dated as you'd call it—for a long time, before we got married. *Then* we finally lived together."

"Maria and I still go out on dates," Darrol said defensively. "Like this morning. We're going to Golden Gate Park to rent a tandem, ride around."

"A bicycle built for two? How very 19th Century of you." She smiled. "But I approve. That's really sweet."

"That's Maria. I wouldn't have thought of it. Never had a bike when I was a kid."

"Never had a bike? Oh dear. Every little boy needs two things: puppy love and a good bike!"

They reached Mrs. Durr's landing. Darrol walked her to her door.

"Thank you," she said, taking her shopping bag and putting it on the floor. "Have a fun day in the park."

Humming 'Daisy, Daisy,' she began searching in her purse for her keys.

Darrol lingered. "The Emperor Norton..."

Mrs. Durr looked up. "My favorite quirky relative!"

"I'm interested in how crazy you think he was, and how much he was actually very clever."

She raised her eyebrows. "Well, both, I've always thought. Crazy and clever. One doesn't rule out the other, you know." She went back to her rummaging.

"No, but I wonder if he was putting on an act."

"Faking it? Oh, I don't think so. The poor man made a fortune then lost it all. That could push anyone over the edge. He was very clever, but afterwards, mostly not right in the head. Why do you ask?"

Darrol shrugged. "Just curious."

"Well, if you're really interested, here's an offer. About once a month I go to visit the Emperor. Perhaps you could come with me. Maybe we could have a date after all!"

"What do you mean 'visit'?"

"Emperor Norton's buried down in Colma. Nice spot in a nice cemetery. My dear Samuel is down there too. It feels good to visit both of them."

She resumed sifting through the purse. There was a faint scent of lavender.

"Sure. I'd like to come," Darrol said. "Could be interesting. I'm free most mornings and the early part of most afternoons. Just say when."

"Aha!" Mrs. Durr raised her keys in triumph. "Well, good, Darrol. I'll be visiting my two men again soon, and I'll be sure to invite you along."

"Guess what?" Maria said, hugging Darrol the minute he came in the door. The kitchen was filled with sunlight.

"Mimi, you know I'm not a guesser."

She pretended to pout. "I only was being retortical." Back to full brightness. "I've packed us a picnic lunch!"

"Great. You put in any beer?" He poured himself a cup of coffee.

"Of course. And Mrs. Quist loaned us an old-fashioned picnic basket. It'll fit on the bike."

"How'd she find out about it?"

"Last night I was down in the store buying picnic things and she came by and we talked."

"Hmm."

"Isn't that OK?"

"I'm not crazy about other people knowing our business."

This time the pout was real. "Darrol, it's only a picnic."

He sipped his coffee. "OK, OK. You're right. If we ever decide to rob a bank, just don't blab about it."

Maria giggled. "Bonnie and Clydesdale, that's us."

"That's us all right." His free hand mimed pointing a pistol. "But it's Clyde."

"Oh." She picked a piece of lint from his shirt. "So, Clyde, where were you?"

"I woke up early and went for a quick walk around the block."

"I meant last night. It seemed really late you got home."

Darrol snorted. "You were passed out. Opened one eye like a dying poodle, said 'phumph,' and went off again."

"A dying poodle? Not very flattering."

"OK, a cocker spaniel. Your hair was quite something, a real whirlpool." He waved his hand in sweeping circles around his ear.

"At least I wasn't wearing curlers." Maria poked him in the ribs. "I know you love those."

Darrol made a face. "Anyway, after we closed, we went out for a few pre-retirement drinks for old Claude Gallatoire. Claude ended up in a puke-fest and we had trouble finding a taxi which'd take him home."

"I wished you'd called. I waited up for a while."

"Jeez Maria." He put down his cup. "You know I sometimes go out after work, let off steam."

"I don't mean that. I might have wanted to join the party."

"Oh." He put his hands on her shoulders. "I'm sorry, Mimi. It was a boys-only sort of thing. When we have an official party, of course I'll ask you along."

"You're forgiven." She wrapped her arms around his waist. "Did Mr. Vero say who's getting Claude's job? You, I hope?"

"Naw, Mr. Black Garters hasn't said yet. The sonofabitch is keeping us guessing."

"Mister what?"

"Inside joke. You wouldn't get it." Darrol stepped back and straightened his collar. "Are we ready to see if we can keep a bicycle upright?"

"I'm counting on you," she laughed.

"Only bike I ever rode was the one I stole. Ten minutes later I crashed it."

"Oh, Darrol. You never owned a bicycle?"

He shook his head. "Never even had a fucking teddy bear."

Golden Gate Park on a sunny Saturday morning is a twirling kaleidoscope of action, a crowded jumble of colors. Kite-flyers, skaters, cyclists, runners, Segway-rollers, Frisbee-players, dog-walkers, chanting monks, drummers, yoga groups, tai chi classes, flower-sniffers, wedding parties, picnickers, photographers, yelling children, parents pushing baby strollers, policemen on horseback and lovers oblivious to all the rest.

In the midst of it all, Maria and Darrol wobbled along on their red Raleigh tandem, slowly building confidence. At the Haight Street rental shop, there had been no debating who would take the front seat, but that meant that Darrol, with very little experience, had not only to share the pedaling and balancing but to do the steering.

Intimidated—but not admitting it—he took them startlingly close to benches, bushes, poles and pedestrians. Balletic on the restaurant floor, he was ungainly on wheels.

"Dork One and Dork Two," Darrol said as Maria took a photo of the two of them at their first dismount, not that far into the park. Darrol had brought them to a halt, ostensibly to adjust his helmet. Or to feel *terra firma.*

"Speak for yourself," Maria said. "All we need is purple spandex, and we'd look like two pros." She collapsed her photo stick and reached across her shoulder to slide it into her pack.

Darrol shook his head. "I don't think pros wear big clunky backpacks."

"You want a picnic or not? Mount up, Toronto."

"I think you mean Tonto."

"Oh," she laughed, "I always get my Indians mixed up."

The cycling became easier. They worked their way further west, the warm air headily-scented with grasses, flowers, shrubs, eucalyptus, fertilizer, mulch and, now and then, marijuana.

"We could get high without trying," Maria called from the rear.

"Stop breathing and keep pedaling," Darrol said, daring to turn his head just a little.

They skirted flowerbeds, museums and the Japanese Tea Garden, cycled past lakes, waterfalls, meadows and groves. The chains ticked softly, the wheels whirred peaceably.

They reached the deteriorating windmill near the ocean end of the park, congratulated themselves on virtually completing the Tour de France, turned, and began cycling back, looking for the perfect spot to have their picnic.

Darrol rejected several possible places—"too many noisy idiots"—and Maria didn't like one open field—"I prefer a little more shade"—but when they were riding near the southern edge of the park, they discovered it: a path which took them into a redwood grove encircling a small grassy area, half in lazy sunlight, half in greening shade. And, for the miracle of the day, there were no other people about.

The only sounds were tiny sharp fragments of birdsong, the hum of distant traffic, the sonorous buzzing of insects, their own light panting.

"This is it, right?" Darrol wasn't really asking a question. He dismounted, held the bike steady as Maria got off.

"Exactly what I hoped for," she said, unfastening the picnic basket from the bike.

They carefully laid down the tandem and stared at the high trees, the crowns seeming to reach far into the cloudless sky.

"Tall guys, aren't they?" Darrol marveled.

Maria gazed upward. "Coastal Redwoods. Sequoias, I think."

"How do you know that?" He rolled kinks from his neck.

"Give me a little credit, Darrol. My head's not in a cake pan all the time."

"Cake! Damn! I'm hungry!"

Darrol took off his backpack, removed a lightweight blanket and cast it like a fishing net. The dark plaid rectangle settled gently onto a partly-shaded patch of grass.

"What've we got?" he asked.

She laid out their feast. "Ham and cheese sandwiches, sweet gherkins, those chips you like. What else? Apples, strawberries. Beer's in that little cooler pack. And, of course, treats courtesy of *La Dolce Via.*" She sighed happily. "It's so nice to have some Saturdays off."

They dropped to the blanket and dove into the picnic.

Maria looked about, chewing contentedly. "So, want any more botany lessons?"

She took his shrug to be agreement. "I see rhodies, of course. Azaleas. That's maybe huckleberry. And over there, maybe some kind of currant bushes. Hm, skunk cabbage. And I think those are sword ferns." She gestured with her sandwich.

"Sword ferns, huh?" He crunched a pickle and flipped the stem into the grass. "I think I need a sword."

"Why would you need a sword?"

"Or a fine walking stick, or a cane with an eagle for a handle."

Maria swatted at a fly investigating her soda. "You want a top hat too?"

Darrol snorted. "A man needs a symbol of his authority."

"Darrol, I can just see you walking down Lombard waving a sword. A SWAT team would be on you in minutes. Better pick a different symbol."

"Yeah, well." He drank more of his beer, crossed his hands behind his head and lay back on the blanket. "Boy that sun feels good."

"Ready for dessert?" She bent over and picked up a small package wrapped in wax paper. "There's an extra one just in case you're really impressed."

"What you got?" He propped himself on an elbow.

"Crullers. But not just your ordinary cruller. We kept the glaze but shot these through with tiny bits of coconut, lemon and ginger. My invention. I call them 'crullers with a twist'."

"Crullers always have twists don't they?"

"It's supposed to be a joke, Darrol." She handed him his treat.

"Stick to baking, Mimi, leave the humor to..." He took a bite. "Lord! It's no joke all right! This is great." He took an even bigger bite and chewed, his eyes closing with pleasure.

As he finished, he sat up straight, puzzling. "Hey, wait a minute, did you take these or pay for them?"

"I sneaked them out."

"Silly Willy is still letting you steal? For no exchange?"

Maria wiped icing from her lips. "Not exactly."

"What d'ya mean, 'not exactly'?"

"I wanted to talk to you last night, Darrol, but you didn't come home until all hours."

"Don't blame me. So, what did he say? What did you agree to?"

Maria looked down.

Darrol read her silence. "Oh, Mimi, Mimi, you didn't just talk, did you?" A knowing expression crossed his face. "OK, I need to hear about it. All of it."

Maria was silent. She hung her head.

Darrol put a hand on her thigh, squeezed and held on. "Spill the beans, Mimi."

She looked at the sun glinting through the sequoias. "Well, I was partly right. Mr. Lenz is an odd duck..."

"That's a given!"

"At first we only talked. It's not really sex he wants, not really. Not in the normal way. What he wants is kinky stuff..."

"Kinky stuff, huh?" Darrol leaned in. "And...?"

"His own special kind." Maria hesitated. "I guess I'd call it bakery kinky."

"Bakery kinky?" Darrol laughed and sat back. "C'mon, Mimi. He screwed you on a breadboard—that it? Did it turn you on?"

"No, Darrol, you got it wrong. We didn't...Well, we didn't make love. Not really. Not like—well, you know—not like you and me."

"Small dick, has he? Big voice, tiny dick. I knew it." His tone mixed scorn and satisfaction.

"Darrol! I have no idea. About his...about that. Can I just tell you what happened?"

Darrol tipped his beer can to his mouth, found it empty, tossed it onto the grass. "Sure. Go ahead." He sat in front of her, cross-legged.

'So yesterday, Mr. Lenz kept me there after I finished. We met in his office. He said all he wanted was to do certain things now and then. Shh!"

Her hand stopped Darrol's impending interruption. "It was weird, kinky, but I guess not that unusual. The ladies talk as we're working, you know, and you won't believe what they say goes on in some bakeries. It's really..."

Darrol threw her an impatient look.

"OK! Sorry." She took a tiny bite of cruller. "Well, anyway, I finally agreed. I didn't know he meant right then and there, but he did. He locked the door and pulled the shade. The next thing I know I'm taking off my clothes..."

"Did he watch?" Darrol was intent.

Maria pushed hair from her face. "I guess so. Anyway, he put a rug on the floor and put a plastic sheet on top of it—he was kinda courteous, considering—and he had me lie down."

"You were butt-assed naked?"

"Um. Yes."

"Go on." Darrol closed his eyes. His breathing had become uneven.

"He musta guessed I'd say yes to his weird ideas, because he had all these supplies close by."

"Supplies?" One eye opened.

"Trays, bowls, dishes, bakery stuff." Maria waved her hands about. "With things like creams and jellies and fillings. You know, pastes, toppings, flours, dough, sprinkles, lots of stuff."

The eye had closed again. "What did he do with all that? What do you remember?"

"I don't really..."

"Try. What did he do? Gimme some examples."

"Well, he spread marzipan in one of my ears and kissed it out. It tickled."

"Marzipan, mm."

"Yes, and then he smeared my other ear with confection chocolate, you know the soft paste, and ate that too."

"That turn you on?"

"Of course not! It was like..." She thought for a moment. "It was like bugs in my ear leaving slimy junk. I was already thinking I'd need a really long shower."

"Mm. Go on."

She sighed. "Are you sure you want to know this?"

"I'm sure," Darrol lay back on the blanket, his eyes closing again. "It's...instructive." He put his hands on his stomach. "What else? You don't have to hold back, Mimi."

"All right," she said. She looked down at her own body. "Well, he filled my bellybutton with something soft and sticky—it might have been cinnamon icing—smeared it around with his hands, and, em, he licked it out. Pretty slowly."

"He was being really cute about it. Ears, navel. What's that? Didn't he go for the major parts?"

"Darrol, this is embarrassing. But OK. If you really... At some point he twisted dough around my breasts, kind of kneaded it all about, one at a time. It started damp and clammy and then got warmer and sort of floppy-sticky. It felt weird."

"I'll bet. Maybe we should try it someday? What else?"

"He left the dough sticking there, and he teased my...my nipples with maraschino cherry stems. You know, just a light little touch. Then he rubbed the cherries around and around in little circles." Maria mimed the action. "Then he ate the cherries, really slowly..."

"Mm. What were you doing? Tickling your little pink friend?"

"No!"

"I can imagine."

"Well, you're imagining wrong. I was doing nothing. Well, except listening to him smack and slurp and chew. I mostly had my eyes closed."

"In ecstasy, no doubt."

"Hardly." Maria frowned. "Do you think it was fun for me, Darrol?"

He opened his eyes, leered, closed them again.

"Darrol..."

"Keep going, keep going. I'm waiting for the really juicy parts."

"Well, you want juicy, you'll get it. But lemme remember. Oh, yeah, he poured some of our best honey all over my...well, my private areas, and well, you know, licked it off. God, that was a gooey mess."

"Was he playing with himself?" Darrol's face was creased, smiling in a broad shaft of sunlight.

"I wouldn't know. Well, I guess I did see his face at one point. He looked very smile-y, I guess you'd call it. Very, very smile-y. A bit dopey. Like you look, Darrol, after you, well..."

"Yeah, yeah. So, all that honey on you, pretty slick stuff, nature's little lubricant, huh? I'll bet next was him sliding inside you?"

"I told you we didn't do that." She considered. "Well, not exactly..."

"Not exactly?"

Maria pulled up a long blade of grass and twirled it between her fingers. "You know those pastry bags, the things we use for decorating cakes and the like?"

"Yeah."

"Willy took one of those—it was filled with orange vanilla cream, some sort of sweet icing like that, I guess—and he... Well, I guess he did put the dispenser inside, a little ways. And then he, you know..."

"He squeezed?" Darrol was watching her again. His voice was husky. "Squirted? Oozed? Filled you with sweetness?"

She nodded.

"Jeez, and then he licked that stuff out?"

"No. I kinda thought he would. But he said we should go slow the first time."

"Are you kidding?"

"That's what he said."

"What else?" Darrol sat back up. "Did you have to do anything to him?"

"I dunno." She fidgeted. "Well, sorta."

"Sorta?"

She drank her soda, dropped her shoulders. "If you really want to know, he had me fit some donuts around his thing. One at a time."

Darrol was agape. "Donuts? Around his *thing*?" He laughed, winked. "Oh, you mean his *Willy*?"

Maria blushed.

Darrol frowned. "Donuts, plural? How many?"

"Several, I guess. Quite a few. He's pretty big."

Darrol's reverie vanished. "I thought you told me you didn't know," he snapped.

"Well, I'd forgotten till now."

"Did he make you lick his *big* sticky thing?"

"God no. But I did have to bite into the donuts, one by one so they fell off."

"Did he come?"

"I don't know. Maybe. But not anywhere near me. He moaned a lot. I told you I kept my eyes closed most of the time."

Darrol hunted for another beer, popped the top, took a long drink. He looked at her. "Did you like it? Did you feel sexy?"

"Darrol, how could you ask that? Does a cream puff feel sexy? Do cakes feel sexy? I felt yukky-icky-sticky, that's what I felt. Couldn't wait to get home and wash."

"Aw," Darrol said. "You're making this stuff up, aren't you?" He burped.

"Oh, Darrol. I wish I was. It's so embarrassing."

Maria got on her knees and rummaged in the picnic things.

"Are you going to do it again?" Darrol asked. "With him?"

"I don't know. I think he'd like to." She turned to Darrol. "Do you want me to? It'll keep him quiet. Keep you in treats."

"I'm not sure if I like my girl getting creamed by some other guy." He brushed crumbs from his pants. "But then...If you do it again, I want to know about it. Every detail. My girl doesn't sneak around, right?"

"I don't sneak around, Darrol. I never would."

"That's my Mimi."

He cooled his forehead with the beer can. "All this happened in his pokey little office, huh?" He pointed the can at her. "Hey, you get the pokey joke?"

"I get it, but I told you there was no poking..."

Darrol watched a young couple crossing the far stretch of grass, tugged by a straining brown terrier. "It's interesting. All these guys keep places at work to fool around."

"These guys?"

"It's not just Lenz. Vero's banging Tekla. He's got a cozy little bang-her closet at the restaurant."

"Really? Tekla? With that phony? Well, I thought you'd have been more her type, Darrol."

Darrol raised an eyebrow. "Me? Nah. She goes for men with money and fake scars."

He drank more beer. "But I tell you, it gets me to wondering about Magnus Quist with that vault of his. His private lair. Probably diddles who knows who back there. The black girl, Georgia. Horny old Della. Little girls. Or maybe he's into boys. I bet he likes that kid who's drumming on things all the time."

"Jamie Turner? The one they call Jazz?"

"Yeah, him. Looks like a shoplifter to me. But cute."

"Darrol, you've got a sick mind." Maria held up a small plastic container. "Hey, we forgot the strawberries. Want some?"

"Sure." He reached over and took a big strawberry. He started it toward his mouth, leaned toward Mari and touched it firmly against her chest. "If we ain't got no cherries, this'll have to do, right?" He began to rub it against her.

"Hey, watch. It'll stain!" She pulled back, but she laughed. "I didn't mean for my story to give you ideas." She selected a fat strawberry and regarded it thoughtfully.

"Well, it has." Darrol bit the top off his fruit. "I think we oughta go home soon and have some fun before I gotta go to work." He grinned. "We got any vanilla pudding?"

Maria smiled at him. She nibbled on her strawberry. "Mm," she said, with a sudden languorousness, "aren't strawberries among the most delicious things on earth!"

She ran her tongue around her reddening lips.

They finished their picnic, cycled back to Haight and turned in the tandem. They decided to take a cab home courtesy of The Merry Widows. The old ladies had liked Maria's vacuum cleaner rolls and had rewarded her with a gift certificate to their taxi account.

"Ride to work in style a few times, dear," Rosa said, finishing an eclair.

"Then marry a rich old *paisan* and someday you can own the cab company!" said Sophia, her smoker's voice a perfect match for Lauren Bacall's.

"Older the better," Rosa added.

The Widows' account was with a decidedly-alternative taxi company. What rolled up in front of the bicycle shop was an old burgundy four-door Morris Minor with a very tall driver.

As they watched the driver un-telescoping his long legs to get out, Maria and Darrol tried to suppress their laughter. Tall man, funky taxi. It looked like part of a circus act.

The driver, opening a rear door, said his name was Dwight and that the cab's name was Miranda. This time they couldn't help giggling.

Maria and Darrol clambered into the back seat. The interior smelled of antique leather with a slight suggestion of wet dog.

Miranda, after some vulgar backfiring, rolled them away toward Mischief House.

Darrol wasted no time. He poked around in the picnic basket, found the remaining cruller, gently smeared it above the opening in Maria's blouse.

"Oh, stop," she said, but she let Darrol rub in some more. He bent over.

"Mm. Coconut," he muttered. "Lemon and honey. Mm." He nuzzled between her breasts.

"No, it's ginger," Maria whispered. "Oh, Darrol, stop that." But she made no move to prevent him.

Darrol came up for air. He noticed that the driver was glancing at them in the mirror.

"Eyes on the road, Dwight," Darrol murmured. "Eyes on the road."

Chapter 17
Uphill, Downhill

The newborn summer fog—incipient explorer, artist, gymnast, dancer, gardener, lover—gently tumbled out of the dark Pacific's cold womb, irresistibly drawn toward the Golden Gate, heeding the pull of warm air rising in distant valleys, lured east by the soft glow of dawn.

Coming to the coast, it found rocks and headlands to investigate, to embrace. It climbed at will, performed incredible flips and back rolls and balances.

Ready to play hide and seek, it flowed eagerly to the huge orange bridge with its long, arcing span, found bold towers and fat cables to encircle, to chase itself around. It fingered the bolts and rivets, stroked and nudged at the paint, whispered of entropy.

It gifted the bridge with playful moustaches, strands of cloud-tinsel, slow-shifting garlands of gray and white.

From below echoed slow moans of pleasure, the deep, ageless sonority of welcome, of warning.

The fog moved on, billowed down over a long, tired tanker, tunneling the vessel in quiet mystery, and baptized fishing boats, their decks and masts bowing, disappearing.

It wrapped the entire Presidio, hid the trees, shrubs and gardens, moistened, refreshed, rejuvenated, suddenly rose, drifted toward the city.

It lapped the edge of the waterfront, pirouetted up high buildings and took in the view. Shuddering, it combined a *grand plie* and a slow-motion *tour jeté,* met sunlight rushing from the east.

Entwined, lovers united, fog and sun danced a *golden pas de deux* into the morning skies.

Darrol loved these spontaneous summer fogs. He often heard people complain of damp, of gloom, of inconvenience, but he thought the fogs only added more charm to his city. *My city.*

Morning or afternoon, the fogs were always unpredictable, always capricious. He identified with those attributes, liked to think they were two of his strongest points.

This Monday morning, the fog had remained low enough that Darrol, walking up Russian Hill towards Nob Hill, could look back and watch the whole dramatic effect below.

As he climbed, he wondered how he could put one of these summer fogs into a drawing without running afoul of cliché. Without running afoul of Miguel Cortez. He grimaced. The critique still rankled. And another assignment was due soon.

Over the weekend, Darrol's list of paybacks had grown. Cortez was high on that list. Karin Holt was there too, although Darrol thought he'd give her a second chance to come around. Radisson Vero certainly made the list. Every night at work, the Radish strutted about like an ass. Or was that a peacock? No matter: Vero was both. The longer he took to say who would be senior waiter, the more annoyed Darrol was becoming. Vero earned an additional black mark every time the creep looked knowingly at Tekla.

And now this business between Maria and Lenz. There was a fair degree of titillation, Darrol couldn't deny that, but he'd begun to wonder if he really wanted that bakery jerk to be messing with Maria. She was, after all, Darrol's. Lenz—or even Maria herself—might need a little friendly reminder of that.

Darrol also had a growing list of lesser irritations. They gnawed at him just under the surface, like nasty little moles with nasty little molars. There was something too smug about Magnus Quist. Jump Jesperson was a crude braggart and likely a liar. Duff Lee didn't deserve the prolonged hero worship.

And, as usual, there were those aggravating parrots, who moments ago had disturbed Darrol's thoughts with a racket right from some Amazon jungle. Darrol was so distracted by the burst of noise, he'd fled down an unfamiliar street. It turned out to be a dead end. No little alleys of escape. No utility easements. Not even a low fence to hop.

As he reluctantly backtracked towards the continuing cacophony—were those birds chuckling at him?—he thought about all the little dead end byways up here. Russian Hill was peppered with them.

Dead End. Not the kind of label he'd want on his street. Not good symbolism. Too many lives in this town were dead ends. They were the lives of dull-eyed people he saw shopping in the 'Norton. Or some of the diners in the restaurant. Stuff your face, guzzle your booze, pay plenty, but get no pleasure. *Dead end lives. Not for me.*

There was a sudden silence. A moment of relief. Darrol stepped back onto Leavenworth, wondering if he could ever do something about the parrots. What would good old Emperor Norton have done? Slashed the branches, cut down the trees with his sabre?

Across the street two large elms erupted in bright colors and even brighter screeching. *The fuckers are reading my thoughts.*

One soloist sounded like it was squawking in Spanish. Sounded like Miguel Cortez on a rant.

Darrol desperately wanted to interrupt their self-satisfied little bird lives.

He walked on uphill, lost in possibilities. Peashooters, slingshots—both denied him when he was a kid—could be fun to wield, but they wouldn't do much. They seemed kind of silly now. Poison, traps: neither of those was terribly feasible.

He thought about catching the Quist's stupid cat, bringing it up here and letting it loose. He grinned at the idea of putting the fat little bastard to work. But those parrots no doubt were smarter. They'd choke it with feathers or drive it crazy with their shrieking.

Well, one of these days, one way or another, he'd get back at them. And at least for the moment, he was out of the screech zone.

He felt around in his jacket and found a toffee. He unwrapped it and popped it into his mouth, savoring the first sweet tastes of caramel. He folded the wrapper and put it back into his pocket. Littering was not acceptable. He hated people who littered. They were no better than the birds dropping their poop all over.

It was getting hot. From fogchill to sweatwarm in just a couple of hours. Darrol loved that about his San Francisco.

Loosening his jacket, he came out of his ruminations and saw that once again he'd wandered up near Grace Cathedral. The pull of the place made him laugh. He wondered if it wasn't some sort of magnetic field, some big lodestone drawing him here.

He inhaled, enjoying the low fragrance of roses, then crossed through the park, intending to bypass the cathedral, maybe loop back toward North Beach.

He sidestepped a young couple sitting on the grass, embracing. A few steps later, he stopped and looked back. The two were oblivious. Nothing intruded on their private little universe. Not the huge church, the squealing children cartwheeling, the jet streaking overhead, the bright-eyed little man leaning into the trash can, the overdressed woman kissing her toy poodle, not even Darrol, standing close and now staring. Heads together as one, eyes closed, their tight embrace was eternal. Exclusive.

He was surprised to think of Maria. He rarely thought of her during the day. She generally came to mind only when he searched in irritation for where she'd put his tux or when he idly wondered what the evening's treat might be.

But, in a sense, here she was, up on Nob Hill sneaking into his mind. In actuality, he supposed, right now she'd be knee-deep in flour or weighing out raisins or rolling dough or... *shit!*

He didn't like the sudden image of the cherries on her breasts. *You can't have it both ways.*

"You can't have it both ways, Darrol." *Oh God.* That was one of the many unctuous pronouncements from Her #4. She repeated it so often he felt it tattooed on his brain. *Jesus!*

"What would Jesus say?" That one slammed into him. Another of her favorites, usually delivered with one fat eyebrow raised, taking her mean little eyelid mole for a ride.

Darrel reeled. It was almost like suffering vertigo. He had to close his eyes to stop the spinning. Slip up and think of Her #4, and she had the power to leap back into the present. Burn her house down and what good did that do?

He reopened his eyes. The cathedral was smack in his face. Escape, sanctuary, a place of answers. Was it trying to lure him again? He'd only been inside once, some months ago, and that was simply a mad dash to find the nearest toilet after an ill-advised street burrito.

But what the hell? Laughing at his natural bent towards sacrilege, he walked over to the building.

He went up the steps under the twin gothic towers and paused in front of the tall gilded bronze doors. A sign said these were replicas of an Italian Renaissance work. The panels, done in relief, all represented biblical scenes. He admired the craft but not the content.

Those stories had been drummed into him, supposedly forgotten after he was no longer in the thrall of zealots, but likely lurking forever in his subconscious, ready to invade and manipulate his dreams. He'd long wished there was some sort of colonic for the mind, a way to totally clean away that old poison.

He entered the cathedral. Cool, dry air breathed toward him. It carried an iota of incense, a trace of cold, objective stone. He found that slightly reassuring.

It was always possible to conjure up the smell of all the churches he'd been forced into. An austere blend of old, lardy floor polish, moldy hymnals, dying flowers and something ineffable he eventually realized was the odor of sanctimony.

None of that here. Chalk one up for the Episcopalians.

As his eyes adjusted to the delicate light and his ears to the low level of sound—a cavernous silence underlain by a low, echoing hum of footfalls and voices—he realized that he'd come here while thinking about paybacks and even about killing. Was that sinful irony? Had he entered paradise already damned?

Or surely was this a place for forgiveness? He remembered that word not with scorn but with a faint sense of yearning. He moved from the entry and looked about.

Awe struggled against skepticism.

This certainly was a place all about height, about reaching. Slender gray stone columns rose forever, rivalling the sequoias in the park. Staring up past dangling purple and blue banners at the distant vaulted ceilings, Darrol felt dizzy again. *Why do we assume God is only above? That makes no sense.* He brought his attention lower.

He took in the giant, ethereal hall, the stained glass windows, the tight rows of plain, dark-wood pews, hunched like soldiers in formation, sculptures modern and old, muted tapestries, stone fonts, uncluttered altars.

Etched on the floor in one open area, splattered with blurred colors from the stained glass, was a large circular labyrinth. People, young and old, were slowly shuffling through its lanes.

Why bother? Why be a zombie? Darrol's eye quickly traced how to get to the center. *You set your goal and you get right to it.* He moved away.

In one alcove, a wooden table held candles which could be lit by visitors, donation requested. Darrol supposed he could choose to light one, leave a candle burning for any person or for any reason. He thought this was silly, probably superstitious, another way for the church to collect money. These were just small bunches of wax tapers, sitting in dishes of sand, idly flickering, burning down to oblivion.

And yet he was drawn to the idea. He stepped closer to the table and watched the flames do their little ritual dances. It was interesting, that flicker. Shouldn't the fire burn straight up? Was there a wind in here, a spirit?

He laughed at himself—inwardly, he thought—but he must have expelled air, as the nearest group of candles bowed. These places played with your mind.

Who would he light a candle for? He had no dead relatives. Hell, no relatives he knew about period. He had no clue if his birth parents were alive. And acknowledging those bastardly cyphers was the last thing he'd do.

Why not light one for the Emperor Norton? The more he thought about him, the more Darrol admired the guy. In an odd sort of way, Norton had made the city his own. Definitely enviable. But why burn a candle for him over a hundred years later?

How about lighting one for Darrol No-middle-initial Yount? Was that weird? This time he laughed aloud, and the flames jumped off their wicks in surprise, wobbled back down. But maybe not so weird. Why couldn't you light a candle for yourself? Not because you're dead, of course. Maybe because you're planning on being dead. Darrol grimaced.

Or maybe, he thought, because you need something. Because you want to state who you are, salute your plans, honor your future. That could be it.

Ignoring the donation box, he pulled a virgin taper from a container, pointed it at a burning candle. The flame willingly, almost eagerly, cloned itself. An eternal flame. *Is that it? Is this supposed to be all about eternity?*

Puzzling, he placed the taper firmly in the sand and watched it burning amid a dozen or so others. A jolly little campfire. *Bring on the marshmallows.*

He thought of birthday cakes. They were a rarity in his childhood—could he remember even any of them?—and only belatedly had birthday cakes become an adult tradition, that because Maria had baked him one on each of the two birthdays they'd been together.

His candle winked at him. *Maria.* Darrol scowled.

He inhaled. Using one substantial breath, he blew out all the candles, shaking his head and blowing until the last taper, his own, gave in.

Happy Birthday!

He stepped away. "All yours," he said to a donkey-faced woman who'd been hovering at the edge of the alcove. She attempted a smile.

He headed for the exit, humming a sardonic version of the birthday song.

The glare of the sunlight—was that the baleful eye of God?—made him shade his eyes and pause on the main steps. When he stopped squinting, he realized he was irritated again. He tried to reason why. Perhaps, he thought, he was annoyed at himself for thinking he'd gain something from the cathedral. Or maybe it was because it delivered nothing for him, nada, zilch. Or it could be both.

He went down the steps, thinking he might go toward Chinatown, find some cheap eats. Though he scorned the Chinese tourists who cluttered up of the city, milling about together like dumb schools of fish, Chinatown itself was OK, Chinese food sometimes just the thing.

Dum sum calling and his mouth salivating, he started to cross the plaza. And stopped.

Once again Gerta Twoshoes had departed her usual territory and was wading in the fountain, holding her dirty green dress above her knees. Her mismatched shoes, today some kind of padded slippers, one beige and one brown, were propped on the rim. Darrol's street people were supposed to be predictable, but maybe something had spooked Gerta, made her give up her familiar places for this, for what might become a new predictable. Or maybe this damned cathedral was putting its voodoo on her too.

"Hey, Gerta," he said. She looked around, saw him, pointed a dirty finger, danced a little jig, her limp spaghetti hair reluctantly bobbing.

"Whatcha gotcha?" she said, tilting her head like a bird.

"Do I have something for you?" Darrol was already rummaging in a pocket.

"Akimbo, Mr. Bimbo. Gimbo, gimbo." Gerta stopped dancing and stuck out her hand. The edge of her dress dropped into the water.

Darrol came up empty. For some reason he'd forgotten to load up this morning. "You know, Gerta, I blew it. How about an IOU?"

Gerta's hand was still out. "Sure, sure. Is it chocolate?" She formed a sly expression. "Them jellybeans is all OK."

"I'm sorry, I don't have anything for you. I'm sorry." He shook his head.

She scowled, jerked into sudden comprehension. "Well, fuck you, buddo."

This was the most direct sentence Darrol had ever heard her utter. He took a breath, tried not to snap at her. "Look, Gerta, I'll..."

But she'd turned her back and was splashing away, leaving her slippers to stare forlornly after her like two needy puppies.

Darrol stepped forward, snatched the beige slipper, jammed it in a pocket and strode from the plaza.

As he made his way downhill, he was intent again on an increasingly-familiar subject, paybacks. He didn't need to add Gerta to his list. What she did and said was eighty or ninety percent out of her control. Maybe totally. He was almost feeling sorry he'd grabbed her shoe. But he certainly wasn't going back up there. She could remain Gerta Oneshoe until she got back down to the mission.

A tourist family walked past him—two parents, a boy, a girl, all wearing 'I Love San Francisco' sweatshirts and small teal backpacks. Each of them was tonguing at a dripping ice cream cone, each thumbing an electronic device. The people looked foolish. The ice cream looked wonderful.

Ice cream.

Darrol's mind jumped like a young greyhound spotting the rabbit.

Cosmo.

Four years ago, when Darrol lived in the Sunset District, his job had been driving ice cream vans out there for Cosmo Malloy. That slimeball, Darrol remembered, kept some sort of handgun in his office. On paydays, Cosmo always popped it out of his desk and flourished it about as though he were a hotshot paymaster.

And Darrol had something on Cosmo. Something big. When he'd worked for the sleaze, he'd ferreted out one of Cosmo's nasty little secrets. The threat of revealing this would easily yield a loan of the gun. Probably make Cosmo wet his pants in the bargain.

Yeah, a visit to Cosmo was a great idea. Soon.

Darrol no longer felt as hungry. He decided to skip Chinatown and loop home a different way. If he needed something to eat, there were dozens of Italian joints to choose from.

"Italian's the best." That's what Maria always told him. He wondered what she was up this noon hour. *Kinky, huh?*

He turned north on Stockton but soon lost track of his surroundings. He was still thinking about driving the *Mr. Sweetie Pies* ice cream vans, the odious synthetic carousel music easily luring kids toward obesity.

There had been some annoyances and provocations that summer, but he'd had some very satisfying moments of revenge. Sweet revenge, how apt.

Every day there were boys and girls who were incredibly impolite—precursors, he supposed, of his adult customers at Lanterman's. There were rude little bastards who shoved in line. Kids who thumped the side of the van. Who raised their voices, who said 'gimme' far too often.

There were kids who maliciously changed their minds right after he'd struggled to dig out scoops of tutti-frutti or strawberry smash from the depths of the frozen tubs. Kids who tried to cheat him, fussed about the money. Even kids who tried to swipe packaged goodies while his back was turned.

For all these little monsters he devised paybacks that, even if they didn't curb the behaviors or the attitudes, they at least gave him—*Daryl*, it said on the misspelled badge that Cosmo never would correct—a scoop or two of satisfaction.

Daryl, aka Darrol, learned how to see the kids coming from almost any angle. He became very good at that, a swivel-head praying mantis, he thought. When eager beavers were getting close, he'd edge the van away, make 'em trot, make 'em fear missing out on their treats. Or he'd just keep rolling away, get his sales quota on the next block.

He learned that two can play at the short-changing game. A bit of sleight of hand, a smidgen of distraction, of volley of doubletalk and he'd have the extra quarter, sometimes the extra dollar. With luck, a kid might even get chewed out when he handed the change to mama.

Darrol became expert at doling out the ice cream, serving under-packed cones, subtly cross-contaminating flavors, keeping some ice cream just below melt level so it would flood at the first greedy licks, dribbled onto their stupid tee-shirts. Oh, he knew how to get back at them.

Now and then he would recognize a certain look in the eyes, that wistful orphan look, that drifting foster kid look. If these children were halfway polite to him, he treated them royally. Big smiles. Extra fat scoopfuls. Maybe an extra dime in their change.

As Darrol's *Mr. Sweetie Pies* days were winding down and his trial career as a server was beginning show promise, he thought he'd go out of the ice cream biz with a bang.

He played around in his kitchen and made a batch of what he thought would be a really dreadful ice cream flavor. Calling it *Peppermania*—among other ingredients, it combined jalapeno peppers, vanilla and butterscotch—he served it from his van at a try-me price.

Cosmo Malloy learned about it, hauled Darrol into the office, read him the riot act, went on about health codes and skirting the rules and being a smart-ass. But he demanded the recipe. *Peppermania* had become a surprise hit.

Darrol said he'd 'try to remember' the recipe. He started to leave. Cosmo told him he wanted the 'fucking formula' then and there. Big mistake.

And then another mistake, even more significant. Cosmo, for all the little crooked enterprises he ran, wasn't that smart. And it particularly wasn't smart to leave Darrol alone with the computer for a few minutes.

It was when Darrol was using Cosmo's computer, ostensibly to double-check some ingredients online and to type out the recipe, that he discovered Cosmos' ugly penchant for kiddie porn. That personal foible didn't seem to square very well with owning a fleet of seductive ice cream trucks.

Darrol never got credit for his *Peppermania* ice cream— which hardly mattered, as he changed the recipe in several ways, so *Mr. Sweetie Pies* couldn't quite get it right, and it was likely awful—but he hung on to what he'd learned about Cosmo.

Good thing, Darrol now reflected, that he hadn't just slammed the cops on the guy. Cosmo's little hang-up was soon going to be mighty fine leverage for getting something more tangible than satisfaction.

Darrol was so lost in thought that he hadn't noticed where he'd wandered. In front of him, sitting against a concrete wall only a few hundred feet ahead, was Burlap Ives. Darrol liked the guy, a master at using burlap for clothing, footwear, sleeping bags, and even rain hats. Burlap could have gone into business, but his mind had jumped the tracks.

Oddly, Burlap often smelled of Aqua Velva. Darrol imagined he could smell the cologne even from here. Better than the odors coming from most of these people.

"Where the hell does he get Aqua Velva?" he wondered to Maria, who always expressed interest in his street acquaintances.

"Maybe he drank a gallon and it keeps seeping out his pores?" Maria sometimes startled Darrol with her quirky thinking.

At the moment, Burlap was intently examining a raggedy rectangle of brown cloth. Before Ives could see him, Darrol turned up an alley, again regretting not stocking up on treats this morning. It wasn't that Ives might assail him as Gerta had. It was a burgeoning sense of guilt, something Darrol didn't like.

He reached the end of the alley, turned onto Union and—*Christ!*—there was Jeepers Peepers set up on a hydrant not ten feet from the corner. Were his street people having a convention?

This time Darrol could do nothing but move forward, especially as Perro Caliente, yipping his stupid little Chihuahua yip, had directed JP's huge eyes along the sidewalk. Or maybe it was the dog with big eyes and JP who was yipping? Darrol's guilt messed up his thinking.

"Hey, JP," he said.

"Yeah, Jack. Shudup, PC." The dog quieted but left his tongue hanging out.

A sliver of duct tape ran across one lens of his Peepers' glasses. The other lens flashed light at Darrol. He was startled to think of Magnus Quist.

Peepers opened his eyes even wider. They were remarkably clear. Bloodshot was the usual flavor of the streets.

"For volume received," Peepers said, "I will tell you about shame."

Darrol couldn't help laughing. "You nailed it, JP. I screwed up today. I'm a little ashamed, and your lesson could be good."

"So whatcha got?"

Darrol's hand involuntarily went to his pocket. "Well, actually..." he began to say, but stopped, feeling something in his jacket. *Gerta's shoe.*

"Well, actually, today I brought something for PC. Is that all right?" He pulled out the beige slipper.

"'zat steak? Beefy stuff?" Peepers asked.

"It's a medium rare slipper."

"OK then." Peepers nodded. "Bombs away."

Darrol held the slipper out to Perro Caliente. PC sniffed with a lot more hauteur that might be expected from a street animal. The dog backed up, paused, lunged, grabbed it, began to chew.

"Bon appetite," Darrol said. Was this mutt gnawing on Gerta? Well, her fault. "OK, JP, you mentioned shame."

Peepers seemed to be staring at Darrol, but it was obvious he was looking elsewhere. "Shame is a collision," he finally said.

"A collision?"

"Your wants and your commy sense run together and go bam!"

"You mean my common sense?"

"On the money, Jack. I lost my sense and dollars on Black Friday, and there I was, bam. Shame's the name." He lapsed into brooding thought.

PC worried at the slipper then settled, guarding it between its paws. Neither the dog nor its owner noticed Darrol moving away.

A short while later, as Darrol walked along an alley to take a shortcut to Chestnut, he stopped, looked for a hiding place, quickly stepped into a covered loading area.

Strolling from the back entrance to the Columbus Motor Inn, oblivious to all but themselves, were Radisson Vero and Tekla Hart, arm in arm. Darrol felt blood racing to his face. What did she see in that prick? *Some people have all the luck.*

He watched until they'd gone past. Seething, he continued up to Mischief House. He purposely looked for insects to step on. He fully remembered his power, the power to choose.

But right now he chose to be lethal.

That night, as he undressed for bed, he told Maria he'd lit a candle for her at the cathedral.

"Candle?" she asked drowsily. "Am I dead?"

"Not dead. Just sleepy."

She cuddled her pillow. "Oh. Well..."

"I lit one because I was thinking of you, Mimi," Darrol said, climbing in beside her. "In the nicest of ways."

"Are you an angel?"

"That's me."

Chapter 18
Courting Trouble

It was one of those rare mornings when neither Magnus nor Alma was working in the 'Norton. Magnus took occasional Thursday mornings off to play bocce, and this particular Thursday Alma had a dental appointment. Since it was only a ten-minute walk to the dentist, she was lingering over a second cup of tea before starting out.

Muted sunlight washed across her corner of the dining table. The smell of toast hung in the air.

"Privilege of the owners, yes?" Alma wiped lingonberry jam from the corner of her mouth. "A little free time now and then?"

"Oh, indeed. We are the privileged class." Magnus, inspecting his set of bocce balls at the kitchen counter, didn't look up.

"Sarcasm so early in the day, Mr. Quist?" Smiling, Alma reached over to stroke Lyckatill, who was dozing in the adjacent chair.

"Not sarcasm." Magnus looked at his wife. "Perhaps a more refined term would be 'cynicism'. I think a cynic puts more thought into what he says."

"Does he now?"

"Sarcasm's a quick jab, most often for effect. On the other hand—" Magnus looked down at the burgundy bocce ball he was holding—"on the other hand, there can be a fair amount of profundity in what a cynic has to say."

He rotated the ball under his stand magnifier. "These Perfettas hold up well, but this one's getting a little battle-weary, *ja?*"

"Do you do battle, Magnus?"

"Now that question holds a morsel of sarcasm." He squinted through the magnifier.

"Does it?"

"In the tone." He rubbed the ball with a small chamois. "Ah. Just a smudge, not a chip."

211

Alma put down her cup. She picked up Lyckatill and let the cat settle on her lap.

"Well," she said, "I have a question to ask in my best neutral tone. No sarcasm, smudges, or chips intended—"

"I hear whimsy, however." Magnus carefully nested the ball in the quilted bag Alma had made for him, gold and blue for the Swedish flag.

He removed another ball and regarded it with a degree of reverence. "But by all means ask."

She put a gentle hand on Lyckatill. "Where did you go last night?" She was not talking to the cat.

Magnus glanced at her. "The usual. Downstairs. My study." The ball went under the lens. "Always the catching up, *ja?*"

"You didn't come back up until one a.m." She picked up her teacup.

He turned the ball. "After all these years, you still wait up for me?"

"After all these years we still have secrets?" She sipped at the tea, made a face.

"I thought you liked that idea, Alma. A few secrets." He chuckled. "*En öppen bok* is not as fresh as one with unread pages."

"That may be, Magnus, but I wonder what you do when you're off 'catching up.'"

He stroked the ball with the chamois. "I still think of having these laser-engraved. Just my initials. An antique font. *Mycket elegant.* But I'm told it could affect the roll."

"Magnus..."

He smiled. "Paperwork, paperwork. A break for reading. Last night, Leif Persson, in *Svenskt.* Then more paperwork. Worry. Worry."

"Worry?"

"The usual, Alma. I don't like the numbers. Our profits are as thin as...your cat's whiskers."

"They're still profits."

"And the apartments." He switched to another bocce ball. "Do you realize landlords on this very street are doing much better than your beloved Mischief House?"

"And are they fair?"

"Hah! Fair has nothing to do with it. The rental market is 'way up there." He hefted the ball toward the ceiling. "We could be doing so much better."

Alma stroked Lyckatill. "Rent controls..."

"That's one big thorn. But also you let the tenants rent at such ridiculous rates in the first place. Look at those lost dollars."

"They're people, not dollars. And we have enough money."

"Do we?"

"Of course, and you know it, *gubben.*"

"Ah, yes, I suppose I should remember which side of the bread my butter's on."

She studied her tea. "Is that cynicism or sarcasm?"

"Eye to eye—" He peered intently at the magnifier. "—we do not see on this." He rubbed the ball, nodded. "So that is what I do at night. Worry."

Lyckatill fidgeted and jumped to the floor. Alma stood up and walked into the living room.

"Well, on a different subject," she said, "I think, despite our living in such deep poverty, I'd like to have a couple of the rooms repainted. This one for sure, probably the bathroom."

He snorted. "There was sarcasm in there."

"In the eye of the beholder."

Magnus looked up again. "You do remember, *gumman,* I didn't suggest that Falun red purely by chance? It very much comes from my Swedish heritage."

"Our Swedish heritage. Of course." She managed a laugh. "I also remember you wanted to have the whole apartment done in Falun."

"And look who won as usual. But let us not throw centuries of Swedish history out the window."

"I wouldn't do that. But I'd like to consider a different color for the living room. Something, of course, which won't clash with your young friend here." She examined the large portrait of the teenage girl.

Alma looked intently at the face. "Some days I think she looks happier than others."

"True to life then." He finished with the last ball, put it in his bag. The zipper snarled shut.

"Change is good, Magnus."

"What I've been saying for some time, yes?" He poured water into a glass. "We sell, we move on." He gulped the water. "I'm ready for someplace warmer. With lots of young people around to keep me feeling young. All, you see, as easy as selling and moving."

Alma didn't take the bait. "I meant small changes," she said affably. "Like painting a few rooms."

She walked toward the coat closet. "And—before you fuss again, Magnus—we could use Falun red as a very lovely accent here and there."

Magnus flicked at lint on his bocce bag.

Alma retrieved a short jacket and her purse. "I think life works very well," she said, "with just a few small changes every so often." She opened the front door.

Lyckatill strolled out, her tail high. Alma laughed. "I didn't open it for you, dummy."

"At least kindly don't change the color," Magnus said, opening the refrigerator, "while I'm out beating the Italians."

Alma smiled. "All right. I promise. But right now I'm off to see Dr. McTeague. I hope to come back with all my teeth."

"I thought his name was Dr. Farley," Magnus said. He put a sports drink and an apple into a paper sack.

"It is, but I often think of that Frank Norris novel. The one with the greedy San Francisco dentist. Dr. Farley has a chair sitting in a bay window just like in the novel."

Magnus reached into a cupboard. "You said greedy. Is he greedy, your dentist?" He pulled out a granola bar and added it to the sack.

"Dr. Farley? I don't think so, he charges a fair price."

"There you are. We should charge a fair price, yes?"

"Magnus, you're incorrigible."

He smiled broadly. "I'm glad my English isn't perfect. So your big word goes right over my head. Should it be sarcasm, I mean."

He waved the paper bag at Alma. She blew him a trifling kiss, went out, closing the door.

"**D**arren, my man! Want your job back, huh?" Cosmo Malloy sat behind his big desk, its surface verging on chaotic.

Malloy was chewing gum with high energy. One long strand of his thin reddish hair bobbed on his forehead, keeping time. "I knew you'd show up again, Darren. You guys always do."

"It's Darrol. How're you doing, Cosmo?"

Malloy's eyes narrowed, but he managed to maintain a semblance of a smile. "It's still Mr. Malloy to all but a few. And you ain't one of the few, are you? Or have you hit it rich and come to buy me out?" He let loose his smoker's laugh. "Offer me a coupla million and you can call me anything you damn well want."

"Still running a dozen scams, Cosmo?" Darrol said pleasantly.

The gum-chewing stopped. Cosmo leaned forward. "On second thought, no openings. See yourself out." He picked up the sports pages and began to read.

Darrol stepped closer. "I'm here to make a little trade."

"Trade?" Cosmo dropped the newspaper. "Where the fuck is Edith? Why'd she let you in?"

"Edith's always liked me, Cosmo. Treat someone nice and they like you. And I brought her a donut with sprinkles."

Cosmo stood up. This didn't provide much more authority. Darrol still had almost a foot on him. "Get to the damn point," Cosmo said.

Darrol shrugged. "OK, I want to borrow your gun."

Cosmo scowled. "What gun?"

"Don't play games. The gun you bring out on paydays. The one that almost shot Ari's ear off when you were proving it really worked. The nine millimeter."

The chewing started again, faster. Cosmo looked slyly at Darrol. "Oh, you mean this nine millimeter?" He leaned down and brought up a pistol. "Ear, hell. I shoulda shot his little Jewish prick off. He was cheating me. Did you know that?"

Cosmo aimed the pistol at Darrol. "Hell, you was probably cheating too."

"I should have. Wasn't, but I should have." Darrol grinned. "But enough reminiscing. Here's the deal. You lend me the gun and I continue to keep quiet about your ugly little habits."

"Habits?" The chewing stopped. "What're you talking about?"

"Cosmo, my man. How'd you think all those parents out there would feel if they knew a creepy-peepy was peddling their kids ice cream?"

The rosy face turned white. "I never touched a kid in my life." The gun drooped.

"Maybe not. But you look. You drool. You get hardons. You—well you know what you do."

Cosmo sank into his chair. Darrol nudged against the desk.

"I don't judge. Have your fun, Coz. I'd just like to borrow your little pal there."

Cosmo thought about it. He took too long.

Darrol was inspired. "How'dya think my friend the D.A. would feel? He has dinner with me about once a month." *The half-truth will set you free.*

The gun was almost in Darrol's hands when Cosmo yanked it back. "You gonna kill someone with this? Pin it on me?"

"No way. Not even gonna rob a bank. Got critters in my back yard need taking care of. A little target practice, that's all."

Darrol took the gun. It was cold and hard. "Just a loan, Cosmo."

"Yeah, yeah. Crummy blackmail."

"No, no, a trade. You'll get it back in a week or so." Darrol slipped the gun into his pocket. The pocket sagged. "Oh, I almost forgot—I need to borrow the silencer too."

"What silencer? I ain't got no silencer." Cosmo had grown very sullen.

"Oh, Cosmo, you're such a funny man." Darrol wiggled a playful finger. "The one you keep in the third drawer down. On the right."

Cosmo, morose, handed him a matte black tube, seven or eight inches long.

Darrol hefted it. "Can't make loud noises in my neighborhood," he said. "Might wake the children."

"I get it," Cosmo said, standing again. "Are we done yet, or do you want my brass knuckles too?"

"You're a gentleman and a true wit, Mr. Malloy."

Darrol opened the door and paused. "Hey, what you said a moment ago would make a great name for an ice cream. *Crumby Blackmail.* I like it. Just don't ask me for the recipe."

T his was a morning of rainbows.

As Magnus walked along Columbus, heading for the bocce court, he could see a filmy sliver of prism arcing behind Coit Tower. Earlier he'd seen a rainbow up Russian Hill, dropping, no doubt, on some rich person's mansion. There was always a pot of gold off there somewhere. Somewhere else.

It stirred a memory. Soon after he'd moved to San Francisco, Magnus had been driving back from Hunter's Point on his motor scooter. As his murmuring old Vespa splashed along the wet streets, Magnus watched the full arch of a rainbow seemingly not that far off. It was flirting with Potrero Hill, where he was living at the time. He noticed how his changing streets shifted the illusion. He could almost control where one end appeared to come down. The end, his Aunt Greta had told him, was where the pot of gold was, or at the very least, good luck. For a brief moment, he'd managed to drop the end right onto his distant apartment house. The rainbow was gone, of course, when he arrived home.

And yet, he later thought, that was the very week he met Alma Falk.

This morning's arch interested him. He'd been working on his volo throws, lobbing the bocce ball instead of rolling it— perfectly legal and quite deadly in the hands of an expert— like an angel of death descending from the sky.

Did he want a perfect, rainbow arch or one with a long upslope and a short descent? Intriguing problem. He'd tried drawing his options on graph paper. Reaching the pot of gold required forethought.

He arrived at Joe DiMaggio and went through the gate. The others were already settling in around their regular court.

Magnus was the only non-Italian in his group. It was hard to crack into a game where heritage was an unspoken qualification. But last year the Italians had noticed him playing pickup games in the adjoining court, and sometimes they'd talked to him.

He got to know their names: Aldo, Marco, Sal and Giorgio. They called themselves *I Magnifici Quattro,* or, as Giorgio added, laughing, "the Pretty-good Foursome."

Magnus told them he was fairly new to bocce but that as a kid in Sweden he'd been an avid player of a game called kubb. The children threw batons at wooden blocks, trying to knock them over. Kubb, he said, supposedly originated with the Vikings.

"Did you know those *cazzo* Vikings made it to Italy?" Aldo informed them with a sudden bit of clearly self-satisfied scholarship. "The idiots attacked some poor little city near the coast. Thought it was Rome. Dumb, eh? No offense to your ancestors, Magnus."

Some months later, when Sal became confined to a wheelchair, he had suggested the group give 'the Swede' a try to complete their foursome.

"Our rules are easy," Aldo told Magnus, "They're *tutto quello che vogliamo*—whatever we want!"

"In Swedish," Magnus said, "that's roughly *vad vi vill*. I practice that myself."

Sal still frequently came to watch, his wheelchair pushed by a tiny, rivulet-faced man known only as Il Bonfato, who sat close by, smoking big cigars, ignoring city rules. Sal ate cheese and salami sandwiches, drank Chianti from a cloth-covered bottle and occasionally commented on the play.

Normally, the group played two against two, but this morning it was going to be a one-on-one tourney, Aldo against Giorgio, Marco against Magnus.

The winners of those games would then play for a twelve-year old bottle of Montepulciano. Magnus knew the 'Norton carried a better vintage, but he withheld comment. The prize didn't matter. He just wanted to win. Wanted to see Alma's face when he told her.

Magnus took a deep breath. He smelled the earthy petrichor of the recently-sprayed court, the acid darkness of Marco's espresso, the spicy meat in Sal's sandwich. He settled down to watch the first game.

Aldo, in top form, needed only a dozen or so frames to beat Giorgio by four points. Beaming, Aldo shook hands all around. Sal offered him a gulp of his Chianti.

Marco crackled his knuckles, laid out his red bocce balls, smiled at Magnus.

Magnus smiled back. He unzipped his quilted bag, took out the green balls. He carefully placed three of them near the baseboard. He held the fourth for a moment, slowly moving it up and down as he flexed his wrist. It felt like power in his hands.

Marco, a good player, was at his most skillful. He had a habit of clicking his teeth, and today the balls seemed to click together in response. He'd also perfected the art of the annoying smile, the kind which can upset an opponent's concentration, and he wielded that smile frequently.

But this morning Magnus was focused in the extreme. He said nothing, played crisply, his eyes intently assessing. He put ball after ball in the right place. In the middle frames he achieved a perfect *baci*—his winning ball sat touching the pallino.

Their sneakers crunched on the oyster shell court. The balls clunked softly. Children yelled from the playground. Cable cars clanged over on Columbus. Giorgio murmured the score as the numbers rose.

In the last frame, Magnus had the final throw. He looked again at the ball positions and calculated. Torque, angles, backspin, secondary deflections. It was like trying to read his father's dizzying architectural plans. Magnus' mind spun. Then it cleared.

With no further thought, he unleashed a blur of furious green. There was a loud crack. His impossible, viciously-hard throw sent the four red balls scattering from multiple collisions and left two of his green in triumphant proximity to the pallino.

No measuring was necessary. The round belonged to Magnus, 12 to 11.

"*Santa madre di Dio!*" Sal was halfway out of his wheelchair. "A cannonball! Pow! You throw like you had a grudge."

Il Bonfato spoke, a rare thing. Belying his size, his deep voice came from bedrock. "*Torre di bocce! Torre di bocce!*"

"From him, that's a compliment," Giorgio told Magnus. "But don't let it turn your head. Aldo is ready for you after the break. And today he's a mean one, *non è vero?*"

Marco, wiping the back of his neck with a red-and-white bandana, wandered over to Marcus.

"So how's your store doing, Quist?"

"It's surviving. But I never see you there, Marco." He bit at a granola bar.

"Ah, my Dora, she does the shopping. She likes the Safeway down by the Marina."

"Well, would you please to ask her to try the 'Norton?" Magnus stuck the granola wrapper in his pants pocket.

"*Sicuro.* Sure thing. Dora jumps at my every word."

The others laughed. Sal hiccupped. Il Bonfato released a stream of smoke.

"You oughta sell everything, Quist," Marco said, tucking his bandana into his bag. "Be retired, like us lazy *barboni.*"

"Good idea," Magnus nodded. "First thing tomorrow, *ja?*" He took off his glasses and cleaned the lenses. Without the glasses, his long, pale face looked like a winter sky awaiting storm clouds.

This time it was Aldo's forest green against Magnus' quiet burgundy.

Magnus seemed to draw inside himself. His vision narrowed. He moved only when necessary, though sometimes with a sudden aggressiveness.

He rapidly considered each throw, tensed, released, willed the ball to specific spots. He struck hard, surely. Twice burgundy smacked green so concussively, everyone winced as if expecting an explosion.

But Aldo was a crafty player. He thought far ahead, placed his balls in clever positions, found success with his low-arc volos and proved better than Magnus in using bank shots.

At ten, the score was tied. Tied again at eleven. One point to go.

In the final frame, Aldo blocked the target pallino with a small phalanx of green. One of the balls was very close, an almost-certain winner.

Magnus' eyes narrowed. Everyone tensed for an impossible attempt, a wild, angry toss, the kind of throw which might bounce off to the horizon.

Magnus relaxed. Closed his eyes. Opened them again. Refocused. He stepped back, stepped forward, lofted another volo, a high throw in a graceful rainbow arc.

It seemed to float before dropping into the cluster. It hit Aldo's ball and the pallino, sending them speeding to one side where one of Magnus' burgundy balls waited.

"Wow! Gonna be close!" Giorgio called. Marco and Aldo hurried to the end of the court. Magnus, spent, trailed behind.

Giorgio ran to get their official distance marker, a cord with beads on each end. It wasn't in his bag. Others rummaged in their gear without success.

Sal spoke up. "*Merda!* It's here, in my wheelchair. No idea why." He held up the string.

Marco came over and took it. "Measuring your salami, Sal?" There was dutiful laughter.

Giorgio bent over the battlefield, held out the string, checked the distances. Pallino to green. Pallino to burgundy. He rechecked, looked up, nodded.

"Our tall Viking wins!" Giorgio declared. "By a whisker. *Molto bene*, Magnus!"

"*Jag vet.*" Magnus, smiling, polished his glasses.

D arrol had never handled a gun before.
After seeing other boys his age with BB guns and Daisy rifles, he'd pleaded with Him #4, one of his more benign foster parents. The most that yielded was a

plastic pistol which shot plastic sticks tipped with rubber suction pieces. None of those fearsome projectiles ever travelled more than a couple of feet or stuck on anything.

In short order Her #4 took away the ineffective toy, chastising her husband. "What happened to 'thou shalt not kill'?"

Cosmo's gun weighed heavily in Darrol's pocket, but it weighed pleasantly on his mind.

As he rode the crosstown bus back toward North Beach, his hand slipped repeatedly into his pocket. He fondled the dense cold metal of the grip, fingered the stubby barrel, ran his hand lovingly around the trigger guard, rubbed lightly across the sighting nubbin. He looked about a little nervously, remembering the guilty pleasure of a small boy trying to look innocently elsewhere while touching himself through his pants.

A young Hispanic woman in gypsy-chic came up the aisle, her dark eyes zeroing in on the empty seat beside him. He quickly took his hand off the gun, swung his legs out a little but didn't stand. He tried to look bored as she squeezed past. The swirl of her dress stroked him with patchouli and taffeta. She settled, looked out the window.

As the bus swayed, her firm leg touched his, rocked away, touched again. Darrol thought about Sheryl Duncan's ample body. He resisted, pushed the images away. *Old business.*

His mind jumped to Karin Holt, body yet unexplored. *Unfinished business.*

He could sense patchouli-woman stealing a glance at him. He gazed forward and slightly upward, offering her his full fine profile. *Sorry, all you get. Too much on my plate.*

He pulled his elbow against the gun. Wouldn't want the thing tumbling out. Letting them see a hard-on was one thing. Letting them see a pistol could lead to real trouble.

Darrol's stop was coming up. He stood, giving the woman his burn-down-the-house smile. He liked leaving a little longing in his wake.

As he stepped off the bus, his stomach rumbled. Thanks to the early trip to Cosmo's, breakfast had been rushed.

Coffee and a pastry were in the cards. And not hard to find. *The Wakeup Call* was within steps of the bus stop. Darrol went in, ordered a latte and a blueberry muffin and turned to look for a place to sit.

He saw the perfect table. Occupied, but still perfect. For coffee and jousting.

"OK to join you?" Darrol was almost fully-seated before Magnus Quist looked up from his magazine and registered who it was.

'Ah, Mr. Yount. Yes, please." The tone didn't hold very much 'please', but at least it was neutral. Magnus adjusted his glasses.

Darrol pulled the sugar dispenser across the table. "Out banking again? Stashing away the millions?"

"No. I treat myself to a little time off for bocce." Magnus drank some coffee.

"Bocce? That what the old guys play in the parks? Roly-poly?"

Magnus considered. "It looks simple, but there's much skill involved. You may think it's a group of elderly men creaking about, *ja*? Hoping not to die before the last ball is rolled? *Nej*! It involves skill, deception. Thinking. It can clear your head of other things."

"Huh." Darrol waved to a server holding a tray. "You any good?"

"I should be modest, but I will tell you I won this morning's tournament. All those Italians and but one Swede. And who triumphed?"

They watched as the server placed Darrol's coffee and muffin on the table.

"So," Darrol said, "I'm in the presence of a sports star? A bocce jock?" He grinned.

Magnus picked up his bagel. "Very droll, Mr. Yount. It's easy to be *hånfull* , em, flippant, but if you played, you'd learn bocce is about dexterity. About flair. Even about power."

He bit into the bagel and chewed with vigor. Butter dripped from his fingers.

"Power, huh?" Darrol pulled soft raisins and bleeding blueberries from his muffin and popped them into his mouth, one by one.

"And control, of course." Magnus wiped his hands with his napkin. He gulped more coffee. "That would appeal to you, yes?"

Darrol ignored the jab. He reached for the cream and felt the pistol bulging in his pocket. "Ever go hunting?"

"Hunting?" Magnus looked puzzled. "Why do you ask?"

"Oh, I was thinking of power and control." Darrol said easily. He poured cream into his mug. "Life and death." He drank some of his latte.

"A big leap from bocce, yes?" Magnus sat back. "But no, I've not hunted since my father took me out once as a boy. My eyesight was not up to the task. He let me use his rifle, and I killed, as I remember, an oak tree, a wild rose bush and a trash bag which looked very much like a bear."

He gestured at Darrol with his mug. "You, of course, are a sharpshooter?"

"No." Darrol shook his head. "No real fathers, no guns, no hunting. No chance."

"But these days you are hunting, I think?" He drank.

"Why do you say that?" Darrol said, too quickly. He looked down. The gun was not visible.

"Metaphoric, I think the word is. A young man hunting for his rightful place."

"Shit. Are you a shrink, Magnus?"

"No, indeed. Just a humble merchant struggling to keep the doors open. But I observe things from my little corner in the store."

"You and that fat spider up in her corner too. Quite a pair. Watching and waiting."

Magnus smiled. "Now who's the shrink, Mr. Yount?" He leaned forward again. "But you're right. I watch, and I see plenty. And you, I can tell, are the other kind of spider, the hunting one."

"Huh."

"But I must go." Magnus folded his paper napkin. "Mrs. Quist expects me. Today we try to design a promotion to counter-position Joe the Trader."

"You mean Trader Joe's?" Darrol ate a piece of muffin. "Why not just blow it up or burn it down?" He enjoyed the hint of incredulity spreading on the older man's face.

Magnus pushed his dishes aside. "Should I to take that seriously?"

Darrol smiled. "If you want, take it metaphorically." He leaned closer to Magnus and dropped his voice. "But there are faster ways to deal with competition, TJ's included."

Magnus raised an eyebrow. "You have experience, of course?" His tone verged on derisive, but there also seemed to be some curiosity.

Darrol sat back. "My boyhood wasn't as pleasant as yours, Magnus. When I was a kid, I found ways to set fire to just about anything. Got away with it. Arson is every child's dream, you know. And I told you about 'The Destructors.'"

Magnus stood up. "Fiction, you said, *ja?*"

"Ya. Yes. In that case, fiction. But real life is always just around the corner."

"I think you tease me," Magnus said, sliding his chair to the table. "Such ideas might better be put in your artwork. Try painting a burning bridge, for instance. A jumper aflame."

Darrol's smile dropped into a black hole. "How the hell do you know about my artwork?"

Magnus straightened his glasses. "We watching spiders do tend to gather information, *ja?*"

He picked up his bocce bag. "Well, *adjö.*" He nodded and walked away.

The espresso machine hissed.

Darrol stabbed at the remains of his muffin. After two attempts, he dropped the fork on the plate and looked out the window.

Magnus, jaywalking, was loping across the street. Darrol remembered a word a sadistic twelfth grade English teacher had drilled into him with other bits of useless, haute couture vocabulary. *Supercilious.* Synonym: bastard.

He picked at muffin crumbs and drained his latte. He wondered again how Magnus might know about the painting. Did Cortez come into the store, yakking about his putdowns? That could be it.

Cortez. He needed putting down. Something really good. As to Quist...that needed more pondering.

The parrots, meantime, Darrol thought, fondling the gun again, would get theirs in the next couple of days.

He walked home and hid the gun and the silencer in the metal box he kept at the bottom of his sweater drawer. Maria would never look in there. You could always count on Maria to be predictable.

"So I told the fat slob to back off," Gracie said, waving her biggest spatula. "An' he did. He took me literal-like. He backed right into the melted butter vat, and—bless me, Betty Crocker, I ain't lyin'—we had the biggest mess since the sewers failed in '99. With him slidin' about on his kerwheister in the middle of it all. Unsalted, even."

Maria and Maureen laughed. Tiny flakes of flour danced in the air.

Gracie smiled. "And that put my love life back on hold." She used the spatula as a backscratcher.

Another day at *La Dolce Via* was winding down. Cleaning, shelving, readying things for the early morning staff, trading stories familiar and new.

Willy Lenz wandered through, humming a tune which by now everyone knew to be from *The Marriage of Figaro.* He often joked that the staff recognized more arias than anyone did at the Opera House.

After saying goodnight to Tito and Gracie, winking at Joyce and congratulating Maureen on her new grandchild, Willy gave Maria the look she had learned meant 'come to my office,' or meant—as she and Willy had begun to jokingly refer to it—'stay after school'.

"I look forward to our talks more than anything," Willy said as Maria turned from closing the door.

She came over and sat beside him on the green leather loveseat he'd recently squeezed into his office. The loveseat still smelled of furniture showroom. It squeaked as her nylon uniform slid across the cushion.

"I like them too." She put her hands in her lap.

"Does Darrol still think we're doing the hot and heavy?" Willy sang 'hot and heavy' a second time, drawing out the syllables.

Maria laughed. "The hot and kinky, yes. But I'm going to run out of things to tell him."

"So you need more recipes for our misdeeds?" Willy's face shone. He was like a little boy who'd been given the key to the bakery. "I can come up with a few..."

"I bet you can." She thought for a second. "So far we haven't rolled in shortening. And I'm thinking maybe something with rolling pins. And I haven't used your silly little dill-dough idea."

"It's not silly at all. A well-baked pun, if you ask me." His giggle was operatic. "Or maybe that's a well-baked bun?"

He stopped laughing. "But why don't you simply tell him the truth? We're only friends, you and I."

Maria rubbed stowaway pastry from her knuckles. "We might be too far into it now, Willy. I wonder if the truth would hurt him more. I dunno. I get confused. I'm not cheating on him, not really, but he thinks I am, but of course that's not really cheating since he knows about it, and it even seems to turn him on, and..." Her voice trailed away.

Willy took her hands in his. "*Che gelida manina*," he sang. "That roughly means that you have gelato on your hands," he told her.

She laughed. "Willy, you've told me about poor Mimi before. I know exactly what you're singing." But she pulled her hands away and rechecked her fingers.

"Actually," she mused, picking at another speck of flour, "a couple of times Darrol has wondered if I was making it up."

"Has he now?"

"Yes, but it's just the kinky stuff he doubts. Otherwise he believes you and I are...well, you know."

Willy sat back. "Oh, Maria, Maria. And no, I won't sing that." He cleared his throat. "But enough about your boyfriend. Let's talk about my wife."

Maria was startled. "Your wife? You really want to talk about her?"

"No." A grim little laugh. "I was kidding. But then again, let's. We probably should. I haven't told you how Judy and I met, have I?"

"No."

"It's a lesson for all of us. Don't simply jump at skill or talent. First learn about the person you think you admire." He went to the credenza, poured two glasses of water, gave one to Maria.

"See, I'm a mechanical klutz." He gulped his water, put down his glass, sat on the edge of his desk. "I was apprenticing at a bakery in Stonestown. I came out from work and found my old Fiat was kaput. I was standing there in the parking lot with the hood up—I know how to do that much, put hoods up—and this cute young woman came by, offered to help. She diddled and twiddled, and my Fiat starting purring like a Maserati. Not that I know if those purr, but you get the point."

"So it was love at first...spark plug?" Maria smiled shyly. She sipped a little water and put the glass on the floor.

"Maria, you're very funny, you know that? I guess it was. But that's what I'm saying. I was so taken with Judy's mechanical skill—and she was soon drooling over my Viennese tortes—that we hooked up without the right foundation. If I can make a joke worthy of you, I'd say neither of us really looked under the hood. We've dragged the marriage on—I think that's called inertia—far too long. One of these days..."

"You seem so happy."

Willy sat beside her again. "I am happy. Here, anyway. I love the job, and I'm crazy about all of you. But at home these days we mostly go our separate ways. Thank God there are no children..."

"Do you want children?" She blurted the question, but Lenz didn't seem to notice.

"God, yes, but we didn't discuss it back then. Can you believe it? Turns out, she doesn't want kids for now, maybe not ever. Engineering is her baby. And you wanta know another funny thing? I didn't find out until last year that she doesn't even like opera. She says all my serenades do for her is give her headaches."

"Some of us like your singing, Willy." This time Maria took his hand. "At least I do. You can sing me that gelato tune any time."

Chapter 19
Fighting Dragons

Darrol admired the extra inches his lifts gave him. He adjusted the collar of his new shirt, glanced at the clock and cursed.

He grabbed his portfolio case and rushed out of his bedroom, almost colliding with Duff, who was dragging a small exercise bicycle down the hall.

"Hey, Duff. What the hell's that? Doing the Olympics?" Darrol opened the coat closet and rummaged.

"For exercise." Duff rubbed at the seat of the bike.

"I thought you work out at a gym." Darrol pulled out a jacket. The hangers rattled.

Duff looked almost sheepish. "I do." He gestured at the exercycle. "For my room. More convenience. More privacy."

"Whatever floats your bike." Darrol put on his jacket. "Say, slain any more dragons lately? Golden or otherwise?"

Duff flinched, paused, straightened. "You know Confucius?"

"The bartender at the Wicked Wonton?" Darrol laughed again. "Oh, you mean the other Confucius. What about him?"

"Confucius would say, 'The dragons we must fight first are those within ourselves.'" Duff's assertiveness fled. He looked at the floor.

Darrol regarded him sternly, found a sudden smile. "Uppity, Duff. You're getting uppity. I like that! Well, gotta run..."

He opened the apartment door. "...I got a female dragon to slay. Ain't that a coincidence?" He dashed out.

Darrol moved briskly down Chestnut, his new loafers clicking authoritatively on the sidewalk. The afternoon breeze was its usual puckish self, undercutting the day's warmth with small chilly swirls. Someone on a lower block was having an early barbecue, lots of tangy sauce. Darrol's stomach pleaded, but he ignored it.

This was his day off from Lanterman's and also the day for his next-to-last art class of the summer. He had a plan for reenchanting Karin Holt. She'd simply not given him a chance. She'd been too distracted, obviously, by end-of-term projects. Today, if he intercepted her between classes, suggested a more leisurely time and venue, well then...

Several tourists were admiring the outside of the Art Institute. A portly man was taking photos of a not-so-slim couple posing by the Italian cypress. Three women in bright pantsuits stood watching. They partially blocked the entrance. Darrol, tapping his portfolio case importantly against his thigh, got the desired effect: this little gaggle parted. He granted them an imperial nod, strode through the arch and into the courtyard.

He went directly to the rooftop. He'd learned enough about Karin's schedule to think there was a fair chance she'd be up there taking a breather, having coffee or doodling in her sketchpad. In any case, he didn't want to stand around outside the ceramics studio.

The sunny quad was busy with chattering students and with tourists gawking at the panoramas. Darrol ignored the people and the views. He checked the café, the outside tables, the benches. No Karin.

He looked at his watch. His drawing class began in ten minutes, and Cortez always threw cutting remarks at latecomers. Darrol didn't want to be skewered again. Not for any reason.

He remembered there was a smaller upper deck, the battlements, as he thought of them. He climbed the stairs quickly, a gust of wind attacking his hair.

It took only seconds to find her. She was standing by the outer wall, gazing toward the bay. He smoothed his hair, slowed his breathing and stepped toward her.

Before he said anything, Karin turned. She was as beautiful as he remembered her, as he dreamed of her. The smudges of clay or chalk or whatever it was on one cheek only made her look more intriguing. She squinted her lilac eyes at him. Was she shortsighted? That only added to her appeal. She looked puzzled. But her smile, when it came, seemed genuine.

"Oh, hello. How are you, Darrol?" She pushed her dark hair back from her forehead.

This time, she remembered his name. A good sign. He mumbled an inane greeting. *Sheesh.* He needed to do better.

"Thinking about flying away?" he finally managed. *Flying? Christ, she's not a witch.*

"Just came up here to calm my nerves," she said. "Today's the day."

"The day?"

"In a couple of hours my ceramics class opens its exhibit. We heard the Dean's coming—which isn't that scary—but also the art critic from *The Chronicle*—heaven knows why— and a couple other bigwigs."

"Some of your art's in it?"

"One piece, a ceramic sculpture. I'm pretty nervous. I don't remember if I told you what I was working on, but it's different than anything I've ever tried. Really intricate."

Darrol recalled the kind of semi-philosophical comments she liked. "Good to stretch yourself, isn't it?"

She nodded. "It is."

"Confucius says something about taking on the dragons inside ourselves." *Inspired.*

"Confucius? You surprise me." Karin laughed. "But I'm not sure I have any dragons. Butterflies maybe. Lots of those."

"I understand about butterflies," he said. "Especially if you're facing a critique."

"Oh, your bridge drawing, Didn't go well, did it? I'm so sorry."

His smile collapsed. "You know about that?"

"Didn't you tell me? Anyway, you'll bounce back." She looked at her watch. "Look, I have to go. Odds and ends to finish."

Darrol was still puzzling something out. Karin touched his arm briefly.

"If you want, come to the opening tonight. Six-thirty in the Walter-McBean galleries. You can judge my crazy work for yourself."

He found his smile again. "Maybe a drink afterwards? Give you my critique?"

"Oh." Karin seemed flustered. "I'm not sure... But let's see, shall we?" She walked quickly to the stairs.

Darrol watched until she was out of sight. He put two fingers on the place where she'd touched his arm, leaned back against the wall, not certain what had just happened. Had she snubbed him? Or was her invitation a start? He swatted at a fly, turned to face the city.

How did she know about his ill-judged drawing? He tried to replay their conversation but recalled only fragments. He mostly remembered her provocative eyes, her lilting voice, her soft floral perfume, how her blue skirt, peeking under her white studio apron, swung against her tanned legs as she walked away.

The fly buzzed him again. Annoyed, he swung at it. Karin was toying with him. She didn't deserve him. But he wanted her. He was aroused and angry. He had a sudden image of picking her up, feeling her luscious body as he threw her over the parapet, her white apron and blue dress wildly flapping, her legs spreading apart, everything he wanted crashing into the boulders and shrubbery far below.

Or why not a lovers' leap, go over together? His knees trembled, his heart flipped. He gripped the top of the wall and found it warm, imagined it was where she'd pressed against it.

Now he laughed. *Over the wall.* Another idea for a drawing? Another chance for a putdown from Cortez.

Cortez? Shit! Class in three minutes.

He got down there on time, but one late-arriving student had to bow before the master and receive a caustically-witty rebuke.

During the critique period, Cortez poured praise on a drawing called *Psyche II.* It looked to Darrol like a hallucinogenic trip through a sky filled with sagging hot air balloons or maybe, as he whispered to the woman beside him, "the spots you see before your eyes when you get a hangover."

But Cortez, in between swigs from his suspect canteen, went on and on about the technique and irritated Darrol further by suggesting the artist's concept was 'daring'.

Another work, *Never a Dull Horse*, appeared to suggest several racehorses astride their jockeys in a frantic charge for the finish line. One of the jockeys seemed to have a tail. Everything was abstracted enough that the drawing might actually have been the blur of a very rain-streaked windshield with hairy debris caught in the wipers.

Darrol had to hold back a smug chuckle when Cortez decided to tear into this one.

"Do I smell manure?" was one of the teacher's more memorable lines. It was almost possible to feel sympathy for the artist, a skinny man in a western shirt and cowboy boots who shrank in his seat, comment by comment, until he'd virtually disappeared, leaving only his spurs, spinning.

After class, Darrol went back upstairs to the café. He ate an unusual burrito which he thought might have included tropical fruit and walnuts, but he wasn't curious enough to peel back the tortilla to check. He was focused on the hour ahead and how best to strengthen the thin connection to Karin.

He decided that he'd better not blurt out his immediate reactions to her sculpture, especially if he didn't like it or didn't understand it. He'd size it up thoroughly, move to the side with the inevitable cheap wine and cheese and prepare some very astute remarks.

Later, he'd take her to Random Schotts, impress her by knowing Herbie, the owner. Then...

He picked a sliver of what might have been bamboo or pineapple from his teeth, headed to the restroom to complete freshening up.

Promptly at 6:30, Darrol arrived at the gallery. It was already jammed with noisy people. He tuned out the hubbub, which he knew would be awash in pontificating, clever remarks and self-serving comments, and he edged through the mob, trying to be casual, hunting for Karin.

At last he saw her off to one side, looking wonderful in a deep blue dress. She was conversing with a short, bearded guy and a tall woman who looked like she also had a beard until a second peek showed it to be some sort of brown ruff or an explosion of neck jewelry. Karin was letting these other two do most of the talking. Darrol could see a very attractive flush on her cheeks. She did not look his way.

He went looking for her sculpture. He was ready to observe it closely, stock up on shrewd comments, if necessary pilfer remarks from experts. Shouldering through the throng, he moved from display stand to display stand.

There were multicolored nymphs, a pink coital tangle which seemed to be mostly about big genitalia, complicated geometric abstracts poised improbably on meager stalks of clay, delicate starfish encrusted with sparkling faux jewels, a clever post-earthquake cityscape with tilting buildings and an open fault line, On and on, some pretty, some ingenious, some baffling.

He found nothing by Karin. Had she been teasing him? Playing with him? Being coy all this time? Slowly reeling him in? That would be fine. More than fine. He liked a conquest, but he liked a flirtatious chase almost as much. He glanced toward the place he'd last seen her. She was no longer there.

In the middle of the exhibition there was an extra concentration of people. They were looking at something blocked to his view. He edged forward, bumped an elbow, nudged a shoulder, resisted the temptation to push at a couple of well-shaped bottoms. A heavy man in a dark suit still was in the way.

Finally, an opening to the side of the big guy. Darrol pushed ahead, took the space.

And there it was. Without checking the tag, he knew this had to be Karin's work. He was staring at the life-sized head of a young woman, done in porcelain with pastel colors and subtle overglazings. The face was serene, almost angelic. It had realistic, peaceful eyes, not the enigmatic blanks on the Greek busts Darrol had seen. The perfect lips held just a suggestion of a knowing smile.

It was an amazing piece of sculpture, alive with shapes and textures.

What was most startling and most lovely was the hair. It was filled with flowers and vines, many quite detailed, and with tiny birds, some alighting, others ready for flight.

Slowly, Darrol edged around the pedestal. He saw clusters of even more complicated flowers. An oval nest with miniscule eggs. A hummingbird. Bees. And—he laughed, making the lady next to him jump—two butterflies. *Butterflies!*

Earlier, when Karin mentioned having butterflies, obviously she'd been making a little joke or even speaking with double meaning. God, was she smart.

"Medusa without the snakes," someone nearby said. Darrol turned to glare, ready to defend Karin, but the same voice added, "and so wonderfully-effective. A truly neat turnaround. Delicate and beautiful."

Hm, he thought, *maybe my opening line.*

Finishing his walk around the work, he leaned in between two people to read the printed tag. *Spring Waiting – Artist: Karin Holt - Not for sale.*

Yes, Darrol thought, Karin was not for sale. She was to be all his, a keeper.

"It could have been absolute kitsch," said a well-dressed older woman at his elbow. "But instead it's lyrical. Pure lyricism, don't you think?"

"Ah, yes, lyrical." He fished up one of Karin's words. "And intricate. I love the double meaning of the butterflies." He nodded professorially and left the woman leaning in for another look.

Moments later he found Karin again, off in a corner. Now she had attentive fans on both sides—the bearded duo from before—and what looked like a receiving line of people edging forward to greet her one by one.

Darrol joined the line, standing behind a thick-haired, fidgeting young guy who stank of sweat and linseed oil. *God, don't these artists know how to bathe?*

The line moved fairly rapidly. Few people got more than a handful of seconds with Karin, but Darrol was confident she'd allow him as much time as he wanted. He continued rehearsing his profound comments.

Darrol had two differing attitudes about the successes of people he knew: usually he tended to be wildly envious, jealous, resentful. But if he could somehow ally with the person or the achievement, Darrol often felt he was making the success partly his own. So make Karin his, and her talent was his too.

As a well-wisher stepped away, Karin looked out at the line and seemed to recognize Darrol. Her smile broadened and she gave a little nod. Almost a secret nod, he thought. He returned the smile, barely avoiding adding a wink.

Karin didn't react, and Darrol realized she might be connecting with someone behind him. His jealousy meter sprang into the red. Before he could sneak a turn, the line moved quickly and Linseed Oil was shaking Karin's hand. He said something in a European accent and stepped aside. Darrol was up to bat.

This time, Karin's smile was unmistakably for him.

"Glad you could make it, Darrol," she said. "Quite a crowd, huh? So what do you think?"

He was glad that the beard and the ruff seemed to be staying politely back, their eyes elsewhere. "A lyrical Medusa," he babbled. "Delicate, and em, so unkitschy."

Karin laughed. "You're not very good at paraphrasing, are you? What do you really think?"

He reddened. Somehow rallied. "I like it. It's quite something." A thunderclap of inspiration. "It's all about anticipation, isn't it? Not so much about the here and now as about what's to come?" *Shit. Did that make sense?*

"You surprise me again," Karin said, with genuine warmth. "That's a lot of what I was hoping to show. Thank you, Darrol." She offered her hand, royalty dismissing the subject.

Darrol took her hand but didn't let go.

"How about afterwards?" he said, trying to keep his voice low. He could feel the line pressing from behind. "I know just the place to celebrate..." Her hand felt like porcelain. His palm felt like a swamp.

She pulled him a little closer. His heart leapt.

"I'm sorry," she murmured. "It's not going to...I don't think we're...And I'm not really... Well, anyway, good luck." She freed herself from his grip and straightened.

Dismissed.

Moving back from their one moment of intimacy, Darrol managed a sick smile and turned away.

Rejection was not something he often experienced. His breathing was shallow. His mouth was dry. His cheeks burned. He wanted to get out of here. But the push of the crowd forced him to circle along the wall to try for an exit.

Partway around, he couldn't help looking back toward Karin and her fan club.

Nausea rushed up. Miguel Cortez was standing close to Karin. Very close. Too close. They were laughing. Cortez put his arm around her and ushered her toward the center of the room, the crowd parting willingly. At the same time there was a general shush-shushing, and some sort of announcements began.

A solid, masculine woman who Darrol vaguely recognized as Fanny Lorsing, one of the ceramics teachers, started going on about the quality of her students. Blah blah blah.

Darrol forced himself to look again at Karin and Cortez. Even though they'd arrived near Lorsing, the asshole still had his arm about Karin. Darrol felt like he'd walked into a sucker punch.

"And here's the great news." Lorsing's drill sergeant voice rolled over the crowd murmur. "Thanks to the generosity of Herb and Cynthia Snowden"—she gestured to the side, and the couple with the beard and the stupid ruff took small bows—"thanks to their generosity, the amazing, technically-astounding piece by Karin Holt, *Spring Waiting*, is not only to receive the Holzheimer Award but will shortly go on display in the show window of the *Elan* gallery on upper Grant."

During the sustained applause, Cortez gave Karin a hug, followed by a kiss on the cheek. Both actions were innocent enough, but Darrol saw the grating truth underneath.

A high, mean little voice in his head demanded he pay more attention to his payback list. Much more attention.

Chapter 20
All in a Day's Potshots

Two birds with one stone. Or, better put, two birds with one pistol. Darrol grinned wryly. It was early the next afternoon. He left Mischief House and began a thoughtful walk uphill. He badly needed to vent. He had not forgotten the parrots. Or the fact that he had Cosmo's deadly little friend in one pocket, the silencer in another. As much as he'd like to take serious target practice on Miguel Cortez— and, at times, he thought maybe even on Karin—shooting some of those obnoxious birds would be easier and much less likely to put him in jail.

He'd decided The Grand Parrot Vendetta might best happen after lunch when kids were still in school, workers were still at work and the retired were once again snoozing. And no snoopy postal workers: the mail carrier always delivered by noon on the block of Green Street where today's lucky flock of parrots loitered.

Green! Was that why the parrots chose that particular street? Could those birdbrains be that smart? Darrol chuckled at his whimsy.

He climbed steadily, part of his trek facing him directly into the sun. Dribbles of sweat rolled from his neck and sought refuge under his shirt. He was wearing large, dark-tinted sunglasses, a gold and red 49'ers cap and a lightweight tan windbreaker. Everyday attire for half of the city: the perfect disguise. Sweat was a small price to pay.

Darrol often took advantage of the sun. He particularly liked to put it behind his shoulder when he talked to people, letting them do the squinting. If he was lucky, he knew it might give him a halo. That really worked well with his street people. Darrol liked the idea of being an angel or a demi-god.

When the direction was right, he'd watch his shadow walking with him and guide it over sidewalk weeds and cracks, run it partway up walls and posts and hydrants. He knew how to bulk it up or make it slender. He enjoyed stretching it out in front of him, long and thin, an advance guard for his oncoming.

He was aware much of this came from his boyhood, when often his shadow was his only companion, one of the few who'd listen and not argue or put him down.

As he turned left onto Green, today's foreshortened shadow swung like a compass needle and pointed downhill. *Getting close.* His excitement rose, for the moment pushing aside the nagging remembrance of Karin and Cortez at the art gallery.

He thought through his preparations. After Maria left for work, he'd had plenty of time to learn how to fit on the silencer and how to work the safety, things Cosmo hadn't offered to share. It took him a while to figure out the magazine. He was relieved to discover it held ten bullets, another thing that bastard Cosmo didn't discuss. Ten bullets ought to be more than enough. If there was too loud a noise, he might have to settle for one or two quick shots before sneaking away.

Seeing their buddies dropping dead might be enough for the parrots to get the desired message: *move on.*

Darrol snorted. *And they flew the coop.*

He touched the pistol through his jacket. This could be good. Really good. And what the heck, he joked to himself, if the gun thing didn't work out, he'd steal the fake sword from the 'Norton and come up here hacking and slashing like a pirate. Parrots, pirates. It all kind of fit. And then...

He heard something, glanced back.

A hairy brown-and-white dog, a small street mutt, had fallen into step behind him.

Darrol stopped. The dog stopped. Darrol made a horizontal chopping motion. It accomplished nothing.

The stray stood there, watching, its tongue lolling out, dripping. It stank of filthy fur, moist garbage, and other shuddering things. *Do you eat parrot? If you don't, get lost.*

Instinctively, Darrol growled. The dog whined, hitting the high pitch of a dental drill. Darrol growled again, much louder. The dog took a few uncertain steps backwards.

"Go home," Darrol barked, mustering up all the sadistic authority of his sixth grade principal, a wielder of long detentions.

The mutt blinked, turned, diagonaled back across the street. Darrol watched it go. A small conquest, but very satisfying.

Turning, he headed again toward the stand of trees. His shadow dutifully trotted along. One block to go.

He was halfway there when a razzing burst of sound interrupted his thoughts. A chubby boy buzzed past on a red mountain bike. Noisy, protesting cardboard flailed against the spokes. *Shit.*

The boy was no older than ten or eleven. Why wasn't this stupid kid in school? Private school holiday? Sloppy home schooling? Playing hooky? Ordinarily, Darrol might have cheered on that last idea, but this kid, making a lot more noise than twenty silenced pistols—and now performing wheelies up ahead—could draw people to their windows, their fences. And even if that didn't happen, the boy himself could be a witness to Darrol's assassinations.

Darrol kept walking, but his mind was again in a turmoil.

His first thought was to shoot the bike's tires. He imagined an exciting, even spectacular, somersaulting crash. End of noise, end of wheelies. But hardly the way to avoid drawing attention. He wondered if another vicious growl might send the fat little bastard whining off. If a growl told the dog he meant business, it could work for the boy. But it also might bring an angry mamma onto the street.

The bike flashed past in the other direction, tires humming on the road, the card contraption on the spokes blowing a disgusting raspberry. The parrots started screeching again, making it all a thoroughly modernist symphony. Darrol hated symphonies.

He was almost to the trees. If he had telekinetic powers—something he often yearned for—he would have sent the boy ETing to the moon. But the best he could do now was to will the kid not to return. Apply formidable, focused mental energy to keep the bicycle away. He tried it.

Get. Lost. Kid.

Darrol looked back. No bike in sight. He had willed it, and it was so.

King of the hill. The rush of satisfaction almost made him forget why he was here.

But the parrots quickly reminded him. How many were up there squawking? A dozen? Three dozen? All shaking their evil little talons and shrieking at him, making fun of him. The wild blotches of color fluttered, the dark branches shook, the trees quivered helplessly. The noise was ugliness personified. Darrol's temperature rose.

Show time.

He looked quickly in all directions. He seemed to be the only person on the block. He pulled out the pistol. Fitted the silencer. Fumbled at the safety. Took it off.

He pointed the weapon at a small cluster of the least active parrots. Breathed in. *Polly want a cracker?*

Darrol squeezed the trigger.

The recoil: insignificant. The sound of firing: no more than a sharp-edged burp. The effect: magnificent.

A split-second of blessed silence. Flying feathers, something splattering, falling. A volley of enraged squawks. A sudden, unified airlift, an entire flockful of vivid reds and jungle greens and bright yellows moving up and out as one, scattering into the sky.

For once, the caterwauling didn't bother Darrol in the least.

His gratification felt almost sexual. He let out a deep, fulfilled sigh. Only one kill, if that, but he'd shattered the impudent complacency of these invaders. He'd shown them who was boss.

It was unfortunate those birds probably had two-second memories. When you inflicted trauma, it shouldn't be short-lived. But still...scratch one up for the good guys.

He heard a vehicle coming from his left. He turned calmly to his right, slipped the pistol, its silencer still attached, into his jacket and zipped up. He began walking unhurriedly in the direction he'd come from. Just another innocent enjoying an afternoon stroll on Russian Hill.

When he found a quiet stretch down Jones, he separated the gun and the silencer and stowed them more securely in his pockets. One of these days he'd need to get this stuff back to Cosmo. *But he can wait.*

By the time Darrol neared Mischief House, the day had become annoyingly hot and his euphoria had vanished. The images of the parrot incident had already lost their ability to soften his general irritation. He'd gained only one small checkmark against his list of scores to be settled.

A vague discomfort threatened to hover underneath most of his activities. He'd known that feeling before. At minimum it was disquieting. Often it was disruptive, much in the way chronic constipation undercuts feelings of wellbeing.

Something sweet, he thought, might provide immediate distraction. He went into the 'Norton and walked passed the registers. Magnus Quist, busy enthralling a customer with wielding his iron weights, didn't look up. Darrol saluted Hilda Brown, adding a click of his heels. After receiving her usual blush, he went to the ice cream chest, slid open the glass and searched for temporary happiness.

The rising cold was pleasant. He reached in and moved frozen containers and bars around, looking for any slightly-healthier goodies.

He saw a familiar brand which made him think again of peddling crap for *Mr. Sweetie Pies* and of one repellent little creep in particular. This brat always took a wad of chewing gum from his slobbering mouth and stuck it on the counter while he made his choices. The gum was Darrol's to clean off.

Darrol paid back the little boor in the best way possible. The kid liked one of *Mr. Sweetie Pies'* exclusives, a Super Snowchunky bar. Darrol collected the used chewing gum and inserted the pieces into the bars, nicely tucked between of nuts, pretzels and chocolate chips. He gave the twerp his own medicine.

Darrol smiled at the remembrance.

"Are you pretending you're a polar bear?" Jump Jesperson, obviously amused at himself, stood close. Too close. "Some of us might want ice cream before you melt it all, buddy."

"Sorry," Darrol mumbled. He grabbed an Eskimo Pie and stepped aside. Jesperson brusquely pushed forward and began assaulting the chest.

Kicking himself for not launching a snappy comeback at the fraud, Darrol took his ice cream to Hilda's register. He waited behind a tall black guy who was having trouble fitting a receipt into a fat wallet.

Muttering, the man finally moved away, and Hilda bent to shift a shopping basket. When she looked up, Darrol was right in front of her. His huge smile pushed her backwards. More blushing.

He put the ice cream bar and a five dollar bill on the counter. "Here you go, Eva," he said.

"Mrs. Brown's first name is Hilda." This came from Alma Quist, stocking batteries in a nearby display stand. "You do know that, don't you, Darrol?" Her voice was neutral.

"Our little joke," Darrol said. "Don't mind, do you, Ev— Hilda?"

The blushing commenced. "No, no. I don't mind." Hilda gave Darrol his change.

"But if you'd rather be called by your real name," he said, "I can manage that. Oops! We're off by a nickel, Addle-Head."

"Darrol!" This time Alma's voice was sharp.

Hilda's blush rocketed to crimson. "*Verzeihen Sie mir!*" She fumbled in the cash drawer, rattled out a nickel and gave it to Darrol. "But please to say it as Adelheid."

She turned to Alma. "My birth name is Adelheid. My mother said it means 'noble.'"

"And noble you are for putting up with... Darrol, how do you know her name?"

He peeled foil from the ice cream. "I keep my ear to the ground." He took a bite, his palm up to catch any falling chocolate.

"Indeed," Alma said, regarding him thoughtfully. She finished with the batteries and slowly walked up the aisle.

Darrol wondered if he'd given anything away. Ice cream dripped onto his wrist. Frowning, he licked it off.

"I will pray for you," Hilda murmured.

"What?" Darrol said.

Hilda, fondling the little silver cross which dangled from her neck, was already turning to another customer.

Darrol wandered toward the front doors. He stopped to look at Emperor Norton. The crazy old guy was a magnet. Darrol bit into more ice cream.

"Don't get on her bad side," Magnus said quietly. He was flicking his feather duster across a display case.

"What?" Darrol wiped his mouth with the back of his hand. "Who?"

"Mrs. Quist is very generous, but she has a sting. It's sheathed like Norton's sword, but when it comes out..."

"Why should I care?"

"Aren't we to be all one happy family here, *ja*?"

Darrol took another bite. The ice cream was beginning to taste flat.

Magnus' eyes flicked to the doors. His slight smile widened.

The bell jingled and the Green girls burst in. Magnus moved toward them. "So! Right on time! I can set my watch by you."

"You don't wear a watch," Pig said with tentative insolence.

"How observant." Magnus bowed to her. "I am impressed."

"Why don't you have a watch?" Pug asked.

Magnus stepped nearer "Ah," he said conspiratorially, "I have this little machine up here"—he touched his forehead—"which ticks away moment by moment. Tick, tock. Tick, tock. Would you like to hear it?" He bent down, bowed his head.

"No, thank you," Pig told him. She brandished a piece of paper. "It's a long list today, so we must start." She yanked a basket from the stack.

Pug, already forgetting about watches, was headed for the gumball machine. "Look, Pig, lots of new greens!"

"Just for you," Magnus told them. "The Greens, yes?"

The girls didn't seem to get it.

"C'mon, Pug. First we gotta find Mom's stuff," Pig said. She pulled on Pug's arm and dragged her sister away.

Darrol was still standing by the Emperor. "You're quite the ladies' man," he said to Magnus. "But I prefer them a bit older."

"And maybe less innocent, yes?" Magnus adjusted his apron.

Before Darrol could sling something pointed back, he felt a hand on his elbow.

"Darrol!"

Mrs. Duff had popped up from nowhere. She seemed very pleased about something. *Another crazy one.*

"Join me for a cup of tea and let's arrange our visit to the Emperor!"

"He's right here." Darrol stuck an impudent thumb in the direction of the cutout figure.

"I'll grant you a small laugh for that," Mrs. Durr said, tugging at his sleeve, "but I'm going to give you the chance to stand before the real Emperor Norton."

She led Darrol toward the Nook. He felt the pistol bounce in his pocket, and he shifted his body to keep it well away from her.

Mrs. Durr claimed the last two seats at the bar. She plunked Darrol down—"Hold the fort!"—and went to the service area.

The Nook was busy. Three elderly ladies playing Scrabble dominated the big table. Lukas Knudsen, Jump Jesperson and Brian Gates, an Iraq War amputee, had the smaller table. Jesperson was into another war story. Darrol shook his head. *Get a life.*

"All right, dear." Mrs. Durr clinked cups and saucers and settled down.

"So," she said, dipping her tea bag repeatedly, "you can have a choice. We could go to the cemetery this coming Friday or else on Monday. On the weekends, too many people are out there tripping over the tombstones." She giggled. "Or lining up for a space."

She put the teabag on the saucer. "We could set off at a reasonable morning hour and still have time for a decent visit."

"Maybe Friday then," Darrol said. The tea was bitter. It burned his tongue. He put down his cup.

Click. Jesperson was cutting his nails in public again. *God.* Did they grow at warp speed? Was this supposed to be entertainment? Did it turn him on to hit others with his clippings? Darrol tried to pay attention to Mrs. Durr.

"I hope that might suit," she was saying. "A picnic lunch is a tradition in some cultures. They eat right on top of the graves. Can you imagine? We could be a little more polite. If you say yes, I'll take care of providing everything."

"What does the Emperor eat?" Darrol wasn't much into levity, but he needed to try something to take him from the rudeness at the other table.

Click.

"Funny you should say that." Mrs. Durr poised her teeth over a small slice of pound cake. "I always take him a little something, often a sweet. It's always gone by next time, so he must like it." She bit into the cake and nibbled happily.

Click. Laughter. Jesperson made a joke about klicks, apparently some kind of military distance.

Click.

Darrol thought he saw a slice of nail flying past. Enough was enough.

"Hey, Sergeant Jesperson," he said, swiveling to face the three men. "Did they teach you that at Fort Ord? Or was it Benning, Sarge? Cutting your nails in public?"

"I beg your pardon?" Jesperson's face had turned the color of swamp water. "If you're talking to me, it's Colonel Jesperson."

"Well, I've heard of self-promotion, Sarge. But you win the prize."

Darrol looked at Gates, the Iraq veteran. "You know how Sergeant Jump here got his nickname? Jumping outta beds, jumping outta windows when the husbands came home."

"How dare you..." Now Jesperson's face was red.

"Darrol..." Mrs. Durr's hand was on his arm. He ignored it.

"We all got secrets, Jumpy, but yours is a doozy." Darrol blitzed them with his biggest smile. "Hey, but don't let me interrupt, fellows. Enjoy your stories. Just kindly don't fire any more shell casings over here."

He swiveled back to Mrs. Durr, found his cup and drank some tea. There were no more clicks—or klicks—from the war zone behind him.

A chair scraped and someone walked off.

Mrs. Durr leaned over and whispered. "That seemed awfully harsh, Darrol. Old men need their war stories."

"There are stories and there are stories." His tea tasted better. He reached for a piece of cake. "So what would Emperor Norton have done? About Jump and his lies?"

"Hard to say. The Emperor made up more than his share of stories too." She sipped her tea. "But on Friday why don't you ask him yourself?"

Chapter 21
Nary a Dull Blackmail

"Y ou ever wonder why there's only four people of color workin' here?" Xavier Shea was folding the last of the big linen napkins. "And we're all at the bottom of the totem pole."

"It is kinda suspicious," Darrol said, laying out extra serving ladles. Tonight Joe Rosa would be making his notorious and wonderful bouillabaisse—among Joe's secret ingredients were rumored to be a very fine whiskey normally not used in cooking and a tropical fruit no one else would dare include—and demand would be high. *Lots of slurping tonight. Lots of messy tablecloths.*

"For that matter," Xavier went on, "there's only one female. Lanterman's isn't exactly your equal opportunity hotspot."

Darrol adjusted his cummerbund. "In a word, I'd say it was tradition. They keep trying to honor the tradition of that old bridge-jumper August, who sounds like he had one leg in the 19th century."

"You saying intolerance and bigotry are traditions?"

"Hadn't thought much about it, but that could be part of the problem. It's sure become the way of the USA." Darrol held up his hand. "But God, X, let's not fight over it. I'm on your side. I'm just saying this place is a throwback. Is that the word, throwback?"

"Throw what back?" Radisson Vero sailed in out of nowhere. Sometimes Darrol could tell Vero was approaching by an advance wave of syrupy hair cream, but tonight that irritating fragrance trailed, arriving after the man.

"Throw what back?" Vero asked again. 'I hope you're not talking about Joe's halibut. You can tell our customers it was on the boat just hours ago. That's more or less true." He gave them his limp version of a smile.

"We were discussing tradition," Darrol said.

"Yeah?" Vero adjusted his cuffs. "Well, the tradition I want tonight is the best service in San Francisco. And don't forget to lay it on thick about the featured wines."

"Which ones are those again?" Darrol knew Vero was too lazy to have checked.

"Look 'em up, learn 'em, sell 'em." Vero trotted off. *The Radish has spoken.*

"So why do you stick around, X?" Darrol asked. "For the love of that guy?"

"Man, you got a sick sense of humor. But the pay's really good. Guess they don't wanta lose us superdudes to those new five-star places."

"Bribery wins loyalty, right?"

"Hardly. But I finish college next year. I like the stability till I'm done." Xavier picked up a small stack of trays. "Why are you here, Darrol? You're too smart for this place."

"I get Claude's job, stay here a bit longer, stash some cash. Got lots of irons in lotsa fires. This town's gonna hear from me, X. Big time."

"OK, then." X gave him a thumbs up.

Darrol set out a last decanter. "Guess I better go learn those damn wines."

The mandatory coaching meeting dragged on. Darrol tuned Vero out and spent his time reliving shooting at the parrots and remembering the ghastly expression on Jump Jesperson's face. Shell-shocked, that's what it was. How appropriate. Little things, but they brought great pleasure. He imagined Cortez' expression when—

"It's a little earlier than planned," Vero was saying, "but Claude here has moved up his departure so he and Mrs. Gallatoire can take that cruise they've always wanted. The boat wouldn't wait for them, can you imagine? So..." Vero toyed with his lapel flower.

Darrol's attention snapped to alert.

"So..." Another pause. Vero cleared this throat. The asshole also was toying with the staff. Any moment he would attempt to twirl his ratty little moustache.

"So," Vero repeated, rising to his full level of pomposity, "we'll be having a couple of changes at Lanterman's. Claude's last day will be a month from this evening. At some point, we'll organize a little farewell do. Stay tuned."

"And..." Vero cleared this throat again. "And I'm pleased to announce that our new Head Waiter—the person will lead our service staff toward new heights—will be...our very own Douglas Duggan. Let's congratulate him." Vero led the applause.

Who? Darrol's mind was mush. *Who is Douglas...? What did...?"*

Spike Duggan, the exemplification of smirk, was shaking Vero's hand, patting Claude on the back and looking like a seriously-overinflated balloon. Darrol yearned for a pin. A big, sharp pin.

"Sorry, Darrol," Carey Modoc whispered. "But look at it this way. Spike will be kissing asses and flicking at crumbs here till he's 80, and the rest of us will be long gone."

"Sooner rather than later," Darrol whispered back, but his brain was already calculating how to unravel the deal. He wanted the extra money, the better tables, the added prestige. And he wanted to leave on his own terms, not because pricks like Vero and Spike conspired to deny him his due.

Vero clapped his hands again, but no longer in applause. "Right, folks, let's get to it. And busboys, try for zero fumbles tonight, OK? Don't forget, X marks the spot!"

Darrol, fuming, missed Xavier's nightly eye-roll.

It was not Darrol's finest evening. His work slipped to a listless A-minus. Few would notice, but Darrol knew he was less sharp than usual. Anger roiled about beneath his best professional smile.

Tonight even the best of the kitchen's usually-sublime aromas irritated him. Too sweet, too savory, too much cumin and paprika in the air, seared beef which rankled, vegetables too goddam earthy, Joe's world-class bouillabaisse too fishy.

It didn't help that Spike slid around with a perpetual look of one-upmanship.

"If he holds his nose any higher," Darrol muttered to Allan Schultz, "he'll fall over backwards."

"One can only hope," Allan said, raising his tray with a flourish.

On top of it all, Jon Gulliver came in to hold court with two rapt young men. Gulliver didn't have a reservation, but Tekla quickly accommodated him.

Darrol drew the short straw and had to work the unexpected table. Ordinarily that would be fine. Despite his flaws, Gulliver was a big tipper.

But tonight Gulliver seemed at his most annoying. He blabbed loudly about his books, told off-color jokes and, worse, constantly kept Darrol on his toes with requests, changes of mind, and impress-his-pals types of questions— "Where does this sea salt come from, Darrol?" "Was this Malbec harvested the old way? I swear I can taste someone's toenails." "Hey, Darrol, by any chance do you know the square root of ginger?"—and he kept Darrol at the table while he told everyone a story. "You'll like this one, Dar."

After making sure that he had everyone's attention, Gulliver went on. "I know this Iraq war veteran, Tom, who loves it when a dining companion says the right words and sets Tom up for a little trick. So recently, Tom's having dinner at a nice restaurant with friends, when one of them, Pete, excuses himself to go to the restroom. Tom's antennae go up.

"Sure enough, as he's leaving, Pete says that familiar phrase, the one Tom's waiting for: 'Would you please keep an eye on my food?'

"Tom says, 'You bet!' And he reaches for his face, pulls out his glass eye and puts the thing on Pete's plate. Smack on top of the prime rib."

The young men went into dutiful hysterics. Gulliver roared at his own supposed originality. "Get it? 'Keep an eye on my food.' Good, huh?"

Darrol forced a smile, checked the wine levels, started walking away.

Gulliver crooked a finger and summoned Darrol back. "You're up, Darrol, my man. The corollary question, just for you, is how often a really good waiter carries off someone's unfinished food."

"Very rarely, sir," Darrol said, adding silk to his voice. "A really good waiter would call the busboy to take it away."

Gulliver wasn't prepared to be upstaged. "Thank you, Dar," he said, trying to smile. He waved Darrol off but made sure Darrol heard what came next.

"There's a smartass inside many a monkey suit."

Darrol didn't reward him with a reaction.

It seemed to be a night for scintillating repartee. Darrol, prepping at a serving station, heard Spike Duggan bragging to the bartender.

"Well, he sure wouldn't pick one of those Johnny-come-lately, part-timers, would he?" Spike said. "The only reason we even call those guys 'waiters' is because they're waiting to move on."

Outdoing the skill and speed of a chameleon's tongue, Spike snatched a maraschino cherry, popped it into his mouth. *With any luck he'll choke on it.*

Just after closing, Darrol managed to get Vero alone in a back corridor. He jumped right in.

"OK, Mr. Vero," Darrol said, maintaining a reasonable amount of civility, "we won't even discuss the merits of who's best for Claude's spot. You're going to have a little—what's the word?—recession, rescinding. Error made, had the wrong envelope, blah, blah, blah. I get the job and Spike can go lick his ego."

"Really, Darrol? And why is that, pray tell?" Vero's little scar sneered.

"Who the fuck says 'pray tell' nowadays?"

"Are you going to correct my speech or will you let me know why I'm going to do anything?"

"Do I have to spell it out?"

Vero took an unusual interest in his fingernails and said nothing.

"I guess I have to." Darrol had trouble keeping his voice down. "Item one: certain seamy trysts in a certain linen closet. Item two: certain meetings in a motel over on Columbus. Item three: a certain devoted wife. And item four: a certain prudish little restaurant owner."

"Are you *certain* all that equates to the stuff of blackmail, extortion, whatever?" Vero didn't wait for an answer. "Here's

253

what you obviously don't know, Darrol. Item: My wife and I are bigtime estranged, and she could give a rat's ass what I do or with who.

"Item: my partners know full well about my relationship. They don't care as long as we're discreet in the restaurant. I have to admit the linen closet thing was over the top, but that won't happen again."

Vero adjusted his rose. "And item three, or whatever it is, Vinnie Lanterman and Miss Hugo personally approved Duggan as our choice. Get that? Our choice."

"What's Miss Hugo got to—shit, is she the silent partner?"

"Does it matter?" Vero's European accent seemed to have vanished. "Regardless, you've got nothing on me. I oughta fire you right now, but trouble is, you're an asset to this place. Is that ironic or what? And Miss Hugo really likes you."

"Then why...?"

Vero straightened his jacket. "Duggan's clearly a lifer. You're not. We're not counting on you to hang around forever—or ever to be respectful to me—but in the short run, we'll take what we can get. Now, kindly excuse me. I have things to do."

Vero pranced off, leaving a stinking trail of hair goop and self-satisfaction. Darrol felt like someone had kicked him in the gut.

After work, some of the others headed for drinks at a popular place over on Broadway, but Darrol declined to join them. He was not up for phony small talk. Instead, he stopped at a smaller tavern and drank two beers, circling the wet glasses constantly on the bar and fretting.

His walk home was paved with bad intentions. His list of infractors—another word he'd latched onto to impress people—had just grown. For sure, Miss Hugo was on it now. All those times he'd served her, how could she sit there simpering and nattering, hiding the fact she was one of his bosses? Worse, how could she vote for Spike?

And there was Vero, of course, slippery, slimy, sliding out from his affair, which should have been enough to give Darrol a big hold over him. And Jon Gulliver, master of snotty remarks. Tonight, one too many.

And what about Spike? Darrol tried to be fair—he prided himself on being fair when he meted out justice—after all, Spike was a bit like a cockroach, just doing his thing, not really responsible for being obnoxious. But it might be best to nail Spike on general principles. *Nail Spike? That's almost funny.*

A motorbike snarled by, seeming far too close. Darrol turned onto Powell and almost tripped on three less-than-sober collegiate types who were playing marbles on the sidewalk. *Marbles?*

He wanted to step in, kick the things, scatter glass all over, watch someone stand on them, lose his footing, roll, fly, fall.

He remembered the cherished red cat's eye he'd had as a kid. It was one of his favorite found objects, not stolen, just lying there in the dirt, winking at him, moments after he'd set a neat little fire in Mr. Mason's shed.

For a long time that marble was a co-conspirator, a pal, a confidant, a touchstone in his pocket. Until one of those fat-ass Fosters lost it in the laundry. Not a bit of sympathy either.

As he crossed onto Columbus, Darrol realized his beloved cat's eye, long-gone, had just done him a favor. It had interrupted the catalog of grievances which had been churning through his mind in a constant loop.

With a clearer head, he thought, maybe he would put those names on paper and decide how to mete out their rewards.

He reminded himself that it wasn't all aggravation: paybacks could be fun. *Think parrots.*

Almost cheerful again, he walked up Chestnut, idly wondering what treat Maria had brought for him.

When he entered the apartment, Maria was not in the hall. Not in the kitchen. Not in the bathroom. He went to their bedroom and opened the door.

Maria was already in bed, asleep. *Shit.*

He debated awakening her, but he wasn't ready to reveal he'd not been given the promotion. He didn't want to talk at all. All he really wanted was his evening pastry.

He returned to the kitchen. He looked on the counters. No treat. Checked the refrigerator. No bag of goodies. Stared at the table. Nothing but a dying banana.

He went back to the bedroom and gazed down at Maria. She'd left a small lamp switched on. She looked so small, so defenseless. She was lying on her right side, a hand tucked under her head. Darrol leaned closer. One fingernail was edged with a sliver of pastry. A dark curl on her forehead shivered as she breathed. There was a minute trace of flour under one eye.

He had an odd upwelling of affection, almost immediately contaminated by a vision of Maria and Lenz at play, a fat cock dripping with honey. Parted lips, waiting.

Arousal and jealousy tussled with each other.

He went back to the kitchen, found some cheap whiskey, had a shot. It burned but didn't satisfy.

After a time, he went to bed, turned out the light and lay still, thinking, listening to the distant underground cable rattle on and on.

Eventually he slept, but fitfully.

The growing litany of transgressions looped around and around, tormenting his dreams.

Chapter 22
Time's Winged Chariot

"**B**y the time you make it into your 80's, you've piled up quite a few secrets. At least if your life's been of any interest." Mrs. Durr seemed amused. "You like secrets, Darrol? I bet you do."

"I don't have your wisdom, Mrs. Durr..."

"...please call me Jo." She shaded her eyes from the morning sun. They were standing by the Mischief House stoop awaiting their taxi. "And you deflected my question."

"Jo, OK. You caught me. Well, I'd guess secrets and lies are part of everything."

"Lies too? Did I uncover a cynic?" Her eyes danced. "And you so young?"

Darrol smiled. "People have been lying to me from the get-go. Right from when I was born. As to secrets—poke a stick into anyone, you stir up a hornet's nest of secrets."

He put Mrs. Durr's big wicker picnic basket on the stoop. "Sorry, this is getting heavy."

"It's my thick sandwiches." Mrs. Durr said. "And my concrete cookies. So, you want to trade a few secrets? Could be fun."

"Trade? Sure. But how'd ya know I won't be lying? Just making things up."

"I've learned how to filter. Or like my gold-grubbing ancestors, I've learned to spot the little glints of truth among all the sludge and the tailings."

"I thought the crazy old Emperor was your ancestor."

"Darrol, dear, Joshua was one branch. The other branch— well, if you want crazy..." She tapped the side of her head. "Gold fever's in the DNA of many Californians. You might cure it by striking it rich, except then you can develop another kind of sickness."

"Greed?"

"You're also smart for someone so young."

Darrol looked down the street. "Well, speaking of secrets..."

Duff Lee was walking toward them. He had an oversized gym bag slung over one shoulder.

"Good morning, Mr. Lee," said Mrs. Durr cheerily. "More martial arts?"

Duff half-nodded. "I try to keep in shape. Body and mind."

He moved to the stoop but found the picnic basket in his way. He stopped to stare at it.

"We're talking about ancestors, Duff," Darrol said. "Crazy ones and greedy ones. You have any of those?"

Duff, turned, his eyes apprehensive.

Mrs. Durr clucked gently. "Don't mind Darrol. He's wound up today. I'm taking him to see Emperor Norton."

Duff gave her a puzzled smile. "Ah. Well, goodbye."

He stepped around the basket, quickly tapped in the key code and entered the building.

"Secrets indeed," Mrs. Durr said. "Was that a little baiting there, Darrol?"

"Possibly." Darrol lifted his face to the sun. "Duff has a secret or two."

"Well, that may be, but..." Mrs. Durr glanced down the street. "At last! Our cab!"

The taxi groaned to a stop and double-parked, wheezing.

"Check your ignition timing," Mrs. Durr told the driver, a young Arab man, as he opened the door for her. He looked bewildered.

Darrol carried the picnic basket to the other side and climbed in. The cab's interior smelled of incense and pine.

"Montgomery BART station, please." Mrs. Durr said, fastening her seat belt. She turned to Darrol. "I always use Montgomery when I go to the cemetery. It's less confusing than Civic Center, where everyone's going every which way. Life should be more orderly."

They began to move. Darrol looked at the familiar buildings from this unfamiliar vantage point.

"As to secrets," Mrs. Durr said quietly. "If I may say so, Darrol—and this is purely the observation of someone who likes you—lately you've been a bit rough on our little group of friends. Their secrets are for them alone to share. It's not up to the rest of us to spill the beans."

He stopped watching the buildings. "What do you mean?"

"Well, Hilda wants to be called Hilda, for instance. Not that addled thing. She's very sweet and bears no grudges, but Alma didn't like you saying it, and Magnus is really annoyed."

"Oh he is, is he?"

"Very protective, our Mr. Quist."

"I'll bet."

"And the other day, you hurt Colonel Jesperson's feelings. It was like you stuck a bayonet in the poor fellow." Mrs. Durr held up a restraining hand. "Not that I don't think our Jump isn't a bit of a gasbag." She tittered. "But if he's really not an officer, what harm? It's his secret."

Darrol toyed with his shoulder harness. "He irritates the hell out of me."

"Me too," she said placatingly. "Reminds me how years ago, the old *Saturday Evening Post* ran a series called 'The Perfect Squelch.' Each little anecdote ended with a perfect putdown of some truly irritating person. You'd have liked those."

"I guess I would."

She smiled. "If I could have thought of a perfect squelch for Jump Jefferson, and been daring enough, I'd have used it myself. Now that's a little secret from me, Darrol!"

She settled back and watched the traffic.

On the BART train, they sat on two seats reserved for seniors. Their fellow passengers seemed to be a mix of harried business people, earbudded students absorbed in texting and tourists dragging luggage to the airport.

"Since we were talking about secrets," Mrs. Durr said. "I'll break my own rule about sharing the secrets of others and tell you an important one I know about Emperor Norton. It's what connects him to me, so he'll forgive me for revealing it. See, I believe that in the 1850's, Joshua Norton had a lusty fling with someone. That bit of nonsense produced a son, Benjamin Algoa Kearny."

"Algoa? The aluminum company? You're related to that?" Darrol's expression suggested he was tallying the millions.

Mrs. Durr yelped in delight. "No, no, not at all! That's Alcoa. This name, Algoa, I discovered, is a place on the coast of South Africa. Joshua Norton spent time there as a boy. Anyway, when his little bastard was born, Norton must have diddled the records to keep him out of it, and the boy was adopted by a respectable family. So ultimately, the bloodline leads through that illegitimate son, right down to me. I'm the visible end of the Emperor's secret."

"Can you prove any of that?"

"Unfortunately, no. I'm definitely Ben Kearny's great-granddaughter. The Emperor Norton part is just a piece of family lore. But I certainly believe it to be true."

It was obvious that Darrol was puzzling over something else.

"And no," Mrs. Durr said, with a mock sadness, "I've inherited neither the Emperor's money—all of which was lost anyway in one terrible investment—nor his madness. Unless you think I'm crazy?"

"Gosh, no," Darrol said, with an unusual earnestness. He slid the picnic basket toward him as a standing passenger crowded in too close.

"Mind you," Mrs. Durr went on, "many think I'm nuts or at the least scoff at me. But my lineage is real. I know it." She laughed. "I can feel it in my bones!"

"So I was right when I called you an empress?"

"Alas, no! I'm not an empress for one very good reason. Dear old Emperor Norton's title was self-proclaimed. He was no more an emperor than this handrail."

"He was all bullshit?"

Mrs. Durr dabbed at her nose with a small lace handkerchief. "Well, if you must put it that way, dear, yes."

It took only twenty minutes for the train to arrive at the Colma station. Darrol and Mrs. Durr were among the few getting off.

They went out to the street. The air was warmer, grittier. It had a glare to it as though the place were frowning about something.

"It's a fairly short walk to Woodlawn," Mrs. Durr said, unexpectedly wielding a cell phone, "but I'd rather save my strength for walking in the cemetery, so, as usual, I'm going to splurge." She made a quick call.

They found a bench and waited for the taxi. Darrol felt drowsy in the warmth radiating from the sidewalk and from the concrete walls behind them. His eyes began to flutter shut.

"Sleepy little town, Colma," Mrs. Durr said.

"Just right," Darrol murmured.

"Also sleepy in the sense of death."

That brought him alert.

Mrs. Durr dug in her bag and took out a small oriental fan. She flicked it open and began waving it slowly by her face.

"It's a town full of cemeteries," she said. "Seventeen of them. The main business here is death."

"So it's not mattresses and bedding?" He was awake enough to joke.

She smiled, flourished her fan, went on. "This is where San Francisco brought all the bodies after the city decided to close most of its cemeteries."

"Why would they close the cemeteries?"

She gave him a dazzling smile. "Your word of earlier, Darrol: greed. Unmitigated greed. Land, development, streets, all those predictable things. Anyway, as a result, Colma has infinitely more dead than living."

"Huh. And the Emperor?" Darrol found a blade of grass by the bench, tugged it free and chewed on it.

"He was buried in a nice San Francisco cemetery in 1880—with lots of fanfare, especially for a lunatic pauper—then they moved him down here with lots of others in the summer of 1934."

"Lock, stock and bones?"

Mrs. Durr waved her fan again. "Darrol, you're funny enough to be a mortician." She folded the fan and returned it to her bag. "I think that's our taxi."

Darrol flipped the grass aside. "Will the driver be living, dead or a zombie?"

"Any of those is fine with me," she said, rising. "As long as there's a driver of some sort. Those driverless vehicles are too weird."

A yellow cab rolled to the curb and an older Pakistani man jumped out.

"Ah, the famous grave-robber," he said. "How are you, Madam Jo?"

"I'm fine, Ranjhoo. And your little family?"

"Thank you, also fine." He began opening doors. "For one week, Mizha is down in San Jose with a sick auntie. The children, who knows? Perhaps off plotting terrible things."

"Is it safe to say that nowadays?" Darrol asked, putting the picnic basket into the cab.

Mrs. Durr climbed in. "It depends on who's listening, right, Ranjhoo? If you're worried, Darrol, Ranjhoo's daughter, Nazy, is a doctor in Palo Alto, doubtless plotting terrible, terrible surgeries, and his son, Saif, is a Silicon Valley engineer, at this very moment doing awful, awful things to electronic devices."

Ranjhoo's eyes met Darrol's in the mirror. "Madam has a fine memory," the driver said. "And a fine sense of humor."

"He means for an ancient lady," Mrs. Durr added.

Ranjhoo put the taxi in gear. They moved slowly away from the station.

Minutes later, they pulled up in front of what looked very much like a castle. A gray, granite-block castle with dark pink tiled roofs. Mrs. Durr paid Ranjhoo—adding a very generous tip to the small fare—while Darrol gaped at the buildings. *What is this, Disneyland?*

A three story, hexagonal-roofed tower commanded the central portion, and the two side wings were adorned with smaller turrets. Leading to the cemetery itself were two archways, each big enough to drive a car through. *Or a hearse.*

Mrs. Durr took Darrol into a smaller pedestrian arch. They walked along an echoing stretch of cool, granite-edged shadow.

Darrol's mood shifted rapidly from cynicism to sudden trepidation. He shivered, expecting within moments to sniff the odor of death.

Instead, as they came out into the sunlight, he smelled new-mown grass, fertilizer, and familiar and somewhat-reassuring juniper.

He saw perfect grass slopes, occasional large trees, white Greek columns on a distant rise and a sprinkling of upright headstones, many of them a muted reddish color.

"My dearly-beloved ancestor is in a left section, back a bit," Mrs. Durr said, gesturing. "But first let's go see my husband. He never did like me to keep him waiting."

She led Darrol away from the paved driveway, and they crossed up a sloping lawn. It was like walking through a very large park, though with tombstones instead of swings, plots of flat headstones instead of garden beds, small white crypts instead of gazebos. The San Bruno Mountains shimmered in the hazy distance.

"Quite lovely here, isn't it?" Mrs. Durr said. "Nice views."

"Why do the dead need views?"

"Well, they don't have television, do they?" she said, maintaining a straight face. "But for the living—and for those of us barely creaking along—the views add a bit of solace, a touch of peace. At least that's what works for me."

They passed scores of gravesites, several ponds, more freestanding Greek pillars and a number of mausoleums, some of which looked like miniature versions of Fort Knox.

"Is your husband in one of those things?" Darrol asked.

"Hardly. Even if we could afford it, he wouldn't have approved. Sam was not unlike our mutual friend Magnus Quist: a bit of a skinflint."

"You think Magnus is a skinflint?" The heavy picnic basket thumped against his thigh.

"Skinflint, cheapskate, whatever you call it. It's mostly Alma's money, you know. Inheritance. Insurance. But I think Magnus resents spending it on the store and the apartments. I get this from her. I've no idea what he'd rather spend it on. Perhaps new bowling balls." She smiled. "I recognize the stingy trait. My Samuel, maybe because he was a child of the

Depression, was unnecessarily frugal. He was so concerned we'd run out of money, that life ran out on him while he was still counting pennies. At least his frugality left me comfortable enough."

Darrol wiped sweat from his face. "When you come to this cemetery, do you talk to your husband? For that matter talk to the Emperor?"

"Of course. One reason for coming out here."

"Do they talk back? And that's a serious question."

She stopped and stared toward nothing in particular. "Well," she said, "my serious answer is yes, sometimes. Not out loud, of course. It's all in my own thoughts. But sometimes I feel their voices shaping what's said." She resumed walking. "Hard to explain."

They climbed a grassy bank and stood above a large open field checkered with scores of dark rectangular indentations, flat grave markers staring blankly at the sky.

"We scattered my daughter's ashes near Point Reyes," Mrs. Durr said. "She'd have liked that. No fuss. No corny epitaphs. But Sam was old-school, and he always said he when he kicked off, he wanted a spot of land and something to recognize him by."

She started down the slope. "So he's just over there, on the right edge," she said. "He'd appreciate that I went for the simplest plot possible and the least expensive type of memorial."

The plain slate rectangle sat neatly in the well-kempt lawn.

SAMUEL M. DURR
April 2, 1933- February 5, 2001
He tried.

Darrol put the basket on the grass. He bent over to read the inscription. "What does that mean, the last line?"

"Exactly what it says. Sam tried to be a good husband, tried to be an OK father, tried to run his business honestly. Tried, I guess, to be a decent person..."

"And?"

She gazed at him. "Know anyone who's perfect, Darrol?" She tilted her head with knowing coyness. "Besides you, of course."

"Besides me? Not hardly."

She sighed and sat on the basket. "Earlier we were talking about sharing secrets. Well, here's one of mine. Gratis. Sam didn't die in a car accident as is commonly thought. In his late sixties, he ran away with a former madam. I understand San Francisco is full of those. Anyway, he died in bed trying to prove he was still young. Odd, the Emperor had his secret affair, Sam had his brothel-keeper. What does that say about the men in my life?"

"And you forgave him, your husband?"

"In forty years of marriage you get a lot of practice at forgiving." She looked toward the grave. "Isn't that right, Sam?" She appeared to listen for a moment.

"Did he say something?" Darrol asked.

"He hoped I didn't spend money on a cab to come out here." She laughed, struggling to push herself away from the basket. "Give me a hand, would you, Darrol?"

He helped her up.

She waved casually toward the grave. "See you, Sam!" She straightened her dress and smiled at Darrol. "Well, duty done. Let's go see the Emperor. And have lunch. I'm hungry!"

They strolled to the left side of the cemetery and moved further into the acreage.

Darrol looked at the markers they were passing. Many of stones bore Asian characters.

"What's with all these Chinese?" he growled.

"They die too, dear."

"Well, it looks like they're everywhere. Taking over, just like those hordes of Chinese tourists in the city." He switched the basket to his other hand. The wicker rustled in protest.

"Where would you suggest these people should be buried? Surely not in China?"

"Now that's a fine idea," Darrol said. He sidestepped a well-worn slab. "I'm just kidding, Jo. Anyway, this bunch is a lot quieter than their buddies in San Francisco."

"*The grave's a fine and quiet place...*" She did a little jig around another marker. "I used to know a lot of poetry, but I rarely had a chance to drop it into conversations."

The picnic basket was making Darrol lean to one side. He halfheartedly waved off a bee. A few clouds flirted with the sun, sent frayed shadows across the grass, moved on. The full midday brilliance returned.

"All right, here we are!" Mrs. Durr led Darrol towards a medium-height headstone flanked by two well-manicured shrubs. "I always think of those little bushes as his bodyguards."

Darrol put down the basket and stepped in to look at the marker, a smooth tablet of rose granite sitting atop a rough block of dappled gray stone. The inscription was incised in simple lettering.

NORTON I
EMPEROR
OF THE UNITED STATES
AND
PROTECTOR OF MEXICO

———

JOSHUA A. NORTON
1819 - 1880

Darrol touched the headstone. It had a cool, silken firmness. He ran his fingers over the words from top to bottom, side to side, a blind person reading. There was an odd grittiness as though the letters had just been cut. Darrol wiped his hands on his pants and stepped back.

"And he's right under there, huh?" Darrol was standing directly over the grave. "You think he knows or cares we're here?" He did a soft shoe routine.

Mrs. Durr, standing to one side, looked down. "Joshua, this impertinent young man is my friend Darrol Yount. He's somewhat of a fan of yours, so go lightly on him."

"Actually, I'm a *huge* fan," Darrol said. He laughed when he realized he too was talking to the grave.

He turned to Mrs. Durr. "I really am a fan, Jo. It just amazes me how he pulled off having the whole city eating from the palm of his hand."

"Eccentricity can work wonders," she said. "Let's get our lunch, shall we?"

She opened the wicker basket. Improbably, she had a blue wool blanket crammed inside. That and a banquet: a bottle of French Chablis, still fairly cold. Thick roast chicken sandwiches. Two deli salads. Vegetable wedges, containers of hummus and blue cheese dip. Fat slices of chocolate cake in triangular plastic boxes. A little bag of Jo's homemade sugar cookies.

"And here's the Emperor's treat!" she declared, hoisting a small foil-wrapped object and waving it like a pennant. She crossed to the headstone and leaned her gift against the base. "He likes chicken legs," she said.

"I suppose that'll be gone the next time you visit?" Darrol asked as they spread the blanket.

"Why of course. And can you tell me with certainty, Darrol—certainty, mind you—that it's not the Emperor taking the food?"

"No certainty here. I hope he enjoys it."

Darrol smoothed the blanket over the spongy grass. "Why didn't you bring something for your husband?"

She was opening the wine. "Why bother? He never had much of an appetite." A small snicker. "Well, an appetite for women, but not for food."

They sat with their backs to the sun and had their feast. The Chablis made Mrs. Durr even more talkative.

"My great-great grandfather Joshua over there—or do I need one more great? I never remember—anyway, he blew his whole fortune in a stupid attempt to corner the rice market. Everything gone at once: kablooey!" Little pieces of chicken leapt from her mouth and flew over the blanket. "And then his mind too: kablooey!"

More aerial chicken. Darrol leaned back.

Mrs. Durr didn't notice. "But when he proclaimed himself Emperor and the word got out, somehow it all clicked. The town pretty much supported him and his loony antics for over twenty years."

She drank a little more of her Chablis. "When Joshua died, thousands of people came to his funeral. Lots of genuine mourners. He was beloved."

Darrol spooned curried slaw onto his plate. "Think someone could do that today—declare himself King of Russian Hill, for instance—and become a loveable crazy? Own the city?"

"Not a chance. Today, they'd lock him up, lickety-spittle. And anyway, today we're all so in it for ourselves we'd never give an inch for a harmless street bum, no matter how charming or entertaining he was. Another of these?"

Darrol chewed his second chicken sandwich and thought about his street people. Mrs. Durr continued with her stories.

"Mind you," she said, pausing for a satisfied burp, "there were grains of sanity, even genius. For instance, the Emperor was the first to suggest building a bridge from San Francisco to Oakland. There are still people today who'd like to name the Bay Bridge after him."

"Seriously?"

"Oh yes. And gosh, as his descendent, I'd like to be the one to smash a big bottle of champagne into one of the spans! Kersmash! Can you imagine? Me dedicating the Bay Bridge to good old Joshua? Here, let's toast to that!"

They clunked their plastic stemware.

"The guy fascinates me," Darrol said, picking up one of the plastic triangles of chocolate cake. The container opened with an inviting snap.

"You and everybody else. Especially back then. And even at his reburial in this cemetery. He'd been dead, what, over fifty years, and thousands came down here for the service. There were speeches, choral tributes and lots of band music. Dignitaries laid wreaths, a bugler played Taps. There was a military honor guard, no less. Quite something."

"Christ, even after he was dead, he had 'em where he wanted 'em."

"I suppose he did."

"We should all be so lucky."

She giggled. "Lucky how?" She loosely counted on her fingers. "Going broke? Going crazy? Being dead? Or having someone tooting a bugle over you?"

Darrol licked a last piece of chocolate from his lips. "All of the above." He twisted so he could see the Emperor's headstone. "So what do you suppose is really under there? A skeleton? A skull? A bunch of bones? Dust?"

Mrs. Durr grew solemn. "I prefer not to focus on that. This is merely a place to honor and remember him. But the important part—his spirit, soul, whatever you choose to call it, is likely somewhere else."

"Think so?"

"I hope so."

Darrol curled his arms around his knees. "I just realized something."

"Oh?"

"I've never had to deal with anyone's death. Never. I was raised by a bunch of strangers, and I don't know or care where they are. I didn't have dying grandparents or dying parents. No brothers or sisters, aunts, uncles—none of those to go dying on me. I guess I've never known death up close and personal."

"Or known grief either?"

"No. Whadya suppose that says about me?"

She broke a sugar cookie in two and gave him a piece. "I suppose on one hand you're very lucky. But on the other hand..." She nibbled at her half.

"What?"

"I think death up close is very humanizing."

His smile was shallow. "You think I need humanizing?"

"I can't possibly say what you need, Darrol. But we never can have too much love or tenderness towards others, can we?"

"Don't know about that, either." He finished the cookie, the last sprinkles falling like gold dust. "But these are tender. Tasty too. Can I have another one?"

When lunch was over, they lingered while Darrol tried making a few sketches. He moved the pencil rapidly over the small pad, merely hinting at grass, tombstones, clouds. Mrs. Durr learned over and peeked.

"Those look very...tentative. But interesting. Are you any good, Darrol? I'm no judge."

"Maybe. I'm working on it." He closed the pad. "But I don't know if death's my best subject."

"OK, then stick to life," she said brightly. "I suspect it's far more fun."

They got up, folded the blanket, crammed things in the picnic basket and turned to leave.

Mrs. Durr took a last look at the grave. "See you next month, Joshua. Don't go anywhere!"

In silence, they began the walk back toward the castle. Their feet whispered through the grass. Two white and yellow butterflies kept them company.

After a few minutes, Mrs. Durr spoke. "So, I should ask. Do you believe me, Darrol?" She sounded tired and a little shy.

"Believe you? About what?"

"About me being Emperor Norton's descendent. Most people think I'm bananas."

"Of course I believe you." He slowly swung the basket forward and back. "And I still think we should call you Empress.

"Thank you, that's sweet. But just leave it at Jo." She retired into her thoughts.

Darrol's feeling of levity quickly vanished. His inventory of annoyances was nagging again. He began a mental game. At each alternate swing of the basket, he checked off an irritation.

He continued swinging and refining his list until they were almost back at the entrance, at the improbable castle guarding the green fields of the gone.

Chapter 23
Out of Sync

It doesn't take an earthquake to cause the city to tilt toward San Francisco Bay on Saturday mornings. It only requires the usual stampede to the farmer's market by the old Ferry Building.

The locals are there, loading their baskets with fresh supplies for home-cooked meals. The tourists are there, lining up for the fabled crepes and other breakfast salivaries and hoping to find sunny places to sit and eat with minimum spillage.

When Maria had a Saturday off, she rarely had to drag Darrol to the market, but today his enthusiasm seemed limited. On their walk toward the Embarcadero, he didn't talk much to her, but he showed plenty of interest in dawdling to greet his street people.

Pipestem Jerry, who as usual had nothing to say, chewed toothlessly on his mangled meerschaum and listened, bulging-eyed, as Darrol expounded about headstones.

Billy Pickleface, who tumbled out of a doorway like a drunken soldier tottering from a sentry box, was rewarded with half of Darrol's pocketful of treats and a lecture about abstract art and bridges. Maria struggled to avert her eyes from the man's pulsing scars, abstract art in themselves.

Unsinkable Dolly was rolling her battered toilet on wheels far along a side street. Darrol led Maria on a detour to see Dolly's sloshing collection of goldfish. He dropped cookie crumbs into the scum-streaked bowl.

While the fish churned the water like golden piranha, he tried to get Dolly to discuss the merits of goldfish over parrots. Dolly remained mute, but her mouth moved in a pulsing moue.

"What's going on, Darrol?" Maria asked as they finally came within sight of the Ferry Building. "Is something wrong?"

Westminster chimes began proclaiming the hour.

"Could be. Look up there." Darrol pointed at the tower. "See that? Incredibly, those two clock faces aren't quite in sync. Is it 9:59 or 10? You think the other two clocks are out of whack also? Four different times? Ooh, ominous. End of the world stuff."

"Darrol, you're worrying me." Maria pushed strands of hair from her face. "Can we talk?"

"Sure, but the signal's changing. Let's get over there first." Without waiting for her, he moved briskly into the crowd using the long crosswalk. Maria, her shopping bags bouncing on her arm, had to run to keep up.

Darrol stopped on the far sidewalk. "Hey," he said before she could speak, "do you think Magnus will find out we're down here buying some farmer's kumquats instead of the 'Norton's?"

"I'm sure he knows we browse here, but he..."

Darrol was already walking away. Again Maria had to jog. She didn't reach him until he stopped at one side of the outdoor plaza. He was eyeing the booths nearest the pier.

"Whatdya say to something cheesy?" he said as though she'd been alongside the entire time. "Great blintzes back there somewhere. Or we could have blueberry."

"Can we talk?"

"Food first." He exaggerated licking his lips, turned and headed for the blintzes. Maria flew after him.

They purchased their food and pushed through the crowd toward an edge of the pier, hoping to find seating. Darrol, leading the way, automatically clicked his mental fingers. *Abracadabra!*

He did an immediate, gleeful double take.

Exactly where he was looking, three teenaged girls were getting up from a low wooden bulwark, like lazy gulls preparing for flight. They clowned for a last quick selfie and departed.

Darrol dashed over and dropped down in the middle of the newly-empty space, barely acing out a young Asian couple pushing an overloaded stroller. Giving them his best 'so sorry' look, he placed his food and coffee on his right and leaned to guard the spot on his left.

Maria met the mother's eyes and offered a silent apology. Darrol gestured magnanimously at the bulwark.

"All yours, Mimi. But mind you don't get splinters on your backside." As she started to sit, he mocked a frown. "Or do you already have splinters from Willy's rolling pin?"

"Darrol!" Her tone was shrill. The young mother looked back at them. Maria blushed.

"Oh, I don't mean *that* rolling pin." Darrol dropped his voice, but not by much. "Didn't you tell me he rolled snickerdoodle dough across your bottom?"

Maria glanced to her other side. Two middle-aged men were absorbed in feeding dripping crepes to each other. "Let's not broadcast it, OK?"

"I like snickerdoodles. Can the two of us try that trick some time?"

"Darrol, why are you so exasperating this morning?"

He picked up his blintz. "Not my usual charm, huh?" He began to eat.

"No, not really." She studied him, sighed and made an attempt at her own food. A fat blueberry squirted free and plopped into her shopping bags. She ignored it.

For a few moments they ate without talking. A cargo ship blatted from the bay. Gulls screeched above the crowd murmur. Espresso machines made rude noises. A street musician floated sweet high flute notes over it all.

"Ah!" Darrol put down his plate and picked up his coffee. "That's better."

Maria napkined a fragment of blueberry from the side of her mouth. It left a purple stain on her chin. "Good. So can we talk? Will you tell me what's going on?"

"Sure." He shifted to face her. "Here's the deal, Mimi. You know my instincts. Well, it just seems to me lately you've really not been the same. That's all."

"Not the same?"

"You seem different. Maybe since you've been...well, you know, playing patty cake with our Mr. Lenz."

"Are you jealous, Darrol? You said it was OK. And it's kept him quiet about..." She glanced at the two men beside her. "About the stuff I take."

Darrol peered at her over his tall paper cup. "That's another thing. You don't bring me goodies every night like you used to. And you don't always wait up either."

"Oh. I don't have an excuse, Darrol. I'll try harder."

"That's my Mimi." He scrunched his napkin and wiped the purple from her chin. He remained close. "So, did you really do that thing with the creamhorn?"

"What? Oh. Yes." She checked her neighbors again. They seemed intent on studying the debris bobbing on the water. "He wanted to do it twice. Butter vanilla, and then I think it was that orangey Cointoss flavor."

"Cointoss? You mean Cointreau?" He nuzzled her ear. "Mm. We should go home and try it."

She leaned away. "Shouldn't we do our shopping?" She picked up the bags.

Darrol's face clouded. "Shopping? Right." He jumped up. "Let's get to it."

His smile returned. The gruffness left his voice. "All those free samples we'll score, that'll be good." He stepped toward the first line of booths. "Peaches, peaches, where are you?"

Maria quickly gathered their trash, stuffed it into a receptacle and hurried to follow him.

An hour later, they'd finished buying fruit, vegetables, two small wedges of artisanal cheese and a few overpriced homemade chocolates.

Darrol had hoped to find kumquats to wave in front of Magnus, but they were out of season. He settled for a few figs.

The long walk home seemed extra tiring, and Darrol declared a break before they tackled Chestnut's uphill slope.

They sat on a scuffed green bench in Washington Square opposite the twin dusty-white towers of Saints Peter and Paul. Tall Lombardy poplars and standing yoga posers mimicked the upthrust of the spires. The park teemed with picnickers, seniors trying tai chi in hyper slow motion, dogs and their owners sniffing each other.

The hot air quivered under the sounds of laughter, shouts, barks, traffic, cable car clangs and twanging from poorly-played guitars.

Maria drank water from a plastic bottle. Darrol stripped the skin from a fig and bit into the fruit. "Just like old times," he said, juice dripping down his chin. "You and me."

She capped the bottle and faced him. "What is it you really want, Darrol? Out of life, I mean."

"Whoa! Big question."

"Then how about a big answer?"

"Well, I want same as you I'd guess." He rubbed a pinky along his teeth to hunt for a fig seed. He found it, slid it onto his tongue, swallowed. "Get ahead in life. Come out on top."

"What does that mean, exactly?"

"It means someday I'll be the boss, the owner, the guy everyone recognizes when he walks into the joint. Any joint." He savaged the rest of the fig.

"You mean the restaurant?"

"No, not necessarily." Darrol wiped his mouth with the back of his hand. "I'm speaking in general. I'll be the one who runs a big chain of businesses, not just a mom and pop store or some stupid ice cream wagons. Or maybe I'll be the artist they all kowtow to in the best galleries. Or maybe I'll find the right gimmick and let the town keep me high on the hog. Like the good old Emperor."

"Why are you so vexated on him?"

Darrol rolled his eyes. "I'm not *fixated* on him, Mimi. I just think he had the smarts, especially for a crazy guy." He put his hand on her thigh. "And you know I'm not crazy, so that puts me way ahead. I've just got to figure it out."

Maria made foot circles in the dirt. "And what about us? How do we fit in?"

He squeezed her knee. "We keep doing what we're doing, baby, and then"—he shrugged, removing his hand—"we see what's what." He looked at the church towers.

"Willy says we..."

Darrol whirled. "I don't wanna hear what fuckin' Willy says, Maria. I'm getting tired of that guy, and maybe it's time you told him to back off."

She struggled to control the tears. "Willy and me—we're just friends, Darrol."

"Yeah, friends with a can of cool whip and a schlong dipped in butterscotch."

"It's not true. I made that up." She tried to take his hands. He pulled away.

"Sure you did." He rummaged in the bag. "I want you to stop this thing, OK?"

"I—"

He found another fig. "Lenz can't report you now anyway, can he? He's in too deep." Darrol guffawed. "Shit, that's a bad choice of words." He peeled the fig and took a bite.

"We're just friends."

"You said that." He looked at his watch. "Damn! My shift starts in a coupla hours. Let's get back, OK?"

"Oh, it's time?" Maria made one last half circle in the dirt. "OK. But you never asked me what I want. Can I at least tell you on the way home?"

Darrol grabbed the shopping bag. "Sure, why not? But let's go."

They left Washington Square and walked along Columbus. Maria was silent for a few moments. Darrol finished his fig, glaring at the inevitable clusters of tourists who got in their way.

"It's pretty simple," Maria finally said.

"What's pretty simple?"

"The things I want. I've thought about it a lot. I've talked to...to myself about it."

They had to stop and wait for a moving van to negotiate a tight corner. Other pedestrians crushed in on them. Maria didn't continue until they'd crossed and the congestion had thinned.

"What I want," she said, "isn't much, just a couple of things. I'd like to become a head baker, maybe someday own a small bakery, make high quality stuff."

"You could do that?"

"I know I could," she said with a rush of enthusiasm. "I really could." She gave Darrol's arm a little poke. "And you know what the other thing is?"

Darrol feigned puzzlement.

"I want a little family," Maria said. "Marriage, one or two kids."

His doubt was not feigned. "And you think you could juggle all of that?"

"With the right guy, the right support." She smiled at him, an invitation. *The right guy.*

Darrol chose to ignore it. "Mimi the juggler?" he mused. "I'm impressed. Got it all worked out, huh?"

"'No," she said quietly, "but I'm certainly thinking about it."

They said little more as they made the slow climb up Chestnut Street.

When they were a few steps from the entrance to the Mischief House apartments, Brick Zimmer came out, yet another pretty woman on one arm, a red shopping bag on the other. He waved the bag at Darrol and Maria and led the woman up the street toward the 'Norton.

Darrol watched them walking away. "That guy has all the luck," he said.

"Really?" Maria said. She hooked an arm into Darrol's. "So what does he have that you don't?" She pointed emphatically at herself and at their shopping bag.

Darrol chose to laugh.

Upstairs, his mood blackened when he saw the tracks in front of their apartment door.

"Goddam cat's been here again. If that idiot Duff's let the thing inside..." He unlocked the door.

Maria could see it was not good news for Darrol's temper. The cat's tracks crossed beyond the threshold.

They found Lyckatill dozing on their sofa.

Darrol, in a state of frozen apoplexy, stopped at the archway and stared. Maria walked into the room. The cat opened an eye, got up, stretched and purred. Maria sat beside it and stroked its back.

"That's how you punish it?" Darrol's lips were barely moving.

"Darrol, she's only a cat. She doesn't know she's broken your rules. She's just sweet little Good Luck." Maria gently patted Lyckatill's head. "Come over here and make friends with her."

"I'll come over there and throttle her," Darrol said, enjoying Maria's immediate cringe. "Just kidding."

He walked to the sofa. Maria looked at him apprehensively and resumed her stroking. Lyckatill slowly blinked her light green eyes and watched Darrol with apparent indifference.

"What do I say? 'Nice kitty?'" Darrol asked. He reached toward the cat. Lyckatill raised her head and licked his hand.

"Christ!" Instead of pulling his hand back, Darrol scooped up the cat. She wriggled boldly, but his arms clenched around her. *So, now what?*

He remembered gripping Her #4's fat tabby before slinging the sly creature the length of the kitchen. He'd nabbed the beast on the counter as she was crunching his cereal. That cat never dared look a Cheerio in the eye again. *Here's another one.*

Maria interrupted his thoughts. "Darrol, what are you doing? Don't hurt her."

"Naw, don't worry. Maybe I'll take her down to the Quists. Yeah, that's a good idea. A personal delivery. Get the door, would you?"

Maria frowned, but she did as he asked.

Darrol carried Lyckatill downstairs. He felt her heart thumping. Her orange splotches looked like dried blood. Not his favorite color.

The door to the Quists' apartment was slightly ajar, and Darrol could hear voices. He stood close to the doorway and listened. Amazingly, Lyckatill had quit struggling and was settled in his arms.

"We are permitted to raise it up to 3%, are we not?" Magnus was in his hissing mode. "Maybe more."

"Yes, but that doesn't mean—"

"We're not running a charity, Alma. They should to be renters not freeloaders." Magnus added something in Swedish. It didn't sound pleasant.

"Can you shut the door, please?"

"I was about to go down to the store."

"Then let's talk about it later."

"If we must." Another Swedish expletive. The door swung open and Magnus strode out.

Only Darrol's quick footwork averted a collision. Magnus pulled the door shut and turned. He scowled.

"*Vad fan vill du ha?*"

"Huh?"

"What do you want, Mr. Yount?" It wasn't clear if the glare was meant for Darrol or for the cat. Or for both.

Darrol thrust Lyckatill forward. "This animal was in my apartment again."

Lyckatill mewled loudly and began squirming. Darrol hung on.

Magnus folded his arms. "It's Mrs. Quist's cat," he said, a saucerful of cream suddenly in his voice. "Be so kind as to deal with her."

Darrol pulled the wriggling cat tight to his chest. "I don't like this thing in my apartment." He sounded like a small, misbehaving boy on the defensive.

Magnus showed teeth. "As I said..." He turned slightly and knocked loudly on the door with his knuckles. "Mistress of the rents, mistress of the cat. She will take care of you."

He knocked again and listened. "Ah...her majesty arrives, *ja?*" He adjusted his teal apron as the door opened.

"Oh my," Alma said. "Are we having a little *ménage à chat?*" She reached out to stroke Lyckatill. The cat purred noisily.

"Mr. Yount found something of yours, Alma," Magnus said.

"She was in my apartment," Darrol relinquished Lyckatill to Alma. He pointedly dusted the front of his shirt.

"Very kind of you to keep her," Alma said, without irony. She smelled of cloves.

"I didn't—"

"But don't expect a rent reduction," Magnus said. "In fact, soon we plan an extra charge for cat visits."

He walked toward the stairs. "But I must get back to the store." He vanished, descending with his usual silence.

Alma pulled Lyckatill close. "How are you doing, Darrol?"

"OK, I guess." *God, that was lame.*

"Have you found your cheerleader yet? To cheer for you, I mean." She stroked the cat.

"It's still myself. Rah-rah, remember?" *Yeah, rah.*

"I do remember."

"Well, I gotta go. Work calls." Darrol drew himself to full height, sans lifts. "Meantime, could you please keep that cat under control?"

"I'll try my best." Her grandmotherly smile was underlain with the best Swedish steel.

As he went upstairs, Darrol thought about Mrs. Durr's notion of perfect putdowns. *Squelches.* He'd missed another opportunity. He wished that a minute ago he'd sent Magnus off with a good one. *"And I bought my figs somewhere else."* That might have been the thing to say to the arrogant bastard.

Or maybe even better: *"I don't give a fig!"*

When he reached the upper landing, he kicked hard at the baseboard. The tiny dent and the ugly brown scuffmark provided little satisfaction.

Four clock faces, four different times. Something needed fixing.

Chapter 24
Points of View

They lay on the kitchen counter awaiting final judgment, three mute prisoners before the bar.

When he'd sketched these pieces, Darrol had been confident in their appeal. But now, only an hour before the last class of the term, he found himself seeing them through the spiteful eyes of his art teacher. Not one of them would withstand Cortez' sneering analysis.

Cortez had told his students to bring two or three quick charcoal sketches to the class for an "immediate reaction test."

"Can you grab the viewer by the eyeballs right off? Show me your masterpieces, *mis pequeños artistas*, and we'll see."

Darrol chewed on a licorice whip and looked at his work.

The first sketch thrust a windmill into an agitated sky, the blades twisted and fantastical, reaching in crazy prayer toward churning clouds.

A few days ago Darrol had admired it. Now he squirmed, guessing at best Cortez might declare it "mad Van Gogh gone ever madder."

In the second image, a sinewy female figure leaped about in a fountain, water flying everywhere.

The other day, Darrol thought he'd drawn freedom, abandon, lightness. It didn't look that way to him now.

"Madre de Dios!" He could hear Cortez using a favorite expression and commenting about "ascending cow patties" or "a scarecrow caught masturbating."

Darrol laughed grimly. The actual critique wouldn't be that tame.

And there was this: a ghostlike Emperor Norton sitting nonchalantly astride his tombstone, a sabre dangling from one hand, a beggar's cup held out in the other. A few clever strokes in the background suggested vegetation-cum-buildings bent in obeisance.

Cortez surely would demolish it. "What is that, Mr. Yount? Uncle Sam selling soup bowls? And so many gratuitous curlicues! *Madre de Dios!*"

Darrol grimaced again. The sketches weren't that bad. Until you put them into the grinder.

He tore off a last piece of licorice and stared out the kitchen window. Lately, nothing had been going his way. This was his one evening off. Did he really want to start it with Mr. Gauchopants tormenting him? Spend a long hour and a half with visions of Cortez and Karin going at it every time he looked at the teacher?

When he was a kid, he'd played hooky. More than once. So it was tempting. And if he skipped class tonight there'd be no truant officer sniffing around. Except maybe the one in his mind, the one telling him to get going, even all those scores, move on, move up.

He watched lithe strands of fog spiraling down the street. Weird, as the late afternoon sun was still washing most of the roadway with brightness. He liked what that summer combination—crazy fog and astonished sun—did to his town.

And now it reminded him of one of the best viewing points anywhere. *Why not?* It'd be a good place to go to think and figure important stuff out.

He put his sketches carefully in his art drawer. They'd keep for a more honest audience. *Cortez be damned.*

He found a can of Bud and drank it as he made a large ham, gouda and tomato sandwich with plenty of mayo, assembling it on *La Dolce Via's* Pugliese bread. The loaf was big and friendly. It looked like it had come right from some busty Italian *mama mia,* which in a way it had. Maria hadn't stolen this biggie. She'd bought it for them, using her discount.

Maria. As he chewed on the sandwich, he chewed on another idea. He could stay home, surprise her. They could splurge on mussels and fries down at that Belgian place. Come home, watch TV, fool around. A nice surprise. He chewed some more.

Then again, the surprise could be on him if Maria didn't show up, if she was off playing cherry strudel a la pussy with

Willy Lenz. He chewed more vigorously, thinking about that. The image quickly ceased to be arousing. *Shit.*

He tossed the unfinished sandwich into the garbage. He'd go out. Screw the surprises, either way. Maria wouldn't know he was cutting class. He wouldn't know if she didn't come home when she was supposed to.

He dug his heavier jacket from the closet, went out to once again play hooky. And to think.

After a short walk and a not-short-enough ride on a crowded Muni bus—as much sweat and garlic as he could stand for one night—Darrol stepped out along the fog-strewn pedestrian approach to the Golden Gate Bridge.

It was cold, even in the remaining sunny patches. He put on his watch cap and pulled his jacket tighter, glad he'd thought to bring it. But he was pleased that the chill and the fog had substantially trimmed the number of tourists. It also helped that it was now well into the dinner hour. Tourists loved to eat. If not to tip properly.

The breeze burned his cheeks and wrapped him in the smells of the ocean and fumes of the busy bridge traffic. Emission laws only work so far, he thought. You can't fool the nose.

The foghorn was already asserting its boomy dominance over the low, constant conversation between tires and roadway. Gulls, screeching, sneaked in and out of the sunhollows. Darrol understood their annoyance. They wanted this place to themselves. As he did.

It was all a meteorological glitch, an anomaly of nature and geography. Here it was, the last few hours of a hot, luminous late-August day, and fog, of all things, was threatening to steal the show from the sunset.

He crossed above Fort Point and reached the place where the bridge began its suspension over the water.

Despite the traffic noises, he heard waves churning on the rocks below. He stopped, peered down and saw yellow-green foam curling high, tonguing the air.

He thought again of the slimy green bathtub where Him #2 liked to hold him under then tickle his little boycock before pulling him up, sputtering, confused.

"All in play, kid, all in play." Him #2 had knuckles crawling with black hair and breath like a mustard jar.

A sudden wrackstink of seaweed rose from below. Darrol wrinkled his face. He'd read that the smelly algae were invasive and getting out of control. Like memories.

He resumed walking, scowling at the ugliness of the temporary chain link fence they'd put along the railing. The fence had something to do with the ridiculous suicide barrier they were slowly installing below. After four years of construction and hundreds of millions of dollars, what would they have? Two long sets of gray steel wings to lift the bridge up in a storm, fly it to Kansas, Dorothy.

In the meantime, if you really wanted to jump, a quick scramble would still do the trick. When he was younger, Darrol had climbed many a chain link fence. You went up fast, especially if angry homeowners—or your own demons— were chasing you. Up, up and over.

The thought of jumping from this considerable height made his knees tingle, quiver with unbidden electricity. Not for the first time, he wondered if he was following in the very steps of August Lanterman.

As if to see Lanterman's footprints, he looked down at the sidewalk. A gust of wind tried to nudge him into the fence. He resisted. Startled fog leapt over the edge. There was no splash.

As Darrol continued toward the midpoint of the bridge, he encountered more people than he'd expected, considering the hour and the weather. Some, their heads down, walked along intent on thumbing their electronics, views be damned. Some ambled, arm-in-arm, lost in blissful coupleness. Some stood at the railing, watching the competing atmospherics turn the partial cityscape into a battlefield of light and mystery.

All ignored him. Which was just fine with Darrol. He was contending with his ever-growing list of grievances, disappointments and setbacks. His irritations were scrolling through his mind, over and over, sometimes in clarity, sometimes shrouded in confusion, a perfect parallel to the environment around him.

Near the midpoint, he found a quiet stretch of railing, oddly free of chain link fencing. And free of people. He claimed the space.

At first he ignored the water. He turned his back to the bay and stretched his arms along the rail to each side as though he were ready for crucifixion. He looked at the two red-gold towers. The supports closest to the deck were visible, but topiary fog creatures, ever changing, gnawed at the tower midsections, at times making entire segments disappear.

Far above it all, ignoring the billowy tumult, the twin tops rose incredibly high, bright and elegant, awaiting the first rays of sunset.

Darrol unkinked his neck and looked at the deck. As vehicles rushed by, the low road edge lights blinked an amber code at him. The message was undecipherable.

Fog fronds floated downwards, parting delicately for the hurrying cars and trucks, or being flung upwards, accident victims in spectral slow motion. Darrol smelled brine and asphalt and paint. A burst of cold wind swept those away. He thought he tasted blood.

He turned to face the bay. He was not afraid of heights, but sometimes he was more than a little scared of what he might do with them. Gripping the rail and fighting off more little zips of electricity in his knees, he leaned out and looked down through leapfrogging strands of fog.

The water was a surly gray, swelling spasmodically, whitecapping more Morse code. Dits and dots and dashes meant nothing to Darrol except for the SOS some guy had taught him years ago, tapping it out painfully around the birthmark on Darrol's thigh. *Dot dot dot, dash dash dash, dot dot dot.*

The present watery message, Darrol supposed, could be *save the planet.* But at the moment the planet was not his concern. He ignored the whitecaps and looked towards the city. *His city.*

Much of San Francisco was hidden. The eccentric summer fog was winning. *And maybe cheating.* The fog didn't actually need to wrap the whole town. It had cleverly interposed itself between the bridge and the shore. A few clumps and tufts and billows fifty feet out from the bridge effectively hid everything beyond. He tried to think of a way a little trick like that could be applied to his own life, to his current problems. Nothing came to him.

Behind him the traffic murmured and muttered. Every few moments, the foghorn shredded the air with menace.

Jon Gulliver had imagined that August Lanterman heard his own heart beating out here. Maybe the asshole writer was on the money, because this dull, steady wallop sure as hell sounded like Darrol's heart. Still holding on, he pushed close against the rail, trying to slow the beat, trying to defog his thoughts.

He watched the darkening water, this time assigning each white surge a grievance and thinking how it could best disappear—he watched it heave, bob, flash, vanish—but there was always a resurfacing—heave, bob, flash again—and soon there was no satisfaction in this little game.

The hard, coarse chill of the railing iced his hands. He wished he had gloves. He hung on, afraid to let go. A gelid mist hovered, trying to suffocate him. He breathed in harder and scoured his lungs with dampness.

In the distance, the fog and low clouds had become tinged with bands of fire. Darrol glanced sideways. A mellowing glow was trying to push through the thick eddies of mists. Sunset was arriving to join the game. Too little, too late. At least on the bridge.

Here, the fog seemed determined to linger until darkness seeped in from wherever darkness lurks all day. The pedestrian walkway, still without its lights, was fast becoming an alley of gloom, a tunnel of shadows. Darrol remembered reading about foggy 19th century London, about Jack the Ripper ready to pounce. He laughed under his breath, but he felt strangely uneasy.

And then he saw Emperor Norton shuffling toward him from the north.

The bulky figure edged through the murk, the sword held out as though Norton was commanding the dusky soup to part. Clinking medals flashed on the broad chest. The high plumed hat bobbed slightly, a slow march tempo. The face, partly obscured, was a pallid oval with a hint of deep-set eyes.

Darrol stopped breathing, stopped moving. His mouth hung open.

His initial feelings of dread and confusion gave way to an odd sort of delirious joy. He wondered if he should stick out his hand or bow. Whether he should speak or be silent. Instinctively, he removed his watch cap. An inner voice clucked that Norton was not a real emperor, so thoughts of obeisance were silly. But the sense of elation and awe refused to diminish.

That made the disappointment all the more profound.

As Emperor Norton came closer, he transformed into an exhausted, overloaded hiker, a thick blue woolen hat bounding on his head, a plastic yellow flower clinging to its sagging tip, an array of travel buttons on his black vest, the clinking coming from metal oddments dangling below his backpack, the 'sword' a sturdy walking stick.

Darrol closed his mouth. He growled something between a deflated "oof!" and a depressed groan. Unheeded, his watch cap dropped to the deck.

The stranger nodded tiredly and shambled away. He coughed once—*Open sesame!*—the mists eddied, and he vanished into the high, dark hedge.

Darrol stared slackjawed at the mute tumble of fog. His heart swung a leaden mallet against his chest, his pulse stuttered. He tried to push the faux emperor out of his mind.

Trembling, he stumbled back to the railing. His hand reached out blindly and grasped the wet iron.

Something roared and pounded in his head. Blood. The accumulation of letdowns and failures. The grim waters waiting below.

He pulled himself closer to the edge. Looked down. Clutched the railing like a gymnast about to vault over a pommel horse.

He took two short breaths. Hesitated. Took two more breaths.

His shivering became violent. He closed his eyes. The foghorn let loose a long, derisive beseeching.

Yessss.

Darrol flinched. His eyes opened. He untensed and looked quickly away from the void. With a sad, self-deprecating snort, he forced himself to turn toward the mist-hidden city.

At that moment, like a jet plane in urgent, steep ascent, the closest snarls of fog flew upwards.

A ghostly, faintly-glistening San Francisco, in the caress of a rosegold sunset, appeared behind a thin gauze of clouds.

Almost instantly, to the bidding of an unseen stage manager, this scrim parted completely.

Darrol gazed on the full, splendid, majestic glory of his city.

His city.

He felt his hair stand on end.

He might not know Morse code, but he understood this message. This message sent directly to him.

He had the power.

His pulse began to settle, his breathing slowed. His knees stopped quivering, he relaxed his grip. Slowly, beneficently, he smiled at the glittering panorama.

With night hovering in the wings, he remained at the rail for some time, thinking, planning.

He imagined the real Emperor Norton standing by his side.

Crazy or sane, they both could hold this city in thrall. Adversaries and adversity could be overcome. Snails could be stepped on.

Renewed, Darrol turned to walk back off the bridge. The departing sun caught a glass tower high on Russian Hill and gave him a knowing golden wink.

Yes, he had the power.

Chapter 25
In the Beginning was the Card

Darrol thought of it as warming up. A smaller payback exercise to flex his imagination, stroke his satisfaction and give himself a bonus: the pleasure of making Duff Lee squirm.

"I can't do this, man." Duff, dull in his Muni browns, dull in his demeanor, was preparing some kind of health food crap to take to work. The scattered alfalfa sprouts looked like they had already taken root on the kitchen counter.

"Can't or won't?" Darrol made it sound like he was a counselor guiding a patient toward the right answer. When you got them, you toy with them. He bounced lightly about on his feet, like a boxer in training.

Duff tried to fold plastic wrap around his little plate but only dislodged more sprouts. "I'll get in trouble." He crammed his food into a brown paper bag.

"No you won't. Chinese tourists are stupid—forgive me if they're your ancestors or something—and you'll be long gone before the message sinks in." Darrol put an arm around Duff's shoulder. "It's sort of quid pro bono here, Duffo. You do what I want, and I continue to keep quiet about, well, everything."

Duff cringed loose. "I gotta get to work. No time."

"Not a problem. You write out the cards in the next coupla days, and we'll give 'em to the Mongolians Friday morning. It's your day off, right?"

"My martial arts day."

"Aw, you'll be just a little late to get to your Martians, Duff." Darrol's tone hardened. "What do you guys do at that gym anyway?"

A sudden shift in Duff's eyes told Darrol he'd accidently struck more pay dirt. "Well, well. Don't we love those locker rooms and showers? So we'll keep it all between us, OK? Just like your other little pecker-dilloes."

289

By Friday morning, Duff had the first part of his assignment ready. Reluctantly, he handed Darrol several dozen small blue cards.

On one side, written mostly in Chinese, was a meaningless discount offer. If *Su-Chang's Superior Gifts* really existed, Darrol thought, maybe they'd get some extra business. But that wasn't too likely, considering what was on the flip side.

That held a printed message, also in Chinese, advising the reader in extremely impolite terms to get back on the bus and scoot out of town. There was an extra suggestion, even more impolite, about a new place to put chopsticks.

"I'm trusting you here," Darrol said, shuffling the cards. They made a pleasant little whirr. "If you diddled me with a different wording, the hammer will fall. And hard." He gave the cards back to Duff.

"These are what you wrote." Duff hung his head. "I am ashamed, but they are correct."

"Oh, get a grip, Duff," Darrol said. "It's all in good fun." He put on a cheap navy windbreaker and slipped his sunglasses into a pocket. "OK, let's head out. The first busses will roll in pretty soon."

They walked down to Columbus in silence and crossed to where the tour busses usually pulled up. Darrol led Duff to a spot well back from the curb and near the window of a still-closed souvenir shop.

Darrol sniffed the air appreciatively. "Breakfast. Mornings around here always smell like breakfast. It's like bacon and waffles in stereo. We're right between that little café round the corner and the one over there." He sniffed again. "Hash browns. Coffee. God, I'm getting hungry." He grinned. "But I bet you're a Rice-A-Roni kinda guy. You're missing out, Duff."

Duff studied the cracks in the sidewalk. His hands were in the pockets of his old brown sweats. He said nothing.

"You know what to do, right?" Darrol saw Duff's faint nod but went on anyway. "Give them a few secs to get off the bus. They'll mill around in confusion like they always do. You wander through, a fellow Chinaman. Say hello in Chinese, hand the cards out, move on. They won't even see where you went."

For the first time, Duff looked up. "Where will you be?"

"Don't worry about me. I'll be here and there, watching the reactions. As long as I don't laugh too loud, no one'll even notice me. I'll be a cypher, a ghost." Darrol looked at his watch. "Ooh, getting close." He did his little boxer's dance. "Hey, howzat go again, the Chinese hello? *Know-how? Kowtow?*"

Duff frowned and muttered something.

Darrol grinned. "Yeah, *knee-how*. But you gotta be lots louder." He faked a couple of jabs.

Duff managed not to flinch. But he tensed and looked up the street.

Darrol turned. Three large tour busses were coming toward them. Toward ground zero.

Duff stood nervously in place. Darrol put on his sunglasses, jauntied a navy baseball cap onto his head, sauntered a few feet away.

There was a series of clunks as someone unlocked the doors to the souvenir shop. Further along the sidewalk, a young Amerasian woman appeared from another shop and set out a sandwich board advertising things in Chinese and English. Tourist choreography, Darrol thought. Like Chinese cuckoo clocks, popping out to mark the hour.

Cuckoo. Knee how.

Brakes hissing, the busses eased in tight formation along the No Parking curb and stopped.

Higher-pitched hisses, sleepy doors opening, youthful Chinese-American guides leaping down, a noisy disgorgement of Asian tourists, some smiling, some looking bewildered, many immediately raising cameras and smart phones. To shoot what, who knew?

Darrol moved near the curb, downstream of the action.

The guides, yelling instructions, spread everyone out as they waited for the stragglers.

Duff had summoned courage from somewhere. He pushed off from the building and began to thread quickly through the tourists, his fixed smile as ghastly as the grin of a New Year's dragon. Nodding politely and murmuring, he passed out the cards, giving the guides a wide berth. Everyone accepted his offering. As Darrol had guessed, no one at first really read the cards, giving them only the briefest of glances.

Duff was gone before the ripple of reactions began.

Darrol, the invisible Caucasian among the throng, saw puzzlement, frowns, scowls, confusion, disgust, shock, even fear. One or two dropped the cards on the sidewalk. Several waved theirs in the faces of the startled guides, obviously clamoring for explanations, for direction. One elderly man opened his eyes so wide he almost forced the glasses from his head.

No one laughed. Except Darrol, and he kept that laughter inward as he crammed as many images as possible into his memory.

He had a street map opened as though he were another tourist, but his eyes were beyond the map, taking in the aftermath of his nasty little prank. *Prank.* That's all it was, really, not serious payback. But the exercise was rewarding.

And more intense paybacks would soon follow.

No one got back on a bus. Most of the cards went into trash containers, though a few, Darrol was interested to note, went into pockets.

The guides finally regained control. Two led their charges into the welcoming arms of the gift shops. Others took the remaining Chinese up Lombard, heading, Darrol knew, to the foot of the block where the crooked section of the street corkscrewed from above. There they would stand and gawk and shoot hundreds of photos as other idiot tourists gingerly zigzagged their vehicles down the red brick roadway.

This slope was hardly the Great Wall of China, Darrol thought, but for the gullible—which seemed to be most of these people—the hype made a mere curiosity rival a wonder with thousands of years of history.

Darrol walked back to Mischief House whistling. He'd enjoyed this fine, if tiny, stab at some of his perennial irritants.

He thought about his plans for that crooked street and for the long processions of tourist clowns who drove down it.

Someday, when he could find the money and work out the details—including how to remain unobserved—he would lay out some neat little camouflaged tire-spikes on the curves.

How many tires would shred before anyone figured out what was wrong? He imagined a fine little traffic jam and a tricky task for tow truck drivers trying to go in reverse up the switchbacks to haul down the unlucky cars. And, he chuckled, there might be people trying to put jacks under their axles as their teetering vehicles—and, for that matter, their replacement tires—threatened to plunge down the hill.

All great fun to watch.

Darrol arrived at Mischief House in a really good mood. He went into the 'Norton, bought a licorice stick, jabbed it playfully at The Emperor, sailed out, whistling.

He bounded upstairs, two steps at a time, still relishing the big scowl he'd earned from Magnus, who pretty clearly wanted to clobber him with the flyswatter.

All in all, a good morning. And tonight, after work...

The anticipation made Darrol whistle even louder.

Chapter 26
Under Glass

That evening, had there been judges at Lanterman's holding up scorecards for the Great Waiter Olympics, Darrol would have scored nothing but perfect 10's.

He buried his resentments, frustrations and dislikes and became the flawless professional. He was charming, graceful, thoughtful. He was fast when required, measured the rest of the time. He was witty when appropriate, remained silently engaged when necessary. There was an almost-continental flair to his service. If he'd spoken with a French or German accent, diners wouldn't have been the least surprised.

The staff eyed him with everything from wonderment to suspicion. Radisson Vero, sashaying about in fine brilliantined splendor, tried hard to find fault, but couldn't. Spike Duggan, despite having secured the senior position, still made little attempts to goad, but failed. Emilio and the other harried chefs managed to spoon out smiles as Darrol negotiated each order with tact, persistence and praise. Tekla all but flirted, Carey tossed him admiring looks—was that flirting too?—and Xavier, absorbing the positive energy, bussed with high efficiency and a disarming smile.

Many of them would have lost all bladder control if they'd known Darrol had a 9mm pistol hidden in his overcoat. One hint of that weapon's presence would have had them assuming the worst and calculating the nearest escape routes.

But Darrol wasn't mindlessly punitive. Nor was he going to shoot anyone or anything in the restaurant. He always shook his head when he heard of employee rampages. Why walk in, bang away and wait for the cops to end it all? At best, surely, you got a semi-erection and few cut-rate thrills before needless oblivion.

If you were subtle, clever, you could pay back grudges in so many other, more satisfying ways. And you could live to move on.

In any case, Cosmo's pistol was reserved for something far more interesting than *carnage a la café*. One shot later tonight would send the luscious Karin Holt back to the drawing board, perhaps literally, and give Darrol an immense amount of pleasure.

In the meantime, table fourteen, smitten with excellent service, was ripe for a little upselling, maybe in the line of an extravagant dessert, expensive liqueurs, fine cheeses. With a fatter tip to follow.

T he North Beach blocks of Grant Avenue—in contrast to the blocks in Chinatown—were mercifully free of tourist throngs. And it was much quieter here at this time of night.

A little after 10 p.m., Darrol, dressed in his respectable black overcoat and a wide-brimmed black fedora he'd bought at a thrift store, strolled over from Lanterman's, for the hundredth time thinking through the possible challenges, the chances of being seen, and how to linger long enough to fully take in his handiwork at the moment of execution.

He liked that word. *Execution.*

The night before, he'd also detoured to Grant Avenue after work and had performed some careful reconnaissance.

Elan was a smaller, snootier art gallery, obviously proud of its simple but elegant storefront, daring only the cognoscenti and the richer patrons to come in. It was not for most tourists.

The lone display window, framed in dark, ornate-molding—as might be found, Darrol guessed, at a gallery in an older European city—held only one object. Well-lit, sitting on a high, subdued pedestal set quite close to the glass, there was Karin Holt's *Spring Waiting*, as beautiful as he remembered it.

No one had questioned Darrol's standing in front of the window, apparently looking at such an alluring sculpture.

But last night, the ceramic wasn't his main interest. He'd been trying to ascertain the thickness of the pane (sturdy and probably safety glass, but not unduly thick), whether it held strands of alarm wire (it didn't seem to) and whether there were gallery security cameras aimed at the window (none were in evidence). Nor could he see any CCTV cameras covering this part of the block.

He'd been pleased to learn that *Elan* and its immediate neighbors—both small, upscale boutiques—closed at 6 p.m. That was true of most other businesses in this half-block, two of them also art galleries. The nearest bar was several hundred feet away, across the street, and it was a connoisseur's establishment, not a Bud Lite joint. It was unlikely there'd be groups of rowdies joking on the sidewalk in front.

So, the moment of truth.

Tonight he focused totally on the porcelain sculpture. He liked the innocent face, the calm eyes, the complex hint of a smile—"it outdoes the *Mona Lisa*," he'd heard someone say at the opening—and he was captivated by the intricate flowers, birds and butterflies in the hair. The pastel colors were restful but engaging. The complicated shapes and textures were intriguing. It added up to mystery and beauty.

Too bad. Too bad.

But his regrets diminished when he thought of Karin and her smiles of rejection. No *Mona Lisa* ambiguity there, her message all very clear.

He smelled pizza and a hint of marijuana. Was someone hanging out in a doorway? Well, let them as long as they stayed away.

He checked in both directions. The nearest sections of sidewalk were clear of pedestrians. The haphazard street lighting created broad patches of light and dark. He tried to remember a word Cortez had taught them. *Chiaroscuro.* That was it. High tonal contrasts. Lovely in art. Good for creatures of the night. *Chiaroscuro.*

His smile vanished. Just that briefest thought of Cortez gave him additional angry resolve. He pulled down the brim of the fedora and reached into his pocket.

Even though he'd only fired it once—*goddam parrots*—the gun felt pleasantly familiar. Keeping it close to the shadowed folds of his coat, he stepped slightly away from the window, stopping at the point he'd calculated was best for penetration without deflection, but also a point where he'd least likely to be nicked by flying glass.

He stood still as a car passed, the radio obscenely thumping. A faint twang of country music seeped down the street. Darrol's stomach rumbled from hurried bites of veal piccata and morel risotto. His pulse stratosphered.

He raised the pistol. Took a breath. Aimed.

The sculpture stared benignly into his eyes. A strange twinge of sadness hit him. Hit him hard. He paused and assessed this. Not doubt. Just sadness.

Get on with it.

He took another deep breath. Aimed again.

Fired.

His mind, completely in the zone, took in and later remembered a multiplicity of images, most in slow motion.

The bullet punched a small hole through the window. The pane hung there in astonishment, its new mouth agape.

Spring Waiting, hit between the eyes, flew apart, seemingly bit by bit, with fragments of pastel beauty, glinting in the gallery lights, rising and scattering like fireflies. Flowers and vines twirled into nothingness. Tiny bees and birds hovered, disappeared. Two butterflies rose, collided, dropped delicately out of view.

And slowly the window wept. Silvery veins spread from the bullet wound in grief and shock, faster and faster until inner layers of the safety glass began fracture and to slide, and slide, a glacier calving, leaving a broad gauze of glass hanging in shame and confusion.

To Darrol's ears, the gun had made only an apologetic little hiss, the window puncture a high calliope sigh. The internal collapse of the glass was no louder than teardrops falling into milk. Behind the pane, the sculpture itself died in silent grace.

Now Darrol wondered if he were hearing an alarm—he wasn't sure, for his mind was in awe—but good sense sent him moving steadily away.

He turned round the nearest corner, quickly walked another block, turned another corner. Removing the hat and overcoat, he slowed his pace. He noticed a lounge a few doors down, went in, sat at the bar, ordered a nightcap. Somehow peppermint schnapps seemed just right to accompany the amazing sense of triumph, the lingering images of retribution. If only it could have been filmed. Or recreated in a masterful sketch.

Some day.

Later, still glowing from his adventure and from two drinks, Darrol entered Mischief House and stopped in the vestibule. He looked thoughtfully at the back door to the 'Norton.

Perhaps it was a trick of light reflecting from a wall sconce, but the keypad seemed to have a beckoning gleam. He walked to it and stood, his hand poised—just a little unsteadily, he noticed—over the numbers. He wiggled his fingers.

What did he want inside? Were there more useful things to learn? Was there anything meaningful he could remove? What subtle havoc could he manage? *Subtle havoc.* He liked that crazy phrase.

He glanced at his watch. It was only 11:46. Magnus still could be in there, lurking in his spider web. *Not quite yet.*

Darrol walked upstairs. His tongue slid around the faint taste of peppermint.

Maria had not waited up. That habit had begun to slip away, and he'd let it. He went into the bedroom. Her silly little purple octopus nightlight was on, enough to let him see that Maria was sleeping.

But as he put the gun in his metal box, he heard her stir. He closed the sweater drawer and turned. Maria was propping herself on one elbow.

"Late, huh?" She blinked and tried to put on a smile.

"Had to unwind. Stopped for a drink. One shot was all I needed." *The truth shall set you free.*

She switched on her bedside lamp. "I brought you a surprise. A nice thick slice of *frustegna*. The cake with the figs."

"Oh yeah?" He removed his jacket and tossed it on a chair. "Guilty about something?"

"Only about neglecting your treats."

"Yeah, well." He sat on the bed and took off his shoes. "So what's your latest bit of hot and heavy with Lenzy-Blintzy?" He flipped a shoe and caught it. "Rolling in raisins?"

"Darrol, I told you I was kidding about that. But in any case, it's not for your personal gratisfaction."

"You mean gratification? Or you mean satisfaction?"

"That's what I said. But either. Both. No more."

He pistolled his fingers and took aim at the cherub figurine on Maria's dresser. "Think I could learn to shoot?"

"Why would you do that? Maria sounded alarmed.

"Oh, I dunno." He popped his lips loudly as he mimed firing. "Might come in handy now and then."

He grabbed her leg through the coverlet. "Hey, wanta fool around?"

"Not really." She pulled her leg free. "I want to get to sleep."

"Well then," Darrol said. "Maybe I'll have to get my gratisfaction elsewhere."

"What?"

"Little joke." He went to the closet, found his sneakers, sat on the bed and put them on. "I'm thinking of going downstairs for a bit of air, that's all."

"OK." Her eyes fluttered.

Darrol stood. "9-1-7-4-6."

Maria switched off her lamp and sank back on the pillow. "What's that mean?"

He moved to the door. "Oh, they're numbers I thought I'd try on a lottery ticket. Sound about right? 9-1-7-4-6? I figure I'm due to come up a winner."

"Mm. Good luck then." Her voice was lined with fuzz. "'night, Darrol."

"'night, Mimi." He quietly closed the door.

Chapter 27
Real News, Fake News

"Well, that's a bit of excitement, isn't it?" Mrs. Durr stood at the Nook's service corner, pouring her morning coffee.

"Pretty big fire!" Olga Grekhov seemed enlivened by someone else's misfortune.

"Olga exaggerates," Ilia Grekhov said, looking at his wife. "A Russian trait, you understand, exaggeration. It stems from the vastness of our country. Our huge geography exaggerates itself. We merely follow."

"My husband, the profound thinker," Olga said, fondness competing with a touch of scorn.

Even at this early hour, the Nook was already half full. Lukas Knudsen was at another table, talking to a sleepy-eyed young woman. Two unfamiliar customers were on the counter stools.

Mrs. Durr joined the Grekhovs. "I don't pay much attention to the news these days," she said. "At my age, most of it seems irrelevant."

"Yes, but Trader Joes is almost part of the neighborhood." Olga bit daintily into her muffin.

"Another slight exaggeration," Ilia said. "But regardless, it wasn't a significant fire, it's out, and the place will be business as usual by tomorrow."

"Are you talking about the fire at Trader Joe's?" Alma Quist walked in, carrying a plate of muffins.

"Apparently a conflagration worthy of Nero." Mrs. Durr smiled at Olga.

"Well, yes," Alma said. "I'm sure Nero was down there fiddling away." She put the plate on the counter. "Have any of you seen my cat?"

There was a small chorus of no's.

"I'm a little concerned. She's not supposed to be in the store, of course, but I can't find her upstairs."

"Perhaps she sneaked into one of the apartments?" Mrs. Durr asked.

"Maybe. But most of you are quick to chase her out. Well, I'll keep looking." Alma hurried away.

At the checkout counters, there was more consternation, but it wasn't about the fire. Or the cat.

Shortly after opening, Magnus had noticed that the Emperor Norton currency wasn't on the wall. No one on the morning staff remembered when they last saw it.

When he wasn't helping customers, Magnus peered under counters, hunted behind cabinets, checked wall shelves.

Hilda Brown, close to tears as though she were a suspect, searched in drawers and cubbyholes. She was on her knees peering behind a health bar display when Alma came to the front.

"Surely you won't find the cat there, Hilda," she said gently.

Red-faced, Hilda stood. Her knees creaked. "I look for the Norton money, Mrs. Quist."

Magnus gestured dramatically at the empty space on the wall.

Alma put her hands on her hips and gave a tsk-tsk. "First the cat, now this."

Magnus straightened his glasses. "Do we have gremlins on the premises, Mrs. Quist?"

The bell jangled. Darrol, yawning, came into the store. "'morning," he said.

He started his usual salute for Hilda, saw Alma's frown, kept his hand moving and brushed his hair back. "Wow, I just heard there was a fire at Trader Joe's."

"Did you indeed?" Magnus gave him an ironic smile.

"More customers for you, huh?" Darrol went towards the candy shelves. "Bring 'em on."

"Darrol—" Alma stopped herself and softened her tone. "Darrol, have you seen Lyckatill this morning?"

"Nope. Can't say I have." He selected two pieces of licorice twist and took them to Magnus.

"Mrs. Quist's cat appears to have vanished," Magnus said, "perhaps even running away with our prized Norton currency, *ja?*" He nodded at the blank space on the wall.

"Wow. The Emperor's money? Some customer swiped it, huh?" Darrol put two dollars on the counter.

Magnus turned to Alma. "Who was on checkout duty last night?"

"Jazz Turner. I assume he'd have noticed if it was gone."

"Maybe not," Magnus said. "That young man has a habit of practicing his drumming whenever he can. Perhaps he was thumping on the ice cream cooler and had his back turned." He handed Darrol his change and slammed the drawer shut.

Alma went back to Hilda. "Let's keep looking for Lyckatill. You try the shipping area and I'll re-check the hallways." They walked away.

"Worth a lot, was it?" Darrol took a first tug at the licorice. "Norton's money?"

Magnus gave a coy shrug. "Yes and no."

"What does 'yes and no' mean?"

"The Emperor put a face value of ten dollars on that note." Magnus began ringing up an elderly man's purchases. "The cash value, of course, was nothing. However, the collector's value today might be several thousand dollars. But—"

He cut Darrol off. "But, the truth is, what our *klibbig-finger* thief got was worth, oh, one dollar for the frame."

"Whadya mean?" The licorice stopped short of Darrol's mouth.

"Eight seventy, sir," Magnus told his customer before turning back to Darrol. "You see, *min vän*, I take precautions. After that attempted robbery a few years ago, I removed the original note and put up a copy. Good thing, yes?"

"A copy?"

"Your change, sir, thank you." Magnus watched the old man walk to the door. "Yes, a copy, a fake. Yellowed a bit, my little touch."

Darrol cleared his throat. "A fake?"

"Happily, yes."

Magnus grabbed his flyswatter, smacked it hard on a ledge, nodded with satisfaction. "But it is nonetheless serious that someone would take it."

Darrol's licorice was hanging by his side. "That sabre, the sword, whatever it is, is that fake too?"

"Yes and no." Magnus ran his hand gently along the sheath. "Oh, this contains a very real sword. And quite sharp indeed. I keep it so. But it's always been merely a replica, alas. In any case, it is now harder to steal, yes? After our last earthquake, I put small devices here...and right here...and here...that you have to release or it will not easily to come off the wall."

Magnus walked back to the register and restacked the shopping baskets. Darrol, absently chewing another piece of licorice, looked thoughtfully at the sword.

The bell jangled. The Green girls giggled into the store.

"How doth my little crocodiles?" Magnus said. "You girls are very early."

"A picnic," Pug told him earnestly.

"Mom said to ask if you have pumpernickel." Pig said.

"*Ja.* We have that very thing. I will show you where."

Pig shook her head. "We'll find it." She grabbed her sister's arm. "C'mon, Pug. Get a basket."

Pug let Magnus hand her a basket, and the girls sped up an aisle.

"A tisket, a tasket," Magnus called after them.

He turned back to Darrol, who was staring out the window. "Was there anything else, Mr. Yount?"

"What? No. I was just..."

The door opened and Della Rossiter and Karin Holt came in.

Darrol stepped closer to the counter. Karin gave him a tired nod. He hid his surprise and mustered a decent smile.

"Magnus, have you heard?" Della's husky voice was very loud.

"The fire at Joe the Trader's?"

"No, not that." Della said. "It's awful. Miss Holt here tells me her prize sculpture was blown to smithereens last night."

"Smithereens?" Magnus tweaked his glasses. "I don't know the word—"

"Pieces, Magnus," Della said, her eyes wide. "Blown to pieces. Someone shot her sculpture in a gallery window."

"*Väldigt ledsen.* I'm very sorry, Miss Holt."

"My gosh," Darrol said. "I hope it wasn't that piece you did of the woman's head?" *Right between the eyes.*

Karin turned to him. "I'm afraid it was. Months and months of work shattered."

"Who would do such a thing?" Della said.

"Don't know," Karin said. "Some jerk with a gun and a sudden impulse to use it. At least he didn't shoot a human being."

"World's full of crazies," Darrol said.

"That's for sure," Della sighed.

"I saw Karin's sculpture at the Art Institute," Darrol told them, his voice full of respectful authority. "Ceramic. Quite wonderful. The head of a woman with flowers and butterflies in her hair. Really lovely. Amazing execution."

"Well, I'll start again," Karin said wearily. "And now, Mr. Quist, I need to distract myself with your best wine and cheese and chocolate. I kept my roommates up all night, so I'm going to treat them to one helluva picnic."

Karin collected a shopping basket from the stack. "Nice to see you, Darrol."

"You too," he said, keeping his voice appropriately somber. *Right between the eyes.*

Della took Karin's arm. "I've got to get to work," Della said. "I'll walk you as far as the wines."

Alma and Hilda returned. "This is not good," Alma told Magnus. "We can't find Lyckatill anywhere."

"Very likely she curls in a shoe box, Mrs. Quist. Your closet provides abundant opportunities."

"She's not in the apartment. I searched everywhere. And Hilda scoured the store, didn't you?"

"Yes." Hilda reopened her register. She smiled to the Green girls as Pig plunked a basket in front of her. "Let's see what you have, girls."

"Maybe it's like the nursery rhyme," said Darrol, "the cat ran away with the spoon. Or with the Emperor's ten dollars."

Alma pursed her lips. "Darrol, that's not helpful." She looked at the girls. "We seem to have lost our cat."

Pug turned the knob on the gumball machine. "We saw a very pretty cat, didn't we, Pig?" A red gumball tumbled into her hand. "Outside."

"Yes," Pig nodded. "On the sidewalk. Out there." She pointed at the front window. "A splotchy kind of cat."

"Lord, it's got to be Lyckatill!" Alma said. "She must be scared to death. Hilda, you manage here. Magnus, we need to circle the block. I'll go down, you go up."

Slowly shaking his head, Magnus removed his apron. "The entire block?"

"If necessary. And all the doorways." Alma started to leave. "Darrol, if you'd care to help for real, you could go out the back of the store and check the alley."

Mischief Lane no longer sported any of the horseshoe-wielding bullies of yore. Apart from the 'Norton's small loading dock, the alley held only a few dumpsters and trash cans and homely back entrances to the buildings which crowded around it, frequently throwing much of it into shadow. It was not on any of Darrol's walking routes.

Darrol stood outside the 'Norton service entrance. If I were a cat, he thought, wrinkling his nose, would I choose to prowl out here? The principal odor was a low admixture of poorly-washed garbage containers. This was topped by a peculiar over-layer of flowers, perhaps gardenia. He grimaced. Sickly or syrupy smells reminded him too much of one of his foster mothers, and not in a pleasant way.

He wasn't sure why he'd bothered to come looking for the damn cat. What was the point? But little Alma Quist, sometimes a surprising force, had more or less propelled him. He'd been easy prey for her, as she caught him while he was still processing several things.

He was chagrined about the fake Norton scrip. His big coup had been significantly undercut. His metal box held a zilch sheet of paper, not a treasure. Yet the theft of the piece, real or not, still chucked enjoyable confusion at the Quists.

He congratulated himself on his good fortune of getting to watch Karin telling of the shooting. *Execution.* That was the right word for it. *Or maybe assassination.* He only wished he'd been able to toss out a few more clever comments without creating suspicion. Or better, that somehow he could have described last night's action, bit by delicious bit. *Right between the eyes.*

Ah well. He started walking.

He refused to call out "here, kitty-kitty" as Magnus and Alma doubtless were doing. That was just dumb. But in case anyone was watching, he made a show of going to the dead end of the alley, peering about, looking concerned. He encountered a dime and a penny, several cigarette butts, three empty beer bottles and one forlorn-looking condom.

Christ! Was someone at it back here, practically under his apartment? He tried to banish sudden thoughts of Maria and Lenz, no longer the least bit arousing. Those two were rapidly moving up on his payback list. He turned and walked slowly toward the street.

Nary a cat nor a rat nor even a cockroach to be seen. But there was movement at the open end of the alley. There, coming toward him, was Magnus Quist, fully lit by the morning sun. Darrol wondered exactly why he didn't like the guy. Quist was an arrogant asshole—plenty of those around—but there was something else.

And at that very moment, Darrol figured it out. Magnus Quist had Darrol's number. That rankled big time.

He watched Quist approach. Darrol laughed at his next unbidden thought. *High Noon.* But which of them was the sheriff and which the gunslinger?

"Well, Mr. Yount, any luck?" Quist called.

Darrol shook his head, said nothing and kept walking, wishing he had Cosmo's pistol ready to draw.

They met in the middle of a fading oil stain, half in sun, half in shadow. Quist appeared relaxed, not in the least concerned over his wife's missing cat.

"I take a shortcut back to the store," he said, shifting slightly so that the band of sunlight fell below his eyes. "I have no desire to go round the entire block. If a cat has no wish to be found, it won't be found, *ja?*"

Quist nodded at his own observation, squinted at Darrol. "Did you play hide and seek as a boy?"

"I'm still playing hide and seek." *Figure that one out.*

"Interesting. Back in Sweden we called the game *kurragömma,* which roughly means 'courage to hide.' I was quite good at it."

"Were you?" Darrol moved, and the sun again caught Quist's eyes.

"Yes, both hiding and seeking." Quist wiped sweat from his brow. "So, Mr. Yount, do you think our arsonist at Joe the Trader was up to the task?"

Darrol watched a dribble of sweat slide down the other man's nose. Any moment it might fly off, a skier jumping into open space. But it stopped and hung over a nostril. "Maybe it was only a trial run," he said.

Quist frowned. "That would be odd. Or perhaps a little scary. But regardless, I think inept arsonists are—what is the phrase?—oh yes, a dime a dozen. Petty vandals, nothing more. If you had started that fire, I assume you'd have done much better."

"Why do you say that?"

Quist showed too many teeth. "You told me you were experienced, even as a boy. Arson was your dream, you said."

"Well, not quite."

"And I recall you suggested a little fire down the street would be good for business up here."

"I did?" Darrol pulled his second licorice twist from a pocket. "You've got a good memory, Magnus. Then again, maybe I said a little fire up here might be good for insurance?" He bit off a large piece.

"Some would find that not so funny, Mr. Yount."

"I guess some would."

Quist stared at him for a moment. "Well," he said finally, "we've both done our bit. As per the cat, I mean. A busy morning, yes?"

He stepped past Darrol and went toward the 'Norton loading door, his thin shadow hurrying after him.

"Keep the home fires burning, Mr. Quist," Darrol called.

Quist went into the store without looking back.

Chapter 28
Eying the Prey

Lanterman's closed at 8:30 this Thursday evening, a rare event, but Claude Gallatoire was a rare old bird. He'd earned his sendoff. The only question was whether Claude would manage to stay awake while they honored him.

Or perhaps, Darrol thought, they'd simply prop him against the wall and party around him.

Claude was wearing his vintage tux. Super-broad, if shabby, lapels. Fading satin striping down the pant legs. A sagging black cummerbund which looked like it had caught more than a few crumbs in its time and refused to give some of them up. The outfit hung loosely on him. Claude had shrunk since the era when he used to wear it regularly. His wife declared that had to do with his carrying too many heavy trays for too many years.

"Think about all those two-pound Porterhouses," she said to Darrol. "Nothing subtle about the old-school diners in this place." She drank champagne like she was chugging water on a hot day.

Glenys Gallatoire was still a knockout. Tall, unstooped, an intelligent face with animated blue eyes. If wrinkles could be refined, then hers had gone to finishing school and Bryn Mawr. Darrol had toyed with several older women but never anyone in her 70's and few as attractive as Glenys. He wondered how doddery old Claude had hung on to this one.

Glad he'd put on his highest lifts, Darrol poured champagne into her eager glass. *I'd go on that cruise with you, Mrs. G.*

"Don't monopolize Glenys, Darrol." Miss Hugo was at his elbow, smiling. *A traitor's smile.* He dipped into his emergency reserve of charm and nodded pleasantly.

Miss Hugo led Claude's wife away. Darrol watched them, thoughtful. Very soon he'd award Miss Hugo her payback. She was sure to be mortified, and, with any luck, she'd also be in a satisfying spot of trouble.

He looked across the room. Portly little Vinnie Lanterman was in a blue velvet smoking jacket. *Good God, did that belong to August, rescued right from the dripping coffin?* Vinnie had his fat hand perched chummily on Radisson Vero's shoulder. They were in close conversation. Every time Vero spoke, his scar danced a can-can.

Lanterman laughed and Vero grinned. What a pair of jerks. Birds of a feather. But there was another grand moment soon to come, two birds with one payback, a helluva stone.

Darrol nibbled at a roast beef canape, wincing at the pungent sauce. Was there curry in these things too? Maybe the kitchen staff had their own bit of revenge going. As if to confirm that, he saw Emilio, Joe and Chips, each startlingly shorter without his chef's hat, sharing laughs near a food table. Or maybe they were simply happy that some of the party had been delegated to a catering team.

"So what's the plan, Dar?" Xavier Shea appeared from nowhere. Instead of his bussing uniform, he wore a beige sports coat and brown slacks. He looked every bit like a serious grad student mingling with the hoity-toitys.

Darrol raised his glass. "I'd tell you my plan, X, but if I did, then you'd become—what's the word?—complicated, conflicted."

Xavier raised an eyebrow. "You mean 'complicit'?"

"Shit, yeah. Maria's vocabulary's rubbing off on me."

"Well," Xavier said, "I don't want to be complicit or conflicted, none of that. Just keep my head down, work hard, get my degrees, grab this town by the balls."

"Woah! You're talking my language." Darrol gulped the rest of his champagne. "But I'll skip the degree part. And I'm going for the jugular."

The restaurant was overly-warm, the air a mixture of expensive perfumes and colognes, buttery odors from the chafing dishes and the heavy scent of the lilies on the tables.

Darrol had a bartender pour him one of Lanterman's most expensive whiskeys—*this one's on your tab, Vinnie*—and found a slightly-cooler corner. He sipped, surveyed the room and went over his plans.

Spike Duggan was talking to a clearly-wilting Claude Gallatoire. Duggan's wife Louise stood by attentively. She was annoyingly-pretty. But perhaps, thought Darrol, that might make his intended comeuppance for Spike feel a little more delicious. The wife was to be a part of the fun.

Radisson Vero was chatting with Glenys Gallatoire. Tekla Hart was by his side. She kept an appropriate employee distance, but Darrol thought he could read hints of intimacy in her expression. *Black panties, black garters.* At the moment at least, he didn't intend any retribution for Tekla. The fact she'd chosen such a dumbo seemed punishment enough. But the Radish would share in the aggravation Darrol was shortly going to bring to the restaurant owners.

The other two were now over at the dessert table. Estelle Hugo, hobnobbing with Vinnie Lanterman, had to stand back a bit to avoid Vinnie's protruding chest. Short as she was, Miss Hugo still was taller than the diminutive Vinnie, and she leaned down slightly when she talked. *Another pair of richwits.*

Darrol chafed at not having guessed that the wealthy Miss Hugo, so often in the restaurant, was the silent partner. Now she would get a double whammy: her share of the restaurant's problems he was going to create and the personal bit of trouble he'd planned for her.

And over there, by golly, talking closely with an adoring Carey Modoc, was none other than the hotshot writer Jon Gulliver. Claude had been asked to provide a list of his favorite customers for possible inviting, and apparently Gulliver had made the cut. Darrol had needed to do some homework, but he was almost ready to sic some delightful stress on the stuck-up Mr. Gulliver.

So many of his targets in one room. At the very least a trifecta. It felt like a heady time, enhanced not a little by the well-aged whiskey.

If Maria and Lenz had been here—and maybe Miguel Cortez—that might have made it perfect. Beyond perfect if you threw in a bonus: Magnus Quist, who deserved taking down a peg or two.

Well, all was in the works.

Darrol savored another sip of his whiskey. It burned beautifully. His determination burned. He smiled.

What a fine party.

Chapter 29
Frame by Frame

Over the next few weeks, Darrol accomplished so much he thought what transpired could have made a very fine documentary film, with himself as producer and director.

The obvious title: *Getting Even.*

Whenever his memory screened everything he'd done, it all unfolded in a long, grand series of montages.

Roll 'em.

The film opens with a bit of backstory: Darrol claiming his due from Ari Steiner, a former co-worker at *Mr. Sweetie Pies.* Shades of crooked Cosmo Malloy! Apparently the ice cream business freezes many a moral code.

Ari, a self-taught computer expert, had been diddling the books, twiddling the numbers, lining his pockets, in other words hoarding all the clichés of embezzlement. Predictably, Darrol found out but promised to keep quiet. Against a future need.

And that need was now.

Cut to the present and a sequence of brief shots. Ari, clearly proud of his expertise, helps Darrol set up anonymous accounts for email, Facebook, Twitter, and all the rest. Could they be traced back to Darrol? Possibly, if Ari was a double-crossing code-writer. But you can tell that Ari halfway loves Darrol, and in any case Darrol will use only public computers, and so he seems reasonably safe.

Montage: Darrol busy at different computers in library branches. His keyboarding is not the best, but he works with great concentration and determination. We see him completing on-line forms, sending, printing.

Insert: As he works in the libraries, Darrol notices street people taking refuge in the stacks. He thinks of Emperor Norton, circa 1879, coming into an early city library, leafing through newspapers, finding accounts of the Emperor's imperial doings.

Darrol snaps to with a rueful smile. He certainly doesn't want his own activities recognized, clever as they are.

The music changes to a jaunty Latin beat, and the next sequence takes us to the Art Institute.

Miguel Cortez is in a classroom, wittily mouthing off to distraught students in front of their easels. The teacher sends the class whimpering away and strolls out of the room. Waiting in the hall are two ICE agents, wanting to talk to him about his immigration status.

Are you Miguel Luis Cortez? Yes. Do you have your green card handy? Of course not—who carries such things around? The agents, played by familiar character actors, show tact, but they are more threatening than sympathetic. That's been the nature of ICE the last few years. Let's check with the personnel office. Let's see the paperwork. Whether Cortez' status is legit or not, the stain of doubt is out there. The annoyance is real.

The sequence ends with a nice big blotch of paint wiping through to the next shots.

Insert: Darrol typing faster and faster. He's getting better at this. We see hints of an official State of California Seal, more forms, the NAACP website, Darrol's triumphant expression.

The score switches to elegant music. We zoom in through passing pedestrians to the brass name plaque outside Lanterman's of North Beach.

Dissolve to the restaurant interior. Time: mid-afternoon. The three owners are sneering at fate by sitting at table thirteen, enjoying pre-opening drinks and gloating over financial updates.

Miss Estelle Hugo sips Darjeeling from a fine porcelain cup, Radisson Vero beams over a vodka martini (close-up: one olive bobbing), and Vinnie Lanterman eyeballs the exquisite amber-ruby color of a rare Barbadillo sherry moving languorously in a Lalique crystal tasting glass.

Mini-montage, mostly close-ups with dramatic lighting: official-looking mail arriving, envelopes opened, cell phones answered, knuckles rapping on a door, sweat on Vinnie's brow, tea spilled in Miss Hugo's saucer, Vero's mouth open, a half-chewed olive landing on the table.

The state's Department of Fair Employment and Housing wants to look into Lanterman's hiring practices. So do federal EEO people. NOW and other women's rights organizations have come politely calling. The NAACP wants to chat with the restaurant's employees of color.

Sammy Horton, the junior dishwasher, grins and tosses a towel. Xavier Shea politely clears the stunned owners' table. They don't see his thumbs up as he walks away.

X marks the spot.

The editing tempo changes again. Cut to: grainy close-ups of Facebook pages scrolling, Twitter entries pulsing out word by word, cursors, screen arrows, icons. The words *Jon Gulliver* appear almost subliminally. And the word *Plagiarism.*

The montage continues with a female TV news anchor green-screened over photos of a scowling Jon Gulliver and a collage of his book jackets.

Reporter audio: "Today, popular Bay Area author Jon Gulliver denied that his bestseller *Oh, Baby, Baby,* is cribbed from the script of a porn film. Gulliver also denied that parts of his *Abandonment* series come from D.H. Lawrence and Henry Miller."

Up-tempo music, perhaps with comic overtones.

Headline montage: *Will Fans Abandon 'Abandonment'? - Lady Chatterley's Ripoff? - Did Gulliver 'Borrow' from 'Tropic of Cancer'? - Plagiarism Dogs Jon Gulliver - Gulliver Travels from Success to Suspicion*

Close-up of the same news anchor, appropriately solemn. "Whatever the truth, Mr. Gulliver, who declined to be interviewed, now seems tainted with plagiarism."

Two-shot with co-anchor. "Well, Doug, I guess the taint ain't going away soon."

Doug, flashing ridiculously white teeth: "No, Suzy, 'tain't."

Zoom in as a banner is slapped over a *Jon Gulliver Reading* poster. The banner reads *Cancelled.*

Did Darrol hit a bullseye or two? Was there actually some truth to his allegations? He knew it didn't matter.

When you drop something into the social media pond, the ripples go on forever.

Lights up. The screening was over, but Darrol would play it again and again, relishing every scene, every payback.

And there was yet more fun to be had.

After finishing his busiest period of getting even, Darrol worked in a bonus for Miss Hugo.

He'd long known that Miss Hugo illegally parked her big black Lincoln outside the restaurant, using a blue handicapped placard to which she wasn't entitled, a card she'd kept for herself after her disabled sister died.

While Miss Hugo, at table one, was sipping her duck consommé, Darrol made an anonymous phone call to the parking authority.

A short time later, as the old ingrate was salivating over poached sea bass with saffron *petits pois*: angry red lights outside the front windows.

Xavier, bless him, drew her attention to what was happening.

Miss Hugo soon looked like she was choking on a fish bone, gasping, no doubt, at the thought of considerable embarrassment, a command appearance in front of a foul-tempered magistrate and hefty fines to come.

That same evening, Darrol provided a little present for Spike Duggan. And for Spike's adoring wife Louise.

Spike liked to brag how Louise tended to his every need, including picking him up from work, doing his laundry, and making him gluten-free vegan suppers in lieu of the staff's food choices. He ate Louise's main dish during Vero's nightly oration and chomped on a special dessert about eight o'clock.

After that, Spike's prized lunchbox—far too cleverly in the shape of a cable car and far too frequently shown smugly to everyone—sat in the staff room waiting to be handed back to Louise.

Darrol pilfered a skimpy red silk and black lace thong he'd once given Maria—something she didn't like to wear anyway, so this was a worthy repurposing—and wrapped it in pretty red tissue paper, also taken from Maria's things.

Using his best imitation of feminine handwriting, he wrote a note on stationery he'd swiped from the St. Regis—he remembered how the very needy and surprisingly-muscular Mrs. Oakley had treated him to two rompful days and nights in a 20ᵗʰ floor suite, swearing she'd leave her husband if Darrol only said the word—and put the note in Spike's lunchbox with the thong.

The note said, with all simplicity and with all full promise: *S...Until...C.*

Tucked under a piece of crumpled foil, these treasures sat in the cable car lunch box, awaiting Louise's discovery. *Clang!* And her suspicion. *Clang, clang!* Duggan might try to pass it off as a prank, but Darrol knew that jealousy, when it's aroused, doesn't quickly go back to sleep.

Indeed, in addition to gleeful imaginings of that confrontation, the next night at work, Darrol took great pleasure in watching Spike. The guy looked sleepless. He was withdrawn, irritable. He made mistakes.

There was no culinary cable car in sight. Maybe Spike wasn't hungry. Darrol, on the other hand, had an excellent appetite.

He finished his shift and walked home, smiling, not even noticing the light rain. He was thinking about Magnus Quist and Willy Lenz.

He still needed a couple of refinements to the big comeuppance he'd mete out to Quist. But the basic plan was hot stuff. *Really hot stuff.*

As for Lenz. *The crumb-bum.* Tomorrow afternoon, with any luck—and with one simple, properly-timed phone call—it would be problems of operatic proportions for Willy Lenz. Let him try to sing his way out of things. It would be sour notes all the way.

Of course, Maria was bound to be collateral damage. That was almost too bad, except that afterward she'd come running home to Darrol, doubtless sniveling or bawling.

At that point, she would provide a superb opportunity for Darrol to wield his magnificent snail power. He'd have a choice. He'd take his time, make Maria wonder which way he'd go.

Crush her. Or spare her.

He was beginning to like that a lot, the power of choice.

Chapter 30
In Flagrante Delizioso

The Merry Widows weren't the least bit merry.

It wasn't that their taxi was stuck in rush-hour traffic. It wasn't that their nightly cocktails would be delayed. It wasn't even that neither had time to dress properly for their sudden mission to *La Dolce Via*. It was the thought of it all.

L'idea stessa! Really.

"Who was on the phone again?" Rosa asked, trying to fix her makeup as the cab lurched and stopped, lurched and stopped. It was hard to hold the mirror steady. The taxi was starting to smell like a beauty parlor.

"He didn't say." Sophia partially opened her window to let in a little air. But it also let in more street noise. She raised her voice. "Very polite. Very firm."

Rosa tried to smooth her rouge. "Someone at the bakery?"

"Very likely, though I didn't recognize the voice. Certainly not Henry or Tito." Sophia closed the window. "*Dannazione!*" She glared at the traffic.

Rosa snapped her compact shut. Crumbles of peach-colored powder leapt into the air. "They are actually doing it? You know, *rapporti sessuali*, right in our business?"

Sophia nodded. "Screwing, yes." She tittered. "In the lusty days of our marriage, my Antonio called it 'buttering the breadstick, *affinando il panino*.' As if the kids didn't know what he was talking about." Another titter.

Rosa glanced at the taxi driver. He was watching the traffic and nodding his head to earbud ministrations. The cab lurched again and moved slowly forward.

"My Emilio was a prude," Rosa said. "Not much of a typical *Italiano* in the bedroom department." She lowered her voice. "Sometimes I had to beg him to...well, to go above and beyond."

Sophia bellowed. "And behind?"

"That too," said Rosa, laughing.

318

Their driver sounded the horn. The taxi crept another few feet.

With difficulty, Rosa tried to compose herself. "So the guy who called us said what? That if we time it right, we'll find them *in flagrante,* rolling in cream and *marzapane,* whipping themselves with *grissini*?"

Lots more laughter.

Sophia took out a tissue and patted her eyes. "Something like that. The caller used the word 'kinky.'"

"Our Willy? Kinky? Hard to believe."

Sophia sighed. "Oh, these days I believe anything." She put the tissue away. "And frankly, I don't mind what Willy or Maria or anyone else does." She chortled. "The kinkier the better, and more power to them, I say. But it's completely inappropriate at our bakery."

"Completely inappropriate. I agree," Rosa said, her voice stern. "Even if it's after hours. But..." She put a hand on Sophia's arm. "But..."

"But what, Rosa dear?"

The laughter returned. "But I hope we get to see something really interesting before we read them the riot act!"

"**D**arrol's gotten pretty maniac the last couple of weeks." Maria trapped sunbeams in her iced tea. She slowly rotated the glass. Ocher circles patterned the walls. Ice cubes clinked softly.

Willy smiled. "You mean manic? Rhymes with panic." He was standing near the window.

"Yes, manic. Silly me. But I don't think panic applies." Maria patted the empty space on the loveseat. "Come sit."

"Maybe it does. He remained standing. "These days maybe panic applies to me."

"It does?"

"I'm starting to think so. But forget about me. You were concerned about Darrol and his mania."

"That's so typical of you, Willy, putting others first. One of the reasons I like you."

She patted the loveseat again, spilling drops of tea onto the floor. "C'mon. It's hard to talk when you're up there like a gorilla waiting to jump out the window."

"A gorilla?" He sat beside her. "That's not terribly flattering."

She blushed. "Oh, I didn't mean that you were one. I meant..."

"I'm joking, Maria." He struck a thinking pose. "I wonder if male gorillas sing tenor. Or is it always bass?"

Maria sighed politely.

"Sorry." Willy gave her his full attention. "Tell me about Darrol."

"Not much to tell. Just that he's been really intense lately, really busy, always got this silly grin in his eyes. He's up to something." She put her glass on the floor.

"Does he still think we're lovers? Cream puffs and dill-doughs and everything?"

"I'm not sure. I tried to tell him it was all made up, but..."

Willy took her hands in his. "We're almost lovers, don't you think?" He rushed to finish. "I mean in a way. A very chaste way."

"Chased? You mean by Darrol?"

His laugh was melodic. "That's one of the things I love about you, Maria. Your refreshing bursts of sweet naivety. I meant chaste as in pure."

"Oh. But it's more like bursts of bad grammar..."

"...and I love your sense of humor." He grew serious again. "But I'll tell you why I use the word 'panic'. I'm beginning to feel trapped, like Radamès running out of air in the tomb."

"That's in *Aida*, right?" She looked at him expectantly.

He beamed. "On the money, *Celeste Maria*. Soon you'll know more about opera than I do."

She shook her head. "But what about this trapped thing...?"

There was a buzzing. Willy stared at a fly moving on the window. "You know all about my miserable marriage. I gotta stop dragging my feet."

He turned back to Maria. "And I'm trapped here too. I like my job—and I'm crazy about all of you—but I want to run my own bakery, not someone else's. Here or maybe further south. So I've started looking around."

He pointed at his graying temple. "And you can see the clock is ticking."

"Willy—"

There was a rustling in the hall, footsteps, whispering. The door slammed open. In poured *Le Due Vedove,* Rosa Lombardi and Sophia Russo.

"Aha!" Rosa exclaimed.

"Aha what? Excuse me?" Willy jumped up.

"Where's the whipped cream? The jelly rolls?" Sophia looked a little disoriented.

Maria was equally confused. "I'm sorry, what?" She stood up hesitantly.

Rosa frowned. "We had it on reliable authority that there was, em, unauthorized activity here."

"*Si,*" Sophia said, peering about for evidence.

Willy gave one of his patented bows. "*Signoras,*" he said, "it's so nice to see you. But what to what activity do you refer?" He glanced at Maria. "Ms. Grimaldi and I are having a friendly talk about our work. Is that truly 'unauthorized'?"

"Well, we..." Rosa looked to Sophia and found no help.

Willy jumped into an aria. "*Un solo istante, ah, l'ira frenate!*"

He let the last note hang then whispered to Maria. "Donizetti. A little complaint."

"Mr. Lenz—Willy—there's no need to sing of anger," Rosa said. "It's clearly a mistake."

"Or a practical joke," Sophia murmured, with visible disappointment.

"Then a happier song!" Willy let loose. "*'O sole mio...'*" His creamy tenor sped directly to a very high volume. Rosa flinched. Sophia's hair blew back.

"*Che bella cosa è na jurnata 'e sole!*" Willy finished and gave a boyish shrug. "All about sunny times," he told Maria. She was smiling broadly.

"You should be at the Met, Willy," Rosa said. "But we're glad you're here. In the meantime, our apologies." She turned to Maria. "To both of you."

Rosa took Sophia's arm. "Come on, *cara*. We can still make happy hour."

The widows left, quietly closing the door. Maria and Willy managed to hold for a second before bursting into laughter.

"Aha!" Willy feigned surprise. "Aha to you too, ladies!"

"Jelly rolls?" Maria sputtered. "Whipped cream?"

"Unauthorized activity indeed. Oh dear." Willy took out a handkerchief and wiped his forehead.

Maria stopped laughing. "It must have been Darrol."

"Some 'authority', eh?" He pushed papers aside and sat on the edge of his desk.

"That's going too far." She propped herself beside him. "He's gone too far."

"Then maybe you're ready to..." Willy studied the ceiling.

"Maybe I'm ready to what?" She began to swing her legs forward and back.

He slid back, sat fully and moved his own legs.

A moment of quiet, companionable swinging.

They looked at each other, noticed they were in sync, smiled a little shyly.

He touched her hand. Her smile widened.

"Well now, Maria..." Willy's voice was sweet and hopeful. "What do you think about San Luis Obispo?"

Chapter 31
A Little Night Musing

Most likely it wouldn't be a very big fire. But, with luck, it might be vicious enough to damage a nice chunk of the 'Norton. The store's old sprinkler system wouldn't be able to keep up, not if the fire was set properly.

Darrol had thought about using explosives. He'd loved to have outdone the boys in Graham Greene's destructors story, ingeniously bringing the whole thing down all at once.

He thought fleetingly of leaning on his former sleazy associates in the demolition company to fork over the right gear, but, unfortunately, he had no firm hold over them, and besides, he was quite rusty with things like nitro and dynamite. Not a wise choice.

But fire would do it. And he'd thought it all through.

He'd avoid messy and traceable accelerants. He would simply cause an electrical spark or short to start everything going. The wiring of the creaky old building was downright funky. Everyday store items would make easy combustibles. Not a lot of work required. In, out, done. Almost as quick as aiming the sun's eager rays through a small boy's cheap but effective lens.

If arson was suspected, blame most likely would fall smack daberoo on Magnus Quist for trying to diddle the insurance companies. That would add to the joy of it all.

The Mischief House tenants? Well, the fire wouldn't get that far, or if it did, their smoke alarms should get them scrambling. Besides, the Collins were out of town again, Brick Zimmer was flying in Asia this weekend, Maria had left a note she was visiting her mother for a few days—more likely she was off somewhere licking her wounds after being canned by the two widows—and Duff, well, who cared about Duff? If necessary, that over-muscled Chinaman could swing himself down a building like King Kong. Or maybe it was King Hong Kong.

The Quists would take care of themselves. They'd dash into the store. In one aisle Alma would be squirting soft drinks and juice to suppress the flames. In another, Magnus would be looking for things which would easily burn. Yin and yang or whatever the Swedes called their opposites.

But what about Jo? She was not a bad sort. Couldn't let her perish. Darrol's inspiration was quick to arrive. Should the fire threaten old Mrs. Durr, one intrepid Darrol Yount would get her out safely, carry her in his arms if necessary.

Be a hero. Skip the cape, but, yes, be a hero. Another bonus.

Just after midnight that Saturday, Darrol, wearing black, went out onto Chestnut, crossed the street and looked over at Mischief House.

There was the usual faint greenish glow from inside the 'Norton. The only lights in the upper windows were those of the apartment stairwell and of Darrol's living room.

He peered higher, looking over the tight gathering of buildings on the block. Through the silvered brume of light pollution, he could see the smears and smudges of a few bolder stars.

The neighborhood was quiet. A slight breeze carried the morose humming of the cable line. A dog barked sharply, twice, shut up. Darrol listened to his blood surging.

It was time.

He walked back across the street, smelling popcorn, gardenias, his own nervous sweat. He reentered Mischief House.

The vestibule was empty. He heard no one on the stairs. He went to the private door to the 'Norton.

He worked the keypad quickly, slid into the gloom of the interior hallway, closed the door. He let his eyes adjust and removed his backpack. He thought he had everything he'd need: wire cutters and strippers, a few screwdrivers and a headband light. For good measure he'd added a pair of gripman's gloves stolen from Duff's room.

The backpack also held what he joked to himself was his high-tech fire-starting backup kit: a box of matches and sheets of newspaper.

He'd thought about including Cosmo's pistol but decided there'd be no need for that. This was arson, not armed robbery.

He put on the headband and flipped the switch to low. He turned to his right. The narrow beam fluttered across the door to the vault. Most likely the vault was fireproof. If the flames got this far, whatever secrets Magnus kept in there might be protected. *Damn it.*

Della Rossiter's door was closed. As Darrol passed, its window's dimpled glass rippled and tossed eerie reflections onto the walls. He stopped and adjusted the headlight so its aim was lower. The plastic click seemed inordinately loud.

He stood very still. Then he grinned. Who was to hear? Emperor Norton, cardboard and all?

A quick, savage jolt.

Darrol staggered, put a hand on the wall.

There was another miniscule shake, very timid in comparison, then everything was still. *Earthquakes can be so inconvenient.* He chuckled at the incongruity of the thought.

He waited to see if more tremors would follow, but everything remained quiet. He calmed his breathing. He could hear the low grumbling of the store's coolers, a thin, high whine of something electronic, a minute scratching sound—a mouse?—and the crackly buzz of the neon light over the arch to the Nook.

He left the hallway and entered the store, smelling the mingled odors of fruits, groceries and fusty old building, the blend he found so strangely pleasurable. A pity that wasn't likely to be around after the blaze.

He was surprised to be thinking of things he'd miss.

The figure of the Emperor would be one of those. He decided to take a final look. He turned off the headlamp, let his eyes adjust again, walked quietly to the checkout area and stood in front of Emperor Norton.

Softly illuminated by ambient streetlight, the guy seemed a little different. There were things Darrol hadn't noticed before.

He'd never spotted the small silver American eagle among the crazy plumage sprouting from the brim of Norton's top hat. He didn't remember there was that much gray in the bottom half of the straggly beard. Or was it the remnants of a sloppy oatmeal breakfast? He'd never noticed that one fat brass button on the military tunic was undone. Was that some sort of symbolism? Below the cuffs of the ill-fitting, slightly-baggy pants, those were not boots, but worn-down soft shoes. *Huh.*

Darrol studied the Emperor's expression. Tonight it appeared more feverish than fierce. Norton's dark eyes stared out with imperial command, almost with anger, but they also seemed occupied elsewhere. Some sort of dual vision. It was unnerving.

It was even more unnerving when the Emperor spoke.

"Are you going to get on with it or not, Mr. Yount?"

Darrol's mouth dropped. He froze.

Magnus Quist slid out of the shadows. "I thought maybe one of these nights, *ja?* And here you are."

Quist was holding a revolver. "I considered hiring you—expert fireman that you are—but free labor is so much better. And..."

He stepped a little closer. "...and this way you will make a fine piece of evidence. What do they call that? Misdirection, *ja?*"

Darrol found his voice. "Midnight craving. Back door was open. I came in for some licorice."

"That is almost funny. *Väldigt kvickt!*" Quist gestured with the revolver. "But now we will go back there, and you will start pouring the fuel you brought."

"Fuel? What fuel?"

"Don't to toy with me, Mr. Yount. I could merely shoot you as an intruder. Instead I will let you to play arsonist. Too bad you will be incompetent and will burn yourself up, *ja?*"

"I don't have any fuel." Darrol began to open the backpack. "Look here."

Quist dropped his gaze. Darrol swung the backpack up with as much force as the limited angle allowed. The revolver clattered into the darkness.

Cursing, Quist teetered back against the counter. His hand connected with something and he came up swinging wildly. With the flyswatter.

Darrol laughed.

But Quist took a second swing and the flyswatter smacked across Darrol's face. It stung like a whip. Darrol touched his cheek. He remembered whips.

Quist grunted and dropped the mangled flyswatter. He fumbled again behind him, grabbed one of his iron weights and flung it.

It was little more than a bocce toss. Practice made imperfect. The weight thumped Darrol on the shoulder and did no damage.

But it was a distraction. Quist scrambled to find the gun. Darrol tried to spring after him but knocked over the gumball machine. The globe smashed open. Gumballs rattled across the floor.

Darrol swerved, lunged behind the counter, ripped the sabre from the wall. The security pins spun off, clinking in protest.

He tried to tug the sword out of its padded sheath. The gold braids flailed.

Quist charged, swinging a small fire extinguisher. Darrol countered with the half-sheathed sabre. It hit the extinguisher with a huge *thunk*.

The sheath split apart, belching out its stuffing. The extinguisher banged onto the floor. Quist staggered back amidst a rustling shower of papers. He muttered in Swedish.

Panting, Darrol hefted the sword. The torn sheath writhed like a dying snake, flopped to the floor, falling among a few still-rolling gumballs.

"What now, Yount?" Quist was breathing hard. He eyed the sword warily. "Will you carve me like a Christmas ham?"

Darrol tried to puzzle out his options.

"Or I could pay you after all," Quist said, almost sounding reasonable. "But it shouldn't look like arson." His glasses flared in the streetlight.

"It wouldn't have looked like arson," Darrol said, sudden petulance in his voice. "I know what I'm doing."

"Then perhaps..."

This time the vicious jolt wasn't a solo. It brought violent company. The building shuddered, shuddered again. Shook hard.

Darrol reeled, slipped on gumballs, stumbled forward, dropped the sabre. He braced himself on the counter.

The paroxysm continued. Cans and bottles and boxes clattered and smashed from the shelves. Plates and glasses skittered in the Nook and shattered on the linoleum. The bell over the front door clamored frantically.

Then the shaking stopped. A final cup fell and shattered. Emperor Norton tumbled onto his face.

Darrol was pushing himself upright from the counter when Quist hit him very hard with the fire extinguisher.

High in the corner, the spider began to check her web for prey.

"**H**ow do you like the irony, Mr. Yount? The arsonist done in with a fire extinguisher?"

Darrol tried to focus. His head ached. His neck hurt. His back and his legs complained loudly. His wrists and ankles pulsed uncomfortably. Something was pinching them. *Tied.* He was hog-tied. He looked up slowly.

He was scrunched on the floor, propped in a corner of a cool, gray-walled, gray-floored room. There was a leather loveseat, a small wooden desk, a metal file cabinet. The space smelled lifeless. There was no sound. *The vault.*

Magnus Quist loomed a few feet in front of him, perched casually on a leather chair rolled onto a small oriental rug. *The king on his throne.*

Quist used his teeth to tug a bite from a licorice twist. He waved the remainder toward Darrol. "Want some? I believe it's your favorite."

"You've had your fun, Magnus. Let's get back to business."

"We have no business. Darrol." He gave malicious emphasis to the name. "I brought you in here in case Mrs. Quist comes down. But that's not so likely, *ja?* Alma sleeps through most earthquakes. She certainly never notices my comings and goings."

Darrol tried to flex his shoulders. "So what is this—the place where you play with yourself?"

"How droll. Is that the word? Or is it 'troll'? You're very much a troll, Darrol." He punched the name again.

Darrol strained against his bonds. Useless. He saw that he was fastened with cable ties. He laughed inwardly. He'd used the things himself when he and Sheryl had played at a little bondage. *Aisle six, bottom shelf.*

Despite his aches, he managed a wink. "Or is this the place where you play with the girls? Big ones? Little ones? Got a lot of pictures here, do you?"

Quist stiffened. "Shut your mouth, Yount."

He dropped the licorice and stood. "Here's how it will be. After I make sure the coast is cleared, we will put you in the store and start a fine smorgasbord of tasty fires." He laughed harshly. "Don't worry. We can get plenty of fuel from the generator, some even to bathe you with perhaps, troll. Tsk, such a careless arsonist."

Darrol wriggled even though he knew that the cable ties could only go one way: tighter.

Quist moved to the heavy door. It was slightly ajar. "You shall have a very nice, truly first-hand view. The best seat in the house, Mr. Yount."

He went into the hallway and pushed the door from the outside until it was almost closed.

Darrol tore with his teeth at the cable ties binding his wrists. The ties were obdurate. His gums and lips began bleeding. He tried to stand. His body refused to cooperate. He tried to slide up the wall. His legs felt too weak. He rolled sideways and tumbled over. He tried to roll to his knees. Too woozy. He was a fetus. A fetus awaiting delivery. Or the abortionist.

He lay still, his mind sorting useless options.

The door swung open. Quist came back into the vault. "Ah, Mr. Yount, I see you've been a naughty boy. But no matter, you'll still get your reward. I find all is clear out there. And all is prepared for—what do you call it in this country?— yes, a wienie roast."

He walked to Darrol and looked down, sighed. "Well, in any case, as the walrus said, the time has come."

Quist bent over, grasped Darrol by the shoulders, twisted him about, began dragging him slowly backwards.

Darrol slumped into a dead weight.

Quist paused and tried for a better grip. "Make it harder if you want. But dancing and bocce, they build the upper muscles, *ja?*" He resumed shuffling backwards.

"Hey!" Darrol let his legs trail. He tried to dig his heels into the hard floor. "Hey, this is really not a good idea. Lemme go."

One heel caught onto the rug. They stopped again.

"You're so much heavier than that stupid cat," Quist said. "Even *död* she was a heavy little bitch."

"I'm not a damn cat. Those people upstairs are not cats. What about them?"

"Yes, what about us, Mr. Quist?" Alma's voice rose, echoing from the hallway. "And what did you do to poor Lyckatill, my little Good Luck?"

Quist started. He dropped his hold on Darrol and turned around.

Alma, wearing a prim navy robe, stood in the doorway. The store's revolver was steady in her right hand.

"Stay there, Magnus."

"Alma..."

Alma shook her head. She gave the gun a tiny flick. "Now move back and sit on the floor by the wall. Don't forget I know how very well how to use this. *Sitta, du bastard!*"

Glaring, Quist sat against the wall. He pulled his long legs in and wrapped his arms about them.

Alma watched him. "Very sloppy of you to leave our gun lying around, Mr. Quist."

Darrol had squirmed around to face the door. "Alma, thank God. Can you get something to cut me loose?"

"What, so you can set fire to the store?" She stopped his protest with a firm gesture. "I've heard a lot in the last few minutes, Darrol. None of it very nice."

He lifted his bound hands in supplication. "I can explain..."

She shook her head. "Forget it. Magnus has long wanted rid of this place. And now I learn he murdered Lyckatill. You, Darrol, it turns out, are just plain sociopathic. I tried hard to give you the benefit of the doubt, but..."

Darrol gave her a broad smile. "You misunderstand me, Alma."

She smiled back but said nothing.

"*Vad ska du göra,* Alma?" Quist said impatiently. His eyes were still fixed on the unwavering gun.

"What I'm going to do, *sötnos,* is shut the door, let you two enjoy each other's company. I'm sure you have scissors. You can choose to free Darrol or not."

"And then what?" Quist's tone was less certain.

"I'm going to think about things. Maybe I'll come free you in the morning. Maybe not."

"*Gode Gud,* Alma..."

"If I choose not to come, well, sorry, but I certainly won't burn down the 'Norton. Not tonight, not ever. I'll improve it or turn it into something meaningful. Maybe a Russian Hill Center. And I'm going to find Thea. I'll try to fix whatever you did to scare her away."

"Oh, and what did you do to Thea, Magnus?" Darrol found his taunting voice.

Quist lashed a leg at Darrol. "Shut up."

Darrol wriggled a half-turn. "Does Thea have a nice Swedish birthmark on her butt like her mother? A purple one?"

Quist looked at Alma. He gaped like a very dead herring.

Alma shook her head in disgust. "He's only playing with you, Magnus. But regardless, why would you care?"

"Mrs. Quist." Darrol shimmied around again. "Alma. I can help you find Thea, I really can. It won't take long."

He put lifts into his voice. It rose to full charm. "And I can help you make Mischief House a museum. You know how I love history. I'm practically Emperor Norton's right hand man."

Darrol smiled warmly, knowingly, on full eight-cylinder smoothness. "And if there's anything else you need, say on the very personal level..." Even in the vault's dim light, his eyes shone with promise.

Alma seemed to consider it. "And I supposed we'd just leave this cat killer, this twisted man here?"

"Of course? Why not?"

"So tempting, Darrol." She reached her free hand out to the wall, felt for the lock override box, pulled off the cover, yanked a wire loose. "Very tempting." Her fingers working like busy spider legs, she removed the battery. "Quite an offer."

Slipping the battery into a pocket, she slowly backed away. "I'll give you my answer when I come to check on you boys tomorrow..."

She was almost in the hallway. "...or maybe in a year or two. Good night, gentlemen."

"Alma, wait...!"

"*Och lycka till*, Mr. Quist."

She stepped back and swung the door shut, cutting off the shouts.

There was a heavy, hollow clunk. Sealed tight. Two fast finger jabs activated the electronic lock.

She went quickly to the control panel, flipped the circuit breaker. No alarm. No lights. She jerked out the vault's telephone plug. No phone. No modem. No internet.

That seemed to be everything. Cell phones didn't work inside the thick vault. Magnus had almost been proud of that. His own little hidey-hole. Lucky him.

Alma turned away from the vault. She stopped to clean her glasses before going into the store.

Light from a few fluorescents was enough to reveal the messy cascades in the aisles. She thought only for a moment before deciding that most of the cleanup might wait morning. She would ask the staff to come in early.

Crunching on glass and gumballs, she went to the front and checked the doors. They were still secure.

She turned to the fallen emperor and tested the supports at the back. Nothing broken. She stood the figure upright and examined the image closely. Minute dents, not significant.

After sliding the Emperor over to his rightful place, she stepped back to look at him. He stared past her once more with all his grand imperial madness.

She walked behind the counter and picked up the fallen sword. The blade caught the light and glinted. The sabre was heavy in her hands. It didn't appear to be damaged.

But the scabbard was in three pieces, perhaps repairable, perhaps not. There was a bit of stuffing dangling from the largest section. She pulled it free and glanced at it. It seemed to be a handwritten official document, maybe fairly old.

There were other papers on the floor. Puzzled, she gathered them, set them near a cash register, turned on a small counter light.

Everything was written in a formal, almost elegant hand. Casually, she read some of the yellowed pages. Read other parts. Sorted the sheets. Reread everything much more closely.

Alma began to smile. She started laughing. She laughed a great deal.

When she returned to the hallway, she had regained her thoughtful mood.

She stood by the big steel door of the vault. She stared at the large metal rings of the fancy but impotent control wheel. She looked at the keypad. Long ago she'd found and memorized the code. There wasn't much Magnus could keep from her.

Five simple taps of her finger and the door would unlock. And then life would be...what?

Or she could ignore the vault for weeks, months, years. No one else in the 'Norton ever had any business with it.

When asked, she could say "Oh, Magnus went back to Sweden. Poor man was homesick in the extreme. He may well stay there. That sort of thing hits many of us when we get older."

"Darrol Yount? I've no idea. Maybe he went to Sweden with Magnus!" A nice little chuckle. "But seriously, he's an ambitious young man. Probably off seeking his fortune."

Alma walked slowly up and down the hall. She guessed there'd be air enough for quite some time, heavy breathing notwithstanding. No need to decide now.

And in the meantime, there were those papers. She began laughing again.

She made a final check around the store. Before she turned off the lights, she walked back to the Emperor and planted a soft kiss on his cardboard cheek.

And then, still laughing, she went upstairs to bed.

Epilogue

To get on top in life, you've gotta be trading in secrets, lots of them. You find things out, you hoard them till it's time, then you use them. Secrets are like ammunition.
[Attributed to a Mr. D. Yount.]

The indigent person who called himself Emperor Norton died on a San Francisco street corner in 1880.

For almost a century and a half, his old cavalry sabre apparently masqueraded as itself, which is to say, it passed very nicely as a "replica of the Emperor Norton's Sword" and moved from owner to owner through the world of collectibles and curiosities. No one thought it more than an imitation.

At no time—until the sword tumbled from the wall of a Russian Hill grocery store during the Farralons Earthquake—did anyone suspect that the scruffy leather scabbard held anything other than padding.

The papers hidden in the scabbard—including notes written by Norton himself—revealed a truly fascinating tale.

With museum curators and historians standing by—salivating—and many lawyers in attendance—billable hours ticking—the papers were copied, recopied, examined by the court and one by one authenticated. Among the secrets uncovered:

In 1856, a wealthy San Francisco businessman, Joshua Abraham Norton, unmarried, had an illegitimate son with Nelly McAllister, a barmaid at a Barbary Coast saloon. Nelly died in childbirth.

To avoid scandal, Norton created a fictitious birth record and arranged for a secret, double-blind adoption.

He had one stipulation: that the boy's first and middle names be Benjamin and Algoa. 'Benjamin' was after a favorite uncle and 'Algoa' from a beloved place in South Africa where Norton had spent much of his youth.

The baby was adopted by a childless San Francisco couple, George and Evangeline Kearny. Norton knew who the adopting parents were, but they were not aware of his involvement.

Soon after the adoption, using another double blind, Norton opened an interest-bearing account, depositing $12,000 at a San Francisco bank in the name of Benjamin Algoa—in this case with Algoa serving as a surname. Norton intended to make the account known to his son—and possibly to reveal the true paternity—when Benjamin reached the age of 21.

Norton thoroughly documented all of this, making scrupulous notes about the affair, copies of the birth and adoption records, and detailing the process for accessing the secret bank account. He wrote a will, naming Benjamin Algoa Kearny as his sole heir. At some later point he hid these papers the lining of his scabbard. And forgot about them.

After losing his fortune in a major business gamble, Joshua Norton also lost his sanity and declared himself to be Emperor of the United States and Protector of Mexico. He became one of San Francisco's favorite and favored eccentrics and remained so until his death. Even beyond.

Benjamin A. Kearny never learned about his true father or about the secret bank account. Kearny was lucky enough to survive the Great Earthquake and Fire of 1906, but the following year he died in a somewhat-ironic accident, killed by a cornice falling from a new building.

Eventually, with no one claiming it, the "Benjamin Algoa" bank account was taken over by the State of California.

In 2003, California banking laws changed, disallowing further payments of interest on such unclaimed property. By that time, however, the money had been earning interest from banks and from the state for over 146 years. The total had reached $441,433.81.

The sole heir and legal claimant to the Benjamin Alcoa account, and also the person proven irrefutably to be the sole living descendent of Joshua Abraham Norton, was one Josephine Kearny Durr.

From local news:

Mrs. Josephine 'Jo' Durr, recently discovered to be the great-great granddaughter of San Francisco's infamous 19th-century eccentric, the still-beloved and forever-intriguing Emperor Norton, co-hosted a fabulous party last Sunday at the heritage Russian Hill building known as Mischief House.

Mrs. Durr has donated a major portion of her surprise inheritance to a trust set up to preserving and restoring the building.

"Not all secrets are bad," said Jo. "In fact, once they're let into the world, some secrets are truly wonderful."

About Emperor Norton

Although *EMPEROR'S REACH* is a work of fiction, the 'Emperor' himself was very real.

Joshua Abraham Norton was born in England, c. 1818, and raised in South Africa. He moved to San Francisco around the time of the Gold Rush. Norton became a wealthy businessman. However, when he attempted to corner the rice market, his efforts failed disastrously, and he was forced into bankruptcy.

In 1859, a destitute and none-too sane Norton declared himself Emperor of the United States (and later as the Protector of Mexico). The San Francisco newspapers loved and promoted this, and 'the Emperor' immediately caught the public's attention.

For more than twenty years he roamed the city as a beloved eccentric, some might say as the quintessential freeloader. Penniless, he usually found free meals and free lodging. He 'inspected' city works, printed his own currency and issued decrees and proclamations (including one ordering the dissolution of Congress).

When Norton died in January, 1880, thousands came out for his funeral. He was buried in the Masonic Cemetery in San Francisco. In 1934, with the city closing most of its cemeteries, his remains were disinterred and reburied, with considerable fanfare, at Woodlawn Cemetery in Colma. Norton's gravesite is easy to find. It's not uncommon to see fresh flowers by his marker.

From time to time there have been serious efforts to name all or part of the San Francisco-Oakland Bay Bridge after Norton, who was one of the first to suggest the idea of such a span.

As far as is known, Joshua Norton had no children. The story of his affair, his line of descendants and the secret bank account all come from the author's imagination.

However, the cavalry sword was real enough, and it is prominent in several photographs of Emperor Norton.

At this moment, the sword, unrecognized, well may be languishing in someone's attic or lurking in a dusty corner of a second-hand shop, its old leather scabbard perhaps holding more than a few secrets.